MTCC NO. 847
1121 Steeles Ave West
North York, ON M2R 3W7

RAVE REVIEWS FOR
J. N. WILLIAMSON!

"Williamson is a master stylist and an author whose work reaches many levels. You can't do better than that when looking for a 'disturbing fiction' fix."

—*BookLovers*

"J. N. Williamson is very much up there with the leading writers in the horror genre today."

—*Masters of Terror*

"J. N. Williamson is a horror classic."

—Poppy Z. Brite, author of *Lost Souls*

"Williamson's lucid, multi-layered prose engages the mind rather than lobotomizes it. A master."

—Mort Castle, author of *Cursed Be the Child*

"The grandmaster of horror!"

—*Dark Matter*

D0830249

Other *Leisure* books by J. N. Williamson:
THE HAUNT
BLOODLINES
SPREE
BABEL'S CHILDREN

MTCC NO. 847
1121 Steeles Ave West
North York, ON M2R 3W7

FRIGHTS
OF
FANCY

J. N. Williamson

LEISURE BOOKS NEW YORK CITY

A LEISURE BOOK®

June 2000

Published by

Dorchester Publishing Co., Inc.
276 Fifth Avenue
New York, NY 10001

If you purchased this book without a cover you should be aware that this book is stolen property. It was reported as "unsold and destroyed" to the publisher and neither the author nor the publisher has received any payment for this "stripped book."

Copyright © 2000 by J. N. Williamson
General introduction copyright © 2000 by Ed Gorman
"When Nature Itself Creates Them" Copyright © 2000 by J. N. Williamson
"A. Pyme" Copyright © 2000 by J. N. Williamson
"Pick-Up" Copyright © 2000 by J. N. Williamson

All rights reserved. No part of this book may be reproduced or transmitted in any form or by any electronic or mechanical means, including photocopying, recording or by any information storage and retrieval system, without the written permission of the Publisher, except where permitted by law.

ISBN 0-8439-4728-4

The name "Leisure Books" and the stylized "L" with design are trademarks of Dorchester Publishing Co., Inc.

Printed in the United States of America.

MTCC NO. 847
1121 Steeles Ave West
North York, ON M2R 3W7

A writer who succeeds in the short story form after first publishing novels is unusual, and so are they who encouraged his efforts.

My fanciful frights were primarily boosted by my wife Mary, to whom all that is best about me is always dedicated, and these helpful people, some also still among the living: Ellery Queen, Anthony Boucher, Robert Bloch, agent Ray Puechner, Martin H. Greenberg, Dean Wesley Smith, Lin Stein, Thomas E. Millstead, John Macaly, Ray Bradbury, Dean Koontz, Tracy Knight, my son Joseph Welhoelter, my daughter-in-law Candace Williamson, Ed Gorman, and my editor Don D'Auria.

Thanks to those people, my frights could become the work of fiction.

CONTENTS

FRIGHTS

OF
FANCY

Introduction

There's an old Hollywood saying: never meet your heroes.

The suave leading man turns out to be a semi-literate drunk. The action hero a braying anti-Semite. And the sweet young ingenue a shrieking junkie.

Every once in a while though . . .

As a relatively young writer (this was twenty years ago) I was reading everybody and everything in the fields of dark suspense and horror. And this meant that I was reading a lot of J. N. Williamson material because he was just then coming into his own, with novels and short stories virtually everywhere.

At one point, I sent him one of my own stories for an anthology he was editing. And he rejected it. But. He took the time to write me a long letter about the strengths and weaknesses of the piece and what I needed to do to make it work. In many respects, he did me more of a favor than if he'd bought the story. I learned a lot.

Since then, I've been in several of his anthologies and he's been in several of mine. And Jerry's continued to grow as a writer. He's written or edited more than fifty books and published several dozen short stories. More importantly, the craftsman has become an artist.

The stories here are fun to read. Some will give you a chill, some will give you a laugh (Jerry's got a sly sense of humor), and some will genuinely move you.

And most of the stories will stay with you. That's the test of the artist. Does his (or her) work stay with you? Several years ago, I bought two stories of Jerry's that I still recommend young writers not only read but outline and analyze. Because they not only stand up under scrutiny, they grow richer with each rereading. You'll recognize them in this collection.

As for Jerry himself, he's a nice, decent guy with a wonderful wife and helpmate named Mary. Six kids. And now grandkids. All this great life experience and life wisdom you can see on eloquent display in the stories gathered here. Because Jerry's the best kind of writer—one who enriches his stories with his own heart and soul and mind. Love, fear, hope, terror, despair—Jerry's known them all. And he's able to translate them into the universal language of fiction.

It's all right to meet your hero, when he turns out to be as bright, kind and talented as Jerry Williamson.

Happy reading.

—Ed Gorman
November 1999

Author's Prelude

If I may borrow an unscripted line from the late actor Humphrey Bogart, quoted by his son*, I can add just a few words and explain why I wrote dozens of short stories in the eighties. The actor said he'd taken so many parts in stage plays because he wanted to "get to the point where he didn't stink anymore."

After publishing several novels, I wasn't being called names as a novelist, but it was only every tenth or eleventh short story that was considered particularly worthwhile, and just about that often the yarn was rejected. My plan was to work so hard at short fiction that I'd become consistent and, like Bogart, *never* stink anymore.

My situation was a strange one, considering what kind of writer God, my talent, and my life

*Stephen Bogart. *Bogart: In Search of a Father.* Dutton, 1995.

had made me. Like most literary-minded people, I'd begun by writing short fiction, but rather little of it sold in my youth. At last I began to craft novels in the seventies, I proved to have a knack at it, and I did what I could to establish myself as a novelist while book-length ideas kept leaping into my mind. For a while they sold almost as fast as I conceived them.

But in 1983 I edited an anthology (*Masques*, Maclay & Associates, Inc.) of short horror and supernatural fiction and, by the time it came out in '84, I was bitten by the bug to write short stories *other* anthologists would want for their books. And that was when I perceived that many differences existed between writing for length and short fiction that were more important than wordage, and that I would have to work extremely hard to grasp and master those differences. In short, novels aren't merely longer, they're something else entirely.

My desire or challenge was given two major boosts, by teaching writing for Writer's Digest School, and persuading F & W Books—Writer's Digest Books—to hire me as the editor of 1987's *How to Write Tales of Horror, Fantasy, and Science Fiction.* For the latter, in addition to two chapters I wrote myself, I persuaded such writers as Robert Bloch, Ray Bradbury, Dean Koontz (two marvelous chapters), Stephen King, Marion Zimmer Bradley, and Colin Wilson to make announced or unbilled appearances—and went on writing short stories, delighted when Martin H. Greenberg invited me to write for *14 Vicious Valentines* (1988).

If I don't think my writing stinks anymore, and I don't, how else do I account for it? And why do I believe I'm a satisfying, professional writer now? Answering these questions is fairly easy, but *you're* the one to decide whether I'm right or not: First, I think I'm one of the most original writers around. It's possible to judge that, in case you didn't know, by doing your best to keep up with what other people are creating, then refusing to use the same material. I also believe that fiction of any length needs an understandable beginning, middle, and ending, and that it's improved when there's a clear point of view. I don't think it matters if most readers may disagree with it; it's a fact that they will never be exposed to your precise viewpoint until you include it in your work of fiction.

Perhaps if I cite the basic horror or problem in several of my novels and then discuss the moral tone I took, or the plot development, you will recognize the nature of their originality:

1. *The Offspring* (Leisure, 1984) was the first novel I wrote, but it sold as my eighth. There was a trick I had to pull off: hide the nature of Lynn, an evil antagonist who wasn't described but was said to be incapable of leaving his bedroom. Seeing an increase in androgyny among performers, I'd created a gigantically obese hermaphrodite with uncanny hypnotic skills that compensated for its inability to walk by mentally tricking others into doing its will. Lynn's grandfather manipulated it for political reasons, and only two normal children kept him from ruling the world; they accidentally started a fire and nothing could keep Lynn from burning to death.

2. *Playmates* (Leisure, 1982) remains a personal favorite because of its originality and my research into Ireland, where I set it, and Irish mythology. An American girl, Troy, eleven, moves with her parents to County Connaught to live with her grandfather, Pat Quinlan. Always imaginative, Troy believes she becomes friends with a wide variety of tiny beings—fairies, elves, even a

banshee. And they are eager to do her bidding! But all this isn't Troy's fault; it's her grand-da who's had a pact, as his da before him, that brings male family members near-immortality. Troy's dad is finally told the truth when, in Da's locked attic, he's shown dozens of partitions containing "perfectly mummified old men . . . (like) a clothing store rack with the suits filled. And the mummy at the head of death's procession . . . lifted a veined and desiccated hand, opened its rheumy eyes, and *winked* at Connor!"

Old Pat says, "This is your *family*, son . . . your living ancestors."

Connor is revolted. And crashing through the attic door is a monster of Irish myth, the huge, round, all-absorbing Nuckalavee! It rolls a line through the "family" like a powerful bowling ball as Connor, seeing Troy in the hallway, rushes to safety with her. And she no longer likes fairies who threatened her daddy.

3. *The Black School* (Dell, 1988) has the clearcut problem of Jill Scott, eleven, being kidnaped, taken to Scotland, then to a literal subterranean hell—there she is enrolled in an evil school. The headmaster knows facts about Jill's teacher daddy, Mike, that he doesn't know and will exchange Jill for the only book ever written by Satan, the school principal.

What gives this book its distinction are the glimpses of hell's denizens, and Mike's teacher friend, Jacob Wier, who seems to be a dwarf—"If you want to discover how many angels can dance on the head of a pin, I'm the one to find out for you"—but is actually an homunculus, who was made in a test tube by Paracelsus in the sixteenth century! It's Jacob who has the devil's bible in his hands and accompanies Mike Scott in the quest

16

to find young Jill and free her, partly because the man-made man hopes his sacrifice will earn him a soul.

The Black School was followed by a sequel with engaging Jacob Wier, entitled *Hell Storm*, in 1990.

4. *Don't Take Away the Light* (Zebra, 1993) certainly is original since I consider it my autobiographical novel. Teddy, age nine, is the adored son of a brilliant self-taught pianist named Evelyn who tells the boy she never lies. When he becomes ill and, bleeding, it doesn't soon coagulate, "Dear"—for Teddy is expected to call his mother that—is upset at one point and tells the bespectacled boy he has hemophilia. He's developed an imaginary friend, Coop, and Dear is afraid Teddy is becoming too independent.

The moral tone of this one is basic. Though Teddy is frightened often by Dear—whose deceased kinsmen often call on her, she claims—he is never disrespectful and believes everything Mother says. What saves him, at novel's end, are the thoughtless things Dear does to herself.

I might list and discuss many more books I have written but I believe I've proved the point I was making about originality.

And with you here in the presence of some sixteen short tales of mine covering a period in my career of some fourteen years, there's really not much to keep you from forming your own opinion.

There's also not much you can do to keep me from doing the same thing—and we writers do tend to base many of our characters on people we've met, even if we do deny it!

I have had the privilege to work—in four *Masques* anthologies and the how-to book I created—to edit,

J.N. Williamson

and to appear with most of the horror, fantasy, and supernatural writers I've admired since mid century.

But the two writers I've probably admired most since then have little or no influence on my professional world, so it's satisfying to make a brief connection to one of them to help complete my introduction.

"It is both an innocent and a haunted Paradise that (F. Scott) Fitzgerald reveals in his first book (*This Side of Paradise*. Scribner's, 1920.)," writes John Aldridge in "Fitzgerald: The Horror and the Vision of Paradise." This is where the connection I mentioned may be found. But perhaps a primary distinction between Mr. F. S. F. and me is that, according to Aldridge, there was something Scott could not portray, while my less-renowned career starts there: "For the beautiful there is always damnation," Mr. Aldridge wrote; "for every tenderness there is always the black horror of night . . ."

There were times when I imagined I had always held those expectations, that they were at the root of my frights if not my fancies or true beliefs.

In the main, however, sixteen other words associated with Fitzgerald remain truer to me and this collection, as listed in *The Oxford Dictionary of Quotations*, Third Edition, Oxford University Press, 1979: "In the real dark night of the soul it is always three o'clock in the morning."

The Writing of "Reality Function"

Until I read Robert Bloch's *Psycho*, I was getting nowhere writing a mixture of mystery and pseudo-sf stories. That wonderful novel opened a world to me, one I hadn't known existed. I was powerfully under the influence of such writers as F. Scott Fitzgerald, Arthur Conan Doyle, and the earlier Ray Bradbury, plus a handful of exceptionally varied science fiction writers.

So I marveled that Bob and I ultimately became friends and was thrilled when he invited me to write for his anthology, *Psycho-Paths* (TOR, 1991), and even more excited when he asked me into its '93 follow-up *Monsters in Our Midst*, because he suggested what kind of psychopath to write about: a high school teacher who enjoyed abusing his authority—and his pupils.

Robert Bloch was one of a very limited number of writers whose ideas for *my* chief characters would be worth hearing out. Bradbury, Matheson, Ray Russell, F. Paul Wilson, Tracy Knight, Gary Braunbeck, Mort Castle, Dean Koontz, Kris Rusch, and Ed Gorman practically complete the list of those I know *and* would appreciatively consider in that category.

In "Reality Function," the psycho teacher Bob urged me to create rides herd again. Study hard, he's a *tough* grader!

Reality Function

"Civilization has separated us from our deep, instinctive will to live, eroded our 'reality function' . . . We are highly vulnerable."

—Colin Wilson. *C. G. Jung: Lord of the Underworld.*

(With particular thanks to my wife and in-house editor, Mary T. Williamson.)

If a single and singular knack—one exceptional attribute—set Matthew Miliken apart from all the other teachers he had ever known, and also made him clearly superior to them, he felt sure he knew what it was.

Mr. Miliken had always remembered just what it was like to be a high school underclassman, and he treated his own pupils accordingly.

What was it like? It was like being a motherless transfer student from a small county school to a

J.N. Williamson

big-city institution, the last eligible pledge to the one fraternity that posed an indifferent invitation, the rawest recruit on the military base, and the newest, lowliest member of the English Department at Salinger High School rolled into one. Matthew Miliken had been all those people, he recalled exactly what it had been like each time, and he treated his own students accordingly.

Just the same way he'd been treated, only worse. More subtly the past seven years he'd served as department head, but definitely, decidedly worse.

Seven years of cleverly weeding out the great unwashed from a department that had threatened to become a benevolent protective society for sheerly titular teachers—people whose copycat appearance implied the worship of some modish, hirsute god frozen forever midway through puberty! Seven years of wielding a scythe with the skill of a neurosurgeon to prune the department of intellectual kudzu and lay bare the brilliant brain gleaming with naked purity at its throbbing center—*his*, eager to take full charge of the responsibility for Salinger's pseudo-students of English! Seven—count 'em!—seven years to make that fool Cross accept his own definition of the word *faculty*. For it was not primarily "a teaching staff," but the other two definitions Webster supplied: The specialized power of a living organism, and an authorization. In short, an empowerment.

Seven, the central, the operative, magic number in Miliken's life. That many years he had been obliged to suffer the inadequacies of his pupils without retaliation. *Twice* seven years ago, he hadn't been so subtle, so skilled at laying plans with infinite attention to detail—and he'd been summarily discharged from his prior post for disciplining some idiot of a youth. Exactly what had transpired had tended until recently to escape Mr. Miliken's memory. Lately, however, he'd started anew to toy with multiples of his favorite number, to recollect the exquisite pleasures of what he'd done to the ignoramus of a boy before several other instructors stopped him, and to feel the stirrings of old delight, the embryonic yen anew. *Three* times seven years into his past he'd been obliged to deal with his army sergeant, during target practice. Not that long a period before the sergeant's accident, he had also needed to get the high-and-mighty fraternity president off his back, but Welch had survived—albeit without taking his diploma. *Four* times seven years ago, when he was a transfer student, the boys who harassed Matthew Miliken had not been so fortunate.

And at age seven, Mother had been the origin of young Matthew's awakening to the fine efficacy of the number seven in his life.

Now it was seven minutes past three P.M., exactly.

Alone in his classroom except for nearly thirty young people who were pretending to focus their attention on a scene from *Romeo and Juliet*, Mr. Miliken lofted his hands from his desk, expressionlessly regarded the life lines in his palms, and extended his ten fingers into the air. He left the five of his left hand up, then tucked the ring and baby finger of the right hand beneath a prehensile thumb. The result provided him with mild enjoyment and so, after gazing with boredom above the fingertips at his pupils' lowered faces, he surrendered to the impulse to smile.

Surely now it was time again. All of them were alive. And so far as Mr. Miliken knew from casually tracking the obituaries—anything deeper would have been compulsive—every student who'd passed through Salinger High's department of English for the previous seven years was still alive.

None had died in the manner of his drill sergeant or the unfeeling boys who had taunted the young Matthew, nor had any died the way Mother and his predecessors as department head had perished—which was the death of preference, where Mr. Miliken was concerned. None of the thick-headed, inconsistent, easily distracted, unruly, and obstinate little gland-dominated cretins had died in any way at all!

His was the patience of Job—no, of a god.

It was time.

Now it was a case of wise choice, particularly if they were to end their space-devouring existences the way that he considered cleverest, most fulfilling, and safest. Selecting half a dozen to die would be egregious; overbearing. Five would bring the closest scrutiny regardless of *how* they exited life, and he could not be certain he still possessed the psychic endurance for the task; one was well to admit the inroads of temporal attrition.

Four then? Awkward. Pastimes of this inventive magnitude demanded the concentration of a chess master. Four was also, according to the ancients, a number of totality; completion. In spite of middle age, Mr. Miliken was trim, watched his diet, never smoked. Twice-seven years from the present, he'd only be fifty-six; *three* times seven—bringing him to age sixty-three—why, with moderation and prudence, his little forays into extracurricular intellectual adventure would not have to end even then!

Well, then . . . three. Not all bad. An appealing number. He shifted in his chair. One-two-*three*;

there were no obvious flaws to it no matter how Mr. Miliken examined it. *Three*. Dropping his left hand, he freed the ring finger of the right in order to allow it to join the adjacent middle and index digits. Head cocked, he studied the finger trio for a moment, noting that the longer middle gave the structure a nice pyramidal look. Very well! For now, for the present purposes, three of them would be ideal. Not perfect. Ideal.

Do I see the hands of any volunteers? he wondered. His round, brown eyes, like chocolate tarts, rolled from face to face, his rare smile a marvel of instructional eagerness to be of help.

From somewhere in the room, a voice—young, female, bell-like in its purity, its clarity! "Mr. Miliken?"

His telepathic powers hadn't abandoned him! "Yes?" he cried, scanning juvenile faces as all of them looked up. He realized distantly that he didn't know any of them well enough to identify their voices.

The fair-skinned teenager was in third-row-left, three back. Mr. Miliken didn't fail to resonate to the perfection of the repeated number. And he did know her; she was the athletic person, possibly track. He'd seen her jogging on the streets often enough to recognize her profile. Unlike most, that was her best side, but she was so alert, so inquisitive, that she always managed to stare back, full face. He peered down at his open roll book. "Yes, *Ms.* Auel?" Megan Auel, and he'd been sure to address her in the idiotic modern idiom.

"I wanted to be sure I understood," Megan began—

"Stand, rise!" he urged her with an evangelist's gesture.

"—What Juliet means here," she finished, rising. Pretty only as an echo of earlier childhood or as a foretaste of what might lie beyond her high school years as a sprinter, Megan had rather close-cropped hair hopelessly lost between a light brown and a blond hue that came out best—like Megan herself—when she ran in sunlight. Her proudest moment had occurred when her coach, Marva Smith-Coles, told her she had less extra body fat than any other athlete Marva'd ever coached. "It says, 'I have an ill-divining soul! Methinks I see thee, now thou art below. As one dead in the bottom of a tomb . . .'" Megan met Mr. Miliken's stare. "She doesn't really see him that way. Right?"

He asked back, "What do you think?"

Megan flushed. "Well, I think she was sorta psychic, maybe." Her tousled head came forward in a sudden, soundless laugh of rueful embarrassment. "I mean, this is *Shakespeare*—so what do I know?"

"Well," he said, "*I* think you may be quite correct. Besides, the Bard wrote for an audience no better informed than this class will be, if I have *my* way about it!"

Laughter rippled. Megan sat, and Matthew Miliken turned his head toward the one student he'd definitely had in mind upon reaching today's important decision. "Lyall," he said softly, "why don't you rise and read Romeo's response to the fair Juliet's visionary apprehension?"

Lyall Dorris stood with an expression of doom on a face that was almost as round as it was long. If his teacher's question had not been rhetorical, Lyall could have answered, "Because I stammer so badly it's nearly impossible to say good morning." Or, "I'm sick of how you call on me three or four times every class, practically inviting the other boys to make fun of me." Lacking freedom

26

or facility, he gripped the thin volume of Shakespeare so tightly in his hands that one page gave way beneath his pressing thumb, and an audible ripping noise drew giggles from the students close to—staring up at—Lyall.

" 'A-And t-trust m-m-m-me, l-l-l-l-love,' " he read aloud bravely, " 'in m-my eye s-so d-d-do y-y-y-y-y-you—' "

"*Thank* you, Lyall," Miliken said, and the boy seemed to disappear as he plumped down into his chair. "I want to see you, briefly. After class."

This wasn't the first time. "M-My b-b-b-b—"

"Your *bus*," Mr. Miliken finished it, unable to resist raising his gaze to the heavens, "won't leave before I'm through with you. I plan to do most of the talking." Amid chuckles, and without the need to read from the book, he completed Romeo's lines: ". . . 'So do you: Dry sorrow drinks our blood.' Mr. Stillings." He recognized an upthrown arm. "You have an observation for us?"

Fifteen-year-old Kenneth Stillings, a year or better the junior of the others, his hand wiggling from the wrist. He who had skipped grades, Mr. Miliken reflected, and might never know love because he was so enchanted with his own IQ. *One, two, three*, he told himself. *Megan, Lyall, and Kenneth—volunteers all*.

"Megan omitted one of fair Juliet's lines." This Kenneth, short and small. Ludicrously, sexlessly small. People today failed entirely to grasp the purpose of education. No student should be allowed to dispense with a year of schooling as if he were discarding a disposable can. This child had missed so much, and now he'd be missing so much *more*. "If I may rectify the omission?" Kenneth's unfeeling delft eyes glazed with memory and knowledge. " 'Either my eyesight fails or thou

27

look'st pale.' Thank you, Mr. Miliken." He lowered himself with almost proprietorial aplomb to his own chair.

"To *rectify*, Mr. Stillings," the teacher said as he stood away from the desk, "is to correct, to put right." He smoothed down his buttoned, brown suit coat. Afoot, he looked tall to most Salinger students, and knew it. Once he'd yearned to own six suits of exactly this color because it was just the shade of his eyebrows, but he had only found one other. He wore one or the other suit seven days a week, and the dry cleaner's people addressed him, without authority, by his first name. "By definition, an omission is an absence, a nothingness. I think the correct word you were questing for was *supply*."

Kenneth, both feet on the floor only when he leaned forward in his chair or rose, returned a two-inch-long smile. It was the most harmonious blend of adoration and envy approximating hatred Mr. Miliken had seen on the human face. "Thank you, sir."

Footsteps were moving in the halls, and soon the buzzer would sound. "Mr. Stillings, am I correct that you're attending biology club after school?"

"Yes, Mr. Miliken." This was the final class of the day and only Lyall, who'd been kept after, and small Kenneth were not rising to rush for the door. "Is there something you would like me to do, sir?"

Miliken nodded absently. Megan Auel was hurrying out without a sidelong glance in his direction and even his nimble mind hadn't yet devised a reason to delay her. Those facts cemented her status as No. 3. *"I think she will be rul'd In all respects by me,"* Capulet's speech played in Miliken's memory. Appropriating it, he added another: *"Well, we were born to die."*

"Yes, there is, Kenneth," he told Stillings. He pretended to appear uncertain. "Your father . . . isn't home a great deal these days?"

Kenneth did a credible imitation of a small statue. Something decorative, more ornamental than statuesque. When the child's lips formed assent, Mr. Miliken recalled small-boy objets in garden fountains, cascading water from tiny penises.

"Your mother frets over you, I know," Miliken continued. "Stop by here and I'll drive you home. I think a little heart-to-heart is in order."

"Did I do something wrong?"

Mr. Miliken liked reading student files from time to time. Learning about the families, the intimate problems pupils confessed to their counselors. Kenneth's mother had gotten religion, his father had not. He'd gotten interests away from home, away from both his wife and son. Little Kenneth's record of straight-A final marks had been no more compelling to him than his wife's born-again status, and neither parent was capable, it seemed clear to the teacher, of appreciating an offspring who was a boy genius. Now that it occurred to Mr. Miliken, nobody was. "You possess a hunger for knowledge, Stillings. It is knowledge I mean to offer you—more than you're likely to get from a room filled with cretins whose truly best hope is that they *will* be . . . born again. Four-twenty then?"

When the child nodded and rushed off to his club, Mr. Miliken turned his attentions to the stammering Lyall with a surge in his intestines that he hadn't known for five-six-*seven* years. The warmth that only came when the major decisions of life were made, the preliminary steps taken, and it became possible to stare down at a pupil from his full height—and eventually discern a *number* beginning to take form on his forehead, just over the brow line.

Often, Miliken had wondered if superior men of the past had shared with him the special gift, this exciting evidence of psychic contact being made between his dynamic intelligence and the scared-mouse section of his chosen victims' lesser brains. Though his reading was catholic, though he had searched for the record of another man with the power to detect the succession of identifying numerals starting to illumine the sloping foreheads, one by one—like bull's-eyes—he'd had to accept the glorious isolation inherent in the likelihood that he was the only one.

He bore up well under it, however.

He approached Lyall arms akimbo, noticing for the first time how like a chipmunk he looked. "Mr. Dorris, d'you know why I asked you to stay after?"

You hate me, Lyall thought. He concentrated, brow furrowing. "Same r-reason a-as t-t-the other t-t-times?"

Mr. Miliken beamed. "I like that. I really do." Big nod. "As stalls go, it's clever. Relatively speaking." Of late, he had rediscovered the delight of arousing hope in student bosoms, then dashing it. Perhaps he'd sensed at an unconscious level that today's decision might be reached, and then primed the pump that was pudgy, stuttering Lyall Dorris.

But until that instant, he had not imagined it was conceivable to begin driving three students to kill themselves—Mr. Miliken's favorite, foolproof preference of method—that very afternoon!

Not that the girl or the brainy upstart Stillings

would be easy tasks. He couldn't even be sure that he could make the Dorris boy do it. That was the thrill, however, and probably why *he* possessed the gift of psychic contact while other superior men lacked it—because Matthew Miliken settled for nothing less than *genuine challenges*!

Additionally, he was not one to grow obsessive over his pastimes. If he failed to motivate any of the three pupils to destroy themselves—

He was perfectly willing to destroy them himself.

"I didn't keep you after school for the same reason, Lyall," he said. "I have given up on you, you see." He shrugged his well-pressed jacket shoulders. "Repeatedly, I've tried to stop your stammering. Over and over I've called on you in class, to read. I've sat here on my own time and listened numerous times to your butchering of some of the best works of fiction in our language. Yet *you*, boy"—skillfully, he lifted a single fine brow— "refused even to carry my recommendations of assistance home to your father!"

Once, in a mood of foresightful wisdom, he had in fact scrawled a note to the elder Dorris in which he stated baldly how consuming Lyall's problem was, emphasizing how disruptive he was in class, stressing that Lyall might "require considerably more than what a speech therapist can provide." He'd added a tactful fillip implying an absence of "social courage," then photocopied the note—believing with all the certainty he had that Lyall would *not* take it to Lieutenant Steve Dorris of the homicide department, a police officer decorated for bravery. He still owned the photocopy and relished knowing that he was obliged to motivate the boy to end his existence rather than taking matters into his own hands. Had the senior Dorris toiled as a clerk or maintenance man, there'd have been literally no challenge to his first student designation.

"Lyall . . . son . . . you're here now so that, without others overhearing, you may learn how hopeless your situation is. I feel I owe you the truth—a commodity of immense scarcity in our time and one almost never conveyed from parent to child. Do you follow me?"

A definite, incipiently terrified bob of the head.

"Life is not what it once was, lad. The infirm are everywhere; recall what you've seen on television. Appeals for funds, for people with spare time to care for the abused or homeless and to serve as surrogate this or that. Doubtlessly you have, yourself, felt pity . . . compassion . . . for those whose very limbs will not work properly."

Lyall nodded slowly.

"Listen to me," Mr. Miliken said, eyes smoldering. "There is not enough money to go around, there aren't enough people with leisure time, to deal with the needs of those like yourself. In the distant past, when the United States was full of small towns, people knew one another, *cared* for one another." Mr. Miliken pinched the trousers of his brown pants, sat in the chair nearest—opposite—Lyall. "Even when a youngster was totally *incapable* of speech, his family or friends looked after him. *No more.*"

The child felt his mouth drop open. He needed to argue, say something; but what he might say was unthinkably rude to an adult, and mired in complexity. His heartbeat hadn't accelerated but fallen so quiet he wondered if he was alive.

"Here are the facts I promised," continued Mr. Miliken, appearing to muster the manliness needed for unutterable truths. "These days, the living bestow honor on those whose nerves are firm. Steady, unflagging. Do not, please, misunderstand. I'm not saying that a youngster must be a genius, or live heroically—like your father, for example—or even have all the answers."

"N-N-No?"

Miliken put out an arm to place one hand gently on Lyall's. "But the *appearance* of those attributes—the very *look* of absolute preparedness, insight, or insider's knowledge, of wit, a flair for repartee, vast social charm—is what wins out." He saw the light of horror in the teenager's eyes needed a bit more support. "Always."

"*Alll-w-w-ways?*"

"They are basic, Lyall, invaluable not just to success—but to survival itself." He made himself pause to let everything sink in. Seeing the lips unadorned even by the possibility of a beard begin to part, he said with his own lips, *Always*.

And then he counted *one*, *two*, *three*, and laid out the rest of it. "Lyall, it is only the haunting dead who could exhibit compassion for your plight. Well, there are your *parents*; but the city's finest are notoriously underpaid, aren't they?"

"The *d-d-d-d-dead*?"

"D'you go to films of fright, boy? Do you?"

His eyes went on saying "the dead." Like neon lights.

"I know they're called 'horror movies,' but I think of them as tales about quivering, trembling, gutless fools who survive merely for the enjoyment of powerful entities—who always know *their* mind! Helpless imbeciles who run to the ground, *high* ground, trapping themselves." Mr. Miliken tilted back his head as if laughing in recollection. "Dying there is the only thing they *ever* do right, isn't it? And if they *can* succeed in speaking, as the unconquerable foe deliberately mounts the steps, the next thing a moviegoer hears is—a *stammer*!

Lyall's hand beneath Miliken's spasmed as he tried instinctively to jerk it away, but it stayed put.

"You know, that's what makes such pictures work, boy." Mr. Miliken leaned more weight on the plump hand. "That moment of amusement and derision shared with the audience when the pathetic, squirming victim *must take* decisive action—or at least come up with a convincing argument for *why* he should go on living!"

The child pulled harder, but the hand was pinned.

"D'you recall the next part, the *last* part, Lyall?" Miliken's fine brows rose and fell, alternately. "It's when the doomed victim—usually a young person these days—finally gets his mouth open. And while his silly eyes practically explode from his head, he looks straight into the camera to defend himself with the immortal—*B-b-b-b-b-but*!"

Mr. Miliken abruptly sat up. Arms folded, he laughed noiselessly

Hand tugged free, Lyall fell off his chair. Pale, he got to his feet with sweat flooding from the temples and fled the classroom with both hands pressed to his mouth. From somewhere up the corridor, he howled.

Mr. Miliken stopped laughing. Simple satisfaction with a job well done was enough, and the boy genius, Kenneth Stillings, would arrive soon for his ride home.

And even before the teacher had made more than a start on the papers he began grading a moment after Lyall's exit, the small and dark-haired image of Salinger High's straight-A-always pupil was waiting expectantly in the doorway.

Ms. Megan Auel's test paper was next on the pile, and Mr. Miliken just glanced at it before inscribing a red-penciled D at the top of the page, then rising.

One-two-three—but not necessarily in that order. "How are things at biology club, Mr. Stillings?"

"Skeletal," Kenneth said. He knew the quip wasn't original with him, but he remembered to add a smile to it.

"Clever boy," Mr. Miliken said. He clapped him on the shoulder and made a show of activity as he loped around him, out into the corridor. "Come along. Your mother will be expecting you." Waving his arm, he rushed ahead.

"I didn't make up that joke, sir." The voice in Mr. Miliken's wake, in common with the rest of the fifteen-year-old, was small. "I heard a football player say it."

Miliken looked back, noticing Kenneth's pullover and remembering too late his car coat in the teacher's cloakroom. Precipitate action was always his potential downfall. "You really do have the most singular fondness for facts."

Kenneth was nearly running to keep pace. "What else is there to depend on, sir?"

They were in the lot behind the building, Mr. Miliken craning his neck in search of his car. He shivered as much from excitement and anticipation as from the winter that wouldn't quite go away. " 'O, thou art deceived,' " he murmured. "Mercutio, I think." He saw his four-year-old brown-for-his-eyebrows car gleaming with near-twilight glory and strode toward it.

"I want to discuss that subject on your ride home. Hop in."

Kenneth opened the passenger door and did so. Hopping, at his height, was the only way to enter a full-sized automobile. "What subject, sir?"

J.N. Williamson

"Reality," Miliken replied. He turned his key in the ignition, waited until the small boy was in. "The reality function, to be precise."

"Oh," Kenneth said noncommittally. The way he looked at someone grown-up with his particularly amazing blue eyes—as veiled by a protective covering of solid facts as an addict's by drugs—might have daunted a lesser man then Miliken. "Is this about religion, sir? Because Mother—"

"It is not," Mr. Miliken said flatly. "Religion is about truth. I want to talk with you about facts." *That should hold him,* he thought, pausing with the car in the street to learn the boy's address. What was needed now was to demonstrate to Stillings that he, himself, possessed superior knowledge or was smarter; preferably both. From studying the student files, he knew not only that the father was usually absent and that the mother was attempting to replace him with churchly matters, but that Kenneth had a weakness: He'd gotten a B+ on a recent weekly exam. In sex education. A psychiatrist wasn't required to know that the father's dalliances combined with the emotional flare-ups of the mother had bewildered a child of somewhat protracted puberty. One who'd do anything to keep his straight-A record intact—

And who was in urgent if unknowing need of a father figure.

To Miliken, the pretty consistency of reliable data seemed nothing more challenging now than a ledge for an egghead to perch upon till it could be made to crumble. Once it did—when small Mr. S. was adequately overpowered by information *beyond his ken*—he would fear what was massing on the ledge with him so much that jumping would become preferable. . . .

36

"I said that I hope to add to your store of knowledge some information that is unavailable at the school library." He looked straight ahead, calmly setting the stage. "You see, Mr. Stillings . . . Kenneth . . . I think you've developed a habit of taking too much for granted. *Rectify* as an all-purpose term, for example. What do you know"—he drew in a breath—"about the atom?"

"I guess I couldn't actually make an A-bomb," Kenneth answered. "But atomic energy isn't a big *secret* anymore." A shrug.

"All right." He shrugged toward the boy. "Then I take it you would not experience much sense of challenge were I to ask you to . . . *show me* an atom."

Kenneth glanced back, alerted. An apostrophe formed between his brows. "If the conditions were right—"

"If you and I stood in *sight* of a nuclear reactor," Mr. Miliken interposed, "*could* I see an atom—utilizing *any* equipment you wish? One single atom?"

"Well, sure," the child said with a laugh. "Of course!"

Mr. Miliken's delight was just marginally concealed. "*Wrong!* No one has ever *seen* an atom!" Fingertips danced on the wheel. "*No one*, Mr. Stillings. So it goes without saying that subatomic particles such as neutrons have never been seen. An entire science—the citadel of fact is based solely upon the *invisible!*"

The mark between Kenneth's furrowing brows was a question mark.

"Words must be defined by an object's constancy, by determining its boundaries. But Kenneth—*Kenny*—particles come and go, like *ghosts*. While scientists *predict* they are there, physicists cannot say that any given particle will weigh such-and-such or even how long it will be around!"

"Like *ghosts*?"

"Ghosts." Miliken turned to nod and quite nearly lost control of his car.

The number "2" glowed prominently on young Stillings's forehead like a gold star.

In spite of it, the teacher had managed before they stopped in front of Kenneth's house to touch on a number of allied topics—the impossibility of comprehending how gravity worked or evolving a theory to explain black holes to every astronomer's satisfaction—and to shatter much of the boy's faith in reality as *he* knew it.

"I swore by the inconstant moon, I guess," Kenneth joked, getting out. His gaze swept to a second-floor window where a curtain was held back by a feminine hand. Looking again at his teacher, his striking eyes were as red-rimmed as if he had been reading.

"Think of Romeo, not Juliet," suggested Mr. Miliken. " 'O, Will I set up my everlasting rest; and shake the yoke of inauspicious stars From this world-wearied flesh.' " He gunned his engine. The numeral on Kenneth's face shimmered in fading daylight. "We continue our discussion before and *after* class tomorrow."

A blink. "I don't know . . ."

"Your sex education teacher told me your record of consecutive A's is in jeopardy." He saw the boy blink again, crimson. "You require the guidance of a mature man . . . *Ken*." And his tires wailed as he sped swiftly off.

One, *then* two (his challenge grew as the numbers ascended) and, finally, three. The increase was predictable, just what made it fulfilling enough to stop after No. 3—pause, actually—and wait another seven years without succumbing to his periodic impatience.

The third choice, though—Mr. Miliken had to concentrate to bring the name "Megan Auel" to his conscious thoughts—demanded clear-headed reflection. They were different, females. Stronger in a certain way. Fewer were suicides, which explained in part why more of them were dealt with violently. *Ms.* Auel gave every indication, also, of being that rare bird, a well-adjusted teenager, even a *happy* one. He turned the car up a street that would return him to Salinger, smiling at his sudden thought: Normal teenagers were mixed up, out of place, grew easily depressed. Since that made this child *abnormal* by psychiatric definition, his attentiveness to her might be viewed as the tender ministrations of a concerned citizen doing his social duty! That made Matthew Miliken a bit of a healer!

An hour of poring through her school records and personal file persuaded Mr. Miliken that he knew the girl well enough to devise a basic plan.

Megan Auel's assets were her potential liabilities. Having been a fourth child and, she felt, an unwanted one—the data coaxed from pupils by psychological profile was *wonderful*—she had kept to herself and become the shyest of children until the occurrence of puberty. Discovering athletics in general and running in particular seemed to have been a revelation and brought her out of herself. A silly, admiring note scribbled by Coach Smith-Coles claimed she was the best female athlete in Salinger High School history.

But those probing tests that evaluated the intelligence also showed the sixteen-year-old capable of earning far better grades; for the most part, Megan was inclined to settle for B's or high C's—

and that was where Mr. Miliken found his opening.

However gifted or skilled, *no* athlete was allowed to participate on a team without achieving a certain (and absurdly low!) grade level. Young people wildly exaggerated the importance of matters. Sometimes they killed themselves because someone with muscles and pimples or a padded bra would not go out with them—and Megan's running was the *sole* activity that brought her a sense of identity, of worth!

It was also the one activity Matthew Miliken could deny her, and drive the child to despair, ultimately to suicide! Why, his intuitive mind had already guided his hand to affix a D to her most recent paper. Unread!

A problem was that the overall grade average couldn't be sufficiently reduced by one teacher's mark. The realization caused Mr. Miliken to frown and ponder until the solution surged into his consciousness with the radiant suddenness of the numerals rising to his selections' foreheads: Any F would get Megan suspended from team practice for the day, and an F final would get her thrown off the team—so he'd *flunk her*!

But he wouldn't lower her present grade from a D. No; Ms. Auel needed to feel fear and tension and not be pushed to the principal's office with a claim that he was being unjust. She had to see *herself* fail—and Miliken knew just how to accomplish it!

Tomorrow, in class, Megan would leave the starting blocks in her greatest race, and her last. Which was, Mr. Miliken promised himself as he graded the rest of the papers, retrieved his coat, and walked without stealth to the darkened parking lot, just where the muscle-bound little female cretin would finish: *Dead last*.

Alone in his apartment, he spent a relaxing evening, retired for the night without giving a thought to any of his school activities (the healthy man compartmentalized his affairs), and awakened the next day fully rested, bothered neither by dream nor nightmare.

But he had been awakened by his telephone jangling, not by his clock radio.

He answered with his mind functioning at noontime proficiency. "Miliken."

"Matthew, I think I have some terrible news."

"Well, Simon," he told the newest and youngest man in English, "I should think it either is or isn't." He stretched his long back, and caught a glimpse of the calendar on a wall round the corner from his kitchenette. He always drew a slash through the day's date with a red crayon before departing for school, and today's date was the 7th. *Auspicious*, he noted, paying closer attention to the caller.

"It is terrible. Tragic." Simon Fontaine lowered his voice as if one might wish to keep what followed secret. "He's a pupil of yours, I think. Lyall Dorris?" Simon paused for a reaction, got none. "He shot himself. Just heard about it on the news." A second pause. "With his father's gun."

Mr. Miliken pursed his lips. He looked forward to going into his bathroom to see the number "7" appear in each of his mirrored eyes. The numeral, black, shiny as pitch, would not linger long. "Thank you for notifying me," he added, remembering his etiquette.

"Kid had just seen a horror flick," Simon blathered. "Wonder if that had anything to do with it. What do you think, Matthew?"

"I think it was probably his stammer." He lifted the arm that was free above his head, yawned. "The poor boy."

41

Then he had twenty-four satisfying minutes to spend in his morning ablutions, with the added feature. His ride to Salinger was uneventful, the day spent largely in listening to whispers and horrified gasps from faculty and student body alike. The sounds served as a delightful counterpoint to Mr. Miliken's private ruminations until, just before afternoon class began, little Kenneth Stillings obediently arrived on time.

"I looked up some of the stuff you mentioned." Standing on the side of the desk opposite his teacher, Kenneth's size and sober face made Mr. Miliken think of history, of boy sopranos whose voices were so pure they were said to have been castrated before puberty, turned for all their lives into adorable songbirds. The old customs . . . "You were right," Kenneth said.

"I was."

Kenneth frowned. "It was kind of hard even to check out some of it."

"Why do you imagine that was, Mr. Stillings?"

A troubled sigh. "I guess some experts don't like to admit it when . . ." He let his voice trail away.

The teacher linked his fingers. "—When reality escapes them. They have no further reason to exist." His elongated thumbs circled one another slowly.

"I don't think I passed the quiz in Ms. Rathman's class today. I sort of knew the answers, but I c-couldn't put them down."

"The sex education class." He saw Kenneth falter, stare down. "You were embarrassed, weren't you?"

Kenneth reddened, wasn't far from tears. "Mother doesn't want me to take that class, 'cause I'm too young, or shouldn't hear about things . . . that way. Or—"

"Kenny." Miliken spoke quietly, gently. *"We're*

men here." The hard glaze over the blue eyes started to melt. "Son," he added, "I understand."

The teenager checked the door to make sure no other pupils had entered. "You do?"

It took an effort made possible only by unstinting practice, but Mr. Miliken bestowed on him the sweetest smile Kenneth had seen on a man's face. "Yes, I do." He held the boy's gaze as he would have held the world's most precious and fragile jewel. "Ken, for some, sexuality is merely an annoyance; perturbation. Are you aware that for some males—healthy, dare I say it, normal males?—the idea of animalistically pursuing a female is abhorrent. And do you know why?" A wait for the head shake. "Because, boy, it is an interference in the cool intellectual activities of life—the superior life."

"Well," Kenneth whispered, "I can see that."

"*You* can," Miliken cried, "of course!" He was at his most affably authoritarian and paternal. "History is full of outstanding men who learned always to *subdue* what the great unwashed call the 'natural' drives." A delicate pause. "Such techniques might be a bit advanced for you at present—not that you'd find a word about them in the school library!"

Footsteps shuffled outside in the corridor. Kenneth went round the desk to Mr. Miliken, leaned down. "What if y-you've begun having . . . a *little* of those drives? Not *much*," he said, cheeks red again, "but what if—"

"Later," Mr. Miliken said, as the others began to file in. His gaze touched the arriving Megan Auel. He hid a frosty smile behind a reassuring clap on Kenneth's arm. "Don't fret, Ken. We'll work together on this problem as long as it takes!"

He waited until his students were seated, and asked for a moment of silence to "honor your poor classmate, Lyall." While heads were bowed, he finished ironing out details in his foolproof plan for the female athlete. When it occurred to Mr. Miliken to pass out the graded papers from yesterday's test, to worry and fluster Megan, he was out of his chair, giving them to a pupil named Martin to pass back, like a shot.

Watching Megan's expression change, he knew he had done the right thing.

Rising, he went round to the front of his desk, sat lightly on it, and explained that he intended to try something "a little different today." He stressed that their marks for that period would depend upon the "performance" of those he called on. There was only one pupil among them, he knew, who could cope well with the assignment, and he did not plan to call on Kenneth Stillings.

"Without opening your books," he began, "I want the pupils whose names I call to tell all of us the story of *Romeo and Juliet*."

The classroom fell utterly silent.

"Is it an unreasonable request?" he inquired. "I don't believe so. We've read many scenes aloud. Surely the majority of you have been adequately intrigued by one of the greatest dramatists to leaf through the rest of the play without my prompting." He smiled sunnily, especially upon Ms. Auel. With her training schedule, she was not likely to have read more than the assigned passages. He'd call on her last; let her stew. And the way she slipped yesterday's paper surreptitiously into a notebook suggested how much she surely hoped he would not call her name. "We begin at the beginning—act One, scene One; a public place, with"—he paused dramatically before choosing Martin, who had dispersed the papers for him—"you."

It was—all of it—a predictable disaster. With an eye on the classroom clock, Mr. Miliken corrected outrageous guesses, supplied names, occasionally described whole scenes, and steadily worked his way round the room to Megan Auel. Despite Kenneth Stillings's periodically wildly waving arm, he pretended not to see him.

At last, as they limped their way into Act V— the churchyard scene —Miliken stood away from his desk, faced Megan Auel. " 'Ah, dear Juliet,' " he intoned with unblinking eyes. " 'Why art thou so fair? Shall I believe That unsubstantial death is amorous; And that the lean abhorrent monster keeps Thee here in dark to be his paramour?' Tell us, my dear, what Romeo clutches in his hand, what he does with it, then be good enough to summarize the remainder of the play."

Since her success in track, she had come to believe that everyone actually liked her a little. Now she sensed animosity, and it made her feel the way she had as an unwanted child. Megan said, "Well, he had poison, and he takes it."

"Does he share it with Juliet?"

She hesitated. Megan knew both star-cross'd lovers died, so the teacher must be asking her a leading question. "I think. Yes, he must have."

"So *wronnnngg*," Mr. Miliken moaned. "She drew Romeo's dagger and killed herself with it, that 'true and faithful Juliet,' as Montague expressed it." He sounded as if the exhaustion they were inflicting on him was too much to bear. "Go on."

"Go on?" Megan repeated, stunned. "They're dead. Isn't that it?"

It was not, and Matthew Miliken was obliged to display his own acting skill in order to seem as let down as he did. "Prior to that question, Ms. Auel," he said with apparent misery, "I was considering a D for the woeful work I've seen today." He returned to the chair behind his desk just as the buzzer ended the class. "Today's class grade is—an F."

The athlete was facing him across the desk by the time he was sitting. "I don't think that's fair to the kids you didn't call on." She nodded at Kenneth, who was waiting behind her. "It's not their fault. Please don't do that to them."

Mr. Miliken pretended to think hard about what she had said. "You have a point, even if it's just possible you're *more* concerned because your D yesterday has descended to today's F." He smiled and pulled his grade book nearer. "Very well, I'll record an F only for you who so pitifully tried to tell the story. I suppose that means you will not be allowed to practice with your team until you bring the mark up?" His smile became a smirk. "Perhaps you'll do better next week and use your free time to become better acquainted with the Bard."

"Sir," Megan began. But her eyes filled with tears. She could not trust herself to speak. So she rushed out of the room silently and left Kenneth with Miliken.

"That was nice of you, not giving the rest of us an F," the boy said.

"I strive, always, to be a reasonable man," Mr. Miliken said modestly. He got unhurriedly to his feet. "What would you say to another ride home?"

The child grinned. "I'd say thanks," he said. And that was done.

A block or two from Salinger, Mr. Miliken reprised the theme of his earlier topic. "You asked me, I believe, what could be done if certain passionate drives were only starting to shake a man's equilibrium. Like subatomic particles, they come and go—and may be successfully diverted."

"It is a real problem sometimes," Kenneth confessed. "I would never mention it to Mother. And Dad—well, he just isn't around much."

"How sad for you." Obviously, Mr. Miliken thought, Kenneth was well into puberty; obviously, Rathman's class had explained what was happening to his body, but not to his mind. Miliken sighed, recalled his own early longings. It was just about then that he had started to become the man he was today. "I told you that certain techniques could prove to be somewhat advanced. However, some of the older students— that football player you mentioned, for example—might know what I was referring to." He shrugged. "Don't make too much of it . . . or too little."

"Sir?"

Miliken stared at Kenneth's puzzled face and said what he meant: "The primary obligation of the superior male is to let nothing stand in the way of his basic plans."

"*Nothing?*"

"Nothing."

"So I ought to go ahead and just—"

The teacher shook his head. "Not so long as *anyone or anything* is there, to free you of the impediment. Reduce tension, so you can return to your chosen course as soon as possible." He was firing the warhead of his design for the teenager. It all depended on his reading of Kenneth. He felt sure the parents had done their part, whether they'd meant to or not, by loading him with the requisite guilt. "A superior man has focus, maintains his course. If he has not *sought* the disease of either human dreams or desires, it is his duty to cure himself of both in order to focus on his own mandated objectives."

"You said 'anyone,' Mr. Miliken?" The glowing "2" was back in the center of his forehead as if the skin were inflamed. "And *anything*?"

Appearing not to hear, Mr. Miliken took his lengthiest pause. "D'you like animals, Mr. Still-ings?" He basked from head to toe in the warmth of the red numeral. "Do you have any *pets*, Kenny?"

And that, he thought, as the child got out in front of his house, was every bit that he could do. A living seed, planted in a timely manner, grew—and ideas were such seeds. How long it took for the crop to reach the state of harvesting was impossible to gauge. But he was sure to give little, troubled Kenneth his phone number at home "in case you have need of me."

He paid his respects to Lyall Dorris in the morn-ing at the mortuary. Because the casket was closed, he did not view the remains. He did intro-duce himself to Police Lieutenant Dorris and the sedated mother. No, he hadn't known Lyall was so unhappy; yes, it could be hard to understand chil-dren these days; blah-blah-blah. Then he inspected the floral wreath he'd ordered during the lunch hour the day before, and left his signature in the keepsake register with a flourish.

That turned out to be Mr. Miliken's happiest moment until the evening.

Megan Auel didn't attend his class. That was highly peculiar, since he'd have sworn he saw her out jogging on her familiar route on his way to the funeral home. In the principal's office, the only fact he elicited from Mr. Cross's secretary was that she'd actually been in school. Mystifying. She wasn't ill, old Cross didn't care that she had cut his class, and the secretary refused to say more.

Wondering what was going on or being kept from him left Mr. Miliken with so much neurotic tension for the remainder of the afternoon and evening that, when small Mr. Stillings phoned him just before midnight, he almost shouted at him.

Kenneth did not seem to notice. "Dad was here," he said. "They're getting a divorce." As he paused, Mr. Miliken swallowed a Medipren. But the child wasn't waiting for sympathy. "I called one of the older guys and he knew what you were talking about. I got some pictures; other stuff." Their connection was remarkably clear and it sounded, now, as if Kenneth was whispering in his ear. "I asked a girl to go out, see, but I don't have a driver's license so—well, I'm feeling a lot of tension. I want to get back on course."

Miliken's heart began to pound heavily. He thought he knew what Kenneth meant, but needed to make sure. "The 'stuff,' he said. "Does it include a—*rope*?"

"Sure. You have to have one, or just the right sort of belt. Sir, thanks for talking to me about not letting dumb things stand in my way."

"The superior male won't permit it." It was delicate now; maybe the brat wanted to be talked out of it.

"Well, that's what I want to be. Not like my father. More like you." He swallowed hard, sounded reassured. For a moment white sound was between them. Then, like that, "Bye." And he'd hung up.

"Well, well," said Mr. Miliken, smiling. He walked down a short hallway to his bath, closed and bolted the door after him. His head was ever so much better. He undressed, then took the chair he always kept in the room and turned it to face the mirror and basin. Sitting, he folded his arms, crossed his legs, and waited. He was very good at it. He believed honestly that he could wait until hell froze over.

It only took him until one A.M. to see the informative black "7" gleaming in the pupils of his eyes.

Sleeping blissfully that night, he was quite prepared to project astonishment and grief when Simon Fontaine and Mr. Cross both phoned to report the sad news about Kenneth Stillings having hanged himself.

But only old Cross had heard the horrifying detail that Stillings had been found naked from the waist down in his closet, the victim of an autoerotic experience. "Photographs, strewn at his feet," Cross said raspily, midway between a kind of furious sadness and disgust. "Was the boy a troublemaker?"

"My, no." Miliken stretched his arm to draw a red mark through the new day's date. Another red-letter one. "He was perhaps the most gifted pupil I've had."

"Well, your afternoon kids are becoming very odd," Cross droned. "Megan Auel, the sprinter, has asked for a transfer to Simon Fontaine's class."

The crayon fell from his fingers. "Why?" The bitch! He'd counted off numbers one and two with an efficiency that surprised even him; now a *female athlete* was threatening the overall plan! And all three of them were *volunteers*! "You didn't authorize the transfer?"

"Sure. No reason not to." No *reason*? "That kid is some runner, and athletes are sensitive these days. Well, there's no rule against it till after semester finals."

Mr. Miliken hung up as soon as Cross again mentioned his sadness about Stillings. *Not in your rules, maybe!* he thought. How could he get to Auel now? She was enrolled in no other classes of his; he couldn't stop her in the school corridors and *stab* her!

Seven *years* he'd been the soul of patience, awaited the proper signs, even eschewed the impulse to pick five or six of them. He'd *let* them put up their own hands, then proceeded discreetly, juggling the trio of cretins as if they were eggs. One was followed by two, two by three—teenagers today couldn't follow the simplest arithmetical progression!

Livid, he snatched up the dropped crayon, broke it in two (SOP for dropped crayons), then tore open another box and drew out the red one. He canceled out the day's date so violently that the tip broke off. Furious now, he threw the rest of the crayons at his wastebasket and missed, spilling them onto the floor.

Abruptly, the need to buy another box or, when tomorrow came, of pinching the tip of the replacement crayon between thumb and index, was an outrage! Megan Auel *had* to be punished, soon! He had even been prevented from going to the bathroom to see the sevens shine from his eyes again! Well, he'd already perceived her to be happy, therefore abnormal; now he had the insight to see her as a lesbian—who else could have stalled his plans by merely transferring from one class to another?

But she had not reckoned (he reminded himself with yet another flash of uncanny inspiration) on his perfect willingness to *help* fulfill their commitments! Colliding with the jut-out of the wall and his kitchenette counter, he read the time shown on the clock and drew in a satisfying, quick breath.

He knew the hours when *Ms.* Auel went jogging and the course she followed—and right *now*, she would be leaving home to do her exercises before the school day began!

Throwing on his suit coat, leaving it unbuttoned for the first time in years, he went looking for her. In general, that would be Archer Road, because it led to the school. But he'd have to hurry in order to get close enough for him to see the "3" on her forehead *just as he ran her down*.

The morning was so overcast and threatening he thought not of *Romeo*, and Verona, but *Macbeth* and Scotland. The world was awry, nature askew, helpless to permit spring because of the ignorance and immorality of today's teenagers. Well, *he* did not lie down and allow the cretins to clamber over him. The Matthew Milikens—the superior men—knew ways to cope with the brats! *He* would not be pushed around or conned by them!

He whipped the brow-matching automobile round a corner with his thumbs folded so tightly round the steering wheel—and so far—that they almost touched. He squinted narrowly through the wet windshield, turned the wipers on. Archer had little traffic flow since the installation of the nearby freeway. These days, the two-lane road was used primarily by other time-wasting joggers or those motorists obliged to cross Archer to wend their way out of or into the bleak older neighborhoods. Mr. Miliken raised his left index finger and two fingers of his right hand from the wheel just long enough to note and count them. *I've even triumphed over mathematics*, he realized, beaming. *For the first time in history, one plus one equals three!*

Rather more than a block ahead, a slender form jogged at the side of the road. A *familiar*, a *female* form. Moving in the direction he was headed, he realized; away from him.

Not nearly fast enough to stay so, Mr. Miliken thought.

The total realization of that thought brought a rising thrill. This young athlete had acquired a reputation—become a Salinger High School superstar—because she imagined, doubtless, that she could outrun anyone. Well, they'd see about *that*!

But there was no rush, no hurry at all, dear *Ms*. Auel. Indeed, there was precisely as much time as Matthew Miliken cared to give Megan before he drove his car *right up her back*. With the windows rolled down then, to hear the small bones of her vertebrae crack and crunch!

"A-one, a-two," he sang and, without accelerating in the least, tooted his horn. But Auel was carrying one of those modern radios, and she couldn't hear him yet. Well, she *would* know he was there! Perhaps he would just eeease up behind her, take the whole process *slooowwly*, permit her fear to build. Then—at the last conceivable second—*Ms*. Auel would finally see him and learn who was *teacher*, who was *superior*!

Suddenly, he was practically on *top* of her! Mr. Miliken had to tap his brake to keep from ending it too fast! Leaning angrily on the horn, he kept the heel of his hand there until the blast might have awakened the dead.

Megan peered over her shoulder without haste and motioned for him to pass.

His brown brows rose, descended, repeated the

exercise several times before he grasped what was happening.

The little bitch imagined she was being pursued by boys from the track team who enjoyed teasing the female athletes. And the noise slamming into her ear from the Walkman was deafening her.

Irked because his next thrill had been thwarted and because he did not like being confused with anyone else, Mr. Miliken allowed his car to pull again within feet of Megan. It occurred to him briefly to go *ahead*, to do it—take no remote chance of letting her escape her assigned numerical position. Then he realized he was not going fast enough at all to be *sure* the car killed her, and had no choice but to cut the wheel to his left and sweep around her.

Yet what happened that instant brought the sunshine back to his cheeks.

Megan *looked directly at him*, and *recognized him*, and the surprise on her face appeared to be matched by a *discernible rise of fear*!

"Three lit-tle words," he sang a snatch of the old melody, his heart tom-tomming accompaniment. When was the last time a number had stared back with a suspicion of his intentions? Exciting! Well, he had only to find somewhere to turn in, make a U, and then he'd be right on the bitch's heels again. This time, he'd build up enough speed during his approach to plow Ms. Megan Auel into the concrete!

Matching action to plan, he spotted a driveway and whipped his car into it at reckless speeds, backed out joltingly, and roared down Archer Road with his eyes rolling from left to right in search of the sprinter. He could thank his stars another vehicle hadn't hit him when he backed out; now he'd rein in the impulse to rush—proceed in a truly systematic manner in order to fulfill the mission.

And as for those "three lit-tle words," they simply meant *I'll kill you!*

—*There* she was! Mr. Miliken's heart soared. Clearly, she thought that he had driven on—probably to school—that she'd been wrong in believing there was menace in the horn blast and his abrupt materialization. She was simply jogging along Archer Road at an easy pace, as oblivious to danger—to him—as they'd all been over the years. *Idiots!* he thought, his well-trained memory providing the apt lines from the tragedy he taught so well: "Doth she not think me an old murderer, Now I have stain'd the childhood of our joy . . . ?" But when he had sped by and looked in his rearview mirror, she still had not caught on, hadn't even *noticed* his car returning on the other side of the road, now disappearing over a ridge!

So he made the second U, then stared at Megan's peaceful form effortlessly drifting along the road. Rain was coming down more heavily, slanting across the windshield; yet *Ms*. Auel hadn't even increased her speed. She was volunteering again! Transmission in neutral, Matthew Miliken raced his car engine, imagined for a moment he was making his own thunder. " 'Three words, dear Juliet,' " he paraphrased, and slipped the transmission into drive. "One . . . two . . . *three!*"

His automobile peeled powerfully away. All he needed to remember now was to focus his attention on the girl's face at the point of contact, so he wouldn't miss seeing the "3" come to throbbing life on her fair forehead. Afterward, when she lay crushed beneath his wheels, he could tilt his rearview mirror down in order to watch his eyes change. Knowing her body was ruined and dead under the car at the instant he saw the black sevens shine like light from the center of the earth might make it go on glowing well into the seven years he'd wait before making his *next* selections.

He began hammering his horn with his balled fist as soon as he was able to make out her close-cropped, light brown hair. "*Look* at me," he willed her—"*look at me!*"

Hearing the horn blare above the music from her radio, Megan did look back, eyes widening in a terror of understanding.

But she looked forward again, too soon for Mr. Miliken to glimpse her forehead, then *seemed to fly*—ran so *fast* that he, in sudden panic not to let her escape, let his foot slip off the accelerator. And before he could have counted three, an astounding *gap* lay between them. Worse, Megan seemed to be looking for somewhere she might *run off the road*! That would force him to stop, chase her *on foot*—and there was no way in hell he could catch her that way!

Entirely unprepared for such a swift reaction, he hadn't moved the car forward an inch when the athlete next glanced back. She was the length of a football field ahead of him!

Damn them *all*, he thought, damn *all the brats*! Fingers and prehensile thumbs tight on the wheel, dizzyingly frustrated, his brown brows working furiously, he drove his foot into the accelerator and floored it.

"One-two-*three*," he muttered. "*Onetwothree*," in a combined prayer and chant. It wasn't possible for her to outrun a car, it was unthinkable for a pupil to destroy his pastime, his world! Through the drenching rainfall he watched the car narrow the distance quickly between them, thought of it as *devouring* the gap. It was *time*, he was *empowered*, he was a *god*! Almost there, nearly to completion! *Look at me*, he ordered her mentally, hurling the thought-command after her—*LOOK AT ME!*

Incredibly, she *did*—and seemed to stumble. She broke stride just as she hazarded a swift, desperate glance over her shoulder—and he was *seven yards* behind her, *six* yards, *five*, *four*, *THREE* . . .

And for a flash it was as if she had *vanished* from Matthew Miliken's sight—because she had jumped a ditch and dashed into the woods! Compelled to crush her, he spun the steering wheel in the direction she seemed to have gone—

And the car rammed headfirst into the ditch, jammed there momentarily on end, then flipped into the air. Not achieving much height, it came down on its top like a man's fist slamming into the earth, its tires spinning as if possessed by an idiot's desire to continue the chase.

Through a torrent of blood he took dimly for red rain, Mr. Miliken saw the upside-down feet of the young woman who would never be third approaching, hesitantly. "As one dead in the bottom of a tomb," he remembered; was that why she wasn't seeing if she could help?

Then, when Megan finally did lean down and peer through the shattered windshield, he observed that she was wearing a school jersey under her unzipped warm-up jacket. The number "7" was sewn into it in vivid crimson.

Because of the way his neck and spine were broken, leaving his fingers clutching the wheel, it was too difficult for Mr. Miliken to decide if the number was a sign or not, perhaps even a benediction. And when he strove to speak, he wasn't able to enunciate more than the beginning letter of the word *help*. Despite all his willpower, the only other thing he could manage was to stare at her, stupidly, brown eyes virtually popping from his head.

Telepathy, he thought, seeking an apt line and, finding it, projecting it mentally with everything he had: *"A greater power than we can contradict hath thwarted our intents."* He hurled the words from his scared-mouse brain to her shocked but well-ordered mind. Now, at least, she would know he was still alive!

Megan Auel stopped well back from the brown car before it burst into flame, and just before the fire got to him, Mr. Miliken was fairly sure she nodded.

The Writing of "When Nature Itself Creates Them"

This is one of the new stories in *Frights of Fancy* and there isn't a great deal I can say about it that wouldn't spoil your enjoyment of it.

So if you feel like it, when you've read it, please return here and read this: I'm not lucky enough to have a drop of Native American blood, but I research myths of the paranormal a lot and there's a tremendous amount to read about in Arizona, New Mexico, and throughout that region. I don't for a second believe I'm right in the premise of this tale, but what else—except Native American beliefs—explains why this most prevalent modern myth began just where my little story takes place?

When Nature Itself Creates Them

New Mexico Territory, 1878

He had been in the saddle since before daybreak, and ridden northwest from the town he called home these days to a ranch just outside of Picacho.

That was where he'd planned to cut out of the herd just enough fine cattle to turn a profit for himself, a notorious loner who had no hands to pay. With spit's worth of luck—something young W. H. fancied he possessed less of than any other commodity—the sale of the stolen cattle would be a fact before they were missed.

Being a loner was just the way he liked it, particularly since he had already spent a little money bribing Four-Finger Spencer, whose usual task was guarding the herd on the eastern border of the ranch. Afterward, Spencer would just tell his boss he had been diverted, drawn off by other noises. Even with the range wars showing signs of slowing down, there wasn't a landowner in the whole Territory who wasn't worried that a bunch of crazy cowboys might make a little mischief simply to raise hell.

For the final ten miles to Picacho, though, W. H. had the recurring impression that he was being watched, maybe followed, possibly getting double-crossed by Four-Finger Spencer. Each time he slowed his mount to a canter, however, listening for the sound of other hoofbeats, his keen ears picked up nothing out of the ordinary. Twice he reined his horse to a quick stop as if they were trying not to vault off the edge of a cliff, but the scrawny rustler still heard nothing unusual. The second time, he glanced around warily and saw little more than mesquite, the kind of cactus every rider hoped he'd never fall on, a couple of prairie hens, and some low-flying quail. When he squinted, he made out, in the distance, a puff or two of smoke that could have been Apache signals but were more likely what was left of somebody's breakfast. They sure as hell had nothing to do with anyone dogging his trail.

He finished his trip without incident, not in the least feeling guilty about his carefulness. The Territory had provided him with more practical knowledge than he'd ever acquired back home. He wouldn't be nineteen years of age until late November, and he had already promised himself that he would drill any man, woman, or child who threatened to end his life while he was just eighteen!

The herd was unguarded when W. H. reached the ranch, just as arranged. There wasn't even a glimpse of ol' Four-Finger, and he set to work at once to cut out the number of cattle he thought he could drive back home with him. The trouble was that the steer he chose to take the lead didn't want to stop grazing and wouldn't seem to panic or even *notice* him. The last thing in the world he wanted was a stampede, but what the young cowboy could never tolerate was being ignored by any creature that was able to breathe.

Finally, the damn stubborn steer snorted and got a mite nervous over his proximity, enough to veer a few feet away—and just as W. H. had expected, a number of cows obediently lumbered after the steer. Reacting swiftly, if not according to the methods he'd been picking up the past couple of years, W. H. withdrew his lasso, made a loop, and lofted it over the big steer's huge head. "Ignore *me*, will you?" he shouted, staring tauntingly into its large eyes before wheeling his horse and heading in the same direction from which the horse and he had come.

The idea was to coax the animal to begin trotting, then running, with the other cattle he had chosen close behind. W. H. would slip the lasso's knot, remove it, and keep them in a southeasterly direction toward home.

But the fool steer started out at a dead run past him, and W. H. merely held on to the rope—while the additional cattle followed in the human's wake, closer to him and his horse then he would have preferred, especially if the latter stumbled. The steer, though, was running so fast it would be impossible for him to sustain the pace for long. A cowpoke was supposed to be in charge, not just let go of his lasso—which he hadn't cinched to his saddle horn when he should have. Eventually, like it or not, he might *have* to release his hold on it and ride out of harm's way.

Steer, would-be rustler, and mount, plus more cattle than the boy had imagined he could successfully steal galloped along in a more or less straight line, forming a design or pattern that might—from the sky—have appeared symbolic or ritualistic. *Maybe I'm wrong*, W. H. thought with hope, *and this fool animal has the strength to go all the way*. Or maybe it'd drop dead. Hell, there were more than enough cows for a damn nice payoff if a *third* of 'em keeled over!

That was when he saw the sun shining down on them like it was noonday—and, right after that, it was so dark it was as if midnight had come. Except a real fast glance out to the left and one to the right told him everything looked as normal as blueberry pie beyond the path they were all taking.

The cowboy stared straight ahead again in time to discover that the steer's powerful legs were still churning but he was *doin' it in the air!* W. H. gripped his lasso with all his might, automatically making sure the animal didn't get away.

And he himself, pulled cleanly from his saddle, was also—*rising into the sky!*

Tilting his face up in fear, he made out the underside and dangling legs of the steer silhouetted against the bright light he'd originally taken for the sun. He didn't know who or what was up there, but he knew that second he was in danger, because he had ahold of the lasso and the other end of it was around the damn steer's neck. They didn't want *him*, they were some newfangled cattle rustlers who were taking what he had worked all day to steal!

For a second he was so confused by his surprise and outrage he considered letting go. But his horse and the now-milling cattle below suddenly looked about half their real size.

"All right, you bastards," he yelled, his voice breaking as he blinked up at the bizarre sight, "if it's a fight you want, it's a fight you're gonna get!"

Now the steer was nearer to the light, and so

was he, and W. H. realized for the first time he was up against some sort of flying contraption, a notion nobody but dumb fools thought was possible. But there it was. That made these rustlers pretty smart, and since they hadn't meant to catch *him*, they might just haul the steer inside and cut the lasso—drop his ass right into the Rio Hondo!

Hellfire, maybe they come up that way, he thought, squinting down at his holster to be sure he was still armed. They'd have to hide this valuable flyin' machine, probably keep it out of sight in the Carlsbad Caverns due south of where he lived, and—the steer vanished inside the machine, and he was only a couple of feet away from it himself. He felt it vibrating! *If they hog-tie me and leave me in a cave, nobody'll see me again till my bones fall through the ropes*!

Without knowing how he got there, he was standing, wobbling, in an oval room with lighting that hurt his eyes. Across the way were six hombres who looked naked for a moment, but his steer and lasso weren't in view. *No time t'get scared, W. H.*, he thought.

When he saw them walking toward him, long arms raised and the palms of their hands open to him, he drew his revolver with the ease and quickness that came with practice—and suspicion of other people's intentions. "I shoulda known you was foreigners," he said scornfully, seeing their faces. "Stop right there, gents!"

Is that a weapon? somebody asked. He couldn't tell which one. *Do you mean us harm?*

"You bet I do," W. H. replied, moving the revolver to include them all in his threat. "Unless you put my steer and me back down and keep out of this Territory. All the cattle you see for a hundred miles is my property!"

We are fortunate to meet you, then, the closest stranger said, stepping forward. He put his long-fingered hand near his waist and an object slipped into it.

The cowboy pulled the trigger of his handgun, firing one unerring bullet into the speaker's torso at just the area of the human heart. The object that had popped into the stranger's slender hand fell to the floor, and so did he. *Violence*, he said, and it was like a wisp of chilly air blowing briefly through the young man's mind. Then the dark, wide eyes of the creature he believed was nothing more than a smart visitor from a far-off land lost all semblance of life.

"You ain't the bright kind of foreigners I thought you was," W. H. said, rotating the barrel of his revolver toward the remaining five visitors. "Anybody else want some of this?"

An exchange was being offered to you, another voice said in what sounded to W. H. like the same one he had heard. The stranger toed the dropped object, a small rectangular thing with a tiny light that glowed green. *It was prepared for a leader among you. It would have told you and all others who we are, our origin, and what we hope to accomplish for your kind and ours*.

A second living speaker added, *It also volunteered data concerning our science, including this ship*. He looked toward the others, his slight shoulders moving. *So little progress over so many years*.

A third speaker said inflectionlessly, *We shall not err again in providing you with either gifts or the opportunity for exchanges of information*.

A fourth stared down at the object with the small light, and it no longer glowed green or any other color. *Nor shall we offer any explanations. They cannot understand*.

"I unnerstand just what you ugly little shrimps are up to!" the human boy snapped. "Wherever you come from, you heard about the price of livestock these days and hoped to make a fast dollar! With the money it took to build this fancy flyin' contraption, you prob'ly planned to raid some of the mining camps too—after rustlin' all my cattle and other holdings!" W. H. was warming to his topic. "I should get some of my—my special police and military after you, while I'm at it."

Another speaker, silent until then, edged cautiously forward. Slightly taller than the rest, he also had extremely wide black eyes, a small nose, and tiny ears placed lower than the cowboy's. His uniform was no less skintight, but showed splashes of color. *It is clear we are in the presence of one of your tribe's leaders, and it is pointless to contact others. Your steer will be returned to the surface as you will be, we assure you. We removed the steer to attempt to solve a part of the great mystery your kind poses for us*. He moved his hand to indicate a long table. Above it, a variety of objects W. H. had not seen before hung in readiness for use. One of them seemed to provide the room's peculiar lighting, but it resembled no gaslight W. H. was remotely familiar with. *Please sit*, the taller stranger urged him. *Seek comfort and answer questions about your world while we are flying you home. Due to your eminent position, you are obviously an authority*.

"I guess it won't hurt none," the rustler agreed, pleased by his host's praise. He perched on the edge of the table, keeping his revolver ready but lowered and including all five surviving strangers in his field of vision. "But don't expect me to give away any government secrets or anything like that— I ain't no damn traitor!"

The tallest visitor stood directly in front of W. H.,

somewhat closer than any people but young girls were generally allowed, with two of the others on either side of him. *We have accustomed ourselves*, the leader began, *to your kind's disposition to want far more than sustenance and progress. What we do not grasp is the seemingly infinite number of things you want, why you desire some of them, and your willingness to take the lives of so many components of your kind to obtain them.*

"I don't want so much," W. H. argued mildly. His eyes narrowed. "You usin' fancy language to insult me?"

Not you as a specific or separate component, a voice answered, though the youth could not be certain the leader had spoken. *Not an insult in any case, but our observations thus far.*

"For example?" W. H. demanded, making his gun rise an inch and wave just a bit. He wished they'd all open their little-bitty mouths a bit when they talked, wished the big shot would back up a pace or stop staring at him like he was a bug or something.

Three of your centuries ago, a voice intoned in his head, *a man called Coronado came to this part of the planet. By stealing many lives, he conquered seven cities whose people were able to do little to thwart him. He sought a golden city named El Dorado, and though he discovered the Grand Canyon, his* want *remained the substance known as gold. Why?*

"Why?" W. H. repeated, astounded. "He coulda bought almost *everything*!"

A different voice—or so W. H. believed— inquired, *Would it have kept him alive longer than the fourteen years he lived after seeking this 'El Dorado'?*

After Coronado, the leader continued, *more of*

those who dwelled here died, many more came and killed before dying—dying as did the first of us to speak to you. People of belief in God, known as missionaries, came for their reasons; then people arrived who wanted to make dwelling places on land where those who first lived here had died. Not all of them were gone, nor all who followed Coronado, so additional lives were stolen. Did the newer visitors have no home-dwellings already or did they lack the gold to exchange? And what made anyone here believe they owned *property to defend or sell?*

"Possession is nine-tenths of the law!" the cowboy shouted. But they just stared at him. "Hell, boys, I don't know. I wasn't born here, I'm from New York."

Each of the five strangers paused. All but the leader glanced at one another. *Another vehicle like this one gathers data from your eastern region and it is no less inexplicable,* he said. *In this Territory there followed what you call 'revolts' and numerous people again perished, although there is much food to consume, and new places to make home-dwellings are often within two days' travel on beasts such as the kind you were forcing to serve as your legs. Why so much* want *with so much land for homes?*

"*I've* traveled, I've traveled a *lot!*" W. H. protested. But he tried to rise and brandish his revolver and could not seem to stop meeting the gaze of the leader. Above him, he imagined, he felt heat, but did not glance up. "I wanta go back down *now!*"

The confrontation termed "war" continues through the years, the tallest visitor said, eyes burning as he stared as W. H. without blinking, *between people such as you and the sort called Apache and Navajo. Now exists a war of the "range." Elsewhere, your kind engaged in a war* with your *kind. Perplexingly, it was called the "civil" war. It seems the primary desire, here, is to kill. Please, explain.*

The youngster lay back on the table, shook his head. "Maybe it's just that we're free. All *I* wanted was cattle to sell to get one of them dwellin' places you mentioned. A nicer one than the Mexes and Indians got. Maybe a nice little woman."

Freedom is good, said the leader; *it cannot explain what happens here.* Lights over W. H. flared; two machines droned eerily. *To reach the root of the enigma your kind poses for us, we have chosen to select and experiment with merely one of the more recent designations of high value you have made. Today we launch our inquiry, to determine why your kind has made only minor progress since our prior contacts with you many of your years ago. We shall not rest—nor will we depart— until our many-faceted investigation enables us to know why you place such value on that isolated example of your wants. Meanwhile, perhaps, we may learn why your kind's aggression is not expressed as an ambition to progress.*

Sprawled on the table, W. H. found himself yawning and fighting the urge to sleep. But he was also feeling deep-down scared and he had to know what the crazy little people were yammering about now. "Which one of our wants? Which example?" he asked.

The taller being from elsewhere lofted a skinny arm. Lights came on above a table closer to the ground. Upon it, legs in the air and large eyes turned appealingly to W. H., was the steer he had cut out at the beginning of their shared nightmare. It looked alive, but it wasn't moving a muscle.

With a supreme effort, a voice spoke in the cowboy's head, *we have come to some comprehension of your kind's proclivity for agreeing upon an exchange value for certain sizes and shapes of paper, of gold, when most of what you need is free. It is harder to grasp the general belief that it is proper to steal the possessions, lives, and home-dwellings of others much like you. We are now forbidden to attempt to understand "war," for it might be injurious to us. So we shall endeavor to learn why you place a steep value on the bovine when nature itself creates them. Many of us theorize the want is sexual, based upon an awareness that cattle offspring are larger, stronger, and have fewer natural requirements. This hypothesis allows for your kind's obvious preference for ever-increasing size and power. Logically, genetics is where our experiments must begin.*

"That's not even a *girl* cow!" W. H. argued, insulted. He tried to rise from the table, but could not; he attempted to lift his revolver, but his hands and fingers were like broth. Groggy or not, that was when his genuine fear began.

He managed to turn his head, glance around. The little-bitty foreigners were grouped, discussing a matter. The leader in the brighter-colored uniform turned back to him. *We are grateful to you for demonstrating that we must never again bring your species among us before your will to destroy has been subdued. Thank you. In exchange, we pledge to return all those we bring aboard to the planet surface essentially unharmed, as you shall be. And to return to the area of your home in the future.*

The cowboy heard a humming noise above him, believed he saw strange tools in several pairs of long-fingered hands as all of them approached him, but he could not focus his eyes. "Now?" he asked, his own voice higher. "Can I go back to the—the surface right now?"

After a brief examination, the leader replied, *to record certain facts about you. From this moment forward you will not remember encountering us. It is for your good and the good of your world, as well as for us.* A round, metallic object descended from the ceiling and hovered over the young man's head. A second descended to a much lower portion of his body which was, though he did not know it, naked. *Tell us the name you were given and the place of your birth.*

"I'm William H. Bonney from New York City," the kid said.

He was kneeling in the dirt in front of the shack he called home these days, fully clad—though his pants legs weren't tucked in—and unaware of how he had gotten there from the ranch outside Picacho. There was no sign of his horse. Shoving himself to his feet, he wondered if it had been spooked by a rattler, thrown him, and run away.

But what happened to the cattle I was rustlin'? he wondered, shaking his head to clear it of several weird images skimmering around in his mind.

He saw, then, that he had succeeded in stealing one of them.

A huge steer lay on its side ten feet away, dead as a doornail despite the fact that he saw no sign of blood. Tottering over to it, stooping, he discovered that its rectum had been cut out as clean as a whistle. There were bruises where its genitals had been, but then, steers became steers because of castration. It looked as if somebody or something had searched for them anyway. What really struck him as crazy was that there were no insects crawling or buzzing around the poor thing's asshole.

He went to bed much earlier that night, feeling light-headed as all get-out, and had a series of the worst nightmares he had ever endured. Shiny lights in the sky were chasin' him, and so was an enormous and glowing steer; then he saw a gang of rustlers no bigger than a minute with enormous black eyes, five-gallon hats, weird tubular weapons instead of six-guns, and he was bucknaked. He had a worse bad dream with doctors dressed in drab gray who had no faces, and they were puttin' something over his pecker—except his pecker *wasn't his*, it was one that belonged on a bull!

Those nightmares were repeated along with different kinds for two weeks until one morning a guy he knew barged into the cabin while he was asleep and W. H. drew on him and squeezed the trigger—and the only reason the man didn't die was that W. H.'s gun had no bullets in it! It had been years since the revolver was empty longer than a minute or two, so that scared him even more than some of the bad dreams.

He took to drawing on anybody who surprised him, shooting some because he was afraid inside they meant to kidnap him, put him on a table, and do something terrible to him. He was still young enough that folks began calling him Billy the Kid instead of W. H., and there were times he liked it and times he didn't and gut-shot them for it.

But whenever anything awful got him into trouble, he always tried to head for home, even if it wasn't any better than the homes of the Mexicans and Indians he had dreamed of back before the nightmares and the shootings started.

Sometimes, when he was home, Billy fell reflective as he sat beside a window at night, alternately keeping an eye open for the sneak-bastards who would someday come to drill him for revenge or reward, and peering up at the southwestern skies. And on rare occasions he'd be honest enough to admit to himself that the latter scared him more than the former, and he would wonder why. It was tied somehow to that morning he'd awakened outside, his horse gone, a steer he recalled tryin' to rustle killed in a way he hoped he would not have to suffer.

And the dreams would return that night, in his own bed. He'd awaken shouting or screaming, and for a little while he tended to remember what it had been like to be W. H. or even "Billy" without two words tagged on that made him a walking target for as long as he lived. Strapping on his side arm, he'd tell himself as he was fixing to ride off that he should never come back, maybe just keep ridin' till he reached New York. There, just maybe, he could begin anew, call himself "Bill Bonner" or something like that. *Hellfire*, he reminded himself the last time he rode off, *it ain't like I'm too old for a fresh start—I'm just twenty-one!*

He went home again though, never seeing the stars that tracked him, and moved, stars that would be back in the same skies decades after he was shot to death and buried.

Home again to Roswell, New Mexico.

The Writing of "Public Places"

Pulphouse, when the first issue was published by Dean Wesley Smith in 1988, had a subtitle: "The Hardback Magazine." And so it was, handsomely published in 1000 copies (plus 250 done in leather). A story of mine was accepted, in editor Kristine Rusch's introductory words, a week after I "saw (their) guidelines."

Kris wrote that "Public Places" suited her "vision of the magazine perfectly" and was also the "antihero protagonist" slot-filler needed for the first issue. Precisely.

At the time Ms. Rusch and publisher Smith bought this tale, I was known, to the degree that I was known at all, as a "prolific novelist" who did a lot of research, a literate editor of two *Masques* fiction anthologies and a briskly selling how-to-book, and an avuncular bird who did a lot of moralizing. More baldly, I was known to believe in good and evil, not an abstract pair of

74

opposites. Each was measurable, a day-to-day proposition, so that growing up in a difficult environment or committing hideous crimes while high on drugs were not excuses to offer me.

Nothing has altered my views, but my take on writing horror fiction began to change when I wrote this story. On occasion, I came to believe, it is well to learn just how thoroughly rotten—how *evil*—bad guys get. Hence, I continued to create antihero types such as Dr. Noble Ellair in *Night Seasons*, Dell and Kee in *Spree*, and those in short fiction such as "No Love Lost," "Herrenrasse," "Goddam Time," "High Concept," "Time Tells Us," "Hildekin and the Big Diehl," and this collection's "Reality Function," plus the tale that follows.

I'm doubtful I'll ever create a more evil "human" antagonist than Stenwall. If the story is out of character for me, at least *he* is out of me, forever!

Public Places

"You done trashed two of Big Buns's little girls over Memorial Day weekend, so he said he ain't gonna give you a chance t'infeck no more of 'em, awright?" Sax Chacker always spoke like a whining parrot, but the self-righteous tone he fell into whenever he quoted his pimp boss made Stenwall feel even more like puking. They were inside the service station, alone, Sax behind the cash register. "Don't you take this personal, but he said t'get yore sick prick into a clinic and keep away from the Farm till you got a clean bill of health. Okay?"

It wasn't close to okay. Stenwall saw Sax glance covetously in the direction of the place they called the Farm, filled with young females, and thought of how Big Buns sometimes gave one of them to this pervert in the western-style hat. Sax, with a razor scar bisecting his pocked face down the middle, whose mug always seemed to be mooning people. Stenwall could care less about the shit Sax Chacker did to the bitches he was paid with, but avid envy was probably already showing on Stenwall's face.

"Since it's the Fourth of July tomorrow, I'm locking up the pumps till Monday." Nervous, Sax tipped his huge hat back on his smooth skull, momentarily stopped gaping out the window toward the Farm, and strove to end their discussion. "So you just get yore doctor's slip and come talk t'Bee Bee in person, awright?"

Stenwall had one more question: the whereabouts of the huge Hispanic guy who operated the Farm. Once he'd learned that Big Buns was in the east, on a procuring trip, he kicked Sax Chacker's ass till the scarred-up pervert couldn't possibly have given a damn how many young hookers Stenwall "infecked."

He hadn't killed Sax, unfortunately. Sax wasn't female.

Meaning to go to the men's for another of his recent, red-hot leaks, Stenwall stormed out of the service station into the broiling desert sunstream and turned toward the side of the building. Mom Baggit preferred for johns to *look* clean, anyway, and he had Sax all over him.

But sizzling motes of light caromed off the station lot, exploding like tiny mushroom clouds, and Stenwall paused to brace himself against the rusty Coke dispenser. Dear Christ, it looked like the edge of the world outside and it also felt that way. If you drove down one unmarked side road leading off the neglected old oven of a highway, you found an air-conditioned converted farm with ladies who took all the heat off—so long as Big Buns wasn't present. He bought a Coke, drank it fast.

But if you drove straight ahead, you wound up

in the desert even before the handkerchief in your
hip pocket stuck to your butt. Shocked by his
insight, suddenly lonely and freshly frightened
for the first time in years, Stenwall saw it as a
choice between heaven and hell. It was another
first for the little enforcer, part-time bodyguard
and spare-time hitman, to prefer the former over
the latter.

Scarcely noticing Sax's hefty three-quarter-ton
truck left on the lip of the concrete drive, Stenwall headed for the men's, thinking. Probably it
was Phoenix where he had acquired the rash. For
a week, that was all he imagined it was. But
another pimp who looked after his ladies had
rejected Stenwall's money and he'd gotten pissed,
then deep down worried, and ultimately headed
for where he'd known damn well he could get
some. Or believed he could.

En route, the fevers—not constant; occasional
ones—had begun. In Taos, two days back, he had
admitted he wasn't at all well. Blaze, Nevada, had
begun increasingly to sound like heaven. Because
hookers were everywhere, but not the sort Big
Buns raised, literally, for fun and profit. He
bought on the unwanted baby market or kidnaped the real cuties, then handed 'em over to
Mom to get the maternal touch.

And every year, a new "crop" came in, ripe for
harvesting. They were nine, twelve, maybe as old
as fourteen; depended on the girl, and how ol'
Mom ranked her.

But Independence Day—July Fourth—that was,
by tradition, the day when the true cream of the
crop was marketed, and all of Big Buns's regu-
lars—like Stenwall—had the date stuck to the
insides of their brains as if Christmas had started
coming twice a year. No moon-faced pervs and no

running goddamn sores were going to keep Stenwall from groping around under the tree to see what the faggot Santa Claus had left for him!

Woozy, he shoved against the men's door, then swore. He could never remember that this building was so damn old the doors opened out, as if the men's had once been part of a private house. Tottering inside, he told himself he'd have this one last virgin—two if he was up to it—then get medical help. After the treatment, he'd be out of action awhile but he'd have this last romp at the Farm to remember while he healed.

If I heal, Stenwall mused darkly. Part of the truth he was having to face was that he never screwed anyone but hookers, and bought two a week. Unlike Bee Bee and Mom's little darlings, they weren't all exactly immaculate.

Another part of the truth was that Stenwall was street-smart but otherwise stone stupid. He lived just to fuck. He stole and chiseled, sold unsavory goodies and would muscle or kill anyone at all, so he had cash-money for fucking. He boasted, told jokes, ate, slept, and occasionally bathed, moved his bowels, and breathed to fuck. And whores were fine, nowadays preferable, for numerous cogent reasons. He even had a speech for the way hookers were cheaper in the long run; another attesting to their infinite variety.

Other women had drawbacks, but Stenwall had no speech explaining that particular viewpoint.

He squeezed into the room, elbowed the front door shut, locked it. At once, his nose wrinkled. The goddamn Sax Chacker made no goddamn effort to keep the place clean, and the men's reeked. If ghosts had followed the scent of their own urine the way animals did, for ID, this was surely the most haunted place on earth. Joseph Smith might have stopped to pee on his way to Utah!

It was also windowless, little more than an out-house that flushed, and Stenwall—whose nose made him don fresh clothes whether he had washed lately or not—bustled to the solitary uri-nal, fumbled for his zipper and idly peered down, anxious to get this over with.

Still zipped, he made a face.

The customary mothball-stinking oval shit lay at the bottom of the upright pisser, disinfectants that failed and looked like the testicles of some-one who had died in Egypt and been mummified over a urinal. Sax had let the thing back up. Vis-cous, golden piss lolled round the nuts and, should Stenwall deposit even a drop, the mess would slosh all over his glossy shoes.

Hurriedly—furious to be Out of There, driving to the Farm—he walked between the two modest par-titions housing the one commode and unbuckled, sweating. Trousers at half-mast, Stenwall paused, abruptly moved by his recent disposition toward hygiene. He unrolled a couple of feet of toilet paper to spread on the horseshoe shaped seat, working with the exquisite care of a father wrapping his child's birthday present. And he took particular care with the horseshoe's break, where Brucie, named years ago in high school, would need to dangle.

Stenwall's precautions had nothing to do with the outstanding chance that he'd contracted a communicable disease and wished to protect the innocent. They stemmed from the harsh warn-ings Ma had given him thirty years earlier, and served—once he was perched cozily in place—to trigger other memories of his past.

As if he had become an aged person, grown

aware of a limited future, inclined to imagine unlimited pasts.

But it hurt again, to whiz. He gasped audibly and simultaneously achieved a rolling, thunderously odoriferous dump—as well as a glimpse of the most intriguing graffiti Stenwall had ever found on a john wall. Instantly, his plan for medical assistance was forgotten in the presence of that kind of panorama that had ever urged Stenwall to inquire into the weltanschauung of existence itself.

An epicurean spectacle of foul legends spread across the booth walls on either side of Stenwall, and a scanning evoked his complete admiration. A lengthier, more thoughtful perusal of graffiti and he was inspired—*elevated*.

After cramming another yard or so of toilet tissue beneath him and rubbing, Stenwall sought a writing implement—anything! Adding his own observations to the marvelous compilation was essential—he could do no less!

But since he scarcely ever remembered to send even a Christmas card to his mother, and rarely dealt in checks, there was no pen or pencil anywhere on his person. The witty, rude jingle he had dredged from memory and meant to write began to fade.

Eagerly then, Stenwall leaped up. He struck the flush lever, yanked his trousers up, mentally saw himself reaching into his pocket for a knife.

But the gee-dee toilet was rejecting his shit. Already it rose dangerously near the seat itself, blackly swarming—

And he saw the other wall, the wall *behind* the lavatory cubicle, with a gaze of rapture akin to the expression of the suppliants who had first seen the Sistine chapel.

Cuh-ryst, Stenwall marveled. From fly-specked ceiling to sticky men's room floor, extending the width of the room, lines of graffiti had been scribbled or carved with such a mood of frolicking, fresh esprit that the gaze of the muscular little onlooker was magically gripped. By comparison to the works he had admired while seated, these limericks, gibes, Kilroys, and innovative genitalia were Miltonian . . . Byronic . . . Shakespearean. There were also feminine names, phone numbers, addresses!!

Awestruck, Stenwall edged closer. Space for more was available, narrowly. But what he chose to add could not be the product of a whim or a stale imagination. Stenwall withdrew his pocket knife, opened it, held it poised in his palm with aesthetic tension, leaned nearer—and froze, surprised.

Half the drolleries were dated . . . *decades ago*. He scanned an amusing anecdotal verse concerning a lass named Jill—"she will"—and the date: May 5, 1928.

Magnetized, Stenwall grunted. He had known Big Buns's place went back a long way, but he couldn't have conceived the service station building was—

Stenwall began to sweat again. There was a neatly crafted raillery about a female named Flora—and three digits: 916! The date adjacent to the signatory, "Foot Long Frankie," was 1909. "916" was Flora's *phone number*?

To feverish Stenwall, distantly disturbed by a sense of apprehension and twinges of pain, what he was seeing before him was renewal. A hallowed Wall of Memories. Chuckling at intricate cartoons, reading more messages, he licked his lips and nodded his approval. It was possible that all the old broads who'd do it, lick it, eat and sit on it, "69d" and loved "every manly inch" were rotting in the ground today.

Yet the things their men said about them

lived. In a way, Stenwall thought as his heartbeat accelerated, these slits were fucking *immortalized*!

Suffused with enthusiasm, he chose a suitable portion of the wall and started to carve in it, remembering the little he'd learned about filigree. Sweaty, he dragged the sharp blade, formed a large, magnificent "F" with a flowering tail and curved curlicue for the cross-bar. Making small sounds, satisfied but self-demanding, Stenwall went to work on an enchanting "U."

—Hesitated, believing he had heard, from the other side of the wall, another, similar scraping sound.

Intently listening, brows raised, Stenwall edged back. *It's fucking heat*, he concluded, retrieving his backward step, raising the knife.

The answering noise of carving began once more but was immediately drowned out by the vastly louder sounds of something massive—ponderous—headed, apparently, toward the door of the men's room.

Spooked, Stenwall whirled, stared in that direction. The room trembled—

And he thought he knew what the rumbling was and dashed frantically to the door, tugged on the knob.

Again, he'd forgotten it opened out. Except, it wouldn't do that now; it wouldn't budge. "Hey," Stenwall called in a small voice. He lowered his shoulder, pushed, did it again with more oomph. Zilch. *"Hey!"* he cried, shoving hard—

The door gave, opened. Fractionally, a crack, a half inch.

And he knew his hunch was right. He really should have killed Sax Chacker.

The scar-faced pervert had backed his three-quarter truck against the men's room door and parked there. The motor wasn't running.

J.N. Williamson

The fucking jackoff pimp's man had *imprisoned* Stenwall!

"Hey!" he shouted, much louder. "Sax, you scuzzball, get your goddamn truck outta the way!" A pause. "Come on." No answer. "Chacker? Dammit, man, move that sonovabitch now—you hear me?"

The white glare in the crack to the outside was late-day sunlight, and all was silence but for the hot, silent scream of desert heat.

"Sax, hey? Yo, Sax?" Staring at the sunny glare was beginning to blind him; his face, reactively livid, was pouring sweat. "Well, I got to hand it to you, man . . . Sexy Saxy, you sure caught *me* by surprise!" The flat, mute strange shriek of sand as far as the eye could see crept up Stenwall's arms, neck, whispered hot and blubbery things in his ear. ". . . Please, Sax? Please, man?"

Outside, way out there, a homebound, holiday semi blasted like the last tyrannosaurus and, giving up, Stenwall spun away from the front door and angrily threw his pocket knife at the closest object, the washbasin. The clatter on the hard floor was a shock. Instantly, he went after the knife and fell to his knees, snatching it up and finding the blade had snapped in two.

Worse, his trouser knees were stained with the crap he had knelt in.

Stenwall ripped a handful of paper toweling from a wall dispenser, hoisted one knee to the basin's edge, awkwardly, and turned on the faucet.

It made a *croak-kukkuk* like an animated frog. Nothing came out of the faucet but rusty-looking puke. He worked the second faucet and not even the lily-pad crowd responded.

He looked toward the sealed rest room door, and the place where a window would be if they'd

84

made one. Stenwall sobbed. Sax had said he was locking up the pumps, that he'd be there awhile—but then he was leaving for the holiday. Tomorrow, the Fourth of July, was a Friday. This was a Thursday, late afternoon.

And neither Big Buns nor the goddamn pervert split-face in the cowboy hat planned to return—until Monday.

Stenwall was stuck in a rundown men's on the fucking outskirts of hell and nobody except a bastard he'd beaten up even knew he was there. *Jesusjesus*. Claustrophobia Stenwall hadn't known he possessed fluttered up along with the realization that the Farm—the little girls—might as well have been on the gee-dee Gaza Strip!

"I could die here," he sobbed. Three and a half days of heat, no food or water—it was getting real to him—he could *die* in a *men's*!

"Wait," he said it aloud, crouched. There was water . . . there *was*.

He sped back to the lavatory cubicle and stared down, heart thudding.

But the john was crammed with the tissue he had used, and it wasn't just water.

Frantic, he began hitting the flush handle. Over and over.

The toilet coughed dryly, overflowed. Stenwall watched the stained and wadded assortment come up and seep under the seat like a goddamn swamp monster. Perspiring, involuntarily crying out, he jumped back before it slopped over his shoes, perceived that he was gagging, and started to vomit stress-bile. Or worse. Suddenly the stench was foul in such close quarters and his guts were killing him.

Behind Stenwall, the three-quarter's big motor turned over. Spinning, running, he got to the blessed crack he had created in time to hear the tires clutching at the concrete and to wonder if Sax Chacker was driving off or merely taunting him. *"Please,"* Stenwall begged—

At that instant the truck backed up against the door again, neatly slamming it shut without smashing the frame, and turned the old rest room into a nearly airtight container. Glancing down, wildly, Stenwall saw that he couldn't even have slipped a note asking for help between the crammed-closed door and the truck. Then the three-quarter's engine shut down. Silence.

He knelt beside the basin, arms draped over it, cheek pressed to the sink's relative coolness. Partly, he slept; partly, he passed out.

It must be morning, Stenwall thought, standing almost arthritically and pulling up the wrist with the watch on it. Electricity still burned in the men's; a bleary-eyed glance at his watch told him the truth.

It was just past midnight. Not an hour or a day later.

Stenwall started to cry, turned it into a near rage instead. Dammit, there *had* to be water in there and, if there was, he'd find it. Because he might very well last until Monday without food, but thirst, the putrid reek, and the smothering heat were already making him need to shut down, pass out; combined with his secret sickness, he felt nauseous, desperately frail.

The urinal, Stenwall thought, blinking at it. Sax hadn't considered *that*—and when he got out of there, come Monday, Stenwall would cut the goddamn pervert's ball off and feed them to him, one at a time!

Enlivened, purposive, Stenwall lurched across

the tiny floor and halted, head cocked. If Chacker was still in his truck, if he *heard* Stenwall flushing the pisser, he'd turn the water off. That meant saving water, containing and preserving it.

Stenwall's gaze darted every which way but felt his renewed optimism and killing thirst for violence dissipate fast. There were no paper cups beside the basin, not even the soft drink bottle he'd almost brought inside with him; there was nothing he could employ to hold the urinal water.

Once more, he started to weep. He hurt now, everywhere; the walls were ready to close in, and he was hot inside as well as out.

But the aged prophylactic dispenser—a tube marked FOR PREVENTION OF DISEASE ONLY—hung from the wall right next to the pisser! Giggling, then covering his telltale lips with both palms, Stenwall slipped over to the faded machine, thinking: If you stretch condoms the way smart-ass college boys do, making balloons, *condoms hold water*.

Tremblingly, Stenwall fished in a pocket for change. His lips made little bursting bubbles when he laughed, chortled—read the two-for–fifty cents price information and realized it was like time travel in this goddamn room! Not that he'd ever used any of those ribbed, pebbled, brightly colored, and scented things, because real men didn't fucking worry, real men wanted to feel—

He didn't even have the right change. *Cocksucker!* Stenwall mouthed the word, dropping his change and seeing it roll, fucking vanish, into crevices as ancient as moon craters. The sweat was dripping into his eyes now, and his nuts felt like somebody was branding them. Through the glass on the dispenser, the packaged condoms

J.N. Williamson

were like belly buttons—or sunken, staring child's eyes. "Tell *me* no," Stenwall exclaimed, and smashed his fist into the glass.

The packets tumbled out, along with red from his wound. Stenwall couldn't tell how deep it was, but it was near the wrist, and it hurt like Christ. Shrieking nonsense, he bolted for the basin before remembering there was no water, froze in panic with his eyes rolling everywhere.

Okay. Clutching one package in his teeth, tearing at it with his uninjured hand, Stenwall ripped the condom out and stretched it the best he could. Then he thrust his whole dripping hand into it. The rubber filmed over with blood immediately, but he seemed to remember blood stopped if air couldn't get to the wound. For a moment, the men's jumped before his eyes like an athlete—

Until the unobtrusive carving noises he'd heard first issued from the other side of the wall.

Dizzy and scared, hurting differently in many places, he allowed his body to slump against the wall, believing his cell was starting to shrink in dimension, but uncertain what terror he should fear the most.

And he knew uncannily that the sun was up, a night had passed, *and* he was being watched.

His wristwatch, past midnight when he had previously checked the time, said it was nearly nine, and also announced that it had stopped. Because he had forgotten to wind it.

Maybe, just maybe, he had passed out for thirty-three hours, not nine.

Stenwall started to stand, and the wet floor threw him painfully to one knee, where he stayed, licking dry lips, noting that the door was still tightly closed, realizing the morning temperature was making the rest room a torture box.

Awareness of thirst instantly accelerated it beyond all rational, tolerable limits. Letting his tongue loll pathetically from a corner of his mouth, he pawed up a dozen or so packets of condoms, cradled them in his arms, and crawled across the floor to the urinal. Tearing the packages open cost him most of his energy, and he peeled off his drenched shirt and worked his trousers down and off, howling faintly at the pressure on his bruised knee. While the pisser had overflowed, he sat, didn't even feel the mess sinking into the seat of his shorts. But undressing had worked the rubber halfway off his wounded hand and it was seeping again, a mixture of blood and puss, and by the time he had formed three condoms into the shape of drooping scrotums and was clambering, slipping, to his knees, Stenwall was talking to himself.

"Trash the little girls, did I, they were trash already, born trash." He extended one of the rubbery devices, midway up the length of the urinal, sick from the disinfectant fumes rising to his twitching nostrils. After nothing whatever occurred, he remembered the obligation of mashing the handle down. "I'll trash the bitches, the cunts, like they always tried to trash me, tried to make Brucie feel dirty."

Instead of a Niagara from the urinal, there was a trickle. He licked filthy fingers, let the contraption just fall off his hurt hand into the drain. Fuck it. He hit the flush handle again, wondering how much blood he was losing, coaxed water into the deformed, quivering rubber, muttering to the faint flow.

Yet he did better this time! Real water flowed

into the condom, pooked-out the nipple, elicited from Stenwall a childlike relief and a shaky yet careful attempt to raise the partly filled prophylactic to his lips.

He dropped it into the repulsive mess, gaping in horror toward the floor in front of the urinal.

A pale brown insect—a huge roach—had been in his water supply. It had been on top of the porcelain contrivance and plummeted straight into the condom while Stenwall was endeavoring to fill it.

He knew that because he saw the roach crawl out of the rubber and begin to sun itself on the anemic, testicular cubes.

"All *their* fault, I shoulda killed the bitches, alla them!" His fists were clenched, raised by the sides of his head. "Shoulda killed *alla* them!"

Cutting sounds. Carving noises—scrape, scrape, jab, *scraaape*—nearer somehow—brought Stenwall's head around so he faced the wall behind the partition of modesty.

Impelled, he started slithering on hands and knees toward the wall, the wall he had so admired, a wall bearing the innumerable and timeless scribblings of other men who had no idea how better to make their mark in the world. Other men who shared a loathing created almost entirely by a near-the-surface certainty of their common inferiority.

It's a rat, said a portion of Stenwall's mind, as he scuttled; it was many rats, gnawing on the other side of the wall. And that message, that notion, seemed immeasurably preferable to a different claim entirely asserted by the functioning bulk of his brain.

When he had crept naked through the reeking overflow at the base of the aged toilet, Stenwall stopped, tried to lift his hand. "I wish I'd killed more of them," he wheezed, hauling himself around the side of the bowl on his knees, getting the hang of it now. Sweat and other things were in his eyes and he couldn't see much, but he had never imagined he had too much to see, anyhow. "I do, I honestly do."

The faint bustling sounds—something new to hear—helped him thrust his head above the level of the commode, and his stinging vision made out a long jagged line exactly like the one in Sax Chacker's face, splitting the wonderful Wall of Memories. Blinking, he saw the split widen and reveal interior edges colored a pulpy pink. "What the hell . . . ?"

The jagged line divided the flowery letters he had succeeded in carving, ran between the "F" and the "U."

And the segments of the wall crumbled—disintegrated—chunks of plaster raining on Stenwall, pelting him just the way the tampons were that were being thrown at him like weapons. More hit him, hurting; one took an eye out, or he believed it did, the pain was too general for him to be sure. Brucie looked out for himself by trying to climb inside Stenwall, and he cupped it with his hands, further protecting the little guy.

Then the attack ceased, or was momentarily suspended.

More plaster broke away from the walls, caught him glancing blows, and Stenwall rocked back on his ass to stare with his more or less good eye at what was apparently trying to kill him.

Dozens, no *hundreds*, of nude women ranging in age from the cradle to the grave were pouring through the rent in the wall. Not a one of them had a face, all were skeletal except for their bosoms and genitalia; a few had hair left on their heads, most did not. Because they could not pos-

J.N. Williamson

sibly see him with great sockets where their eyes had been, he knew this was nothing personal, understood immediately that anybody, almost, would have done—so long as he was male. *Do it, do it to him*, he thought some of the trashed women shouted; *sit on his face, all right . . . 69 him!* Grins of ivory sought to turn into enticing, lip-smacking puckers, but they had no lips left and the mouths split wide, like the wall. Stenwall shrank back against the modesty partition but the bony arms reached out, hands making the kind of obscene gesture he'd always found expressive, more clawing with fingers like the white keys of an old piano. *They* went after him in waves, slopped avidly over him, attempted to mount him any horrible way they were able. The flesh they had left, all that had ever been coveted, slapped against every portion of his terrified body while dozens of furry patches pressed to him, jostling to reach his mouth or penis.

And when he felt he must certainly smother, they stopped.

He opened his eyes to the echo of his own screams and squinted around. The men's room remained barricaded and there was still time to go, days of disease, isolation, and dying for need of water. He found the naked dead women were still there, mostly, pulled back from him, slowly seeping into the split in the wall—some already gone and more going all the time. Those who remained had lowered their arms of bone, and their postures were rueful. The one counter-attack they had mustered at last was abandoned because of what each woman essentially was and would always primarily prefer to be. Unlike him.

Before they left Stenwall—none forgiving him but incapable, even collectively and dead, of the

92

violence that was not of their sex—clearly understanding once more that they alone possessed pity and might generate it—the immortal women shed tears upon their shining, their fleshless cheeks.

And Stenwall knew finally that even one drop of that priceless fluid could have saved him from joining them. Soon. But they had never touched him that way. Not even once.

Perhaps it would happen behind the perpetual Wall of Memories. When all of them were one.

The Writing of "Watchwolf"

"Watchwolf" was originally written as a contribution for *Masques II* (Maclay & Assoc., 1987), the second of what are presently the four volumes of "Works of Horror and the Supernatural" I've edited. I thought it was original and clever; quite amusing.

I still think that estimate is accurate, frankly. However, the same adjectives can be applied to the stories by Stephen King, Bill Nolan, Jim Kisner, Ray Russell, Joe Lansdale, and Alan Rodgers, and I didn't want a primarily horrific anthology to turn into what old movie ads sometimes called a "laff riot." (Not that Tom Sullivan's brilliant "The Man Who Drowned Puppies," an underrated masterpiece to me, could have left "amusing" as the prevalent lingering mood!)

So "Watchwolf" found a home in what turned out to be *Footsteps*'s "Erotic Horror Edition," though it is probably one of of my all-time least sexy yarns!

Watchwolf

He'd hit most of the houses in the neighborhood, using a variation in timing and a directness of approach that were the envy of his larcenous chums, and was cruising around trying to select his next target when he saw the freshly posted sign in front of a house he hadn't burglarized yet: BEWARE OF WEREWOLF. Beneath that eye-opening but ridiculous legend, in smaller hand-painted letters, was the rest of the startling message: "Especially when the moon is full."

In all his six years as a proudly unapprehended break-and-enterer, Nesby Walcott had never been threatened by a werewolf before, and reading this new sign—which consumed more time than that used by the literate neighbors, who'd also gathered on the sidewalk as a product of word-of-mouth amazement—made his day. It tickled Nesby's street-sharpened fancy and challenged unholy hell out of him.

"Sumbitch," he whispered, not even bothering to alight from his car and hide in the forming crowd. He was one among many and knew it. "Ain't that *somethin'*?"

What brought the same tuneful query to his lips for a reprise didn't occur until almost an hour had passed and the neighbors, by and large, had dispersed. Then, at twilight—long before the evening's moon clumped bloatedly into view—Nesby saw the porchlight go on, the front door to the house swing open, and—satisfying reward for Walcott and the patient, neighborly remnant—a *beast* exited the residence and trotted down the steps at an unbeastly pace.

An aging female, tremorous smile and hair the color of the onrushing moon, kept the door ajar. "Do your business, Caesar, honey," she called. "Momma will leave some nice little Pooch-Pleasures in your food bowl."

Nesby Walcott leaned over the chipped steering wheel of his calculatedly colorless, six-year-old Chevy pickup truck and giggled until tears came to his eyes.

The "beast" Caesar, presumably the "werewolf" of the sign posted in the fenced-in yard, raised one hind leg—and what dampened the grass fell no farther than half a foot; seven inches, maybe. When the small fellow finished conducting his business, he raised his terrier-sized head to stare questioningly around the scant handful of chuckling spectators and remarked, quite distinctly, "*Foof*. Foof-*foof*!" Nesby utterly collapsed in the front seat, helpless, causing his hula-dancer-on-a-string to quiver with anthropomorphic empathy. The elderly lady's protector was not only no larger than a Boston terrier, but unable to bark without a marked canine lisp!

By the time he had tooled slowly away from the

curb, melting easily into the elongating shadows of mid autumn with the other grinning onlookers, Nesby had certainly chosen his next home to hit.

The truth of it was that, when the moon became full, or close enough to satisfy the burglar's challengeable side, he was tempted to back out to rob an alternate home. Whatever the old broad was up to—she who owned the absurd Caesar—was actually far more joke than dare.

There were other, alternate explanations for the sign she had put up. Maybe she'd been burglarized somewhere else, mugged or rolled, and meant to be lurking bravely inside the place with a new shotgun across her lap. Or the silly-looking mutt with the lisp might be a decoy, and two giant Dobermans or German shepherds waited ravenously within—unfed for eons.

Either of which would make it abundantly more challenging for Nesby Walcott, who just *loved* slaughtering big dogs and knew all manner of effective, sinister ways to do it. He considered himself even better with old ladies, armed or unarmed.

But his career in crime had instructed Nesby in the many surprising ways of those who seemed to be just aching to be hit upon; and while *this* was definitely something of a new wrinkle, he knew that common sense and the odds alike argued in favor of one, drab, disappointing fact: The old broad had a neurotic attachment to her small pet and actually *believed* that tiny Caesar was powerful or cunning enough to protect her.

He returned to her house three nights later, no longer entranced. He had elected to burglarize her house and garrote, stab, or strangle her animal less because of the challenge than because he'd squandered the loot he'd acquired after fencing stuff from a prior gig, and because, primarily, he had always detested both dogs and old women. And there was the way her sign had attempted to warn him away; that, he thought coolly as he drove, was something a guy could take personally.

Caesar was not in the yard—back or front—when Nesby glanced up, once, at the stony white cyclops eye peering from behind cloud cover, then broke in to the house with the consummate noiselessness of practice, or the grave. Once within, he paused, allowing all his keenly self-serving senses to probe for peril; then he slipped like a wraith through the dark kitchen into the dining room.

A luxurious smile twisted his cruel and capacious yap. Good China—no one was more expert than Nesby—was displayed on the old lady's hutch as if she meant to post a second sign: HELP YOURSELF TO MY BEST THINGS. There was polished, costly silver—top of the line—left in the drawers.

He helped himself, using a voluminous, lightweight cloth sack he'd long ago lined with pockets of sorts, compartments into which the valuables he stole slid easily; without clinking, or clattering. This task took such a small amount of time that he was both disappointed and distantly alarmed. Alerted. The old broad might be neurotic, but that should've made her even more aware of the burglaries occurring all over the neighborhood this past year. Yet she had been so composed, letting Caesar out to pee, so unnoticing of the people gathered there.

Draping the partly filled sack over one meaty shoulder, Nesby shone a slim flashlight across the dining room and followed its beam as if pulled into the richly carpeted hallway by a magnet. What he saw, wherever he looked, as he swung the light in a slow arc that encompassed the large room at the front of the house, rekindled Nesby's excitement and even threatened his customary cool: Any self-respecting burglar who knew what he was looking at would kill to make sure he had taken everything of value before leaving such a place, because it was worth four or five heists of average houses; antiques were everywhere.

And killing was just what Nesby Walcott decided upon—for the first time, actually, despite his bravado; rape and assault were his personal high points prior to tonight—because loot like this meant the old lady had jewelry socked away, too.

Probably in an old-fashioned wall safe in her bedroom, if he knew *her* type. Breathing as shallowly as possible, heartbeat thudding loudly, Nesby sent his beam in search of the staircase—

"*Poof!* Poof-*poof!*"

He froze where he was, arm out-thrust, and grinned. Caesar the Great, all eighteen or twenty pounds of him, was somewhere in that darkness, ready to protect his frail mistress. Nesby's pocket flash had not located the stairs, or the old lady's stupid pet, but he didn't think that idiotic titter of a bark had awakened her. It certainly had done nothing to scare him or make him want to flee!

"Nice doggy," he called, softly, trying not to snicker. His beam washed the midnight baseboards of the quiet old house and suddenly found the first step of the stairway. "Where *are* you, Caesar, you ridiculous little mutt?"

No reply, for an instant.

Then from a point roughly midway up the

shadowed flight of stairs, the most hilarious howl Nesby Walcott had ever heard sent him into uncontrollable chuckling and snorting. It was as high-pitched as a woman's scream, but not at all loud, and it broke the way a new teenager's voice shattered, winding up in a gurgling noise that sounded almost apologetic. Nesby wanted to stop laughing; he muffled his mouth with the palm of his left hand, then followed the crazy howl both with his no-longer-stealthy feet and his rising flashlight beam. For another moment, he saw nothing, partly because his pocket flash was shaking in time to his chuckling and partly because it had occurred to him that it didn't really matter if the old broad heard him. Killing her after he'd banged ol' Caesar's head against the banister and steps until he looked like a toy with his stuffing oozing out would cap off his great adventure, his most successful professional achievement.

"Come on, Caesar, I ain't gonna hurt you *much*," Nesby cooed. "Dammit," he cried finally, taking two steps up the stairs, "where the hell are you?"

Fierce *growling*.

The flashlight beam and Nesby's eyes swung all the way up simultaneously. A third factor became the moon, suddenly filling the curtainless window on the landing, at the being's back. What he saw, Nesby knew, would haunt his waking thoughts for the rest of his life. Or approximately forty-five seconds.

The man-thing heading down the steps toward him, two at a time, was naked—a fact of insignificance, comparable to identifying the Ayatollah Khomeini as bearded, or describing the hydrogen bomb as an explosive. He had a lot of grayish white hair. He stood at least eight feet in height, his eyes were redder than burning coals, and the reason Nesby lived a full three-fourths of one minute was that Caesar found it difficult to squeeze and thrust his enormously wide shoulders between the walls of the staircase.

But he managed, which was more than Nesby could say. Hands twice the length and half again the width of the burglar's head palmed the latter the way an NBA center copes with a basketball. There was not net or rim into which Caesar could exactly *dunk* Nesby's head, but the effect was irreproachably similar when the old lady's protector sent it flying down the steps and, with a commendable amount of English, bounding through the dining room into the kitchen.

"Caesar, honey? What are you up to?" The white-haired person shuffled to the second-floor landing and peered myopically over the railing. "*There* you are!" She hesitated, squinting down at the freshly abbreviated burglar crumpled at the foot of the steps; at his partly filled sack; then at the enormous man-thing illumined by the light from the bloated full moon. "I swan," she said, mildly enough, "there's another of those fellows who never once stop to think that lycanthropy can work *both* ways. You want t'take him out in the backyard and play with him?"

The mammoth pet on the stairs wriggled its buttocks in delight. "*Poof!*" he barked in a clear tenor. "Poof-*poof*!"

The Writing of "The Sudd"

Perfect has been defined to mean "complete in all respects" and "absolute," and I was surprised to realize, after creating roughly one-third of this *Pulphouse* tale, that I was doing such a thing.

Because I know of no rules applicable to all forms of genres of fiction that a given tale must run the gamut of emotion from exciting, funny, sensual, frightening, pertinent, and evocative to illuminating, shocking, and inspirational, I had not set out to create a perfect story before '89. Even now I'm constrained to define my terms more narrowly.

Does a close reading of several lines make the writer see nothing he is feverish to change? It's rare for me to reread a yarn or chapter written a dozen years ago and not want to rework it. In fact, I'd like to begin from scratch every other story in this collection and see how each develops this time! But in a decade plus, I've never wanted to replace a comma of "The Sudd."

Partly, I believe, what happened was that the origin of the basic idea combined with my research to bestow a particular clarity of imagination and insight. That origin was a PBS program about starving Africans, affluent international tourists aboard a ship, and floating garbage.

I said, in an intro to "The Sudd" in its maiden voyage, it's a tale "about blindness and the sudden gift of sight." What I've always wanted to say about it is that it's a revenge story. But it isn't, quite.

But I don't do meaningful, literate horror better than this.

The Sudd

Peter had told him to go to Cairo, and Price Sterling nodded as if he were a minister and God had told him to go to hell. He was only thirty; he had heard a lot already in the movie business. What he hadn't heard was an order that put him on his own, thousands of miles away, with little said about expenses. And while he expected Egypt to be considerably different from hell, the origins of command had seemed similar to a new second unit director.

What Peter hadn't thought to tell him in his customary mercurial manner was *how* Price should go to Cairo, or hell.

Which was why he opted for getting there from Kenya by way of a steamer up the Nile.

After all, Price had reasoned, they'd blow enough film for four new versions of *The African Queen* without approaching Huston anyway, and he knew at least two scenes that would play better aboard ship. With a little location work out of the way, he'd know what to recommend, and might even wind up a hero.

Besides, Price had yearned to take this cruise since Hollywood High. Generations late for believing Tarzan implicitly, he'd been stuck watching PBS one night. The girl's name was long forgotten now, but she had turned on a travelogue that bored him at first, then galvanized him to action, and ultimately motivated him to pursue his career in film. His realization that it was possible not only to travel on a river that ran four thousand miles and be paid for it, but to record for posterity—and for other teenage boys with uncooperative dates—sights ordinary folks would never see, had overwhelmed him.

It hadn't occurred to Price until he sat sweating profusely in a deck chair aboard the *Willem Rotter*—making notes about the eland and beisa seething silkily up the riverbank without noticing him or the steamer—that he could be as ordinary as the girl-with-no-name who had prodded him into watching public television.

Part of the diminution of ego he experienced was linked to the rich mix of nationalities he'd encountered after two days on the steamer. Ahmed Firouk, returning to Alexandria after weeks of undisclosed business, smiled as if taking a screen test. Krapf, no Christian name volunteered, a Durban resident with lips that would've looked great in blackface. Aging Mrs. Marxe from Leopoldville, citing the "e" in her name like an academic credential. Originally British Bruce Smallesmith, from Capetown now. One Carlos Brazza of vague origins by any judgment, destination north of the Sudan. (Price would have doubted the day of the week from that man.) Emma Vanderblatt, a scintillating fifty, asea on

105

revivified charm and her birthday. Stanley Sydney Odney, an Australian who liked enunciating his own name, had been on holiday in Mozambique and mentioned a spot of biz at Lake No.

The girl.

Further reasons for Price's modified ego had to do with his certain hunch that each of them was exceptionally rich. None of them treated him an iota different, or better, when he told them what he did.

Especially the girl, and that was all the intercourse he'd had with any of them up to now.

And the peculiar likelihood that none of the people he had met knew anybody else on ship. Even before he introduced himself to them, he saw that they were already playing specific parts, enacting them as if it were insignificant whether they were good at it, important that they pleased themselves.

That variety of pretense or individuation impressed Price, reminded him he had come this far, partly, in the hope of recalling the way he had been before encountering culture on PBS. People he ran with went nowhere except en masse, en suite; whether they were gaffers or best boys, second unit directors, screen writers, or the odd featured player who got off on slumming, it was central to each that the rest perceive the point of his private little drama. True leadership in Hollywood appeared to amount to how many others agreed to be spear-wielders in one's extemporaneous and open-ended soap. Price thought the reason orgies and drug parties had succeeded was that no one had the foggiest notion of how to be alone. Someone else was always around, and the mere thought of loneliness was literally a fear of the unknown.

Making notes and blocking scenes, Price studied the foreigners playing, reading, drinking on the steamer deck, and wondered if he had booked a passage on one of those old movie boats headed for hell. It wasn't difficult to imagine, even if such films usually lost big bucks. Because it was hot enough for the Styx. Barely twilight, Price's third evening aboard, and the perpetuity of the pounding waves of heat began to seem kismetic as cancer. For a lean, serene, imperturbable man like him, the relentless rising temperatures were like some ridiculous wild girl from Kansas who'd do anything to impress him. He started trying to envision either Khartoum or Cairo as paradise.

Most of the ego sloughing away that afternoon, and now, involved what Price Sterling had been observing on the banks of the Nile.

They had been following that part of the world's second longest river which was called the Bahr el Abyed, or White Nile. As a buff, Price knew that at roughly the time the Nile received the waters of the Giraffe River, their direction would veer slightly, indiscernibly, until his long-planned cruise wound up in the Sudan, at Khartoum. He'd fly from there to Cairo if he had any intention of arriving before Peter and the rest. There were hands of the Egyptian hierarchy to shake, tribute paid before the clasps were broken. Always, it was that way on location, whether the official with anticipatory eyes wore a turban, or a nametag marked MAYOR.

The steamer sizzled along like some smoldering insect on the unchanging Nile, the incomparable river flowing with almost sentient deliberation into channels beyond a cartographer's skills, and Price wondered about skipping both heaven and hell. He thought about purposes or their absence, the girl in the swimming pool, the way meandering waters with an elevation of sixteen hundred feet, here, narrowed to the width of Hollywood Boulevard due west, now, of Ethiopia . . .

One hour ago it had been broad, searing daylight, and he'd caught glimpses of crocodiles as long as cleared banquet tables lolling in readiness between the boat and the people on the banks. He saw weavers; old women with stooped backs, at work; bare brown children whose bellies looked seven months pregnant; young males who ran in razorish Zeekoevlei grass like suicides' shadows haunting a heap of broken green bottles. "The Bantu" was the collective term Krapf from Durban used for the people, speaking full voice. Chin lowered and guttural when he drank illegal skokiaan opposite Brazza, the Afrikaaner also called the people "kaffir." Price grunted. He knew the American equivalent of the word.

More minutes later, stars out like teeth in a necklace, he saw the Bantu had left the bank. *Do they have a dinner hour or are they too smart to schedule pleasure?* Price wondered. When he rose and went to the rail through surges of heat like passionate breath, he could not see the crocs, either. But a pale ibis, sacred still to some human beings dependent upon the Bahr el Abyed, rocketed over the waters as if gusted there by jaws snapping shut a lifetime late.

And when he rested against the railing a yard or two from Smallesmith, the Brit, Price studied the girl in the pool, thinking she might turn into a fish. A pandodant, maybe, or a shiny bichir. Not a mormyrid, or elephant fish. These steamers had been outfitted, Price mused, for the maximum delight of their passengers. While the *Willem Rotter* had never been an aesthetically enticing craft unboarded, it sported every modern convenience—if by modern, Price thought, one meant 1949 or so. The pool was situated at the center of the main deck in order for tourists to watch the bathers, and for the latter to know it was happening.

When at last the swimming girl surfaced in her one-piece suit that was strangely out of date to the Californian, her abrupt exit made him think of seals leaving the water. She virtually squeaked, bare and flat-footed across the deck in what could have been a direct line toward Price Sterling. The swimsuit made him think of new car tires. The bathing cap was brushed by stars hanging low as lanterns at a Beverly Hills pool party, turning her outer space baldish until she was close. When she was as near him as she was going to be, the cap was peeled away and hair as red as Kenyan tamaties rained in torrents.

Merle Oberon eyes, Price thought, saw her gaze touch his tanned face without seeing him at all. Then the eyes and her naked knees dipped the swimmer into a chair beside Mrs. Marxe from Leopoldville. What shocked him was both the way the girl totally did not see him, the incivility of that, and a new awareness that no passenger had glanced for even an instant at the astonishing sights along the river. Not once, he believed, in two days, three evenings.

"She's beautiful," Bruce Smallesmith acknowledged at his side. He didn't lower his voice despite the proximity of the two women in shadows at the table. The hum-and-shudder of the steamer was such a constant that it was easily ignored but, if it hadn't been, still the weight of the African night pressed upon them like a murderer's pillow, muffling sound. Recently, Price recalled, a lion had roared and its impact was no

109

more immediate than MGM's Leo. "But not exceptional."

"Everybody is beautiful in Hollywood," Price said, putting most of his hands in the slits of his tight white slacks. "It's the law."

Smallesmith had cultivated an image of impeccability with such fidelity that he looked innocent as an infant—like a dead man, he no longer aged, just crisped. "You didn't comment about laws obliging Californians to be exceptional."

Price presented a sincere grin. Probably the Brit wanted something, everybody did, but this moment broke the spell of apartness troubling Price. "Well, this happens after you've signed a contract," he explained. "You're exceptional as long as it's been paid."

"I see," Smallesmith chuckled. His gaze, slightly veiled by tinted lenses in his glasses and by his own private purposes, had returned to the swimming girl. Each man noticed she had dried her red hair, but not her body, nor had she donned a robe. "That must be what happened in television."

"I don't . . ."

"When residuals went in," the Englishman explained, "it was like born-again exceptionability."

Price laughed. He wondered, suddenly, if Bruce Smallesmith was also trying to figure out a way to sit at the table with Mrs. Marxe and the unexceptional swimmer. He wondered how the Brit kept from sweating, or from showing it; why Mrs. Marxe didn't seem to have spoken to the redhead and went on reading a novel with a title in a language he didn't recognize; why the girl sat down there or, finally, had come out of the pool at all. He wondered a lot.

"Why don't . . . these people . . . mingle?" He

was half-startled he'd asked it. Yet there were probably two dozen men and women, no kids Price had seen, to whom he hadn't introduced himself, and all were alone. Or, like the women nearby, individually preoccupied. "Why don't they wish to meet one another?"

Smallesmith's brows rose above his tinted spectacles. "But we do know each other, dear boy," he said. "For the most part. The majority of us have met many times, at many places."

So you don't like each other, Price thought without speaking.

The older man went on as if he had. "It's the Nile, you see, Sterling. We're a smidge more sociable when on land."

"It's like commuting, then," Price said, excited as he understood. "Now I get it! People taking the same train to New York every day must get pretty bored, too." He laughed nervously. "I feel like such a damn tourist now."

The pause before Smallesmith answered was long enough for Price to turn toward him. The *Willem Rotter* was rounding a bend, and all the American detected of the other's face were the colored lenses.

"You don't get it at all." The eyes were those of a blinded owl. "All any of us will ever be on this benighted river is tourists."

Involuntarily, Price jumped. "Pardon me?"

"It's sheer mesmerism, one's first time out here," the Englishman said. "When one does not live in Africa." He had lowered his pitch now, and it was sporadically as if his voice merged with the neighboring sounds of purring civets, the squeal of the earth pig, the conversations of lemur families. A stork like snow vaulted into the moon, vanished. "You'll see the lily of the Nile growing wild, Sterling, with exquisite azure flowers—and stalks

111

large enough to encompass a man's fist. Your destination, the Sudan, has grass that reaches a height of ten feet." His features swam into focus, the lips scarcely moving. "The Nile basin extends from four degrees South latitude to thirty-one degrees North. There are alpine flora in the Ruwenzori Range, for God's sake!"

"You're saying . . . ?"

"It's too much, boy, it's too vast." Smallesmith looked incredulous. "Price—they didn't even discover the headwaters of this damn river until 1862!" Slim hand slipped into jacket pocket, he made ready to leave. "We are afraid, dear chap." His free hand found Price Sterling's bicep, squeezed and released it. "None of us really wish to be here, you see, but there's no other way."

"No, I don't see!" Price declared. "What—"

"Here, look at this." Smallesmith withdrew his hand carefully, turned it palm up. Something brown and gross, bloated, clung. "It's called a kenopus."

"A what?" Price said impatiently. He edged a step off before prodding at the creature with a ring finger. "Damn, man, it's *dead*."

"It's not." Smallesmith flexed his fingers. Eyes far too big for it popped; then the creature leaped, cleared the railing, was swallowed by the river. Sweat streaked one of the Englishman's colored lenses. "It's a toad without any tongue," he said. "Fancy that." His gaze swiveled to the bank, back. "From Ethiopia."

"Bruce, I don't get the drift," said Price. But Smallesmith was at the table with the disaffected women. "I don't see at all."

The man stopped without looking at either woman, or anything on the steamer. "It's the sudd, old boy. You may assume that's why we're afraid."

The girl in the one-piece swimsuit looked expressionlessly toward Price. It was the first time he thought she'd seen him. The coal brows of the old woman formed the letter V and dripped perspiration on her open book. An elderly man across the deck gripped a shuffleboard stick like a crutch. Smallesmith was gone, and Price remembered dinosaurs fast-frozen in the act of masticating, ships of fame sinking.

"Nearer," he whispered not quite sardonically as he turned back to the railing and the riverbank, "my God, to Thee."

Uncountable eyes regarded him.

When the lids closed, the African night was impermeable.

It didn't occur to Price until morning, after several solitary hours of muttering imprecations at the inadequate air-conditioning in the staterooms, that he hadn't seen "a Black" among the *Willem Rotter* passengers. Some were employees. Stewards, waiters, a grinning middle-aged man with a tiny boy who accepted the letters Price had written. But the bad part was that he hadn't been conscious of their absence whatsoever until seeing that the paying customers of the steamship line constituted a minuscule minority. And he wondered even before he saw the red-haired woman was back in the pool, how it stayed possible for a people in such overwhelming numbers to be invisible.

Price was in trunks and perched on the apron of the swimming pool, dangling tanned legs and perceiving for the first time how pasty, how unrelievedly white, he looked, in contrast to the others on board.

Except the swimmer in her one-piece suit.

She said, shockingly, "Get me something cool to drink, quickly." Her Martian head and shoul-

ders had sprung from the water at Price's feet.
She was addressing him. She either added the
word *please* or he expected it enough to imagine
she said it.

"Okay, all right." He was standing by the time
he answered her, questing for a waiter, hoping he
didn't have to leave to obey. The young woman
was beginning to assume for him the properties
of a mermaid and, if she again submerged, she
might disappear into a river cave forever.

But he was overeager, had one side turned
when a waiter materialized with a tray, and the
swimmer slithered up beside him and accepted a
glass when the waiter stooped to her. "Hamba
gable," she murmured—and Price realized she
had a drink, as well, for him.

"What did that mean?" He wanted to pay for
the drinks but that, too, had been done somehow.
Maybe she was keeping a tab.

She showed him perfect teeth, a moist red curl
fleeing from the bathing cap, and cleavage that
was exceptional enough, en route to the Sudan
and a world of veils. "Go in peace," she said. She
hadn't told him her name and had yet to look at
him, really, a second time. Perhaps she truly
looked at no one.

"In what tongue?" asked Price.

"In Swahili," the girl retorted. Her upper lip, on
the rim of the glass, was thin; determined. "He'd
have preferred Twi-Fante, but one can't spend all
one's time learning the Sudanese dialects."

"I think it's marvelous you know Swahili," Price
said. His drink, principally, was gin; he was
relieved it wasn't skokiaan, which he'd learned
was moonshine. She smiled and he caught it.
"What's funny?"

"Tourists. The world. One form or another of
Sudanese is spoken by fifty million of them. If

you don't speak a bit of their chatter, you're positively at their mercy." Those Merle Oberon eyes contrived to be covert and put-upon. "There's Dinka, Yoruba, Twi-Fante—I mentioned that one—Fulani, Hausa—that's useful in trading." She stared down at the bottom of her glass, sighed. "God knows what the Tallensi, Mangbetu, or Wolof are chattering away in these days." Her nose wrinkled. "Too much outside influence."

"Where are you going?"

For an instant she didn't understand the question. Then, startlingly, she laughed. "To the end of the trolley ride."

He laughed with her as best he could. "Then what?"

"Then," she said, yanking the suit up snugly over her bosom, "then I'll catch another trolley back."

"What did Bruce Smallesmith mean when he said you were all afraid, out here?" He realized she'd started to slip back into the pool and put out fingers to touch her arm. Skin not nearly as tanned as his felt remarkably cool. "Of what?"

For a moment he thought she wouldn't answer him. She did, expressionlessly once more. "Bruce Smallesmith is *English*." She hissed the curse.

"But what's 'the sudd'?" he called after her, getting to his knees like a perplexed boy attempting to follow a mermaid trail. "Why are you terrified by it?"

She showed her cheek and one Oberon eye to him from one-third the length of the pool away, not even pretending she hadn't heard.

Obviously, she had given him her answer. She had also stayed in the swimming pool.

Before noon, the *Willem Rotter* wended its methodical way into another of the interminable branches of the river, passage seemed to narrow

J.N. Williamson

to the width of a two-lane highway, and Price found himself at the railing between Stanley Sydney Odney, the lanky ex-Aussie in outback shorts that reached the knee, and Krapf, from Durban. All three stared at a number of tribesmen laden with pots and carefully wrapped packages which they pulled behind them on sleds Price Sterling found ingenious.

"Nomadic herders, mate," Odney answered his question, "prob'ly from the Dongola provinces. Off to swap beer and unleavened bread—dates, too, and whatnot—for camels or horses. They're called Kababish."

"Kababish?" Price repeated. "That doesn't sound—"

"They speak a Semitic tongue," Krapf interjected, pursing thick lips. "Aside from that, they're industrious, at least."

"The girl in the pool," Price began, addressing Odney, "she said the blacks on this tub were probably Twi-Fante. How could she tell?"

Odney, to his amazement, broke into laughter. The Afrikaaner crimsoned, glared at Price as if he'd enjoy killing him, and wandered off in the general direction of the man named Brazza.

"What did I say wrong?" Price demanded of the Australian, spreading his hands. "Is there something wrong with the Twi-Fante?"

"Wrong?" Stan Odney repeated, grinning. "Nothin' about the ol' Twi-Fante a well-placed *kisi-ki-kali* wouldn't fix right up!" Odney came closer. "They're Akan people, do a bit of arts and crafts and brass-castin' for their tea and cakes." He cast a discreet but amused glance around. "Y'see, sport, there's only one way the lady could be sure these kaffir are Twi-Fante, so I doubts she knew about the waiter for sure." Whispering, he

116

said, "They's one of the tribes in these immediate parts what's downright opposed to circumcision!"

Late in the afternoon, Price asked Smallesmith what *kisu-ki-kali* meant in Swahili, and the exact translation was "knife-sharp."

After that, it got hot on the Nile.

Price had spent his life in California, rarely seeing any winter except when he went into the mountains to ski. He liked everything hot. But the temperature on the *Willem Rotter* was exceeding anything he'd even imagined. Definitely, he thought, while going down to the lounge with the rest, this was not paradise—somehow, even demons would flee from such a hell.

Sagging at a table with Ahmed Firouk, the customarily self-irradiated Mrs. Vanderblatt, and Brazza—unasked—Price was stunned to think that a man might perish quite easily there. The Sudan, his stop, lay just south of the Sahara, encysted by the tropical forests of Guinea and the Congo. He remembered reading that Ethiopia had been dead in the path of innumerable fortune-seeking types from the east, had been a superior culture-carrier, strategically, to Egypt. All around these people were fortunes, indeed, found and forged and taken; plentiful game had roamed wild around them with nothing but the shoebill heron of the furtive Nile to return, to enlighten them.

"It's warming up," Firouk declared, with the flashing smile of a manic weather man.

Mrs. Vanderblatt, ravishing and golden at fifty, looked away. She hadn't touched the drink she ordered, and the wonder of her cosmetic base was proving as man-made and feckless as her dietary conquests.

Carlos Brazza, doe-eyed and massive of torso,

made a snorting sound and moved his feet heavily under the table. "You'd like them to keep records here, yes? To know if it's near one for this time of year?"

Ahmed was incorrigibly cheerful. "That would be truly interesting." He wafted immaculate shoulders and Price had a glimpse of a Russian word on his suitcoat lapel. "If we must have the heat, an element of sport would be nice, yes?"

"Please," said Emma Vanderblatt, hesitant about departing, but clearly thinking of standing. Her alto was a tiny mouse fleeing across the checkered tablecloth. *"Please."*

Brazza sniffed, swallowed his beer, gestured at a waiter. Price asked if he could help Emma, and Brazza, lumbering to his feet, seemed entertained. "You can't help. Senora heard the captain's report of ambatch, *Umel Suf*, and papyrus." His soft mole's eyes looked amused, but he turned to the Twi-Fante rushing with his drink and snatched it from the small, dapper waiter. The latter ducked his head as if awaiting a blow, winking his eyes shut as if doing so might save him and resurrect something. Brazza put a hand on the waiter's neck but looked at Price. "It's never confined to one channel, and she knows it."

Emma stared not at Brazza but at the Twi-Fante, forming soundless words with lips that cracked. Then she hurled herself from the table, lurched out of the lounge.

Price thought she had whispered, "Kill him." When he started to question Brazza, the burly man was stomping toward the lavatories. Ahmed Firouk also stood, drawing a newspaper from his pocket, smiling pleasantly. He discerned Price's bewildered look, and paused.

"There is always much water loss, due to high temperature, sir." A shrug. "As a rule, there's no

conjunction of a perilously reduced water level—
and the sudd." An index finger that resembled the
Kenopus cautioned the American. "As a rule."

Price sought a nap, couldn't find sleep. Sitting
up, drenched, he had a mental image of something satin with sequins in it, and needed
instantly to know the time. His wrist showed him
white where his watch ought to have been. In a
dimly lit corridor outside his room, he saw the
small, wincing waiter from the lounge, and followed him to the deck for no reason he could
grasp. But Smallesmith was the only man he saw
through a blistering haze, and the Brit crossed
toward him with motions that made Price think
of swimming. Smallesmith's body showed skele-
tally through his soaked clothing, but he halted
before going below, a born explainer.

"The sudd," he said without preamble, "is Nile
garbage, old boy. Floating vegetation." He managed to seem chipper. "It's rather like . . . a mov-
able swamp." He squinted above Price's head. "To
put things into perspective, I should say the sudd
is Africa's equivalent of . . . an *iceberg*."

"But the boat—"

"Is designed to carve straight through. Quite."
His brows lifted, perspiration ran unimpeded.
"All our vehicles are built to get us from point A
to B—even C, or X. The alphabet isn't that reliable, in the jungle."

"Papyrus," Price recalled, aloud, "ambatch . . ."

"Bordered by a remarkably dense growth of
rushes and reeds. You remember them from
Bible class, don't you?" He stepped through the
door, but hesitated. "If the old hulk won't go
through, the trick is to avoid running her
aground. That is messy."

Then he left, and Price, obedient to ancient
needs, turned towards the yawning swimming

pool. The girl he didn't know was gone; he'd see her one other time. Behind him, Krapf came to the doorway smacking his lips over a dish called mabela, which tasted remotely like hot chocolate pudding. A woman of color whom Price hadn't met stood beside but not with Krapf. Neither addressed Price and he never saw her again.

He gazed across the deck and the water, and it was twilight, but he scarcely noticed, even after he had gone to the railing. He did see how narrow this channel was, then for a second doubted his senses and clung to the rail simply to regain every kind of balance.

The banks on either side of the steamer appeared so near he might have thrown a beach ball anywhere and struck dry land. To his left, forest, to his right, forest, each inhospitable and sealed like the gates to heaven or hell. All Price could see whispered, muttered low in its collective throat, and said nothing he was able to understand. He quit striving to penetrate the jungle of night, wetness scorching his eyes, incapable of distinguishing between perspiration and tears.

Which was when the Blacks on board left the *Willem Rotter*, although none of the Whites or Coloreds knew it for two hours, including Price. But they learned of the exodus when the steamer ran aground.

Then came the mosquitoes, the tsetse flies, that summer bug called a miggie. Next, midnight; but their time pieces were slow . . .

Smallesmith it was who told them the radio was out and he said nothing when Krapf swore, said it had happened intentionally. Ahmed observed that it didn't matter, considering the temp, the limited water and food, the distance (as he put it good-humoredly) "to anyplace." Emma Vanderblatt remained in her cabin, and Stan Odney wondered if she was bloody alive in there, but did not go to see. Some old man Price had dimly noticed did.

Brazza pretended to get drunk just inside the mess, holstered revolver brandished on a meaty leg. Aging Mrs. Marxe finished reading the novel in a language Price didn't recognize and began another, sanguine and solitary.

Someone shot himself. The report was its own news bulletin and a few of the rest, Price believed, were envious. Nobody was wounded or ill, no one was hungry, no one was especially thirsty, and they were going to die there.

Alone, Price felt himself start to panic, and went back on deck, where he saw the girl in the swimsuit reclining on a rubber mat beside the pool. He thought she was dead. He heard her humming, the fragile sound as distant as breathless anticipation on the surrounding riverbanks. He stripped off his shirt, mopped his eyes to look at the sudd on which the steamer was grounded, dimly conscious of the captain manfully trying to ram through the colorful floe, the "Nile garbage." The air was redolent of a pleasing, woodsy scent like a cologne he'd bought. Vivid but small, a passerine stood at one of the young woman's outflung arms, but the bird was no longer singing. When Price had drawn close enough, he perceived that she was propping it up with her lolling fingers. Its neck had been wrung.

"Ham-ba-gahhhhh-lee," she sang, off-key, looking beautiful, desirable. The Merle Oberon eyes were glassy. She was wet from head to toe, red hair like a fountain of blood, the rest of her sensual with perspiration. "Ham-ba-gahhhhh-lee."

He bent, dizzy, to see what was the matter with her and recognized the familiar clear-plastic packet of dagga, the Sudanese drug of preference.

Price stripped down completely en route to the railing and the Nile. It looked like an easy swim to either shore, if the crocodiles had fed. Nude, knees bent on the railing, he stared right, then left, into thickets of unblinking, watchful eyes. They stretched to unguessable horizons without malice. He was turned black by night, but that mightn't be enough.

"Kwakheri," called the young swimmer. "Niii-ight."

Price nodded, dove off the railing.

Every pair of eyelids closed.

The Writing of "Mercy"

Among the many things numerous critics are opposed to is the short-short story. In fact, just about the only cavil I saw in reviews of my first four fiction anthologies (called *Masques*, the quartet numbered Super Bowl–style) was that I, the editor, chose too many short-shorts.

Apart from the fact that I obviously liked them and had reasons for including them, my main countering argument is that nobody genuinely authoritative has ever told me the exact definition of a short-short tale. Does it run as long as three thousand words, which I have heard, or no longer than two thousand, which I believe is a good rule of thumb (or pinkie finger)?

This story, "Mercy," is certainly a short-short, so skip it if the length is important to you. Clearly it's not to me. I'll tell you why, in two parts: First, I think written material of any kind—including TV and film scripts—has a natural length to run, and it's the writer's task to write just that far and stop, and it will only be padding to create another page, or another five thousand words; more will be less.

Second, I've worked less hard on any number of four thousand word stories—and chapters—than I worked to tell this little gem. I had a lot to say in rather few words, and I meant it as a murder mystery, not one of horror, a form far more natural to me.

But the surprise turns out to be on me. This 1988 "shortie" is more topical today, on at least two scores, than it was then! How could I not like short-shorts?

Mercy

He'd had little choice but to kill her for quite a while, and he'd known it, but actually *doing* it— that was the hard part. Until tonight.

Because he'd loved her in his own uncommunicative fashion. No longer with the passion of youth, which was scarcely yesterday in Thomas's case, but loved her. Enough.

But now it was clear to him that his new obligation was no longer avoidable. He'd have done the same for a house pet without a qualm, so how could he do less for a wife of forty years?

Dammit, it wasn't *her* fault she had grown increasingly senile and turned every day of their lives into a weird guessing game. "Do you know who I am, Charlotte?" he'd ask, and she responded—if she answered him at all—with the coy expression of a slow-witted child. On some days, the guessing game worked the other way around: "Thomas, is this a hotel? Where are we?

Are we on vacation?" In the house they'd occupied for more than thirty of their forty years of marriage!

Of course, he had felt truly sorry for her, back when it began. He'd hauled her to a doctor, then a psychiatrist. Fed her vitamins and medicine and played the guessing game religiously until, at times, he'd begun to doubt his own sanity and wondered if the time might come when he, too, was unable to recognize his own damn possessions.

Yet Charlotte had gone relentlessly downhill. Finally, they'd told him there was nothing more to be done, and turned his everyday world into a ceaseless series of chores even the sturdy young man he'd hired for the job eventually balked at handling. Without a hint of hope that life would ever become remotely easier; without the possibility that Charlotte would ever get an iota better.

Deep inside, Thomas both resented his circumstances and was terrified by them. Angry, too, at the unfairness. Such emotions were the penultimate ones he'd had to face, to come to grips with, before tonight.

And now that he had, Charlotte was going to die. Now. In her sleep, or what passed for it these nightmarish days, these endless nights. By his own hand, yes—but unarguably, this was a mercy killing, and no one rational could quarrel with that. What was that two-dollar word they used for it? Thomas paused at her bedroom door, thinking and trying not to step on places in the floor that squealed like mice. *Euthanasia*, that was it. He wouldn't be murdering her, he'd be . . . resorting to euthanasia.

When it was over, Jeannette, who'd been Charlotte's first visiting nurse, would be waiting for him.

He whispered "Euthanasia" repeatedly while

he pressed down with the pillow, molding its soft contours over Charlotte's face. He whispered the new word huskily during the short struggle, shouted it at the top of his voice when she nearly wriggled free, as if he had to get through to her, convince Charlotte that this was right, merciful.

Done, exhausted, Thomas sank to the edge of the bed, nerves singing the word back to him. She'd almost squirmed away once, and he was too tired to remove the pillow. "You know," he said aloud, "it was the thing to do." He was rewarded by silence, and a peaceful feeling he found exceedingly reassuring.

Sighing heavily, squaring his shoulders, Thomas reached across the body, groping with one hand for the pillow and, with the other, for the small bed lamp. *Euthanasia*; a pretty, musical word. "It was," he murmured as subdued lighting grayed the image before him, "an act of mercy."

The pillow came away as freely as the shriek of shock and horror from the old man's throat.

Beautiful, sensual Jeannette—who'd understood perfectly why an active and virile man could not go on being saddled by a senile idiot—who'd stood by his side two years ago when he'd put Charlotte to sleep the *first time*—stared palely, sightlessly, up at him.

It came slowly to Thomas's waning memory that, after Jeannette had helped the jury grasp his humanitarian reasoning, he'd remarried. Aghast, he saw then that—somehow, in some terrible way he couldn't conceivably understand—he'd *forgotten* marrying his lovely, exciting, cooperative nurse Jeannette.

And no jury in the world would believe for a moment that the thirty-year-old beauty in his first wife's bed had suffered from Alzheimer's. . . .

The Writing of "The Mother Pact"

In my life I've known fewer than a dozen people who seemed to me to be, by any lights, unforgettable. The first, as close readers know, was my mother, and I've tried to capture aspects of her extraordinary personality at length and in short fiction: *Don't Take Away the Light*, my 1993 semi-autobiographical novel, has "Dear"—my nickname for her—as the secondary character. She's also a minor player in a few other Williamson novels and a stronger one in my short story "I'll Give You Magic If You Give Me Love" in the old *Horror Show* magazine.

But here my mother is the point of discussion, and the voice on a phone call in a setting based on a genuine Mother's Day visit incorporating my wife, two of our six kids, my sister, and my father. Basically, the frightening neighbor called Mrs. Maas is the only fiction in "The Mother Pact."

But I'll be surprised if you don't find it off-putting, probably scary.

The Mother Pact

My family and I came from out of state to celebrate Mother's Day with my parents; but considering the way my mom ran out the back door to
avoid us, you would have thought we'd come
from Mars—by way of a spaceship that hovered
over the entire neighborhood, filled with little
big-headed aliens avid to kidnap nothing but
mothers who wore dark wigs and used what was
left of their musical careers to give neighborhood
children piano lessons.

That was the way it looked to Mary and me, at
least, when my dad and baby sister had haltingly
explained Mother's absence. It took awhile for
them to do that, too.

Sis (all bright-brown-eyed like our mom, but
lacking, at fifteen, most of the weird streak): "She
heard your car pull into the drive. Then she
looked out the window to be sure and made a run

for it through the kitchen and out into the backyard!" She laughed the happy/silly giggle that
seemed brave and dear to me along with her
dancing eyes. She wasn't quite old enough yet to
see the quantity of pain Mother's odd ways
caused in people, and I envied her. "She didn't
even change out of her bedroom slippers."

That was Linette's way of trying to cheer me
up, because the "backyard" was thickly wooded
and extended almost two hundred feet to the
neighbor's fence, and no one had trimmed the
grass since I married Mary. But I didn't want
Mother to hurt her feet. "To be sure," Sis had said
without finishing it, "that it was you, Mary, and
the children." But that was certainly the implication. My God, did Mother still resent my marrying a Catholic girl so much she'd pass up a
chance to see her grandchildren and me?

Mary became expressionless as stone, turned,
and headed for the foyer of the old house. Chuck,
seven, hers from a previous marriage, ours if I
ever made him accept me, followed my wife.
John, on his way out of the twos that hadn't been
remotely terrible in his case, stood rooted in
ambivalence. His gift for "G'ma" was clutched in
his tubby arms, and he was looking from my face
to my dad's, to Linette's, and back to mine. John
wasn't really the cutest little towheaded kid who'd
ever lived (a part of me that stupidly preferred
facts insisted), but he was certainly the cutest
towhead *I* had fathered. Now I was angry; pissed.
But my heart couldn't catch up with the queerly
savage rhythms that went on throbbing at gut
level in that house.

Dad (residually handsome in his dark-and-
wavy-haired, dependable way, except his lips
were pressed together a lot with stress and he

seemed more tired out every time I'd seen him since I got married): "You know how she gets, Ted."

Aware this was about as close to grown-up conversation as we'd ever gotten, I replied with enormous earnestness, "I *thought* I knew." Inside my stirring memories there were unsought images—picture flashes—of Mother telling her little Teddy stories of deceased relatives coming to her at night with mixtures of prophetic and profane advice. Mother referring casually to "coloreds down the block," screaming about "Zionist conspiracies" and "Jew bankers." Mother playing music all night, improvising with innovation I wouldn't recognize again till I saw Michael Jordan shoot. Enemas she'd given me so often my perverse adult bowels had made an eternal pledge to constipation. "But I wouldn't have believed she'd hurt kids' feelings to get back at Mary and me. Or did she run off because my numerology said this was the day I'd set fire to the place, or eat the piano?"

My dad got out his God-I'm-sorry expression, turned his head, and glanced toward the kitchen to hide the look, and because he had his customary desperate hope his wife would do the normal, decent thing and reappear with some sort of rational explanation. What I had said about starting a fire stung him because she *did* set a small blaze out at the side last year. When I'd asked why, on the phone, Mother'd said airily that she'd been mad at *him* (emphasis hers).

As though suddenly realizing Mary and Chuck were waiting for me in the foyer, to leave, Dad rumpled John's yellow hair. Clapping me on the back, he called, "Mary, this is only one of her moods. She'll be back any second."

I sighed, rested the big gift from Mary and me

on the dining room table, ready to follow my old man back into the living room. I was careful not to push off a stack of my mom's sheet music, which was everywhere. Unless there was company—clearly, we weren't it—they lived around it. *Maybe it's just as well she took off,* I thought. I hadn't had the guts to ask Mary not to put her name on the gift tag too.

Sis linked her arm in mine, did a tugging little dance step meant to make her Big Bro laugh. She used to do that to save me from more Mother-inflicted moroseness and sometimes succeeded—just by being an affectionate kid. I wondered how much Linette had had to endure with me gone. We stepped back into the cathedral front room with the ceiling that let Mother's piano artistry reach for the heavens. Mary and our son Chuck were dutifully seated already. On a sofa within dash distance of the door, our car; freedom.

Dad (settling into the old, red chair he'd bought at a garage sale and considered one of the three things that were his): "Ted, your mother told me last night she'd disappear out back if you all came down for Mother's Day."

"You all?" I said, perching on Mother's piano bench (I'd wanted to sit with my wife and older son, but there wasn't room with them and another pile of old sheet music on the couch). John leaned back against my legs, staring at his grandfather. Sis was off answering the phone. "We aren't southern," I added.

"Now, don't get mad—or take it that way." He fumbled for his cigarette pack and lighter, and I wasn't sure the fumbling was because he was nervous.

"What you mean is that we shouldn't get mad at Mother," I said. It was a reference to how he had always defended her, agreed with her that

mothers never lied—and the implicit commandment that they were unfailingly right, and perfect. There'd also been something in my father's
tone that suggested I should have been enough of
a student of Mother to figure it all out myself.
"Because she's a brilliant pianist, composer, and
teacher."

He held my blinking gaze until he realized his
lighter was getting too hot to hold. "Well, she is.
People so talented have to be expected to be a little eccentric."

That was a dead accurate quote from Mother,
and it was one of her excuses for everything
bizarre or antisocial she did. To tell the truth, a
part of me still agreed with it. My mom had
always been the farthest thing from trite. Anybody who wasn't an idiot would have seen how
brilliant she was. Right on the piano next to me
then she'd played anything written down, and
could sight-read the classics or any kid of pop,
then transpose for anyone who wanted to sing. If
I hadn't come along, she might have become
world famous. But she'd always smothered me
with love and attention—till today. Clearly I had
underrated the depth of her mistrust of people
from other faiths, colors, even nationalities.
Because all this shit today had to do with Mary, a
wife who couldn't even receive the sacraments of
her church—because she'd divorced an unfaith-
ful wife-batterer and wound up marrying me!

I broke the gaze with my dad, sighed, and
hugged little John. "Guess I just haven't kept up
on my studies into Mother's ways. The past three
and a half years I've tried to raise a family of my
own instead"—*and tried to make Chuck like me a
little*, I added to myself—"and selfishly concentrated on keeping bread on the table." I looked
back up, pulling my elbow away from contact

with the sacred piano. "I suppose I'm just a little fucking rusty in figuring out what Mother wants on a given day of the week."

Dad: *"Ted!"* Truly shocked. Just as if his wife hadn't ever used the word when she was pissed. Of course, those times of tirade and abuse were merely part of her curse in being both a gifted woman and a mom, and were supposed to be immediately forgotten. "The *kids*," my father added in a breath.

Boogey-boogey, they already got fucked when we showed up here today, I thought. Then I felt sorry for him, as I had a million times, and wanted to go over and hug him—plead for both understanding and an explanation. "Could you just tell us why she'd decide, the night before we even left our home, to take off out the back door if we visited her on Mother's Day? Can you give us that much?" My mind raced; I perceived just then that I almost never addressed my father by any sort of name, possibly because I sensed that would be granting him too much identity to suit Mother. "We came a hundred *miles*, and both Mary and I believed it was our *duty* to come if we could!"

"And that is exactly where you made your mistake," he said, and sat up straight in his beloved chair that didn't match the rest of the furniture, but which he was somehow permitted to retain. His voice sounded nearly joyous, as if this was the *point* to *everything*—maybe the cure to cancer, and the embarrassing heartbreak of psoriasis. "Your mother wanted you to come sometime when it *isn't* a duty—when there's no holiday whatsoever and it's just an ordinary Sunday!" He hesitated, careful to try to explain it just the way Mother had to him. "Not on a day when sons everywhere are visiting their mothers."

Instinctively, I turned my head to seek out

Mary, who'd done the same thing with me. I'd had the impression my unflappable, beautiful, green-eyed wife would never look truly stunned five times in our marriage if it lasted fifty years, and she was using up one of those times. But then, we'd been together fewer than four years; that wasn't nearly long enough to begin anticipating even half of the astounding things my mother could think up.

Awful as it was to admit, I started nodding. I realized with an emotion close to guilt that I *should* have expected this particular performance of Mother's sooner or later, that her reasoning was one hundred percent consistent with her beliefs:

That she and I were special, a word synonymous with *superior*, and had a bond that Mother had forged by dint of adorably and cajolingly seducing my long-ago boy's ego. She'd enticed me into agreeing with her at a time in my life when I may not have even *seen* more than one hundred fellow human beings, because I was "frail" as a small child and she had driven me to and from school until my junior year at Shortridge, thereby effectively closing out most of the world. This bond was predicated on the superiority I shared as flesh of her flesh and her assumption that I was also a free spirit who should never be "plagued" by "mundane practicalities"—not while she, "buffeted by the storms of life" had already learned how "cruel and callow other people are." This premise led her to "dedicate" herself to "shielding" me from "brutal experience" and thereafter gave her the right to make judgments on everything and everyone I might ever happen to meet.

From that premise it followed (in Mother's inventive mind) that neither of us would ever automatically cooperate (or coexist) with any conventions, fads, commonplace desires, or dreads "of those whom God hadn't seen fit to bless with truly independent minds such as ours." So we'd believe what we chose (so long as God was part of the equation), but not necessarily go to any churches, give or not give gifts when we pleased (to show our sincerity, and not necessarily at Christmas), behave any way that appealed to us "in the sanctity of our own homes," and be vigilantly hostile toward "all that is solely of man and mammon"—meaning, I learned as I grew up, Communists and "one-world pinkos," unions, foreigners who weren't aching to come here, and everybody who was not a white Protestant native-born America-Firster "whenever they get out of line."

I need to insert here the fact that my mother had friends who were Jews and Catholics, adored the music of countless black jazz musicians, never took part in any kind of protest march or, I believe with all my heart, considered burning a cross. In ways I have never been successful in comprehending, the people of other creeds and colors whom she personally admired or liked never seemed (in Mother's view) to "get out of line." Except, of course, yours truly. I who brought a Catholic and her Christened Catholic child into the family—and Mother's everyday sphere of things. The fact that these were two people who'd never wafted a rosary in my direction or sought to lure me to "that pagan foreign religion" never entered into it. I'm pretty sure she believed my flesh-and-blood son John had secretly been sprinkled on his fair-skinned little forehead by some "Roman" priest, but that hadn't been part of Mary's deal and mine. Remarrying after her divorce had excommunicated my wife, and Mary wasn't actually too thrilled by the fact.

My Mom, though, appeared not to have believed a word I told her.

Have I digressed too much to make it plain I broke the Mother pact wide open by honoring a convention called Mother's Day—a day that was obviously set aside for "lesser people"? Do I really need to stress the fact that from my mom's viewpoint, *every* day was intended to be a golden opportunity to honor . . . Mother?

Well, my newer, chosen family and I hung around awhile talking with my dad, doing our collective best to behave as if there weren't anything strange about the situation. I agreed with my father that Mother would show up any moment, and found myself sweating like a horse while I attempted to guess what kind of performance we'd get from her. I knew she wouldn't lie and say she'd simply *had* to visit the German family living on the street behind, for a variety of reasons. First, Mary and I might take that as an apology, and Mother offered none. Second, my folks hadn't "neighbored" with anyone since I was Linette's age. But most importantly, they lived on the "good" street in the neighborhood, and the family behind us didn't—and *they* had such heavy accents my mom would never have made such an excuse. She figured anybody lucky enough to come to America to live should speak English like William F. Buckley within six weeks or get the hell out.

But I didn't think Mother's return to the house and an effort made to ignore her own prior absence—to pretend she'd been there all along; in the bathroom, maybe—was too much to hope for. I had seen her pull off much more complicated deceptions, and, to tell the truth, I genuinely believed she loved me far too greatly to pass up a chance to spend a couple of hours with me, and with her honest-to-blood grandson John.

So when we'd all suffered as much stress and tension as we could stand—when even John was becoming crankily sleepy, Chuck was getting as bored as a seven-year-old should have to tolerate, Linette's little-sister grins and good-humored gags were becoming rubber bands of attenuation, and we three adults were swallowing the silences lying on the front room carpet at our feet—

I was amazed and disgusted by two thoughts that came to my mind while we were saying our awkward goodbyes:

First, my mother was the only person I had ever known who literally commanded attention— remained the *center* of attention—without even being present or saying a word. I was much younger then, on that infuriating, ultimately humiliating Mother's Day; but I was reasonably sure I'd never meet another human being with such an imaginative array of off-center, mutually destructive talents—and I *mean* "mutually destructive," because Mother was so oddly principled and obsessive about her own commitment to our "pact" that she'd been entirely willing to sacrifice her own pleasure.

Second, simply put, she had hurt the hell out of me. I'd put my wife Mary on a pedestal, our marriage and the needs of our kids above all else, and Mother had unerringly hurled a ball of shit straight at our heads—but Mary, Chuck, and John would remember only the embarrassment (if that, in little John's case) and some of the anger they felt. *I* was the one who had been badly hurt, and would stay so; exactly as Mother had intended. Because I was the one who had been "special," and now she'd told me I no longer was.

139

Of course, I tried to get even. I didn't phone her during the spring, though I had phoned her nearly every week before that nightmarish Sunday, and when I rang the house in August, I made it a point to call on a day when I knew quite well Mother always went with her brother to put down flowers on Grandma's grave. I rather hoped my dad might have driven them to Crown Hill— so I could avoid speaking to either parent, but pretend to salve my conscience—but he answered the phone on the second ring. For a second I thought that might mean Mother was home, too, and braced myself for confrontation. She might or might not bring up Mother's Day, but she *would* give me an attitude, and *I* would bring up her rude absence.

For a moment, the tone in my father's voice made me think I was getting an attitude from him.

But he "reminded" me it was the anniversary of Grandma's death, and said how much he knew Mother would hate to have missed my call (*Good, good!* I thought)—then he spoke of how worried he was getting about her.

"That day you and Mary were here with the kids," he said quite slowly, clearly uncertain whether he should go into this, "Mother's Day . . . ?"

"Yes?" I said, rebracing myself to the best of my ability.

"She had a supernatural experience, Ted—or that's the way it looks. One that scared the hell out of her."

I almost laughed. This was a maneuver from my childhood. This was a golden oldie, a tactic so overused and outdated it had white hair to the ankles! I'd spent innumerable hours, as a boy, shivering to stories about Uncle Rob promising

Mother he hadn't planted his life savings in any gardens before he died, quaking to reports of phantoms who rearranged the furniture at night or warned my mom of "signs" she'd be seeing soon—omens of enormous and ominous portent. But now, *now*, I had a family of my own, I'd be thirty years old my next birthday!

"I don't know why seeing spooks or even hearing her piano move in the middle of the night should frighten her, Dad," I said. I wound the telephone cord around my wrist till it was taut, noticed, and then almost disconnected my father, in my embarrassed haste to unwind it. Why was I buying another one of Mother's weird tales? When was I going to grow a tail like any good master-psychologist's dog needs to put between its hind legs?

"This wasn't exactly a haunting, and it didn't occur during the night, Ted," my father said firmly in my ear. "It happened Mother's Day afternoon, when you were here." He paused just long enough that I could hope this was only one of my mom's ways of avoiding blame completely; having second thoughts, then concocting a reason for not being there to greet us. "This was something called the Moss-Woman."

Like an idiot, I dropped the phone. Had to pick it up before I could go on talking. Possibly, if I'd ever once heard my dad side with Mother and verify one of her so-called "psychic events" and therefore had good reason to think he was weird, too, I could've maintained my lightly skeptical reaction. But there'd never been a time when Dad commented on her "events" one way or the other. Now he was a believer.

I cleared my throat and asked him what a "Moss-Woman" was.

"For a few days, your mother wouldn't even tell

me what happened. She didn't even use that funny name. But she was pale as a ghost when she came back to the house, and wouldn't even open the presents you gave her. I tried to tell her how cute little John looked—Mary's boy, too—but she sort of sagged on the piano bench without even playing a note."

"Well, what did she say happened?" I demanded, and repeated my question. "What the hell is a 'Moss-Woman' and what did Mother say she did to her?"

Dad took a deep breath. "Just . . . touched her, I think." He clearly knew he was both confusing and losing me, so he made an effort to get the rest of it out, inadequate as his explanation was. "Your mother isn't well, Ted." I thought sarcastically, *Tell me about it.* "She's developed a terrible dry cough, and I think she picked up some sort of . . . rash while she was out running around in that tall grass and those weeds." His inflection said he *hoped* that was all it was.

A new headache kicked into one temple. "Have you gotten her to see a doctor?" I knew I was only wasting my breath, but the question reconnected me to reality.

The click and hiss of his lighter carried to my ear. "You know how she's been about doctors since Mom died." That "mom" was hers: Grandma. "I went to a bookstore, looked up 'Moss-Woman,' Ted. It's a German myth. They look pretty much like anyone else and don't hurt people as a rule, but they want to be accepted as real neighbors." Dad was talking fast now, for him, attempting to tell me all of this ridiculous stuff as quickly as he could. "Moss-Women are great mothers who'll do anything for the sake of their children, and it's important that their kids are accepted."

"Dad," I began.

"Anything a human does for them or to them is repaid a hundred times over," he rushed on, and I realized he was reading now from notes he'd taken. "If you are nice to them, they'll make your workload lighter. But if you offend them, they can make you sick—very sick. Just by"—Dad's voice began to tail off—"*touching* you."

I wanted to tell him that was complete craziness, yet I was suddenly itching under one arm, snuggling the phone to my neck so I could scratch. For me, for my dad, it just wasn't as absurd a story as I know it would sound to most late-twentieth-century Americans. Because Mother had described seeing fairies playing in the grass when I was a kid, and she'd even discerned an eerie light hovering above the grass in our backyard—and Dad and I had seen it, too, but never found out what it was. "There are a lot of trees behind the house, and it's a deep lot," I reasoned the best I could, "but it's no woods. Dad, it's just a big backyard that needs mowing."

"Whatever your mother saw out there, it scared the pee out of her, son. It made her ill enough that she's refused to give me many of the details. Ordinarily, she goes on about ghosts and things for days, she *enjoys* them. Son, I think this really happened."

That comment shocked and spooked me. In a way, it was Dad's tough admission that some of the strange things Mother claimed to have experienced during their years together were not in her imagination, because he had never countenanced the slightest suggestion before that that was conceivable. "But what *did* happen?" I pressed him.

"Every other damn bit of weirdness she's always talked about is fairly common knowledge, or she's said that her mother or some friend told her about it. She's never read books about anything that might be supernatural except for her numerology." His pause was quite brief. "I had to look through around a dozen occult books at the store before I found this thing in an encyclopedia by someone named Lewis Spence, but she called it by its name the first time she was able to discuss it. So where, Ted," he demanded, "would she hear about such a creature except from a *real* Moss-Woman?"

He promised he'd keep me informed about my mom's health, we hung up almost immediately after that, and I knew he had me with that question of his. Logic told me it wasn't impossible she had picked up knowledge about the myth from a dozen different sources. But when an annoying corner of my mind asked me to itemize them, I came up with a TV show called *Sightings*, then drew a total blank. Except for those that had articles about pianist heroes of hers, she didn't read magazines. She hadn't had a close friend in years, which meant no gossipy rumors. And Mother's upbringing certainly had made its mark on me; I watched *Sightings* and most documentaries about both UFOs and hauntings on the tube myself, and I'd never heard of a "Moss-Woman" before.

All this was occurring during a period of my life when I was trying to earn an income for my family by selling space in catalogs for a mail-order firm. It definitely wasn't my *raison d'être*, and I had to hustle for every paycheck. So I kept forgetting to call my folks' house again—I genuinely *believed* I forgot, anyway—except for twice before November, and nobody answered. Mary and I were surprised when Chuck got an unprompted birthday card from them with ten bucks enclosed. Mary was perplexed, but careful to make Chuck scribble a thank-you note to my parents, and then—catching me off-guard— another holiday season lay dead ahead.

Which naturally meant to us (since my wife and I weren't precisely brain-dead) it was okay to ask her father, a widower, to celebrate Thanksgiving with us, but that we shouldn't even telephone my side of the family unless Mother brought the holiday up. I toyed with the idea of trying to get Sis up to our place, because we both wanted her, but she wasn't old enough to have a driver's license yet and the only way it might have worked out would have been for Mary's pop to bring her. Considering the virtual certainty that my mom would have concluded we were converting her to Catholicism on the spot and turning her into Sister Linette with a capital "s," I didn't want to see Sis that badly. It was a pleasant Thanksgiving anyway, till dark.

To my amazement, Mother did bring up the holiday. She phoned around midnight that chilly Thursday in Thessaly, and I was horrified to realize I didn't recognize her voice.

After we'd both said "hello" and she asked, "Did you have a nice Thanksgiving, Teddy?" I knew it was Mother. No one else called me that anymore except my wife, and then teasingly and when we were in bed late at night.

"I'm really glad you phoned, Mother," I said, very nearly really glad. "Yes, we did; thanks." I was appalled by how she sounded: rasping, dry as sandpaper. Her voice had always been fairly low-pitched, but now it was as if it were an effort for her to speak. Instantly, I was wary, guarded, half-expecting it was an act. "Did you and Dad have a nice day?"

For a second there was no reply. It had been her cue to tell me no days were "nice" any longer (implication: since you married *her*), or—however contrarily—bawl me out for not visiting them on Thanksgiving, or at least recite a complete litany of ailments.

Instead, she merely said, "I'm afraid she's gotten me, Teddy."

My God, I realized, after a pause to think, I'd forgotten about the Moss-Woman! Let's see, it was August when my dad told me about Mother's queer experience (*story*, I corrected myself sternly), and it was supposed to have happened on Mother's Day—and that was over six months ago. Surely she wasn't still getting mileage out of that one isolated "event"—unless of course she really *had* fallen ill that day!

I must digress to make it clear I'm not the uncaring bastard I might seem to be. It's possible no mother ever had more effective input on a child than mine. I spent more hours with her, growing up—including countless middle-of-the-night when she was either confiding in me about her spectral visitations or, knowing I'd be listening, playing music just for me—than a modern husband spends with his wife in a ten-year marriage. She taught me not only a lot about the world I knew, more than a little of it nonsense, but everything that had ever happened to her and every dream or fear in her heart. Maybe we'd given each other too much insight into the other, yet her most costly mistake was assuming I would never have any independent ideas, desires, or aspirations of my own. I had loved her more than most sons ever really care for their moms, but living in the same house with her was like dwelling with a local television pitchman who plugs his steak knives or used cars twenty-four hours a day—free of any obligation to hold to the truth or the facts—and I was stuck with buying what he pitched every single time.

Part of the reason I'd loved her more than most boys adored their moms was the fact that, after Dad lost his number one status in her heart (I never did learn how, or why), I was the one who was permitted to see her lovable side. I was her principal audience, not just for the piano serenades but for the deepest longings, beliefs, and loathings that Mother possessed. In a way, I was still incredibly flattered by that. In a way, I always shall be.

"Do you want," I began gently, pulling out a dining room chair to sit in, "to tell me about it?"

"*Her*, dammit!" croaked Mother. "Not it!"

"Okay, 'her,' " I said. "Do you?"

"Darling, I look like the wrath of God," she said. Clearly, I realized, she was trying not to cough. "Like a really old bitch."

Her line didn't amuse me because she was only in her fifties then and she had appeared beautiful in the way that women who can entertain the public learn how to sustain the veneer of beauty longer than others—right up to the time I'd married. "Maybe you need a new wig," I suggested.

"Only if I found one long enough to cover my face and arms," she quipped. But she tried to laugh and I heard this "hsst-hmp-hmph" sound despite the way she covered the phone mouthpiece with her hand. "What the goddamn little bitch did to my skin is . . ." But she allowed the sentence to fade. "I don't want to discuss her, no. There's no point."

The cough Mother had been suppressing escaped like Schwarzenegger and Stallone joining forces to burst out of a bamboo holding cell. I had never heard a worse cough, one that more obviously told the listener that the throat and lungs had to have something terrible the matter with them. "Mother," I said with the firmness of tone Dad had used on me, "you *must* see a doctor about that cough! Please. Promise me you'll—"

"I did, I saw two doctors," she gasped. "The goddamn quacks! One for my skin, one for the cough. I forget which was which, but one of them was some Russian Jew your father heard about; a specialist." She drew in a breath and started sounding better, and I wasn't sure whether it was bringing up some phlegm or saying something snotty about physicians, foreigners, and Jews in the same breath that improved her condition. "Maybe musicians should specialize. Then I could play like Count Basie all the time—badly, of course—and make a fortune, like doctors do!"

I laughed aloud. Mary stood in the entrance to the dining room, wearing just her bra and panties, pointing to her watch to remind me I'd have to arise in six hours for work. When I mouthed "Mom" to indicate who was on the phone and she saw my delighted grin, she looked completely baffled. If Mary's specialty could have been teaching people to stop fighting the unvanquishable realities, we would have been rich. She and my mother didn't breathe in the same universe, and it occurred to me as I found myself aroused by my wife's unexpected appearance that I might have married her mainly because she made reality more interesting and attractive than Mother's world of anomaly and fantasy.

"I think you're going to be okay, Mother," I said into the telephone, meaning it. It occurred to me to bring up Christmas and to verbalize a dream I had of both my families together on a happy day—Mary's father included, if he wanted—but I didn't, and maybe Mother would have agreed this time. It's not that I believe everything would have been different if I'd brought it up; I don't precisely feel guilty about it. It's just that I would like to have seen my mother more or less like herself again, heard her play carols, even listened to her vilifying another nation or religion or two. "You still sound like your old self, except for the cough."

"Pray for me?" she asked in that unfamiliar voice. I said sure, and I did, once or twice. But I thought I heard the very familiar notes of melodrama seeping through her raspiness and I felt guilty about not praying more, or harder. "Be careful if you meet the Moss-Woman, son. I know we have our pact, but you're more like me than you care to believe. Promise me you won't lose your temper if you meet the nasty little Nazi demon?"

I smiled, said sure again. I was watching Mary get ice for the Pepsi she took to bed with her, and my sneaky peek at her through the open kitchen door was charging me up. Supernatural beings in the woods seemed a million miles away. "I won't."

"Give little John—the children—a kiss for me," Mother rasped, and I relaxed mentally until she added with surprising, possibly telepathic aptness, "and for heaven's sake, *don't* have any more kids for a while. You can't afford it!"

I was like a maddened tiger in bed that night, but if anyone really enjoyed it, it must have been Mary. Mother's symptoms, beliefs, and uncanny ways had me in doubt again. And fear.

My father phoned after Christmas and close to New Year's, purportedly to thank us for the unimpressive gifts we'd managed to send despite the fact that almost everybody tended to celebrate those holidays. Then he told me what Mother hadn't—that the two doctors she'd seen could not trace the sources of her persistent cough and skin complaint, but they'd said she was running a consistent temperature, her throat was badly inflamed, and she could severely damage her lungs if she kept whooping that way. Of course, she had refused to "waste money" on X rays. "I'm very concerned about her now, Ted," Dad whispered. That meant Mother wasn't far from the phone. "Her conditions are both worse, and she can't get enough to drink. Except that she finds it hard to swallow."

"Put her on," I urged him. "Maybe I can talk her into getting X rays."

"Well, she almost never speaks anymore," he said. That horrified me. *Mother, not talking?* "Unless she has to."

"Should we come down?" I demanded. And suddenly I got angry. "We can't just stand by while she—" Hell, I couldn't finish the sentence. I was panicking just by realizing what I had almost said. Mother was one of a kind, and I'd never believed such people perished. Bogart, Jack Benny, Marilyn, the Beatles, Bette Davis, Elvis. They were meant to just run down someday in their nineties, when you'd had a chance to *assume* they were dead anyway. They lived so long most of their own families were gone, so some great-grandchild buried them and, after that, maybe they went on talking or joking or singing and playing for the roots of trees. "Dad, what shall I do?"

"I think she's all right for now," said my father in his careful hushed tones. "Come see her on

Mother's Day—and don't worry about that, I'll arrange it. If you came now, she'd be convinced some doctor told me she was dying."

I whispered back, "*Is she?*"

"I'll call you about any change," was all he said, then hung up.

Late in February the phone rang not long after we'd put the kids to bed and were settling in before the television set. Mary ran upstairs to answer it (the house is an old trilevel and we hang out mostly in the lower part) because I'm a big fan of IU basketball and my wife is a considerate person. Coach Knight had the Hoosiers ahead of Purdue by ten—I always referred to the Boilermakers as "PU"—and I was astonished when Mary reappeared on the second step, clearly about to call me to the phone.

"It's your mother," she said, looking surprised. Of course I'd told her Dad had said mother seldom used her voice anymore unless she had to. "I could barely hear her."

I wish I could say I wasn't irritated as hell at first. Basketball works for me like a good drama and sitcoms get other people's minds off their daily lives, and I temporarily spaced out about my mom's health problems.

Then, sighing but enormously concerned, I was vaulting up the four steps toward the dining room, and the phone. Mary stayed with me, watching with concern as I snatched it up.

"Just wanted to thank you for the birthday card." She enunciated each word so carefully and took so long to utter the sentence it was like hearing rusted machinery striving to crank through defective gears. "Tried to thank Mary. Don't think she understood me." Birthday cards were all right; they celebrated an individual's special day.

"How are you, Mother?" I asked. The former IU players broadcasting the game into our lower level might have been discussing something meaningless from a cavern deep in the earth.

But she didn't answer me at once, or didn't seem to, and I screwed the phone receiver into my ear until my wrist and forearm began to shake. "Teddy . . . I can't play anymore," Mother said. "Skin on my fingers . . . comes off. Just about raw."

Dear God, I thought, more sympathetic than I'd ever felt toward any other human being. Mother unable to soothe her soul the only way she could, playing the piano. Incapable of using her voice well enough to speak the many hurtful but also badly hurt words that represented her other means of communication. An image popped into my mind of a creature one or two feet in height, ancient and wizened, covered everywhere on her body except for a smirking and half-toothless mouth with ugly, writhing, mossy growth. I beat the creature off with an effort of will, muttered the loving yet meaningless words of caring anybody might have spoken to her.

"Your father said you want to see me . . . Mother's Day." She paused, wheezing; I heard a glass clink against her phone as she took a sip. "That Mary has to be with—her father." She laughed briefly, horribly. "Catholics have such funny ideas about . . . holidays, don't they?"

I realized how my father had "arranged" my visit, that it would be strictly *my* visit. "I'll be there," I promised, glad Mary's hand was on the back of my neck. "Call me if anything—"

"Won't be making any more phone calls," Mother croaked. A tortured breath. "Love . . ."

I also said, "love," but I was talking to nothing.

152

There was no further contact between either of my parents and me till winter had passed, though I phoned several times, hoping to get an update from Dad. For the first time, it occurred to me how odd it was that two people who rarely left the house at night unless Mother had a piano job never appeared to be home in the evenings these days. I didn't mention that to Mary because I had always wanted her to believe I was nothing at all like Mother, especially where her supernatural beliefs were concerned. But my folks' absence still struck me as peculiar, even as something that was not of their doing or mine.

Then the cold weather had crawled away, spring was shaking its head to get its bearings, and the time for me to drive from Thessaly to Indianapolis was here. This year I took only one gift, and it was more a grandma's-day type of present: little John's clay ashtray or dish or whatever exactly it was that he'd made for her in nursery school. I kept glancing at it during my drive, now and then; I was hoping I could enable him and Chuck to grow up without their brains being filled with unreachable ambitions, plus beliefs that could have some bizarre factual merit to them but might very well be better left to those who required a different kind of belief system.

Before I reached the old house on Pennsylvania Avenue I was aware that the growing proximity to my mom was pulling me into her orbit, psychologically, in an inexorable manner that seemed to render everything else in my life childlike at best, meaningless at worst. To combat the feeling, I tried to think objectively about the woman who had borne me, to be absolutely logical, even detached—which I know now is a serious mistake. In attempting to be the opposite of Mother, I actually complemented her. No rational opposition to anyone remotely like her is possible unless you really *are* that way. By denying any similarity to my mom, I not only replicated her rebellion against the truth and reality, but left myself with nothing to be except an equally quarrelsome, masculine clone of her.

So overpowering was my gifted Mother's hold on my psyche, I saw, that I had rarely given a thought to my sister Linette since I last saw her! We had the capacity for being close; science said siblings were closer by blood than parent and child—and I had last worried about my on-the-scene-and-spot-Sis when we were in Indianapolis a year ago! For a second I couldn't even remember if Mary and I had mailed her a present at Christmas. All of which was an example of our mother's magnetic personality, since in most modern American homes it was the teenager who grabbed center stage—the youth of the teenager that people of middle age envied and tried to emulate.

In Linette's first home and mine, all there was of youth was what Mother remembered of her own and spoke of as if no one else would ever have such experiences, or needed to. Suddenly I doubted that our dad had any clear memory of his time being young before he'd met our mother-to-be.

Sis was waiting at the door when I pulled up in front of the house with the once-ornate stucco siding, hugging me before I'd walked halfway up the lane. "My favorite bro!" she cried, as if she'd had several brothers; then, before I could continue toward the front door, "She's dying, Ted, I'm sure of it, our mama's dying." I felt the brush of her eyelash tears on my cheek like sweet raindrops, but saw she was keeping her face chipper with a disguise of smiles. "Brace yourself for the way she looks and sounds."

"My entire skeleton is one big back brace," I said in low tones, side-by-siding it the rest of the way.

And that was what I believed one hundred percent before I saw Mother.

My dad and I scrubbed one another's five-o'clock-shadow cheeks before the three of us entered the high-ceilinged front room, Linette chattering as if this would be nothing but a little family get-together; and then I saw the person on the sofa whose phone voice I'd had trouble identifying, and didn't want to admit to myself that I recognized her in person.

From a distance of twenty feet, the skin of her face and arms—she'd donned slacks so I couldn't see her legs—looked like that of a fairly dark-skinned African American, or perhaps a native of India. She had applied eyebrow pencil, lipstick, and rouge, and her performer's good judgment in makeup had led her to buy shades of all three that were much darker than she'd ever worn before. Drawing nearer with each step, I saw how immeasurably worse she appeared than from just inside the foyer. The flesh that showed from half a dozen feet away was brown-blotched, as if she'd been beaten, and bruised.

Sitting beside her—making myself kiss red-walnut lips that belonged to a stranger—I believed she had a disease of pigmentation, some awful virus that had confused the chemical substances in her body. One needed to have known her *before*, I thought, to grasp the changes; one needed to have remembered she was a petite, pale woman who rarely ventured into the sunlight (*as she did one year ago*, I recalled) and preferred the night hours. The fact that she had donned her favorite blond wig just made matters worse, turned her even more incongruously into someone whose appearance I scarcely recognized.

"Don't worry about. . . . the kiss," she told me—I'd had to stoop, put my ear to her almost inky lips to hear—"the quacks said I'm not . . . contagious."

I started to chuckle at her nonsense, then realized most of the scant redness in her lips looked like scabs of blood. My fingers flew to my own mouth before I got control of my hand. Beneath the heavy lipstick, her soft flesh was unbelievably dry and cracked. In fact, there were strips of skin on her forehead, temples, and cheeks that seemed to have peeled away, healed, peeled again and were attempting one more time to heal. But wherever it had come back, the skin was an ocher or umber color—and resembled bark.

Tenderly, I raised Mother's arm at a wrist that felt hard, sticklike, to examine her fingers. I doubt I kept her from hearing my gasp. I doubt the FBI could have found any sign of fingerprints. The poor tips glistened with something Linette (I learned later) had put on to soothe them, and they were a light, raw pink with fine traces of laceration acquired (I felt certain) from courageously trying to continue playing the piano. The power of touch is underrated as a sense, I found out that instant; the pain Mother had endured and was enduring was dreadful to consider.

When I had unwrapped John's gift for her and she had momentarily recaptured some of the old sparkle in her large brown eyes, making me promise to tell him Grandma loved his present, she brought my ear close again to make sure she was heard. "Have to lie down," she croaked, "in bed. Think I'm getting . . . rooted . . . to it." Her gaze caught mine, her eyes said more to me than her words. She put her arms over her head to stretch, and what I saw made me turn my head to meet my sister Linette's heartsick eyes. Mother's customarily white underarms, albinolike of hue, had mottled, harshly lined splotches from three to four or five inches in length—such a deep brown of color that it was nearly black—running from the pits of her arms to just above the wrists.

"I made a chocolate cake for you, Mama," Sis said brightly, rushing over to help the dying woman to her feet. My father was on her other side before I could stand. "Your favorite."

"I know that," Mother rasped, the louder remark bringing spittle to her lips. She turned her head to peer at me. "Staying?"

My heart thudded. My thigh muscles tightened, wanted to run. "I'll be here."

She was nodding her satisfaction with that until they were almost out of my sight.

It was then I decided I needed fresh air. A walk in our heavily wooded backyard. "Happy Mother's Day," I called before I remembered our old pact. "Love . . ."

Then I found a roll of paper towels in the kitchen, took one, and blew my nose before going out back.

Dad had put in a patio years ago when we moved in. Once there had been cookouts, and I'd also had a basketball backboard, but now they were the last bastions against the encroaching, still-growing trees and wild grass. Just the pole on which my backboard had been mounted remained, and it reminded me of little but the stake on which they had burned Joan of Arc— or had they tied her to a cross? My thoughts were as much a jungle as the wooded growth into which I was advancing, telling myself I was not searching

157

for anything as fanciful as a "Moss-Woman," as a creature smaller than a UFO pilot with a mossy body and evil eyes—but of course I was. I kept staring toward the grass and weeds; possibly I intended to catch her, or smash her flat if I noticed her before she noticed me, I'm not sure.

I wasn't a Catholic despite my mom's dark fears, but I was a catholic reader, and useless facts sometimes stuck in my memory. Melanin was the chemical that gave pigments a black color, so if Mother was suffering from an oddball skin problem, maybe that was a clue. In Caucasians it was concentrated in moles and freckles. But melanin also existed in plant life. I also thought, as I kept inching my way between the trees, of what little I knew of the fairy kingdom. They were *always* in woodlands and fields, folklorists claimed. Like demonic beings, they could spot a human weak point, a flaw of conscience, more quickly than people could—and Mother had a few; she disliked or distrusted the majority of human beings. The fact that she believed devoutly in a divine Being would only make her a more desirable target to any dark entities she had offended, because they had no choice but to believe in God and they wouldn't be very happy about the obligation.

Those who made a study of mythical people—and assumed there actually were such creatures—said so much land had been occupied and inhabited by us that the privacy-loving beings of legend have lost most of the unspoiled places in which they prefer to live, and have been obliged to adapt to our ways. Logic told me many of the beings must have done this by pretending to *be* people. If I was right, humankind couldn't know where or when we might blunder upon a "door" between the coexisting worlds and inadvertently pass through it. Mother could have trespassed and not known it.

At my feet, a few yards ahead of me, I believed I saw blades of grass bend as if smaller, unseen feet were pushing them down. The skin of my arms and on the back of my neck goosepimpled. Then my hair felt as if it had been rumpled, but I saw no one else around, and there was no wind stirring at all! In fact, it was so still where I stood in my mom and dad's deep backyard that the lack of sound itself seemed eerie. Uneasy as hell, I pushed forward, nearly ran into a tree branch at face level, and a spiderweb swept weirdly across my forehead and one ear. Willing myself to get a breath and quit being so silly, I paused to scrub at my creeping flesh, and squinted straight ahead to get my bearings.

I found myself at the rear of the lot and looking at a fence—the back fence of a house that faced the street behind my parents' property. I knew immediately this should mean something to me, then I remembered what: We'd all known the people who lived in the old house on the other side of the fence— a German family—and my mom felt sure *their* street marked the start of the neighborhood's decline. Everything beyond it, to the west, was sheer slum according to Mother.

Dimly, I recalled chatting with the woman who dwelled in the old house when I was somewhere in my teens, and also a tiny son, a child with those immense, shining eyes some little kids had that said they were born knowing everything, or they would certainly catch up with whatever they had missed. I didn't remember a man.

Suddenly I realized I wasn't only looking at the fence, but staring at the woman herself, who was frozen in place and staring back at me! Apparently she'd hung wash on an old-fashioned clothesline and had decided to kneel before a young tree, quietly working until I'd materialized from the trees. She was digging in mulch and bone meal around the base of the trunk, and she had a homey watering can waiting on the ground just behind her. The tree was an evergreen, I realized—

And I also realized I was continuing to stare at the small, plain-looking woman—she was probably in her late forties, with her graying hair in a bun at the back of her head—as if she actually *was* frozen in place, waiting for my casual inspection to end. "Hi," I said, feeling like a clumsy kid again. "We met a long time ago when I was still living here with my folks. I'm their son, Ted, but I was a lot younger when—"

"I remember you," she said, giving me the flicker of a smile. Or it might just have been sunlight and shadow from the trees passing over her mouth. "You are well, *ja*?"

"Fine, thanks," I replied, going nearer to the fence. "Unfortunately, my mom isn't well at all."

She said, "I heard." Toiling efficiently, briskly, as if there was nothing more important for her to do, she reached behind her for the watering can and began sprinkling at the base of the evergreen as if she knew how many drops were just right. Her round, somewhat doughy face was set in an expression of nearly loving absorption. "I know."

She heard? That surprised me because, as I said, my folks didn't neighbor much. She hadn't said she was sorry my mother was ill, I realized. I rested my fingertips on the top of the simple wooden fence, trying to figure out what was going on, if anything. It was humid out there; stuffy. When I glanced around, I discovered I could no longer see any sign of my parents' house, nor anything but growing, expanding nature. I said foolishly, "I came down for Mother's Day, of course."

"You were a good boy." The comment appeared devoid of sarcasm. "How is the little *Schwester*—what is her name? Lynn?"

"Linette," I said, wondering all at once why the pleasant but industrious neighbor lady was expending such effort on a fir tree when there were a few evergreens growing untended within a stone's throw. Of course, they were on our land, but it still seemed strange to me, when there were all the trees anybody could want to see closer to her property than to my folks' home. "She's fine except for worrying about our mom." That was meant to be a lead line; to give the woman another chance to say it was sad that Mother was sick, or to inquire about the nature of her illness.

"Good children are a blessing all good parents deserve," she replied. She didn't look up, but I saw her frown, observed something born of strong emotion crossing her bland and almost bovine face. Through with her watering, she got to her knees and began carefully picking dried brown needles out of the fir tree's youthful branches. "When the weather warms," she said softly, "I will plant pansies here. *Sohn* always liked looking into their little faces."

I straightened, and nearly took a step back from the fence. The only other times I'd ever heard such emotion in a woman's voice were those when my mom was deeply moved by what she had played on the piano and tried to put her feelings into words. "How is that cute little boy of yours?" I asked. The place where I was gingerly gripping the fence seemed electrified. "Of course, he's bound to have grown so much I might not recognize him. Why—he must be about Linette's age by now!"

"This evergreen is all I have of him," the woman said, and raised her face to peer directly up at me. "He fell sick. He died."

"God, I'm sorry," I said in a breath. I let my hands drop to my sides.

"On another day when *Mutter* was honored," she said evenly, "yours was here, not far from where you stand. She had run from her house, through the woods, and found me here. But I had no evergreen then, young man; only my lawn at the back and my small garden, *ja*?"

I nodded, blinked.

"Your *Mutter* turned when she saw me at work, because she knew I would seek an answer to a question I gave her weeks before." She stood, but kept touching the fir tree, fussing with it with her busy fingers. "I'd wished her to teach my little boy piano, and I had said I would pay her what she asked. I knew she loved music as did my *Sohn*, and he wanted to play a song before he died." The neighbor's eyes did not widen and there were no tears visible in them, but they were so deep I believed for one moment the woman might be blind and actually have no eyes. There was only the blackness. "Your *Mutter*, however, was very angry that day—because, she said, her *Sohn* and his family had come to visit her!"

"I'm so sorry about your boy," I said hastily, feeling a great urge to hear no more, possibly feeling very afraid. "But Mother is *dying*. She can't even *play* piano because—

"She said bad things about *Sohn*, about me. About your family." Moisture showed in her eyes, her black, forever eyes, but her fury and indignation were spent. "She is a woman who did not wish to see her *only Sohn*! Such mystery I cannot solve. Of course I would no longer permit her to teach the lessons to my dying child."

I was again surprised, even prepared to be relieved. "But she didn't say no?"

For an instant it seemed she might thrust her arms in among the branches, attempt to embrace the tree. "I did not ask her once more that day, after hearing her anger for you and your wife." She picked up the empty watering can, clearly ready to go back into her house, then hesitated. "There are those who, dying, find a different sadness; while it may be no better, sometimes the anger flees and its energy serves a different and better purpose. All that of nature has its uses."

As she turned to her house, I was startled to remember her name. "You're going to have a beautiful evergreen here, Mrs. Maas," I called.

She slowed her passage, but didn't stop. "When it's over," she said distinctly, "you and your *Frau* must come to visit. You will be amazed how quickly and well a tree treated lovingly may grow. When it is fine and healthy because you alone have nurtured it, it provides much comfort as one becomes older."

"We will," I said, stepping back from her yard and her fence without yet turning. "Thank you for asking us."

"Don't forget!" Mrs. Maas called, opening her back door.

I waved at her, kept edging away. "Believe me," I said, "I won't."

The Writing of "Small Gift from Home"

Many writers not yet established in short stories center their sights on magazines that pay the most money. My goal was to be chosen by certain anthology editors, such as Robert Bloch, Martin H. Greenberg, Jeff Gelb, and Kristine Rusch, and for certain publications. I called this "signs of making it," and the regular publications in which I dearly yearned to see my work were (more or less, in chronological order) *Ellery Queen's*, W. Paul Ganley's *Weirdbook*, *Weird Tales*, *The Horror Show*, *Grue*, a major men's mag, *Fantasy Book*, *Eldritch Tales*, *Night Cry*, Rod Serling's *Twilight Zone*, *Pulphouse*, The U.K's *Fantasy Tales* and *Fear*, *Cemetery Dance*, *Deathrealm*, *Bizarre Bazaar*, *Terminal Fright*, and *Palace Corbie*. (I forgot *Mike Shayne's* and the short-lived but worthwhile *Mystery Monthly* and *Espionage*.)

Goal scored and yearning fulfilled. The men's mag I cited was *Cavalier*.

One of the first editors and one of the first publications I tried respectively to please and to make was Stuart David Schiff's beautiful booklike magazine, *Whispers*. A dentist by profession, Stuart was one of many small press or speciality house publishers who brought me pain by teaching me that even if they couldn't pay the way *Playboy* did, their standards were just as high. The product of those standards was that almost any writer whose work appeared in such suspended magazines as *Whispers, Weirdbook, TZ, Horror Show, Deathrealm* or Lin Stein's *Dead of Night* felt it was an accomplishment—and readers were apt to *read* your fiction with no naked gatefold girls to divert their attention!

My first success with Stu occurred in 1984 with this story, that convinced me I could move further afield imaginatively and in terms of characterization than I'd dared, until then, to wander. It was roughly my twenty-sixth or- seventh story sale. Thanks for the earlier rejections, Stuart!

Small Gift From Home

Your distinguished chairperson has asked me to stir my aging stumps, but he don't fool me into thinking it's this old fool he wants to hear speak. What he wants to hear is *about*—about my dear friend Q. T. Barrett. And I, for one, do not blame our fine chairperson. Except you aren't going to hear about the legendary Barrett of the sixties, when "Cutie" Barrett—as that smart aleck columnist once called him, at the height of the marches—was a middle-aged man of fifty.

You're going to hear about the start of our friendship, Q. T.'s and mine, for the simple reason that it was around that time—before our heads got white like snow—that I first saw how useful he'd be to blessed Doctor King, and how resourceful Q. T. could be when things got ugly. Resourceful enough to get the help of the most mysterious black woman I ever met, just in time

166

to save his baby sister from a fate worse'n death.

That's it, sit back a spell. You'll be glad you heard me out.

When my story starts, it was a matter of honest fact that you might not have called Q. T. Barrett nonviolent, strange as it seems. It was before Martin, as I've stated, and we was young and healthy together, scarcely aware of what cruel things was happening elsewhere to our people. Neither Q. T. nor I had been hurt more than the average, and I s'pect we believed we was sturdy enough to handle anything.

Leastways, until that old grizzly crossed our path over at Horace's.

As I recall, the structures in this very neighborhood were a whole lot brighter-looking, cleaner, back then. But only on the outside. Inside, they was crammed with folks who looked out for number one in the oldest and narrowest of ways, so there was too much terror for anybody to see how bright things were on the outside. Y'see, fear makes shadows grow inside a human being, and the light doesn't get to it.

Well, it was the giant everyone called simply Big who lengthened those shadows for us. Not that anybody talked out loud about him, leastwise not until Big had noticed how pretty your daughter or your baby sister was becoming. Then it was too late for discussion. Then was when Big really got that sugar-and-honey mouth of his into gear, and put out his huge bear's paw to rake in the sweetest sunshine you had in all your life.

I don't know to this day if my friend Q. T. ever learned more about Big than that; what his real name was, or where he'd come from, or how he'd managed to get all the mob connections he had. To the people who lived in our neighborhood it was enough to know Big's fame fitted him like his tailored suits, and that mammoth ruby ring he flashed from his pinkie finger, and the self-assured way that he handled those two-ton dudes—the ones who always stood next to Big, down at Horace's. They toted the hardware, because guns spoiled the cut of the old bear's clothes.

It began coming to a head that December when Big flashed that gold-gleaming, grizzly smile of his, and proposed his way of saving time. Instead of Big sending out his side-men to choose our women for the rackets, Big opined, why didn't we just march our sisters and daughters right on down to Horace's whenever he asked?

It was Freddie, I think, who was the first to shake his head, No. Freddie was also, for a while, the last one to do a crazy thing like that.

The last, until the night Big glanced up from those sausage fingers of his, causing the manicure girl to stop. His baby finger was raised and the ruby was red, like a pearly drop of blood, as he fixed his tiny eyes on my friend. Oh, he was polite at first. Observed that Q. T.'s sister Zanra was "turning into quite a young lady, hoss, yessir, a real looker."

It wasn't that Big was wrong. Zanra had had a birthday recently and yes, she was the prettiest girl of thirteen in the whole neighborhood. Pretty enough to make herself into just about anything decent she could, none of which was what the old kodiak had in mind.

Right then I should have wondered about Q. T. Because he didn't fly off the handle when Big asked about his sister, he didn't get himself roughed-up or rousted a bit. No, sir, Q. T. did an amazing thing instead.

Leaning over Big's drink-laden table, he *smiled*. Sweetly; all feathery-light, right into the face of that enormous teddy bear. Behind us, the clicks coming from the pool table ceased immediately and everybody started staring. I couldn't take my eyes off Q. T. Barrett.

"How," he said softly to Big, "how would you like to get your hands on a girl who is truly *different* than any you've had before? A beauty, Big, sure to earn a fortune—one who's eager to do what you please? What would you say to *that*, Big?"

Big was suspicious, naturally, but I saw that light in his squinty old eyes. What I hadn't seen was how Q. T. had been watching his sister Zanra grow, how he'd figured this would happen some-day and was prepared for it. I also hadn't seen just how far Q. T. would go to protect his own.

For a while, the bear fired his questions at my friend. He blocked 'em the way Russ used to do it. And at last Big, very surlylike, said he might just bypass Zanra Barrett if Q. T. was on the square. He told Q. T. when to bring "that diff'rent babe," then lowered his head. "I wouldn't be late, brother," Big said pointedly as he gave his fingers back to the trembling manicurist. "If I was you, I'd have that little lady here *on time*."

Now, after I tell you folks the rest of it, you're gonna want some answers to the details of what happened, and where she came from. Please, don't ask. Q. T. never explained it to me and frankly, I don't want to know anymore. But it was close to Christmas when my friend kept his appointment promptly with Big, and I imagine I'll never forget it.

J.N. Williamson

Because he has this girl with him, all right. And they walk right up to ole Big's table. And everybody in Horace's place gapes, first at the girl and then at Big—who never once took his astonished and greedy eyes from her.

She was pretty as a picture. Q. T. didn't lie. Truly, I never saw lovelier eyes or skin in all my life. And a figure that made words grind like hamburger in a man's throat, with a sort of *pouch* held from a leather rope around her waist. Because Q. T. didn't lie when he said the girl was different, either!

Without knowing or speaking a word of English, as I came to learn, she walked right up to Big like she was already owned, and slipped her sweet arms around his thick neck; and that gave the rest of us the chance to see that she wasn't much more than *three feet tall!*

Well sir, why that beautiful Pygmy girl went along with my friend's idea or how Q. T. came to know her, I don't rightly know. Just as I told you. Far as I know, she could have come from Africa, or the Andaman Islands, or from heaven or hell. But that mean old bear Big licked his grizzly chops, and he ordered everybody else but the girl to clear out.

As I turned to follow Q. T., his sister-replacement stayed put, and my heart thumped like the leg of an arthritic rabbit. Snow was pattering down outside, and her teeth were that white. Last I saw of her, she was gripping that pouch close to her side.

For Christmas, Horace's and the other spots always shut down, so I had a chance to ask Q. T. some questions. He just grinned, told Zanra to pass the gravy to me 'cause my spuds looked dry. Then there was their gift for me, beneath the tree; and then it just didn't seem right to bring up

Big or that miniature girl. We was festive! But I hated thinking how Big would make another fortune with a novelty like her workin' the streets. While I understood Q. T. protecting Zanra, I couldn't square his *volunteering* that nice foreign girl—or perceive just why she went so eagerly with Big.

I found out December thirty-first. Never forget it! After all, it wasn't what you would call a standard New Year's Eve with Q. T., Zanra, and me spending part of it at Mobrow's Funeral Parlor.

Which is where Big spent the whole holiday, 'cause *he* was the guest of honor!

Skip forward a minute before I explain. As some of you good folks know, I married Q. T.'s sister Zanra, and we've had a good life. Now and then, I woke up nights thinkin' about that pretty Pygmy girl, but all I ever heard was rumors. Rumors about a kind of voodoo she'd known that was so close to pure science it might have been bottled-up, and sold! Stories that she wasn't actually a Pygmy at all, but from even weirder places.

But mean old Big's dying was an omen of fine change. Soon, all the brothers and sisters began sticking together; and sometimes, at least for our own neighborhood, I considered that it might all have begun that night in Mobrow's Funeral Parlor.

That was the night I saw my friend Q. T. Barrett walk right up the aisle, to pay his last respects to ugly, dead Big. I watched how wise, how mature my friend had become; and as he peered down with his face all sober, the other folks who had surrounded the casket parted—which is when I saw that which I will *never* forget.

Q. T. might talk about it when he rises, today, to speak; but I doubt it. I asked him what had happened many times and Q. T. just shook his head, the way he did at the bier, the way he'd done when I realized what that little girl had managed with her voodoo, or science, or outer space magic, and couldn't tear my astonished gaze from the front of that funeral home.

Because old grizzly Bear's coffin, gleaming like a star and containing the awful rascal's mortal remains, wasn't more than *four feet long*.

The Writing of *"Origin of a Species"*

There are several reasons why I believe the next story is one of my special efforts, and they're tied to fulfilled challenges. The first of these came from the editor Martin H. Greenberg, whose anthology invitation amounted to devising something new to write about one of horror fiction's most well-known bogeymen. When a really fresh idea bubbled to the top, it brought a couple more challenges with it:

Could I do enough research in my own books to write convincingly about a divorced and retiring homicide detective whose hobby was archaeology? I've never been divorced, retired, or a police sleuth, and I knew nothing about archaeology I hadn't picked up from newspapers and movies.

Then, as I worked, I had to hazard a guess linked to psychology, and I had to send my protagonist to a dig in eastern Turkey. I'm awful at geography; all I knew about Turkey came from a lovely girl I used to date, named Nadia. What I had going for me were my central premise and the Biblical portions I'd read years ago and wondered about ever since. I still do.

Greenberg bought the story and basically I liked it then and continue to feel that way about it. As for the title, you'll understand it at the end.

Origin of a Species

When Erwin Parrish decided to go to Turkey to get a look at the dead body, it was (in a way) a busman's holiday.

After all, Parrish had been a homicide detective for most of the twenty-three years he'd spent on the force. He had seen enough corpses to make anyone gag, if the effect of looking at them had been cumulative, and he didn't even have any reason to think that the one in Turkey was the victim of foul play.

But Erwin, at forty-eight, had never seen one that was more than three thousand years old.

For nearly as long as Detective Parrish could remember, his consuming hobby had been archaeology. Even as a stolid, square-built, crew-cut-headed boy of eight or nine, Erwin had been peculiarly fascinated by the origin of things— "things" from people and their ways to the communities in which they lived and their worlds at

175

the particular times they'd been alive. It was as if he had needed to get at the heart of things, trace the happenstance of life to its roots in order to learn why the person or persons and their artifacts had even existed.

But because the folks with whom Erwin happened to grow up were poor and uneducated, no one thought to steer him toward archaeology till his grades were far too ordinary to earn him a college scholarship. By then, anyway, he had decided to become a police officer. Without knowing why, it had seemed like the thing to do.

So as a young cop riding in a prowl car—looking just the same except for growing up and adding a drooping mustache to munch on whenever he needed to keep his mouth shut—Erwin had settled for letting his oldest fascination become his primary reason for getting up each day and doing his work so well he could go home again and read. There, for decades, he had spent his free time studying the exploits of other men who went on uncovering the secrets of the past— men who Erwin Parrish came to believe were little better informed than he.

It might have been enough, except that he also got married two years out of the academy and fathered two sons.

Once, several years ago when Parrish was making a genuine effort to save the marriage, he'd gone to a psychologist named Travis Goodnight, and the man suggested Erwin's avocational interests absorbed him the way they did because his unconscious mind wanted to know the origins of his personal problems, needed him to explore his own past.

Chewing on the fringes of his sandy mustache, Parrish had mulled over his "personal problems."

Never once had he laid a finger on anyone in his family, but Carmen had claimed for years that he "hungered" to batter her and the boys. She was convinced he was a powder keg that had wanted to go off since she met him, that he got sullen and spent a lot of time by himself because police work demanded self-discipline and his marriage mandated it, so silence and study were the only ways he had to keep from turning into a psycho or something.

Well, he'd pushed those notions around in his mind, even wondered if he had decided to be in law enforcement just so he'd learn to keep a lid on his temper and had gotten into homicide for some sort of vicarious goddamn thrill. Except the truth of the matter was that he hadn't ever wanted to belt Carmen until she got those weird ideas in her own head.

And the problem with what Dr. Goodnight suggested about his unconscious need to explore his past was that it was sheer crap. "See," he told the shrink, "I've dug archaeology since long before I even saw my wife." The pun about "digging" archaeology was an old quip meant to deflect the curiosity of people who found his hobby strange.

"I didn't mean the problems in your marriage," Goodnight had explained. "I meant those personal problems you've sensed in your own mind ever since you were a small boy. Everybody has their own kind—but you made no waves for your parents, didn't join the Scouts or go out for basketball, or turn into a brain. You began to study the origins of things in the past at a time when most boys think anything that happened a month ago is old stuff. I'm only suggesting that the majority of people doesn't look for the answers to questions nobody has asked, especially while they are children." Goodnight added softly, "Not unless they're screening questions for the real things people can't yet ask themselves."

Erwin had dutifully pondered the doctor's observations for a week. During those seven days, Carmen conspicuously attempted to keep their late-teenage sons away from him, made Parrish sleep on the couch, and the cop abused no one— except for a recruit in his squad who came very close to losing some valuable evidence.

When he returned to Goodnight's office at the appointed hour of the appointed day, he took his seat across the desk from the psychologist rather quickly. "Doc," Parrish began, "let me ask you some questions for a change. I've really hoped I could hold my family together, but it just isn't happening. So is archaeology a good hobby for me or not? Does it help me to stay nonviolent, or is the whole thing going to go off in me like a bomb someday?"

Although Goodnight was a lot younger, he was smart enough not to ask what Erwin thought. Instead he made some remarks Parrish would not forget. "I'm not even an amateur archaeologist, Detective, but think about this: You're around murdered people all the time in your job. Then— ostensibly for relaxation and pleasure—you yearn to go to digs where you hope to find . . . dead things." He almost smiled. "Dead things such as people. I wonder, Erwin, if it isn't just possible that you're a homicide detective twenty-four hours a day whether in fact or in your oldest dreams."

"I suppose that's possible," Erwin had said with a grunt.

And Goodnight responded by spreading his hands on his desk and practically beaming at him. "Then how can you hope to find yourself in a normal family relationship when the members of your family are *alive*?"

Parrish had stood then and turned, expressionless, toward the office door. "My problem got solved for me in the last twenty-four hours, Doc," he said. "My oldest boy announced his engagement and plans to get married next month, and my other son moved in with the love of his life—a kid named Kevin. Right after that, my wife threw me out. I'd recommend Carmen come to see you, because I think she needs a hell of a lot of help, but I wouldn't do that to a nice young psychologist with a vivid imagination and a family of his own. You haven't got enough insurance to protect you when a woman like Carmen gets *her* imagination going!

That had ended Parrish's counseling sessions, but the neurotic suspicions Carmen had voiced continued to occur to him as time passed and his family was supposed to begin becoming just a memory. He sought to cheer himself up by reminding himself that, living alone now, the powder keg Carmen had believed to be inside him would never go off at anybody he loved. Goodnight's points about his unusual choice of a hobby and the notion that he was a detective of homicide—of death—on a full-time basis depressed him awhile and he wondered repeatedly if there might be anything to the many lousy things people kept saying about him.

For three years or more after the divorce was final, Erwin worked as many hours as he could. When he wasn't investigating a possible homicide or one that was indisputably that, he was boning up—he scarcely recognized the pun—until an important realization dawned on him one afternoon at a death scene: He liked archaeology now one hell of a lot more than he did police work, and he probably always had.

Not only that, Parrish perceived, but he was good, damn good—as knowledgeable as most kids fresh out of a university course! Everything about the vast subject intrigued him, from anthropology and philology to paleography and sheer history. No more than a couple of hundred years old as a social science, archaeology studied the past through the identification of the material remains of human cultures—but also through interpretations. As much as anything, that was surely the element he had taken from his lifelong passion to his law enforcement career. In homicide detection, too, you had to discover all the facts, then be skilled enough to interpret what you had in front of you. In addition, a detective wound up feeling like he was cock of the walk when he'd solved a case. Erwin could only imagine how successful a man would feel when he dug up something at an archaeological site that no one else had ever seen.

But he knew that when the archaeologist did it—and when he *proved* his theories about the dig and its products—the guy was showered with both praise and envy. A police officer who did the same thing might have to watch *his* find, the felon, parade straight out of the courtroom when everybody in the place knew the cop was right!

The trouble was, both disciplines required fieldwork. You had to be there as soon as you could get to the scene, and you had to keep it clean, unsullied. Everything about both kinds of investigation demanded painstaking procedure, enormous care. Just as it was in homicide, an archaeologist had to study the artifacts around a bag of dead bones, the weapons and the tools, if any, the clothing, and the conditions of absolutely everything. Schliemann, Evans, Woolley, and Carter had made the discipline a systemized science in the nineteenth century, taught other archaeologists that even a midden—a refuse pile, maybe human droppings—held huge amounts of significance. Cultivated seeds led to the unearthing of more data; what a skeleton was wearing and how the man had died were sources of additional clues.

Parrish spent all of four regret-filled years bemoaning the loss of his marriage and his failure, as a boy, to pursue his primary interest in life until—pushing forty-nine years of age—he came across a little filler item in his daily newspaper.

Though it wasn't remotely as ancient as the amazing "Iceman" unearthed early in the nineties, a startlingly well-preserved male body had been found on a mountain in eastern Turkey. Parrish read that the remains were revealed when a number of boulders were unexpectedly dislodged and sent down the slopes of Mount Ararat. Clad in full-length robe and sandals—all in good repair—the corpse discussed in the newspaper was particularly interesting because, ten days after its discovery, radioisotopes and other forms of dating failed to establish the fellow's age. All anyone on the scene was willing to say now was that "reasonable estimates placed his period as thirty-five hundred to five thousand years ago, possibly longer," and that "additional tests are bound to bring us a closer fit." The last line of the piece mentioned that the body was damaged in the area of the chest cavity, and the heart seemed to be the only organ that had been damaged.

Erwin tried to make himself lay the newspaper aside and leave for work on time, but he kept rereading the article, all the knowledge he had crammed into his head setting off buzzers. Maybe the general public didn't know it, but, while no dating system devised could establish the birth date of any corpse (including that of someone who perished a week ago), modern science was outstanding in dealing with periods only several hundred years ago. Fifteen hundred years, "possibly longer," was much too large a gap. Not only that, but determining the age of remains no older than five thousand years should not represent any kind of imposing problem.

Parrish folded the newspaper carefully so that the filler piece showed clearly and, shaking his head, made himself rise. The thought passing through his mind that moment came to him as unbidden as any of his recent birthdays. *A far-out explanation for the trouble they're having with this guy would be that he was old as Methuselah when something or someone killed him.*

Erwin turned in the direction of where Carmen would be sitting if this was their home, instead of his lonely apartment, and they were still together. He knew about that aspect of the past—how rumors still existed that a race of men in that part of the world had lived to incredible ages—because of his ex-wife. When she had begun making sounds about getting fed up with him and how he seldom seemed to notice her, Parrish had tried to get religion, too. He'd taken up attending church with her on Sundays, even accepted the Bible the minister offered him.

Then he had made the mistake of reading it, from scratch—"mistake" because the Good Book had gotten interesting to Parrish and further distanced him from Carmen.

Because a good archaeologist was not only a detective at heart but an historian, Erwin had rediscovered something he'd forgotten while he was reading Genesis: A lot of the Bible needed to be taken on faith, but from a certain point in the Old Testament forward, it was just about as reliable a work on ancient history as any book a man could find. People who weren't religious—which Erwin wasn't—forgot that. They even preferred to ignore the fact that the yen for recording anything for posterity—the actual compulsion to *write*—was first motivated by religious beliefs and feelings. Why, Johann Gutenberg's first volume off the press in 1456 was a Bible!

So, because Erwin was a man who was mesmerized by the origins of things, he had gotten so fired up about the story of Noah—not only the parts concerning the Flood, but the recorded ages of men before and after it—that he'd immediately gone back to tuning Carmen out! He hadn't wanted or meant to, he'd even tried to share what he learned with her. Facts, though, even those that were easy enough to understand and had to do with the lives of every creature on earth today, just weren't Carmen's thing. Sometimes Parrish had believed she just liked sitting in a pew dressed in her Sunday best, relaxing.

Erwin realized with a start that the reason he was so worked up over today's newspaper story was that the dead guy discovered in eastern Turkey was lying on the same mountain where Noah's ark was supposed to have come to rest after the Flood finally stopped. He certainly didn't imagine the old boy was Noah, and definitely didn't believe he'd been hundreds of years of age when he died, but everything about the find intrigued Parrish immediately. Hell, there hadn't even been a dig—the corpse in the hood and robe had simply popped into view!

183

On his way to the 32nd Street station that morning, he suddenly remembered he had enough accumulated leave time to fly across the world and go into the field while the Mount Ararat Man—the press named him that—was still an archaeological process as much as an event. Sure, it would set him back a bundle—but who did he have to spend money on now anyway? The boys were grown, on their own. His settlement with Carmen had let her take the house and 90 percent of the furnishings in exchange for paying no alimony. If Parrish wanted to blow his small savings plus all the leave money he hadn't taken on the adventure of his lifetime, there was nothing to stop him—

And nobody, basically, to mourn him if he fell off the damn mountain!

So before he could change his mind, Erwin told Chief Middleton that afternoon that he'd be using all his vacation time in one big chunk, then booked a flight for Ankara. He was sweating freely when he was done, but he felt free, too—free, and younger than he'd felt in thirty years! And if the department found a way to suspend him for such an abrupt action, shit on it, he had his twenty in, he could retire tomorrow if they pushed too hard!

During the four days before he caught the big bird, Parrish had a lot to do, including the renewal of his passport and getting his shots. He also placed a long-distance phone call to a Turkish policeman he knew named Gus—short for Augustus—Ekin. The two law men had met when Gus was in the country to facilitate the extradition of a Turkish national, and they'd liked each other. Cops tended to hang together closely, and Erwin figured his acquaintance might cut a little red tape, point him in the right direction, and put him on the slopes of Ararat more quickly than if

Parrish wandered off on his own. Ekin said he'd be happy to do anything he could.

Ararat was a dormant volcanic mountain, but it hadn't erupted since 1840, Erwin found when he set out, feverishly, to learn as much as possible about the site of the discovery. It had two peaks rising above thirteen thousand feet, seven miles apart, and the fact that oxygen starvation was entirely possible at the summit provided part of the reason why even modern explorers had not been able to sustain a search for the ark of Noah. Other reasons included the instability of the slopes because of snow, and occasional unexpected avalanches of rock.

But Mount Ararat Man, the newspapers had reported, had been a considerate fellow. Whether he'd lost his life from falling boulders or his remains had rolled down the slope for unaccountable reasons, the body had been found fewer than three hundred feet from the foot of the mountain. *Almost*, Erwin mused while he was packing, *as if he finally wanted to be seen—buried, maybe.*

But he had to be careful about drawing assumptions of that sort, pretending to be "interpreting" the facts when he had almost no data to interpret. Even if the dead man he hoped to examine had been born only three thousand years ago, 99 percent of today's customs and most modern beliefs were newer than that, largely unknown to human beings whose lives might have preceded the Flood. Burial rites had been changing throughout history, and they also varied from country to country—and Turkey was bounded by the Black Sea, nations of the old USSR, Iran, Iraq, Syria, the Mediterranean, Greece, and Bulgaria. The Euphrates and Tigris Rivers rose in the east, for God's sake!

And the Armenians called Mount Ararat, Parrish remembered with something akin to a wondering shudder, "the Mother of the World."

Finally aboard the plane flying away to the excellent adventure of his life—to southeast Europe and its bristling interface with Asia Minor—Parrish recalled the carefully detailed story of Noah from the Bible Carmen's clergyman had given him. Folks used Methuselah as a synonym for astonishing longevity, but he had been only one of many whose reported lifespans exceeded those of any modern man or woman. Noah himself was supposedly five hundred plus when he begat Sham, Ham, and Japheth, and most of the males who were cited as living prior to the Flood were said to have been around for centuries: Seth, Adam's son, for 912 years; Mahaleleel made it to 895; Methuselah to age 969; and Noah's father, Lamech, lived to be 777. Of those mentioned in chapter five of Genesis, only Enoch didn't surpass 365, at which point it says, unaccountably, "And Enoch walked with God; and he was not; for God took him."

Of course, Parrish reflected, everyone but fundamentalists usually poked fun at longevity of that kind. Erwin could see why; he just collected the data. Yet the curious thing about the Bible was that its authors usually got things like Ararat itself right and, in recent times, archaeological digs with some regularity had been uncovering city-states located right where the Bible claimed they were. Like the man on Mount Ararat today, they had only been covered—buried—by time.

Critics and "analysts" were the same whatever the field of inquiry, Parrish thought. One of the factors that had hooked him on Genesis was the way it indicated a *clean distinction* between the period of time before the Flood, and after it. Before passing along instructions to Noah, God said (in 6:3), "My spirit shall not always strive with man, for that he also is flesh; yet his days shall be as an hundred and twenty years." By the time Noah's sons were grown and, after the tower of Babel was unwisely constructed, people were scattered abroad "upon the face of all the earth," human beings were living shorter and shorter lives. As early as Chapter eleven of Genesis, Nahor survived only to 119.

The detective ate the meal he was brought by a handsome uniformed woman and perversely wished they still allowed smoking on airplanes— perversely because giving up cigarettes was one of the things he'd long since done to try to please Carmen and keep the marriage going. Man's days would be "an hundred and twenty years." Last month on TV Parrish was watching some talk show and he had heard several modern-day experts on life expectancy say there was no reason in the world the human body shouldn't be expected to last for one hundred and twenty years. The longer Erwin lived, it seemed, the more often he heard things tentatively confirmed that so-called experts had derided in his childhood!

So what had happened to change everything for people starting with the "generations of Noah," and did that have anything to do with the first archaeological site Erwin Parrish would ever see in person? Right after the Almighty's new statement about the longevity of humankind there was a marvelous combination of words that had thrilled and also chilled him every time he'd read them—"There were giants in the earth in those days"—words Parrish doubted that any professional archaeologist believed for a minute.

"Giant" was from the Greek *gigas*, he'd learned, but that told him shit. What had it meant when some unknown translator, hundreds of years ago, had tried to convey a matter of importance; afterward, after all, the Flood seemed to have wiped out everything but Noah, his family, and the mated sampling of life on the planet, and then human longevity had been cut to a fraction of what it supposedly was! Was it possible "giant" was originally connected to a different sort of person entirely, or alternately to the passage of time when there was no such thing as a decent printed calendar? Anyone who knew how to read could see in Genesis 6: 1-4 a distinction being made between offspring and descendants of the offspring "of the sons of God and the daughters of men," or the part about "when man began to multiply . . . and daughters were born unto them."

Almost as if the "daughters" hadn't previously been born to them.

Or, Parrish thought, as if "daughters of men" did not have the same origin as "the sons of God." But what the hell could that mean?

Unless there were not only "giants" on earth, but more than *one kind* of women.

Erwin checked his watch, closed the Carmen-inspired copy of the Bible, and settled back to nap. He was disgusted with himself. For the most of his forty-eight years he'd longed just to be present at an active dig, but he'd never seen anything more wonderful up close than a few touring mummies and a handful of tiny bones from a bird that had lived during the Cro-Magnon period, a lousy twelve to thirty thousand years ago. By archaeological reckoning, that was about the time of the Kennedy administration! Yet here he was on the verge of fulfilling his oldest desire and he was more interested in a bunch of Biblical curiosities any real scientist would dismiss.

Gus Ekin proved to be as likable and pleasant a man as Parrish's memory insisted, but shockingly older. The very next day after Erwin's plane finally touched down on Turkish soil, they were in a jeep leaving Ankara and headed toward the eastern coast, when Erwin realized that fourteen years had flown the coop since the other lawman visited America. Now the white-maned, dark-skinned man with the sparkling black eyes was a semiretired chief who appeared overjoyed to be of service to his colleague from the United States.

Parrish tried again to thank Ekin for easing his way through customs, then entertaining him at his home. "I have enough *otorite*, what you call clout," Gus said from behind the steering wheel, "to get you many places, even take you directly to any of Turkey's many borders. I also have acquaintance with certain Iranian and Iraqi border guards, but I do not think you shall care to meet them—or the Syrian patrols, who tend to dislike the Turkish as well as Americans."

"I'm only interested in the mountain," Erwin told him, "and the dead man they found on it." It occurred to him his remark might sound a trifle brusque, and he managed an apologetic smile. "Apart from old friends, of course."

Lighting another of his endless, foul-smelling cigarettes, Gus grinned back. He had a disconcerting habit of raising his hands from the wheel whenever he turned to regard Parrish. "United States people put a high *fiyat* on friendliness. In this part of the world, at this point in history, there are few friendships and fewer people still who wish to see the Ararat Man. It is probably because of this that I have the good news for you."

"You know someone in government who can clear it for me to see the dig?" Erwin asked eagerly.

"Better yet, I know Professor Dag," Gus replied proudly, "the archaeologist who is representing Turkish rights to this find."

"Gus, you're amazing!" Parrish exclaimed.

"Maybe so! He's agreed to permit you to view the remains—pardon the universal police language, eh?—this night and all of tomorrow." Gus negotiated an especially complex curve in the improbable-looking highway speeding them through the countryside. "You see that it is only *maybe* I am so amazing, Erwin. Dag did not welcome you to his party for a longer period that that."

Parrish leaned back against the passenger seat and munched on the fringes of his mustache. "I don't know whether to jump up and down with joy because you've got me on the slope or to cry because—"

"Because you came so far for one day and one half," Ekin finished for him. "Thank me many times, and jump perhaps once, my friend, because Dag did not wish an amateur there at all. It seems there is more to the Mount Ararat Man than the press has been told. I had to tell him you're the American who helped me return a *fine insan*—a bad man—to our nation, where he was executed."

"I wondered what you people did with that bastard," said Parrish.

"What is often done to the killers in this part of the world," Gus said. Then he lifted his steering hand to watch Erwin's reaction. "You may find it amusing to know what the professor Dag's name means in our tongue. Maybe, my *dost*, it shall explain why you share a common interest."

" 'Dag' has some meaning?" Erwin asked. "What is it?"

"It means 'mountain,' " Gus replied, and laughed so heartily Parrish was afraid he might tip the Jeep over.

But Professor Dag, in person, reminded Erwin more of a molehill when the two met at the foot of Mount Ararat. Aging and small enough to have been called "petite" if he'd been a female, Dag was perfunctory in greeting Parrish, then waving for the American to follow him. There were several muttered syllables that might even have added up to sentences, but either the professor did not speak English or he did not choose to.

For an instant Parrish, wearing a parka that now felt too heavy for the late spring day—he had decided to take warmer apparel thousands of miles from home on the theory that he could always take it off—stared longingly after the departing Ekin, who was both helper and translator. Gus had said he'd be back for Erwin tomorrow night, then left with a cheery wave. It was the first time in years Parrish could recall being alone in an unfamiliar place and being mildly frightened by it.

Then he turned to find Professor Dag, and Erwin's eyes and head rose as he stared up at the twin peaks of the Hittites' Ararat high above him.

Mother of the World, thought Erwin. There were higher mountains—many of them—but a city-bred-and-bound homicide cop seldom if ever saw any in person, and the cloak of snow spread atop ancient Ararat reminded him of a great shawl someone of giant size might have rested upon a pair of monumental maternal shoulders. *"And God said unto Noah,"* Erwin recalled from Genesis 6:13, *"The end of all flesh is come before me; for the earth is filled with violence through them; and, behold, I will destroy them from the earth."*

Parrish's gaze slowly lowered to focus on his grudging host and the small party of professional archaeologists grouped at a roped-off area some three hundred feet up the rocky slope. He began moving up to join them, awed as much by his thoughts as by the scene before him. *Just what, exactly,* Erwin pondered as he climbed, immediately obliged to breathe more self-consciously, *was meant by "I will destroy them?" Them who?* It sounded specific then, in that setting. True, if the story of the Flood—repeated in nearly every religion on earth—was true, he supposed the majority of life-forms (including human beings) had not survived. But almost everybody knew Noah had been told to take with him—

His step faltered, his chain of thought was broken. The five men and two women who were living the life Erwin Parrish had denied himself till that moment were instinctively opening a pathway for him as he drew near. For a moment it was quite like the mourners standing before a coffin in an American mortuary, thoughtfully making room for the newest arrival at the bier. Even small, dignified Dag, gently pulling at his beard, stepped away to admit Parrish.

What lay sprawled in stony rubble a dozen feet or so from Erwin looked at a glance like an ordinary middle-aged white male who's been shot or stabbed to death—last week. Unlike the famous Iceman, who was of enormous antiquity, this did not appear to be a leathery or mummified cadaver with most of the quickly identified signs of common humanity weathered into the undisturbing, alien guise of a life-cessation dating to prehistory. This body, this *man*, did not oblige anyone by seeming as if his death and his life as well had transpired beyond modern-day kinship.

Even when Erwin went closer, this poor corpse somehow made the detective think of men he'd known, worked with, cared about. In a curious, vital way Parrish could not have put into words, the Mount Ararat Man was one of them. Of everyone.

Except, of course, that it was apparent he'd been frozen, and was no longer, that his partly opened eyes—intact—lacked the consciousness of life, and the poor SOB was every bit as dead as any man Erwin had found in abandoned warehouses, alleys, and the wrong women's apartments.

And those things were apparent because nothing that ever lived could still possess a living spirit with a good-sized hole where its heart belonged. When he automatically started to drop to his haunches and get a better look at the wound, a man with a days-old growth of yellow beard rested a fold of the tattered robe over it.

Preferring to think of the concealment as an act of sensitivity instead of an effort to hide something the younger man didn't want him to see ("There's more to this than they told the press," Gus had said), Parrish arose and stared down at the ordinary-looking dead man—who was from thirty-five hundred to thirty-five thousand years old or older. Then he glanced at the other people, expecting little Dag to introduce them. That would have been good manners anywhere on the planet.

So when the professor didn't do it, Erwin introduced himself, nodding his head at each man and the two women. None of them uttered a sound, though the yellow-bearded archaeologist and the marginally better-looking of the women nodded back.

There was a capacious tent a few yards away, smoke filtering through its top, an array of archaeological tools Parrish yearned to seize simply to look at them, and a couple of glittering machines he'd only read about in more recent journals. Feeling that he'd be damned if he let these strangers high-hat him and ruin the only such opportunity of his life, Erwin was thinking of taking matters into his own hands and starting to examine the robed corpse when the woman who had nodded decided to speak to him.

"Chief Ekin said you were of inestimable assistance in returning the serial killer to Turkey," she said. "He is Sherlock Holmes—or Sam Spade, maybe!—in this part of the world, so Dag permitted you to have a look." She had nice cheekbones and wide lips that looked as if they wanted to smile but had forgotten the formulas. "You shouldn't expect him or the others to be very helpful. I'm Andrea Clayborne."

Erwin was so relieved that someone else spoke English she turned beautiful while he looked at her. "You're British, right?" He saw her nod. "Well, I've heard pros in the science can become a bit overprotective. Can you tell them I'm only here to observe?"

Dr. Clayborne wrinkled her nose. "Ekin told Dag that. But it doesn't matter, because they think all Americans know someone in the media and only want publicity—and money, of course."

She explained to him the site was being constantly guarded by members of their group until a decision was made about the proper disposition of the find, so she and the man with the stubble of yellow beard were assigned to stay at the site with Erwin that night. "Ordinarily we might all remain, but it gets pretty chilly on the slopes after dark, even in a heated tent. Tomorrow you can browse around to your heart's content."

Erwin thought of telling her that he was really somewhat more knowledgeable than a common browser, but didn't. "I take it the man who'll be with us isn't Turkish, either."

Andrea's pale brows rose. "How did you know that? His name is Erich Hoffmeister; he's German."

Parrish grinned tightly. "Just a good guess they'd stick two outsiders with the third one for tough duty—meaning we're men, and you're a woman. Who's the other woman married to?"

"Dag," Andrea Clayborne said, giving him a smile that succeeded radiantly in expressing her pleasure that he was astute enough to recognize the situation for what it was.

But what Parrish neither recognized nor understood when she, Hoffmeister, and he were tucked in sleeping bags inside the tent for the night, was *why* Professor Dag, and his other Turkish colleagues, were playing so cozy with an archaeological find that really wasn't exactly spectacular. It was a big deal to him, sure; just lying in the dark tent close to a genuine, active site was a moment he'd never forget.

Gus was right, there was more to this. And even after a cursory glance at the remains, Erwin was fairly sure Dag was either keeping something potentially earthshaking to himself till he had the data to make a huge personal splash—

Or the problems the dating experts were having in establishing the dead man's age were exceptionally special. *"Giants in the earth . . ."*

Moving as soundlessly as possible, Parrish slipped out of his sleeping bag, and groped in the dark for his parka. Before sundown he had sweated like a horse in it, finally removed it. Now, he would be glad he'd brought it. Obviously, he was meant simply to soak up atmosphere tonight, then be watched attentively by Dag and the others when daylight came.

Erwin didn't think he wanted to be a good little amateur anything anymore.

Edging toward the tent flap with Andrea Clayborne and Erich Hoffmeister just shadowy masses as he passed, Parrish realized this thing was a mystery as hard to crack as any he'd seen in detective work—and it might boil down to one question: Who, or maybe what, was their visitor from the past?

Once outside, with the wind whistling down from the peaks surmounting Ararat, Erwin was eager to don the parka. The noise wasn't loud, merely steady, like that produced by a creature with gigantic lungs who had been summoning someone through the centuries. He found it necessary to watch his footing, after he nearly fell; the tent might have been pitched on fairly level ground, but this was still a mountainside. His friend Gus had told him last night that while this site was that of a volcano that was dormant, earthquakes occurred with terrifying regularity and frequency in Turkey. In all likelihood a quake had dislodged the boulders shielding the dead man's remains, then rolled him partway down the slope.

Reaching the site, noticing for the first time that Ararat Man had been provided with a framework of aluminum supports to prevent him from continuing his downhill descent, Parrish knelt and tried to make his vision adjust to the peculiar lighting. The moon was out and there was a mixture of reflection from the snow on the dual peaks and shifting shadows presumably formed from outcropping rock. He had never seen anything like it; the site was simultaneously adequately lit—even shockingly so, to his eyes—and so splotchy it was as if the entire slope was illuminated by something that kept shorting out.

Erwin supposed the impression he had that he was being watched was a neurotic commonplace for weirdly obsessive people like him who volunteered to work on the sides of mountains at night.

Using just a thumb and index finger, doing so as deftly as he had with any body he'd had to see, Parrish slowly brought the fold of the robe away from the awful wound in the chest. Then he leaned forward to examine the gaping hole with his naked eye.

"God saw that the wickedness of man was great in the earth..." No accident occurring when Ararat Man was being unceremoniously whipped this way and that had made this wound. No burrowing beast had made the aperture and devoured the heart, either.

Parrish was a good enough homicide detective to know that one or more persons had either dug into the fellow's flesh with a sharp instrument and cut his heart out or had driven something nice and round through the chest first, *then* removed the heart.

Rocking back on his heels, Erwin chewed on his drooping mustache and asked himself to theorize when the Mount Ararat Man had been killed, why, and by whom. Rumor had it that Chaldean priests of the fifth century B.C. had climbed Ararat and peeled away bituminous coating from Noah's ark. Maybe they also found this robe-wearing body, held some quaint superstitions, and excised the heart. But even the fifth century B.C. was more recent than he was supposed to be; such a theory amounted to suggest-

ing that he had been a *passenger* on the *Ark*, since
most experts placed Noah's survival at approximately 3500 B.C.!

Yet that *would* explain Professor Dag's secrecy.
Human remains from Noah's ark would be priceless, even if they didn't explain how this body succeeded in looking like one that had been living
and breathing a month ago.

Shivering, Parrish remembered the parts of
Genesis concerning "sons of God," "daughters of
men," and the distinction he himself had noticed
regarding a time "when man began to multiply"
and the daughters were then "born unto them."
In hunting for an older definition of *giant*, he had
wondered if men had even fathered daughters
before the Flood. Perhaps the reason the "begats"
tended to concentrate on men alone was because
few females were born!

Erwin shivered. What if the male corpse so
ingloriously sprawled at his feet was a "son of
God" because, like Methuselah, Lamech, and
Noah, he had been a *giant of longevity*?

So one of the daughters of men, feeling her destiny was a short life of drudgery, had attempted to
reverse the position she had with her mate—by
taking and possibly devouring his all but immortal heart? Why, his own ex-wife Carmen had been
jealous of his meaningful work! Imagining he
wanted to "batter" her, she'd stolen everything he
had but his career in law enforcement! Even
Goodnight, the shrink, had said *he* had personal
problems and couldn't enjoy a normal relationship with a living family—that was how pervasive
the influence from the "daughters" had been on
Carmen, his career—on *everything!*

He slid and scurried back to the tent to share
his ideas with the professional archaeologists.
"And of every living thing of all flesh," God had

told Noah, "two of every sort shalt thou bring . . . to keep them alive with thee; they shall be male and female." Suddenly it was clear to Parrish that the mate of Mount Ararat Man hadn't wished to settle for her paltry years, and killed him during or after the voyage; he was probably one of Noah's sons—the greatest archaeological find in history!

Erwin threw back the tent flap as he entered and a pool of light spilled on Erich Hoffmeister whcre he still lay in his bag.

The sleeping bag was still zipped shut, but one end was *soaked with blood*.

Astounded, Parrish rushed over and yanked the zipper down from the young man's face with trembling fingers.

Herr Professor Hoffmeister's throat was torn open, his yellow beard had turned red, and his face was white as the snow atop Ararat.

There were no life signs. Erwin frowned; froze. This man's murder left one other, aside from himself, alive on the slope—and she was behind him. Clayborne must have killed the German, she probably cut out the heart of Ararat Man. She had either faked her credentials or just exploded like the powder keg Erwin was supposed to have inside him, raining her neurotic superstitions like shrapnel.

Waiting no longer, Parrish spun suddenly in the direction of the British woman's sleeping bag, prepared to subdue her any way he had to.

Except someone else already had subdued Andrea, permanently.

He bent forward to peer down at her pale face and, below it, the rent in her throat. *An animal*, Erwin thought, *stalking us* . . .

But after he'd struck a match and looked more closely, he was able to detect the presence of what

J.N. Williamson

appeared to be bite marks under the ear, in her neck.

All right. Okay. It hadn't attacked him, so it must have come into the tent while Parrish was at the site.

Finding both that the tent held no additional surprises and a flashlight he had brought, Parrish took from the dead Hoffmeister the largest digging implement he could find, went slowly to the flap of the tent, and cautiously slithered outside.

Without thinking about it, he shone the flashlight on the roped-off site, and gasped.

Mount Ararat Man was gone!

Running then, rushing to where the remains had been restrained by supports, he found them kicked apart—

And an already-drying trail of snow-dampened sandaled feet leading up the slope toward the distant pair of peaks.

But nothing that ever lived could rise and walk without its *heart*, Erwin realized.

Then he used the beam from his flashlight to aid his vision in the odd, unnerving moonlight—sprayed it up the slope rising above him . . . and saw *her.*

Climbing at a rate of speed that seemed purposive but not hurried, clad in a robe similar to that which the long-dead man hanging limply in her arms wore, but with no hood and a head of flaxen hair wafting behind her, she seemed almost to be drifting up Ararat. She looked to Erwin Parrish to stand six feet or more, and the thought seared through his mind that there was no logical reason why giants had to be male.

Without the slightest plan, he kept the beam centered on the amazing sight, tucked the shovel under one arm, and climbed after them. *Dag must've seen her*, he realized, panting after a matter of yards; *that's why he was so uncommunicative and maybe why he left three foreign outsiders on the mountain—as bait! He'd need proof that such a woman existed.*

Till Parrish was close enough to see the blond woman clearly, she didn't pause in her effortless stride. Then, though—when he was within twenty yards or so and wondering how much farther he could climb—she turned, froze in place, and stared at him.

The Armenians' expression, "Mother of the World," vaulted into Erwin's mind. At a glance, she looked magnificent to him. Her robe prevented him from seeing any details of her figure, but her carriage was outstanding, her courage and sense of purpose obvious. She had wide-spaced eyes that could have been colorless, a widow's peak, and hair so tawny it might have belonged to a lioness.

But she opened her mouth in a snarl that exhibited blood still dripping from her generous lips and teeth, the latter long and jagged except for a tooth on either side that looked inches in length and came to points no larger in circumference than needles. *I have sought him for centuries, dwelling in the ark*, she said, *living on the blood of natives and those they said vanished because they could not draw breath.*

Erwin heard her speak with the voice of mountain wind, deep in his head. Thousands of years danced like motes, particles from elsewhere, between them. "Who *are* you?"

She said, *Noah, son of Lamech, chose to save my husband and me, two of all kinds, from the Flood. But our kind was not favored, so one was sent in the day when my husband slept to slay him. Though his heart was removed, I awakened in time to save it—as I have done for that moment when I might find him and put it back. For our eternal lives.*

Parrish was stunned. Her mate slept by day; his assassin had known he could only be killed then, by something carving into his heart. And *she*, the astounding woman of Ararat, had kept his heart for thousands of years, believing she might reanimate him! Foolish to ask her more about their kind, that which had slaughtered Andrea and Hoffmeister the way she had, when he knew then they were history's first vampires.

Those with you kept me from reaching my husband when his body was at last released, she said as if reading his thoughts, *so I waited longer, then bit them that I might take him. Yet you are from another world; I need not slay you. Leave us and you shall live.*

Erwin's brain spun. Then he shook his head. "You've stolen from an archaeological site, and you're a suspect in two murders." She began to climb, he lumbered after her, weighted flashlight heavy now in his right hand. He had to do this, but he couldn't make himself read her her rights. She was mounting Ararat faster now, scampering, putting distance between them. "I'll see to it you're well-treated, get you a good—"

Parrish broke off because he heard the rumbling sounds, both above and beneath him. He was drained of breath and caught midway between the beginnings of an avalanche and an earthquake! When rock slipped from under his feet, he glanced down in mortal terror.

When he glanced up, the widow carrying her husband's remains had disappeared as if by magic.

But much farther up Ararat, fleetingly exposed when lightning added to the uncanny illumination over the imposing mountain, Erwin saw the hull of an ancient vessel—one that had easily been large enough to displace 43,000 tons and bring to safety the males and females of every major species, including "every creeping thing of the earth . . ."

Rock of every size poured down from the two peaks of eternal Ararat even as Erwin, mortally wounded and losing consciousness, believed he caught a glimpse of a tall, magnificent blond woman running like the wind perhaps in an effort to save him.

He had time to feel glad that he himself could one day be the focal point of a great archaeological discovery and to whisper, too softly to be heard by any living thing, "Mother."

The Writing of "Child of the Sea"

A stranger phoned one day to announce his intention to begin a publishing empire—magazines and books—and add that he wished me to become a part of it. I doubted anyone's ability to set out on such a course successfully. It's the publishing version of a new writer announcing he'll become a household name with his first novel.

But the stranger offered me an absurd amount of money to write a really long story for him, "one with a classic feel to it," and he swore he'd send me part of the stipulated fee just as soon as he got the yarn. It happens that I had an idea I thought would require length to develop, that I thought a "classic feel" might emerge from a tale set in the past, and that I had a yen to write a "period piece"—one that might seem to have been created a century or so ago.

I've been asked when and where the finished story takes place, and I have no idea. Not only that, everything I know about being asea on a good-sized ship is right here in "Child of the Sea," the product of research I did without leaving my house. Mary and I were aboard a houseboat once on a man-made lake, and that concludes my personal experience.

After numerous phone calls, I got a portion of the payment I'd been offered, and I never heard from the stranger again, nor saw anything published by him. A couple of years later I submitted it to Dean Wesley Smith, who came close to building a vast publishing empire via his magazine and company called *Pulphouse*.

In a mini-intro to this "really long story," Dean—who is also a talented novelist—reported that I sent it to him "over three years ago . . ." It seems only fair to the stowaway called Child, Child's victims, and something hideous named *"Teredo navalis"* that they make one more appearance in the present collection. Maybe it's the spirit of Eld . . .

Child of the Sea

"The ship and all in it are imbued with the spirit of Eld."—Edgar Allan Poe, *"Ms. Found in a Bottle"* .

It would take awhile for the square-rigged vessel to take enough wind to carry it so far from the uncharted island that she was no longer in sight. Carmody, the first mate, had waited until the one-legged sailor called Hope rowed back to the ship after leaving the young stowaway on this otherwise uninhabited patch of ground. No doubt the crew would continue staring back as long as possible, returning the abandoned child's gaze till the graceful right-angled sails had blown the *Marie Ellair* entirely out of human view.

And no doubt those men aboard the *Ellair* who had not been privy to what happened while the stowaway was among their number would be disposed to regard Carmody's decision as cruel, heartless—rife with superstitious awe at best.

Child did not care if so much as one of them experienced pity.

Provisions for temporary survival rested in neat stacks Hop made on the beach before slipping back to the ship with its tiers of sails half-furled like angel's wings above the wooden deck. Not once had the peg-legged sailor ceased observing the small person they were leaving to die, once the provisos were gone; old Hop shared the first mate's knowledge of how many had perished and Carmody's insight, too, into why they had died.

Child did not care what Carmody, Hop, or any other seaman believed. Child did not care that there weren't nearly enough kegs of water for a wait of duration, did not care that the island had no name and was therefore not on any route of any sailing vessel on this ocean, and did not care about what would happen to the *Marie Ellair* when it was no longer visible on the horizon.

Wild flowers grew in a vivid panoply of incongruity where the beach ended and the brief woods began, bristling in an etching of imminent night. Child did not notice, Child—who might have seemed any age from under ten to more than twelve depending upon the observer, and probably a "small" ten, eleven, or twelve—cared far more about recalling the satisfactorily interesting events on board the grand but aging three-master.

And without a turn of the head Child reproduced those fulfilling experiences of memory with such dazzling perfection of clarity that it was almost possible to relive them. Standing on the beach with only the trees aft to keep the small person in the ankle-length coat and oversized hat from determining the farthest side of the almost lifeless island, Child saw the recent past—saw it again on the twilit ocean waters.

J.N. Williamson

Aboard the *Ellair*, the sailing men discerned a slow, shy smile taking shape on the scarcely exposed face of the child they were deserting and those few, like Carmody and Hop, who had come to think they knew their stowaway, shared the memories, and shuddered.

Irish Jack Carmody it was who chanced upon the ragamuffin one early watch a week ago when the first mate was on duty. Stows were neither in the expected order of things nor so rare these changing days that there was cause for great fuss, but the clean-shaven Carmody was somewhat taken aback. They'd been to sea for almost two months now and the store in the hold was inspected frequently. It would be easy to view the discovery of a child hiding amid the barrels of grain as a reflection upon his competence as an officer, the efficacy of the training he had given his crew.

Yet all he really saw when he'd ordered the stowaway out of hiding was a yawning mouth and pink, hairless cheeks, a wide-brimmed sea-goer's hat, a wool muffler tucked under the hairless chin, and a badly soiled overcoat so conspicuously too large for the waif that it was probably stolen property. This apparition stood somewhere between four and five feet in height; any better estimate was rendered doubtful because the youth had either been sound asleep or didn't yet have its sea legs and kept lurching from side to side. Mr. Carmody smiled in spite of himself. With the blend of shadows cast from the pyramid of cases in the hold and smudges of dirt on the stow's forehead and ears, there was no way even to be sure it was a lad!

Carmody gave some three seconds to the notion of informing the captain of the matter. Then he recalled that he himself had been urged

Experience the Ultimate in Fear Every Other Month... From Leisure Books!

As a member of the Leisure Horror Book Club, you'll enjoy the best new horror by the best writers in the genre, writers who know how to chill your blood. Upcoming book club releases include First-Time-in-Paperback novels by such acclaimed authors as:

*Douglas Clegg   Ed Gorman
John Shirley   Elizabeth Massie
J.N. Williamson   Richard Laymon
Graham Masterton   Bill Pronzini
Mary Ann Mitchell   Tom Piccirilli
Barry Hoffman*

SAVE BETWEEN $3.72 AND $6.72 EACH TIME YOU BUY. THAT'S A SAVINGS OF UP TO NEARLY 40%!

Every other month Leisure Horror Book Club brings you three terrifying titles from Leisure Books, America's leading publisher of horror fiction.
EACH PACKAGE SAVES YOU MONEY.
And you'll never miss a new title.

Here's how it works:

Each package will carry a FREE 10-DAY EXAMINATION privilege. At the end of that time, if you decide to keep your books, simply pay the low invoice price of $11.25, no shipping or handling charges added. HOME DELIVERY IS ALWAYS FREE! There's no minimum number of books to buy, and you may cancel at any time.

AND AS A CHARTER MEMBER, YOUR FIRST THREE-BOOK SHIPMENT IS TOTALLY FREE! IT'S A BARGAIN YOU CAN'T BEAT!

✂ CUT HERE

Mail to: Leisure Horror Book Club, P.O. Box 6613, Edison, NJ 08818-6613

YES! I want to subscribe to the Leisure Horror Book Club. Please send my 3 FREE BOOKS. Then, every other month I'll receive the three newest Leisure Horror Selections to preview FREE for 10 days. If I decide to keep them, I will pay the Special Members Only discounted price of just $3.75 each, a total of $11.25. This saves me between $3.72 and $6.72 off the bookstore price. There are no shipping, handling or other charges. There is no minimum number of books I must buy and I may cancel the program at any time. In any case, the 3 FREE BOOKS are mine to keep— at a value of between $14.97 and $17.97. Offer valid only in the USA.

NAME:_____

ADDRESS:_____

CITY:_____ STATE:_____

ZIP:_____ PHONE:_____

LEISURE BOOKS, A Division of Dorchester Publishing Co., Inc.

to "demonstrate more initiative," which the mate perceived to mean that the Old Man would not wish to be disturbed because of irrelevant matters. The cap'n had ample on his mind with two passengers aboard, one of them a woman!

"Feed that," he instructed the sailor who had accompanied him on rounds this morning. "Then find a bunk for our 'guest' till we dock at Upper Ingram."

The seaman, now in his forties, would have been a big man if he hadn't had the habit of bunching his shoulders, stooping. The mannerism stemmed from a time when his parents abandoned him and he spent his boyhood flinching from swings of a constable's nightstick. Then Garret went to sea, and now, alone in the world, he had and knew nothing but the *Marie Ellair* and sailing.

"But sir," he called, "what shall I do with the scamp till we dock?"

Carmody hesitated at the foot of the ladder leading out of the hold. "That's up to you," he replied, and remembered the captain's injunction. "Show a bit of initiative, Garret. Show a bit of initiative!"

Then the sailor was left with the urchin and blinking through the shadows at his charge. The child's jiggling about had stopped, at least. Feeling the man's gaze on him, the waif was managing a wan smile. Shaky, uncertain, but a smile—one that evoked in Garret some melancholy yet familiar instant of reminiscence.

Feeling awkward, bulky and beetling beside the little creature, Garret hunched down to his haunches. "What's your name then?"

Eyes that looked at once smoky and backlit by a glint of color the seaman could not remember seeing before glanced off, restless as drifting smoke. There was nothing deliberate about it, Garret thought, no trace of an actual stall—and the man suddenly realized two things he should have known all along: first, he could not be sure this bundled-up scrap of humanity was a male child; second, the poor little morsel was surely scared half out of its wits!

But when he extended a comforting arm to pat the stowaway's shoulder, Garret saw the partly concealed head turn back, the strange, deep eyes fasten on his olive orbs. "Sir . . . what's *your* name?"

Garret caught himself grinning. "Bob," he said when he realized the meaning of the question. "My name is Bob."

The wonderful young eyes widened. "Me, too," Child said, appearing to marvel at the fact. "That's my name too!"

Garret gave his charge the pat on the shoulder he'd had in mind and quite nearly gave way to an abrupt, impulsive urge to hug the boy.

That familiar instant of melancholy he had experienced upon seeing the shy, uncertain, discreet smile on little Bob's face happened because looking closely at this young'un was for all the world like staring into a mirror, thirty years ago.

Violet Whitney could think of nothing during dinner in the captain's cabin except a child she had glimpsed among several sailors in the passageway leading past the mess. The little one had struck her as a perfect rose among her thorns, and she was unable to suppress a question that leaped to her lips after she, her husband Alexander, and the officers were seated.

Though Violet's intuition argued that a Mr. Carmody was not forthcoming, neither Alexander nor the grizzled, distinguished captain seemed to know the child's identity. Indeed, all those at table with the slender Mrs. Whitney appeared to question the very fact that she had seen a young person! Alex was the only one ungentlemanly enough to say as much, however: "My wife is so fond of children that she imagines tiny tots assuming form—rather like phantoms—when she spies a shadow for which she cannot account."

"Still and all," said the captain, "the maternal instinct is a marvel, isn't it, sir?" He made a show of sampling wine brought to him by a steward. "I'm certain Mrs. Whitney would make a splendid mother."

"No question," Alex said, an edge of gruffness to his tone. Almost twice Violet's age at sixty, he had no interest whatever in children. His business empire was so far-flung he always said that he had no time for parenthood; and that was a part of the truth.

Yet the comely and auburn-haired Mrs. Whitney could not force from her head a certainty that a child of some eleven years was aboard a sailing vessel with coarse sailors of every age. The impropriety haunted her even after excusing herself and returning alone to their guest quarters.

The more Violet thought about the matter the more she was sure the poor little thing had also discerned her concern. There'd been the shyest, most modest smile just before the oafish men thrust her down the complex corridors of the ship toward a myriad of mysterious rooms.

Her? Yes, without question—for Violet was convinced the pronoun was accurate. Even a cursory glimpse had revealed to the childless Violet Whitney a delicacy of form, and feature—an image of graceful femininity quite beyond the masculine of gender!

J.N. Williamson

Supine on one of the cabin's bunks, increasingly anxious about the fate of the girl in the ridiculous man's coat and scratchy muffler, Violet cried out audibly when there was a soft, tentative tapping on the cabin door.

"Yes?" she said, sitting up. "Who is it?"

The reply was a high-pitched and unintelligible mumble. Believing herself to be the only woman passenger, Violet went swiftly to the door, then paused before cracking it open a judicious inch.

Child, without the hat, had wavy, mouse-colored hair to the shoulders. The hat was grasped tightly at the breast. "I wonder, madam, if you could help me? I find myself lost." The entreaty came breathily but not with panic. The eyes were cast downward, politely—to the floor—and Violet, peering down too, saw the grimy, enveloping overcoat and footwear that was vastly too large. Worse, one shoe was a brogan which covered the slim ankle, the other actually a soiled riding boot.

"Come inside," Violet said instantly. She took Child's wrist and brought the urchin into the cabin. "Of course I shall help you!"

Child's chin went up only when the woman tipped it in order to look into the youthful eyes at close range. What she saw there would have drawn a pang of sorrow except that Violet had steeled herself, expecting to witness the torment, the loneliness, the clear absence of maternal care. One could stare into such beautifully feminine black eyes and believe in an infinite sisterhood, a bond of burden, neglect, and abuse formed by a seeping red cord being knotted and reknotted in female hearts around the globe. Perhaps only the mighty sea itself could symbolize their isolation and what united them.

Violet was about to offer the girl garments of

212

her own and to wash the grime from Child's face and gently inquire into how she had been brought so low when Alexander's meaty, middle-aged body squeezed into the cabin, shouldering the door to noisily behind him. "What's this?" he demanded, brushing past waif and wife. "Must the churches send these people to us even after we're at sea?"

Violet chose the wrong words. "Oh, Alexander, I told you I saw a child aboard!"

His silence constituted his worst sort of retort and rebuff.

"I said I'll help," Violet whispered to Child, their faces inches apart, "and so I shall. Come to me when you're in jeopardy. All right?"

Child's head bobbed. Child stared back, eyelids up.

Child, outside the door, looked back into the woman's frightened but defiant eyes as long as possible. When the door closed between them, Child heard the start of the first desperate quarrel between Violet and Alexander Whitney.

Child noted that the woman had not asked in what way she could help.

Child smiled sweetly, and knowingly.

Garret was there, paying no mind to finding his little Bob near the guest quarters. His plain face was a mask of tentative reprimand and concern. "Why did you wander off, lad? I've arranged your bunk for you. Answer old Bob!"

Child skipped along with the seaman's fretting pace, nodding dutifully and saying little in response to the man's gesticulations.

They passed first mate Carmody without noticing him; Carmody's approach was from a shorter passageway.

The Irishman overheard Bob Garret say he knew how hard it could be to think about others' feelings when a boy had spent his short life just trying to remain alive. Carmody wanted to smile at the surge of paternal regard. But he had seen the little stow leave the Whitneys' cabin and he'd heard the powerful Mr. W. raise his voice to Missus, and he needed to learn why the urchin was bothering them.

He had seen a strange smile on the bland, filthy young face. Something about that made him believe he should delay questioning the ragamuffin.

Carmody motioned to the peg-legged seaman beside him and they went to examine the rigging. "I don't like this, I don't," Hop muttered. Carmody didn't have to ask the fellow to explain his meaning.

Bob was still attempting to convince Bob that he should be more considerate to people when each of them had hold of mops and were swabbing down the galley. On the *Marie Ellair*, all able-bodied seamen sought to keep the vessel spic-and-span when guests as rich and influential as the Alexander Whitneys were aboard.

A pest called Nick—only the captain knew his full name or past, but everyone knew his sturgeon features, slippery-eel anatomy, and his derogatory remarks—saw Garret counseling his charge. Peering up from his desultory work, Nick wore his usual caustic expression. Most of an hour had passed since the two Bobs began working and the teleostean Nick had used his time to formulate an insinuation. "You're a fair little mom, now, Garret." A feral smirk across the galley. "You want to be called 'Roberta' from now on?"

Bob's hands knotted into fists but he settled for a glare and another swab that left an angry and smudgy swath on the floor—

Then he saw Child's face. The distant eyes were turned from him in boyish mortification.

"Say, 'Mother' Garret," Nick pressed, "how fond of the wee one are you? Is that a boy or a skinny girl under the coat and muffler? Y' might want to *share* your—"

Bob crossed the area between them quickly. Neither he nor Nick heard the first mate and old Hop entering the galley. Bob was occupied by pounding his fists into the other tar, and Nick was busy defending himself from the punches.

Carmody and Hop parted the men, but not without working up a sweat.

Irish Jack went on perspiring while he dressed the brawlers down and recalled the feverishly bright eyes and perplexing sweet smile of the stowaway—a smile that seemed to Carmody to radiate satisfaction, just then, and gladness.

That was the first time he thought he should have informed the captain.

The second occasion was quite late that night. It was a foggy brute that required the effort of all men aboard ship until, close to three o'clock in the morning, as landlubbers reckoned time, the weather cleared and Carmody saw the stow standing quietly at the ship's railing. By himself, staring out at the ceaseless motion of the restless sea.

Shivering, Carmody turned his collar up around his neck. Career sailors would not have been spooked by the turmoil of the past hours— the clear mortal risk, men barking orders and responding with midnight eyes like those of runaway horses. But a child should have been terror-stricken. *A child*, he mused, *would have gone below and covered his head with a blanket*.

Jack Carmody hung back, considered the small figure, studied the nondescript but oddly distorting hat, the narrow shoulders, hips and legs so ill defined by the overcoat, the unmatching footgear, the bony, miniature hand scarcely contacting the wooden railing for balance. The imperturbability of—it.

The androgynous young face then shifted into profile and Carmody watched an extraordinary smile form on the creature's lips. It was shy yet, and distant; but the little aperture of a mouth exhibited a joy that seemed tinged with quite unexpected passion. The smile, he felt, expressed less cunning—or need for it at that moment—and it was queerly gratified, momentarily ... complete.

This was also the occasion when Irish Jack believed he saw love—affection, at least—in the waif's unreadable eyes, though it looked only at the endless ocean which even first mate Carmody, at base, feared rather more than he feared death.

Bob Garret was there, then, next to his charge of less than a day, showing a parent's demeanor of gentle and passive concern.

Carmody didn't see the amazing change of expression on the ragamuffin's face because he had sighed, turned away, and resumed his weary watch. Garret was a grown man. Jack regretted assigning the stow to him, but he *could* deal with a child.

Big Bob sensed Child's apprehension and saw the lower lip start to tremble at the instant the moon, as if it had been beckoned, came out. It seemed to Garret that young Bob was obviously keeping to himself something so stark, beyond his ability to understand, that it drew a feeling of immediate recognition from the broad-shouldered man along with a spasm over his own remembered childhood fears. "Did the fog frighten you, boy?" he blurted. "What is wrong?"

Child's long lashes blinked back the tears. Shame, or guilt, showed in the smoky eyes. It gave the impression that he yearned to say what had gone amiss, and, in another tick of time, it was as if the little tyke had no other choice.

"He says you're going to sell me to him! Must I be his property, Bob—must I?"

Garret pulled his head back in amazement. "What's this about 'property'? People can *sell* people, boy? What are you telling me?"

Suddenly Child's long, skinny arms were wrapped around the sailor's thick middle, hugging Bob as if this would be the way it was forever. "I want to stay with you, sir, I don't want to be *his*."

Shocking possibility left Garret cold. "Who?" he rasped. "You don't want to be his *what?*" He held the urchin at arm's length. "Answer me, little Bob—hop to it!"

"Nick." The answer was a sinister whisper. Child glanced up, down again, abashed. "N-Nick's the one who . . . wants me, says you'll s-sell me. *You* know."

For two short seconds Bob kept his gaze on the roiling waves. Then, without fuss, he kissed the stowaway's chilly temple and spun away. "People don't sell or buy people, 'specially children!" He worked his fists. "Not whilst Bob Garret's on this side of Davy Jones's locker!"

"Where are you going?"

"Stay here, little Bob," Garret said without glancing back, stomping away.

Child didn't. Heart racing, Child trailed after Bob as the man lumbered toward the crewmens' sleeping quarters, stopping en route just long enough to hide something he took beneath his coat.

Unerring despite the inky blackness of the area, big Bob strode toward a lean, lithe figure sleeping in a hammock. Unhesitatingly, he twisted the ropes supporting the hammock, dumping Nick on to the floor. Standing over him, Bob brandished a weighty belaying pin he had taken. "Wake up! Get up!"

Groggy, the wiry seaman sniffed the air warily with his long nose, wiggled into a kneeling position. When the ship hove, a shaft of moonlight revealed Garret, and behind him a mass of shadows like a short but overladen coat rack. "What's this?" He tried his version of humor. "Mother and child lookin' for the sewing circle, is it?"

The art of belaying involves securing a ship's ropes—for a considerable period of time—by winding them round a pin. Such an object must be reliable, sturdy; very strong.

Garret hit Nick in the face with the pin, a blow that began at shoulder height which took the broad-shouldered Bob's arm and hand around to the opposite side of his body.

Then Garret brought his hand and arm back and battered the other man's forehead with the belaying pin, ripping the scalp loose. Geysers of spurting blood were like a Chinese fireworks display.

Bob put the pin down, took aim, and kicked Nick's ribs with all his strength.

Though there was a sharp cracking sound, Nick responded with no more animation than when he was struck the second time.

Child, beside Bob. Somehow the small, comforting presence did not come as a surprise. They squinted through the murky shadows together. "He looks like a fish in a pan, don't he?" Bob said.

Child emitted a hideous giggle. Garret stared down, shocked; little Bob was grinning, but the light at the back of the strange eyes was brighter than before.

"He shan't be ownin' anyone," Bob said fondly. Less than a minute—and one man—had expired since reaching the sleeping area. Bob took another few seconds to see if another man had awakened, seen what transpired, but he saw no evidence of that. "Come on then," he said, stooping. "Help your old pop take care of this."

They hauled the corpse up on deck, working side by side, then carried it over to the railing. Not a soul was around. Together (although big Bob could have done it alone), they let the dead weight drop into the oily waters.

The grandest time of Bob Garret's life came when the little being in the dirty coat and ridiculous hat hugged him, murmured thanks, and, smiling shyly, asked if Bob minded being called "father."

That was a moment in Bob's life that could never be surpassed.

Night is never darker than it is on a sailing ship when midnight has gone unnoticed and yesterday's dawn somehow feels closer than tomorrow's. It was possible to be so far from shore that, if there was no moon, all the meaningful illumination one can find is in memories that cannot be shared with another man.

Carmody felt that way when he dimly recognized the old salt reeling toward him, just outside of the bridge, and the emotions were so familiar to him that the sight of another human being—awake, about—was nearly supernaturally jarring. Billy Salvo, that was the oldster's name,

Jack recalled—*and he is going to tell me something that will alter my life and his for the rest
of time.*

The premonition did not prevent whiskery and
decrepit Billy from doing it. "Nick's murdered,"
he whispered. Words almost snagged on his rum-
soaked, scraggly mustaches. "Bob Garret done
him in with a belayin' pin!"

"You saw it happen?" What was wrong with the
old sot? It was Salvo's last voyage; no one aboard
liked Nick. Why did everything become so complicated?

"Aye. I sawed it." The old man mumbled, nodded, poisoned the air with his rum and his life
without the earth beneath his feet. Perhaps a permanent odor was what the ocean gave back to a
man who had pissed in it for seventy years. "So
did Bob's brat."

The first mate studied the ancient face. "Did the
little Arab help Bob?"

Billy thought about that one. "Not to belay
Nick. They both toted off his remains, though."
He bobbed his bewhiskered head. "I stayed put in
m'bunk, kept m'eyes shut. Lord knows where
they put poor Nicky."

Jack turned his head, peered beyond the old
seaman at the sea; he knew what he would have
done with a corpse. Even the fishes had to eat.

He came very near to seeing Child, who just
stood stock still at the railing within hearing
range of the two men. Child was too small, too
nervelessly motionless, to be easily discovered.

Besides, Child had not wanted to be seen then.

Child wanted to be seen only by Billy Salvo and
in the right light at the right time.

That time came when the old man was teeter-
ing an ambling path back to his bunk, muttering
to and congratulating himself, informing the

ocean and God that he would expect a bit of extra for his pay at the end of *this* voyage, a reward for an honest man who kept his eyes and his wits about him. No killer, silly!

The right light which Salvo saw was in Child's depthless eyes, and it enabled Billy to get the only reward he was going to get on ocean or earth: a clear and unobstructed view of Child waiting for him by the mizzenmast, impeding his progress to the stairs leading to the sailors' bunks.

Child let Salvo see the swamps and sweet springwater of life, floods of accumulated knowledge and belief that had swept through endless time's streams and tributaries—the high seas of triumph and loss, the rapids of beating desire that were never ever slowed to a trickle but were trapped by whirlpools and maelstroms before being rocketed to the skies and thundered back into man's existence and his existences. Child's eyes widened—past the darkness to numbing light—to let Billy ride the surging surf, to become immersed in days and nights he could not even remember but to do it again, and find himself showered into the future Billy'd been making all the voyages of his long present life.

Child allowed an old human being to see the totality of the recorded Billy Salvo so that Child, too, could see, and it stopped Billy's life, halted him dead while also sending the sailor off to follow another light in darkness and hope it led somewhere.

Then Child skipped nimbly around the remnant of a man who had been an informer exactly as Child had wished and sprinted soundlessly through the brief passageways of the doomed *Marie Ellair* to awaken and ruin the woman who'd been as friendly as big Bob.

"They think I did it, that I helped Mr. Garret,"

Child wept when motherless Violet Whitney
threw her cabin door wide. "But I didn't, ma'am,
he *made* me go with him!" It was obvious to Child
that the story was impossible to follow that way
but it would make Violet want to know more.

"Before you go on, let me help you off with
those dreadful damp clothes," she said, drawing
Child into the cabin. "Poor darling, you mustn't
have been to bed at all tonight."

Child looked pathetic and surrendered hat,
muffler, and overcoat.

Child knew that once Violet Whitney saw the
faint swell of a budding feminine breast beneath
the tattered men's shirt, it wouldn't take much
longer. "You said I could come here when I was in
jeopardy, ma'am." Child strove to bat back tears
but they were a foregone conclusion. "I j-just
don't know where else to g-go."

Child started. The burly rich man who had
been sleeping came into the room, saw his wife
embracing a young female. Good. That would
make it harder for him to say no, which he *had* to
say, but this was more fun.

"Please, dear, tell us what happened," coaxed
the woman. She listened intently while she rum-
maged in her trunk, occasionally pulling out this
or that article of feminine apparel. A sidelong
glance at Child brought Violet the mildly surprising discovery that they might be closer in size
than she had heretofore believed. "We shall do
what we can to help, won't we, Alex?"

Grunting, producing a cigar, Alexander Whitney gathered his dressing gown round him and
took a peevish, watchful seat.

Child eschewed the details of a presence
aboard ship that was undeniably illegal and told,
concisely but dramatically, a tale that encompassed the fiction Bob Garret had already heard,

Bob's lie-based slaughter of a man who became (in Child's telling) a lascivious pursuer of undeveloped womanhood, and first mate Carmody's callousness both in assigning a girl-child to Garret's care (without duly notifying the captain) and doing precisely nothing when the same girl-child found grown men appearing to fight one another to death over her.

Child drew to the end of the story wide-eyed with terror and the heaving of a marginally rounded young bosom. "I d-don't know if Mr. Carmody wants me for h-his own, or if he thinks everything is m-my fault." Tears standing on the cheeks brought the account to the brink of an effective conclusion. "I'm afraid he believes I m-might turn out to be a—a hoodoo."

Violet started. "Do you mean a *jinx?*" She turned to Alexander in an effort to enlist his rational outrage at such a patent absurdity. "I thought the officers of this ship were supposed to be educated men!"

The husband made no reply for a moment. Then he raised the cigar he had ignited and wafted the smoke in a gesture of impatience and manly reasonableness. "What a fellow believes is what motivates him, regardless of how foolish it may sound to other men." He expelled smoke, pursed his lips, slowly shook his head. "I don't like this, Vi. We're guests on the *Marie E*; we're miles from anywhere and in no position to defy the cretins. Mutiny over lesser issues than this isn't unheard of."

"Surely you don't propose that we abandon this child, turn her over to their tender mercies!" Violet draped several garments over Child's lap while she stared at her husband with the conviction that she had never seen him so clearly before. "That would be quite unworthy of you, sir."

Hoisting himself to his slippered feet, Whitney permitted himself the first long look he'd had at the slender child with the discreet eyes and mouse-colored hair. The hair, out from under the hat, bunched at the cheeks; the visible skin was an unhealthy pink, in Alexander's view. Still and all, he had the impression that if he went on looking at the child—got to know her—he might have different feelings toward her.

Feelings that would make him really *so* less uncomfortable than he felt just then. "What I propose is that we allow this miss to stay here till morning, when the captain should be fully informed. He seemed a good sort." He ground his cigar out in a tray, avoided looking again at Child. "Let him get to the bottom of things when we dock somewhere." And that was clearly all he had to say.

Violet bathed Child's face, neck, hands, and arms from a basin before she and Child retired; a bond seemed already formed between them. She learned that the young one who so clearly needed her was called Vivian, or Viv—the very name Violet had yearned to give a daughter someday because it went well with "Violet." The fact slipped out as naturally as if they had known one another for years.

Viv raised her timid, bravely knowing eyes to inquire why Violet—since she liked "little children"—had no offspring of her own.

For an instant that appeared to have begun years before and yet extended into a future that suddenly seemed a grim, empty, futile void, Violet did not answer.

Then she turned her head, minutely, to peer at the already sleeping, gray, and rumpled Alexander, and gave Viv a tender hug. "For a very long period of time I believed there was a reason," she whispered. "Now, I feel sure there's not a reason in the world." Young "Viv" hugged back, warmly.

And in the morning, clad in Violet Whitney's clothing, Child went with the woman to see the captain.

On their way they saw a man named Bob Garret tied by a strong hemp to a mast, being flogged by a short one-legged seaman. The snapping force of the whip in the latter's hand denied any suggestion of fragility or deficit of balance afoot. The splitting sounds of the cat carving into big Bob's naked back were what took Mrs. Whitney's initial attention and, for another instant, maintained it—the way any clear and unequivocal evidence of dying is always compelling.

Garret's back appeared to have been turned into a vast navigator's map in which the bisecting lines represented passageways in the most harsh and garish red Violet had witnessed. Morning sunstream pooled a hue between yellow and orange as a background of the still-living map.

Violet belatedly sought to steer her small charge around the scene of awful violence, but she stopped when she saw that the man who was gradually being punished to death was staring mutely at Vivian, and Child was staring back—straight into his mystifyingly startled, wondering, and pain-anguished eyes.

Just trying to stay alive, Garret's lips formed the words. But whether or not that was defense, a wry observation on human destiny, or a question put inexplicably to Child, the moment of contact was brief. Vivian gave the fellow what Violet saw as the sweetest aloof and distant smile ever, tossed her head with disdain, and swished her skirts in readiness to walk the rest of the way to the bridge.

225

Violet wondered why the dying man on the mast also said *Help me* to young Vivian and if the child had not discerned the message or just preferred not to acknowledge it.

First mate Carmody gaped at the two females as they passed. His mouth was open in astonishment.

The husky captain stepped out to greet his visitors, nothing in his expression betraying startlement. Violet realized he had been watching the fulfillment of his or Carmody's ghastly orders from the door to the bridge, and that meant that the Irish first mate already had conveyed his tissue of lies to the captain. Only God or the nearly dead Bob Garret could imagine what claptrap—what arrant superstitious nonsense—had been told about poor Vivian!

For several minutes Violet sought to set matters straight by telling the old captain the truth as she knew it. It was just in the final seconds of her statement that the uniformed man seemed restive, even resigned to his own conclusions; so Mrs. Alexander Whitney added, "My husband is a man of some influence, sir. We shall not tolerate this child's further abuse. Though he jokes with me about my maternal disposition, Mr. Whitney will not sit by while anyone disciplines Vivian—either for the actions of adults in your command or because some of your men put credence in the ludicrous notion that she is a jinx."

"We don't punish children on the *Marie Ellair*, madam," the captain said.

Violet had to blink her eyes. "Well, I should think you wouldn't." She took Child's hand in her gloved one, pressed it to her breast.

"—Regardless of how they get aboard my ship," he added thoughtfully, and gazed curiously at Child. "One does wonder from time to time how they manage it. *Why*. It is tempting to think of tracing their . . . origins. Perhaps it's just that 97 percent of the world is water and, therefore, some young—a few—must find their way to the sea." Gently, he placed his wide palm on Child's pate. "We'll never catalogue all the creatures existing on the ocean."

Child tolerated the touch, squirmed. Violet didn't know what to say. Was he discussing superstitiousness or dismissing the topic? Had he even wondered if Vivian was a jinx prior to their own broaching of the subject?

He smiled at Violet. "Where *is* your husband this morning, Mrs. Whitney?"

The captain's tone was accentless, free of accusation. Yet Vi knew that was what it was, in a way. He was subtly implying that the kind of husband she had delineated would have accompanied her and the child on an errand of such significance.

Violet found the answer on her lips and blurted it out. "He is making the initial arrangements." The mere act of putting her thoughts—her desires—in words made her wish to say them all. "Arrangements to *adopt* this abused, sorely neglected child." She was flushing and knew it and did not care. "She shall be our own, Captain—our own little girl."

He sustained the steadiness of his gaze on her. "I'm sure this is the most fortunate child on seven seas." He spoke flatly and without enthusiasm but forthrightly. "You will make a marvelous mother, madam."

And so I shall, and I will, Violet promised herself when they were again approaching their cabin, *if I can simply persuade Alex to let me try*.

"I must speak with my husband in private, before you come in," she said softly to Vivian, praying she was conveying far more through her hands resting on Child's nearly bony shoulders. She scanned the polite, bland, always somehow distant face. "But would you like to be my daughter?" Her voice scarcely traveled the scant gap between them. "Would you enjoy being . . . our . . . child?"

Child worked the eyelashes, nodded. Smiled. Just so.

Which made it the best moment of Violet's whole life. A shining, truly fulfilling but very brief, very best moment.

Violet Whitney kissed Child's cool cheek, asked her to wait right outside the door, entered the cabin, and would never see "Vivian" again.

The first permanent naval force on the planet probably was the Athenians', and their three tiers of men wielding oars, the *trimeres*, were mostly slaves. Galley slaves.

The captain reflected on that as he descended carefully into the hold of his ship dark there as if it was twilight. This was a task he wished to perform himself, not leave to Mr. Carmody. Despite all reason, he believed it was conceivable that the child Garret and the first mate had thought to be a boy and who now seemed to be a girl might lead to the destruction of the powerful, rich Whitneys. That would have repercussions in the financial capitals of the world, but his real concern was the woman. He had lost his mother, the captain had; this Violet Whitney reminded him of her, when he was a boy. And the first place any of them had seen the stowaway was here, in the hold. The sex of the child didn't matter in the slightest.

In addition to the danger which he believed awaited the Whitneys, what mattered wasn't a case of superstition, either, but sheer fact:

Inside of twenty-four hours, three men had

died—on *his ship*, The unlikable Nick, a poor sot named Billy who'd never done worse than tell tales to his own paltry advantage—

And big Bob Garret, a decent sort. Dead when Hop's orders were carried out.

The captain dusted his hands, decided where he would begin looking. Rome's navy won a victory at Actium that allowed them to rule the Med for four hundred years, he recalled, and some men in their galley had been slaves. Viking ships marauded the European coasts beginning around the year 800, kept it up for some two hundred years, and they had been manned by slaves— slaves whose deaths, during war, were terrible beyond description. They'd suffocated or burned to death . . . closer to the sea waters under their bare feet than to the decks of their vessels.

Such dying isn't natural, it's not even the decent death of fighting men, the captain ruminated, poking into grain barrels and among the kegs of water. An idea came to mind: If haunts ever rode the ocean's waves—if there was anything to the scuttlebutt about ships being found adrift without a sign of life *but no trace of the way the men had met their fate*—then what if restless or lonely souls that survived death had nowhere to go, and sought companionship from time to time? Not true friends or families, no, nothing lasting— because the poor devils' time would forever be *now*, this minute . . . and they might enjoy giving back some of the misery they'd experienced during their lives.

Or there might be other explanations. The captain took a step backward, gasped. The top of a wooden barrel had just come away in his hands and rolled out of sight! *Peculiar*, he thought, startled. It was as if the lid of the barrel had been *forced up*, and *off*.

229

Frowning, sighing because he really did not want to do this, the captain put his grizzled head forward in the partial light to stare into the four-foot-high receptacle.

He saw it at once, but resisted the stern obligation to accept what he was seeing.

It was long, and wormy. Vaguely pink, vaguely translucent, simultaneously flimsy-looking, loosely coiled, vaguely threatening. It was not decked out as if in armor (like an insect of size), yet there were things like tough plates affixed to or growing from the head (what passed for a head; the thing possessed no charm, personality, or even sex that he could make out). It was a bivalve, the captain knew that; he knew it because he was a good ship's captain and it was his obligation to know everything that might possibly be aboard a ship, everything that might happen to *his* ship. So he also knew that this great mollusk—Latin name *Teredo navalis*—had the capacity for burrowing into a wooden vessel's timbers.

He also knew that there were some sailing men who held the belief that it was capable of burrowing—even at its usual size—not just into the hull but all the way to the hold of a ship. As this particular . . . thing . . . had clearly done.

Now he believed what his peers believed because the shipworm he was staring at inside the barrel consumed the whole *space* inside of it! Probably it had been there, lurking out of sight in the hold of *his ship*, since the *Ellair* had embarked—for all he knew it had been on board even longer, maybe it had been born there!

But, why? Why remain there, hiding? To what end?

Pouring perspiration, and filled with a mixture of curiosity, revulsion, and wonder, the captain tried to remember what he'd learned once about a shipworm's nesting habits, its mating rites, how it reared its young—

When jaws he scarcely saw at all began to bore into his neck just under the jaw—going at him, *into* his flesh, that was much softer than the wood of a tree—*grubbing* into him like a worker drilling a hole! There wasn't even much bloodshatter, or spray; the shipworm was tidy and didn't like waste one bit more than the captain had.

But it might have been minimally gentler if it had known Child had returned to the hold and was crouched, smiling, on the stairs. Watching avidly, dutifully.

It might not have burrowed all the way through the captain's throat and out again on the other side, leaving little more than part of the head on top and the legs below. Stopping—finished—when she saw Child.

"He asked where you were. He saw that I didn't have my husband with me to stand up for us! How do you think that made me feel?"

Alex was out of bed now, working his shoes onto his big feet. He'd already donned his trousers; his every movement made his intentions clear: he meant just to leave the cabin, knowing well that no lady would make a public scene by shouting at him on deck!

It wasn't supposed to have gone this way; she had imagined her husband possessed a flicker of compassion, she had not desired reaching the stage of asserting herself—pleading for the oldest rights Violet knew. But he had said, "No," and repeated it—repeated it in the same cold, level tone with which he had ultimately denied her every pleasure, need, and right. No, no, *no!*

"I mean to have that child for my own!" Violet insisted, closer beside him as he slipped into his shirts, then turned to brush his sparse hair. He was sixty but he was large, and the tiny tic in one eyelid warned her he was losing his temper again. The realization enflamed her. "I could leave you, Alexander!"

"Then survive on what?" He peered glacially at her in the mirror. "If you persist in this business with the child you shall have *nothing* from me."

Violet caught a breath, watched him slip by her, took one of his arms with her hand. She was about to play her trump card, but it was fraught with peril. She simply had no time and no patience left for sweetness or tact, when Viv needed her *now*. "There are some gentlemen with whom you do business who won't take kindly to your refusal of the only thing to which society agrees a woman is entitled: the right to mother-hood."

He stopped at the door leading from the cabin. Not facing her, his reaction was impossible to determine, or define. But she knew the muscles in Alexander's forearm had tightened; his entire arm felt like a steel rod.

"I could ruin you, Alexander Whitney," she whispered, daring to utter the rest of it. "If I must."

His other arm, tensed as greatly as the one Violet gripped with her nails, came round with all the man's resentment of the truth they shared propelling it. The power of the blow tore away Violet's desperate clutch and the rest of the moorings of the agreement they called a marriage.

Lifting herself from the floor to an elbow, Violet bled copiously from nose and mouth. "That quaint child senses what you are, Alexander," she said. "I know she surmised—from my answers to her little questions—that you can't have children.

The very proximity of even an adopted daughter would remind you of your own—"

Alex could not hear that, so he kicked her with precision between the eyes.

Then—to the top of Violet's head rather than the eyes or jaw—he hammered his heavy fists over and over, saying (in his customary speaking voice), "No. No. No. No. No. No. No."

She did not have to hear anything he said, at last.

When Violet was both silent and gone, he knew he had loved her.

Neither Whitney departed the cabin or ship alive.

No doubt the members of the crew who survived and who had not had the opportunity to meet Child would go on staring back as long as possible at the abandoned youth standing amid wild-flowers and a limited supply of food and water on the island none of them had seen before and would never see again. The place existed on no charts; probably first mate Carmody had been pleased with that when he assumed command of the *Marie Ellair*. Probably he assumed that he and his seamen were no longer in danger, that the dying had ceased.

Once again wearing the coat, muffler, and hat which eliminated any reasoned inference concerning the small person's gender, Child understood the Irishman fully, now. Carmody had insisted upon these clothes because the sailors who had not made the stow's acquaintance might never have permitted Captain Carmody to maroon a girl.

The memories of the interesting, recent past were experienced by Child as if each event were new; present. Each instructive element had been conveyed, impressed in the brain cells of she who had symbiotically made over and redirected each of them. For the *Teredo navalis*, which thrived on sailing vessels, and the apparitional jinx—whose origin was Greece's *inyx*, a wrynecked bird akin to woodpeckers—first had shared a perverse fondness for the timber of ships and sea travel—

And shipworms would not drown, either, when ships sank. They were no more worms than Child was merely the residue of a whipped and long-deceased human slave.

Just when Child was about to sink into another crystalline reverie that might well have slipped through the waters of liquid time to moments of vengeance preceding the birth of all those people left aboard the *Ellair*, a distant scream brought the little being's partly occluded eyes wide open, staring at a craft on the ocean so small—because of the range between them—it possessed less clarity than sweet memory.

But then, whether tireless wind had borne the terror-stricken sound to the island or Child had only shared it vicariously, it became easier to discern. The *Marie Ellair* was in flames.

Carmody and the others would find little left of the lifeboats, and it definitely was too far to swim. Not that there was much likelihood that many of the sailors could even get to the smaller boats.

Beautiful, the ocean at night, whether upon or just peering out at it. Beautiful, and teeming infinitely with life, even when there was no ship asail upon its cresting bosom—like now. Child rested a narrow back against a tree and sank to a seated position against its unsullied roots. Child smiled.

There was nothing of shyness or discretion about the smile.

The Writing of "Everyone Must Know"

The character named Dr. Martin Ruben was the protagonist in my first published novel (*The Ritual*, 1979) and the publisher was old Leisure Books. A parapsychologist who reminded people of Sherlock Holmes—actor Basil Rathbone, actually—Ruben also appeared in other early novels of mine (*Premonition, Brotherkind, Horror House*), but this is the only short story about Martin—

And I wrote it for Lin Stein's *Dead of Night* magazine to celebrate a decade of survival as a published novelist, and because the poet Ms. Stein is one of the three most considerate editors I've known. Her small press magazine, for which I wrote a column in every issue, is in suspension now; printing expenses took away her chance to break even. If she can ever revive it, I'll be there like a shot. And maybe Dr. Ruben will be, too.

Everyone Must Know

Martin Ruben required only moments with Julian Stanvall to conclude that the little man was probably not mad, no publicity seeker, and quite possibly haunted.

All that came as a welcome surprise to a youthful psychiatrist whose mixed success in one bizarre case had led to a succession of wearisome patients who only wanted to believe their deceased relatives were visiting them, either out of love, terror, or to become causes celebres.

But this Stanvall seemed to be different. He did not claim his house was haunted, he said *he* was. He swore a presence dogged his every step, made all his life miserable.

"Do you sense it," began Ruben, pressing his long hands and fingers together, "or do you see it?"

"Both, Doctor." Stanvall's red-rimmed eyes

were unblinking and he appeared at the point of exhaustion. "Yet I never see the face. And I have to. It's my conviction that I must come face to face with it or go insane." His small hand quivered at his lips as he chose the right words. "But if I do see the entity's face clearly," he whispered, "I shall probably cease to exist."

Ruben made a note. Curious. Why hadn't Stanvall simply said "die"? Everything about Julian Stanvall was a curiosity. Refined features but badly wrinkled; the skin on the cheeks occasionally overlapped, like plant leaves. He seemed old, aged, except every movement was quick, or sudden, the lips were thin yet sensual, and his never-blinking eyes were star-bright, they penetrated like lasers.

"Do you recognize this presence, Mr. Stanvall—does anything about the entity enable you to identify it?"

"So!" Stanvall gave him a vivid smile. "To you it's Dickens's ghostly 'indigestion,' a bit of cheese that failed to go down." The smile did not fade. It ceased. "I don't suffer digestive upset. And I never eat cheese."

Ruben also smiled. "You're aware, of course, you didn't answer my question about recognizing the personality, the apparition, you glimpse?"

"I know him better than myself," the patient sighed. His animated eyes burrowed into Ruben's. "He is cold, merciless. He reproaches all I do."

Curioser, thought Ruben, inscribing a note. He repeated it. "Reproaches?"

"He groans his disapproval. With a ghastly gasp of freezing breath at my throat. With proddings of my arms when I make love. He is akin to chilblains on my bare feet at sunrise, when I retire."

"You go to bed at dawn?" Ruben asked, glancing up.

"I work," Stanvall answered, "nights."

"And you do . . . what?"

"What I must. I'm creative, you see." He sat erect across the desk. "I innovate, freely. Nocturnal air is conducive to my—my freedom of expression."

"And when you sleep, sir," Martin pressed, "you also dream, don't you?"

No answer but a half turn to peer past Ruben to the window. It was as if he responded to night air billowing the drapes, lifting them into a nearly life-sized, vertical form Stanvall found interesting. Or empathetic, perhaps.

"It's not my dreams but my nightmares you may find informative, Doctor," he replied at last. His lancing gaze darted back to Ruben. "They don't cease. However, they have changed, or advanced—gone worse for me."

"I have studied them, nightmares," the lean psychiatrist commented. He meant to bolster the other's confidence. "Variations of basic themes. I understand them."

"Do you?" It was nearly feral, a snarl. "Have you heard the one in which the dreamer dies quite hideously—"

"Unusual," Ruben interjected, "but not unheard-of."

"—Yet the death is not the worst feature of the sleeper's dream?"

"More rare," Ruben confessed. "A trip to hell, suffering for eternity scheduled, is that it?"

Stanvall almost howled, *"No!"* and let his voice trail off. His hands were flung forward and he dragged his fingers, made furrows in Ruben's polished desktop. "A trip to death that ends with the disintegration not alone of my body but my immortal *soul!*"

Ruben clutched an outflung wrist, pinned it. "You see the actual element of soul deterioration in each repeated dream?"

The red-rimmed eyes were pathetic; pitiable. "Every one," he nodded, "in each nightmare."

"Very well." The standing Ruben leaned toward Stanvall. "Then that means you see the priest as he starts to drive the stake into your heart! You hear the thudding sounds and bone breaking . . . you feel pain spearing the cells of your body!" Martin perceived Stanvall's altered expression, his lips parting fractionally, and he pressed on. "You witness your blood geysering from the awful, jagged wound in your breast, do you not?"

The patient tried to yank his wrist away, but it was at an odd angle and the hawk-nosed psychiatrist was bearing down with all his weight.

"Does your soul suffer abominably, your memory recalling all your victims and relating to them, at last? Come, deal with your guilt!"

"You know, then," Stanvall whispered, "what I am?"

Martin released his wrist and patted his hand. "Well, I know what you *believe* you are." He spun briskly away. "It's getting cool, I think." He turned to the windows, raised his fingers.

Stanvall's laughter was cold on Martin's back. "You are cleverly entertaining, Doctor! You might nearly tempt me to prove I *am* a vampire, though I've lived thirty decades frequently laboring to establish that I am no such thing!"

Slender Ruben went to his coffee service, poured two cups. "I assume you prefer yours black," he said drily, smiling. "Tell me, could you prove yourself a vampire, sir? With trumped-up papers dated three hundred years ago, that kind of thing?"

Julian accepted the cup gratefully. "Church records, a birth certificate, that sort of thing wouldn't persuade you?"

"Alas, not these days," Martin said, sitting and dropping three sugar cubes into his own cup. "Nor glimpses of your incisors, for I am no dentist. Since I am Jewish, I have no crosses or crucifixes to make you flinch."

Stanvall slumped in his chair with apparent resentment. "Yet you appear to believe I am, for want of a better word, haunted. Correct?"

"My beliefs must be of no importance here unless you are simply engaging in pointless theatrics. If you'd be good enough to recline on my couch, we might get to the bottom of your difficulties."

"Hypnotism, is it?" The little man raised a brow, saw Ruben nod. Without rising, his laser-like eyes were shining in the lunarscape of his myriad miniatures. "An intriguing prospect. But beneath your spell I should find myself helpless— to fire; to the stake."

"I had not thought you paranoid." Ruben spoke with deliberate pity.

"Touché," Julian murmured. Then he rose and walked to the sofa. He assumed a comfortable, prone position. "Pascal wrote, 'Belief is a wise wager.' So, perhaps, is well-placed trust. You shall not slight my primary conscious anxiety, that of the mysterious presence that dogs me so unstintingly?"

"I think," Ruben said, sitting behind him on a stool, "we may find a common explanation for it and the repetition of your nightmares."

"Proceed, then." He folded his hands on his chest, perhaps protectively, certainly dramatically. "A word of caution before you begin: no posthypnotic suggestions to bark or howl like a dog or buzz like a fly. I can become all such creatures, and any of them would be the size of a man."

"My word," Ruben promised, suggesting a focal point for Stanvall and beginning to induce the trance. *The human mind can believe anything*, he thought wonderingly. What psychiatrists did not know was the total extent of the belief capacity to create for others the appearance of substance.

Little time was needed; Martin knew what he was doing. "Stanvall," he said, not loudly, "you can hear me and respond. When were you born?" That single question should dispense with the nonsense related to his patient's status and age when the tape they were making was played back.

"The year was 1632," Julian Stanvall said in his normal voice.

"Tell me where," Martin said, heart skipping a beat, "and what was your father's vocation?"

"The nation is no more," said Julian. "Father crafted things. He was a wood-carver."

"Your mother . . . did you have strong feelings for her?"

"I did not know either parent well." The eyelids fluttered. "When I was little, they perished."

"From the plague?" Ruben asked.

"From vampires." The lids screwed shut. His voice rose. "Vampires tore out their throats!"

Ruben was shaken, glad Stanvall could not see him. "Who raised you, Julian?"

The patient's Adam's apple bobbed. "Vampires." His eyes rolled beneath the closed lids. "Made me one of them. I was their slave." He started to weep. "I had begged and b-begged

241

them to accept me and, one full moon during autumn, they . . . *did it* for me."

Appalled, a theory nonetheless developing, Martin Ruben studied the badly creased face. Severe problems were involved. If he chose now to dispossess his patient's conviction, he might steal from Stanvall the only past he recalled, regardless of how superstitiously absurd and neurotic it was. Martin knew of no genuine Stanvall past with which to replace the fiction, and it was not impossible that the concoction existed because the truth was something Julian knew would drive him into functionless madness.

"Julian," Ruben retrieved a thread, mind racing, "why do vampires exist? What is nature's purpose for a vampire?"

The eyelids worked, opened partway. Stanvall seemed lightly drugged but lucid, not confused. "In each human life there is meant to be a moment when, for the first time, an awareness of one's own mortality occurs. An exact instant when the person accepts the knowledge that he will die. But people may have no youthful contact with human death because of their family's longevity, and due to quite isolated existences without neighbors nearby, without newspapers, or even television."

"Go on," the psychiatrist urged, fascinated by Stanvall's imagination.

"You see, *everyone* must know of personal mortality, of death, before true maturity is possible. I was taught it is a rule, the inviolable one. Some people, fortunately, don't reach maturity before they're adults." The intensity in Stanvall's plain face was deeper than Ruben had seen before.

Everyone must know, Martin mentally replayed

the haunting idea. "Or?" he demanded, resisting the urge to shake the small man. "Or *what*?"

"Or he shall live forever," Julian said at once, "and where would all the people *live*?"

Ruben blinked. Nothing in his experience had prepared him for this, and the inferences he was left to draw. *I must find a better approach.*

But Julian continued, "Those who raised me told me the rule, and our major role in the lives and the deaths of others. We have the unappreciated task of identifying and pursuing those who might otherwise . . . *slip by*."

The first rule for both psychiatrists and psychologists, Martin reflected, might be refusing to believe and share a patient's illness. But the second rule was probably not ever to deride what was revealed, to scoff or laugh at it.

His next step was to plunge poor Stanvall into his nightmare with the hope, the expectation, of locating the source of those strange beliefs. Once Martin had done that, the man who thought he was a vampire moaned eerily, and sweat ran among the pouchlike folds on his cheeks like trickling water.

"You're physically safe with me, Julian," Ruben reminded him. "What do you see? Where are you, Stanvall?"

"I'm in death, or stasis. I see a man—big, powerful!—with a mallet, a stake!" The words were choked out. "He has found my casket and he has thrown it wide!"

"Is he alone?"

"There are . . . others." A whisper, meant only for Martin. "Two more!"

Three; how representational. "See their faces, look at them, Julian." Martin stood, moved to peer down at Stanvall. "Who is the man with the stake? Is he a priest, Julian? He is, isn't he?"

"Nooooo," Stanvall groaned, hand upraised as if to protect his chest. Again his odd eyes were open, straining in their sockets. "Father, he's *my father!* And—and the next figure"—Julian's sobbing sound was immense but one of relief—"this is *Mother*. My father and mother are here!"

Reason begins to triumph, Ruben mused. Now each man relaxed. "Now, Julian, there's the third person. Can you describe him or her?"

Stanvall's eyes shot from side to side. He was clearly trying to discern, to see the image starkly. Above him, patiently, Martin Ruben waited for him to identify Number Three only as the twentieth-century Julian Stanvall as a boy—as a once normal and healthy lad who had been the receptacle, as with all children, for those beliefs elders wish to bestow. In a way, this patient's "ghosts" were Dickensian images of the past haunting him in the present. Now Ruben saw it as his task to give Julian what he might believe, more contentedly, in the future.

"I see the third presence," Stanvall cried, "and it's—another man!" The report dismayed Martin; this fixation was powerful. "He's seized the stake and mallet!" Julian made a horrible grimace. "He detests me, he disapproves of everything about me . . ."

All right, Ruben decided, placing his bracing hands on the arms of his patient on the couch. "*See* his *face*, Julian. It's not really a man, surely it's a *boy*, isn't it? With features similar to what *yours* were?"

"I see him clearly now," Stanvall said, nodding agreement with his own words. "A man with fine, regular features. A generous, warm mouth; intelligent, bright eyes." Suddenly Stanvall writhed as if to twist out of the coffin in his mind. "He's placed the point of his stake against my *heart*!"

"Come forward in time *now*!" Ruben clutched his patient's shoulders, comprehension arriving too late. "Don't *do* it to yourself!"

Beneath him there was an abrupt and shocking concussion. Stanvall, it appeared then, had *imploded*. And winds surged up from the chest, lifting Ruben, forcing him—staggering backward—toward his window. He glanced down at his shirt and suit, expecting to find them soaked by poor Stanvall's blood, amazed and uncomprehending to see himself unmarked.

The window to his back stayed closed but the drapes rose in ferocious billows before slowly sagging. Without the appearance of life.

Then Martin rushed to his patient, forced himself to look down . . .

The only noticeable alterations in Julian Stanvall were the facts of his death stamped in awful terror upon his face, and the absence of the pouchlike wrinkles that had disfigured him. Gone now, Julian was far younger, regular-featured, and marred solely by the fright he would take to his real and permanent coffin.

If I do see the entity's face clearly, Julian had said, *I shall probably cease to exist.*

Ruben kneeled at the couch, a slender hand resting gently on his patient's arm. Stanvall had been haunted. By the younger man he could have been but was not allowed to become.

And the ghost of the future that never came had resentfully disapproved of everything Stanvall had done, whatever it had been.

The Writing of
"The House of Life"

Working with and for John Maclay of Balti-
more—then a publisher, mostly, now primarily a
versatile writer—was what got me my first flush
of notice as a full-time "man of the written word."
I must put it in some such way, because that
notice was primarily taken of the hardcover
anthologies *Masques* (1984) and *Masques II*
(1987). I edited them; Maclay & Associates published them.

Between the two, John donned an editor's hat
and self-published a theme anthology entitled
Nukes, to which he invited Jessica Amanda
Salmonson, Mort Castle, Joe R. Lansdale, and
me. Priced at $4.95, it won rave reviews and
proved what appeared on the back cover: ". . . Who
are better qualified really to show you what IT
would be like (nuclear war), to awaken you to the
need to prevent it, than writers who envision horror every day?"

Want to know how right John Maclay was? The Soviet Union stopped being communist! Who says the pen is no longer mightier than the sword?

The character Colin in "The House of Life" was based on a now-deceased, beloved friend of mine named Nigel. I wept over what befalls him here.

The House of Life

"When the house of life is thus thrown open, there may enter in that for which we have no name..."
—*Arthur Machen*

1.

When consciousness at last returned to Colin, it came in a rush to life so fast that agony itself wasn't instantly identifiable but a bewilderment which, instinctively, he knew was portentous. A sheer, evil omen. He found that he was crumpled at the bottom of a steep, damp shaft plunging down into the broken earth. Although he did not know how he'd gotten there, the fact that he didn't wonder about it was less the product of confusion than young Colin's nature. He'd always been pragmatic; an accepter, an adjuster.

What did trouble Colin was twofold: First, he

seemed trapped, and freedom of movement was always one of Colin's basic requirements. Second, all the sounds he heard in the world were his own raspy breathing and fierce winds that whistled far above his head. As if mocking and questing for him, summoning him.

In the next several moments, pain became fully identified and, for the time being, mentally filed away. Feeling disoriented, he crouched low against the dirt floor of the shaft instead of trying to rise, evaluating the extent of his injuries, seeking to retrieve his customary resolution. He didn't like abrupt change, never had. As a rule, the absence of noise had served as a kind of archetypal message to Colin's orderly brain that it was time to sleep. People had kidded him about that way Colin had, in the clipped days of winter, of beginning to yawn soon after the sun went down.

But craning his neck and staring up, he saw that it wasn't quite dark out; the combination of stark silence and unnatural illumination confirmed his initial judgments. Worse, while it decidedly wasn't bright, it didn't resemble sunshine, and Colin blinked at the radiance, then glanced away, nearly whimpering. Concentrating and trying to bring himself to greater awareness, he caught a deep breath—

Odors, disagreeably complex, smotheringly hot, filtered down from the earth above him. He saw then that he'd been knocked unconscious by the fall or he would surely have detected, immediately, the smells of cooking.

Smells of cooking, and charring, flesh.

2.

"You're well along. Certainly into the third trimester." He was that kind of man who generally moves so fast and so nimbly that his mouth worked and his eyes focused badly when obliged to stop. Hiding a glance at his watch, he strove to avoid speaking sharply to the pregnant girl. But the absurdity of being fairly sure he'd be delivering a child in such a place combined with his own youth and busy ways to make his tone inevitably peremptory. "How far?"

"I don't rightly know, Doc," she told him.

"See here!" He settled back until his well-tailored rump rested on one of the crates they'd been using for makeshift chairs, trying to ignore the oppressive, inches-thick door above his stylishly trimmed, curly head. "Your *boyfriend*"—the doctor paused, pointedly—"convinces me to drive all the way out here on what the fool survivalist has the gall to term 'an errand of mercy.' But meanwhile, he and his let's-pretend army bolts into the hills—leaving you behind in this—this jerry-rigged bomb shelter! Please be decent enough to answer my questions, *Miss . . . ?*"

"You're just riled because you should of let the City handle me, right, Doc?" She pushed up from the cot, leaned on her elbows. Despite how dirty she was, how very pregnant, she was a remarkably pretty child. *Of seventeen, eighteen at the outside,* Darren Hopper concluded. And she didn't try to tell him that the father was her husband, so at least she was honest. Her maternity apparel amounted to unzipped, faded jeans and a man's shirt. "Didn't you know that do-gooders can't be choosers?"

He watched her force an unmalicious smirk through a surge of expressive pain and knew he was right, that she was in labor. Which was why her vigilante lover had phoned, two hours ago. There might be time to move her if they'd had a phone installed in their underground tin can!

Hopper again glanced round, saw the generator, pyramiding canned goods and bottled water, five other neatly made cots. Sure; one for the anti-establishment yokel plus a quartet of cots for two additional couples. He saw a card table with candles that were burning and a crumbling Trivial Pursuit game; a Bullworker muscle toning device; a cheap Osco alarm clock; plastic-covered boxes filled with peanut butter–layered crackers; a broken shotgun and some shells.

Hopper saw no crib or bassinet, clothing, or food for an infant.

"I never seen no baby, Doctor," said his patient. She was cooperating, coloring with embarrassment as she spoke. "But I reckon I'm just over six months and"—she looked away—"m' water broke right 'fore you got here."

Dr. Hopper was up, running a hand over his long, black-curled hair. "My *God*, girl—you should be in a hospital! A preemie's chances in such—"

His stare of professional worry was centered upon the girl's somewhat bucolic, phlegmatic face and did not, to his knowledge, move as the first explosion came. Yet, somehow, he was gazing straight at one of the candles next to the old game and the candle began to shimmer, to streak yellowly as if frightened before expiring. That anomaly and a sudden descent into darkness, rapidly followed by pale illumination from beyond the shelter which hadn't previously penetrated it at all, concealed from Darren the other facts: that he'd been thrown to his knees, that the detonations were the loudest he'd ever head, that only his outflung arms had kept his pregnant patient from levitating into the air and falling to the floor.

It was the girl who, stretching from the cot, found and relit a candle and told Dr. Hopper what the two of them had heard. When he continued to gape wordlessly at her she also explained the meaning of the backlighting at the shelter door.

He could not take his eyes from her. When, again, she spoke, he stared at her lips as if he could no longer hear. "See, *that's* why Lloyd 'n the others went up in the hills." Her voice was so calm, so steady, that Hopper was increasingly appalled. "Ol' Jimbo, *he* got some kind of tip. We had ourselves quite a network, ackshally, and now my Lloyd's in charge." Incredibly, she brightened further. "Maybe—of everything!"

"But . . . he did not take *you*." Still on his knees beside her, he enunciated clearly because it seemed terribly important to be factual now. Entirely truthful, as if they were being observed and might be graded. "He left you behind—you, *and* his *baby*."

"Well, Lloyd wanted t'kill it two months back, so this ain't *his* fault." Her charming face showed pain as she shifted on the cot. "He warned me not t'get peegee 'cause they is no *place* for children in the world anymore. Jimbo tole us that most little children will be"—she paused, raising her huge eyes in self-derision, and grinning—"a-tom-ized."

Internally, the word did something to Hopper. That second incapable of speech, he nodded with gravity as if grasping that all she said would be important; a glimpse of fact, of penultimate truth. Then he began to stand. His knees did not support him and he dropped heavily upon one of them where he began to cry. In an instant, sighing, she put out her plump arms to draw his weeping face to her bosom, saying, "It'll be all right, hon," over and over.

Eventually, when he'd half unlocked, half battered open the door leading from the wrecked shelter, Darren Hopper stood on the vanished survivalist's barren ground, feeling heat coiling there like the insides of a space heater, and saw, rising from the center of the leveled city, his time's most common image of horror—a devilishly clever logo no ad man would have conceived. Dimly at best, he remembered he'd heard that, if you could still see the mushroom growing, see it filling out like some bloated lung inhaling humankind, you had looked your executioner in the eye and he had not blinked.

They is no place for childern now. Hopper, thinking limitedly, found himself free only to wonder about a human child who was being born at that exact moment when the world ended.

3.

Colin perceived that his vision had become accustomed to the semidarkness of the shaft and also saw that one wall had collapsed. Gouts of ghoul's earth had formed a hill, of sorts; it sloped from the wider base where now he stood, panting and claustrophobic, to a much narrower peak, ending at the top. At what Colin perceived as freedom. It was, he calculated, possible to escape by gathering every ounce of energy and *running*—faster than he'd ever run in his life. To freedom. Already he'd tried calling out for help and heard no reply but wind snuffling, swirling up dust.

There was no food, there was no water where, in last-second bondage to uncertainty, Colin crouched, craning his neck. There were no other options.

He was midway through his now-or-never rush up the rubble hill when, the hard way, he was reminded of his fall-incurred injury. A leg began throbbing as if small bones had been snapped in sequence; the leg could not go on functioning if the chain reaction spread. He kept going even while imagining—right before reaching the top— that he was doomed to tumble all the way down. Finding purchase, Colin suddenly burst back into the world and sprawled upon an earthen ledge, regaining his breath.

At once he covered his nose and shivered.

The wind and odor were far stronger here, but he didn't know which was making him shiver.

4.

He popped into the dining room entranceway with the air of a jaunty, honored dinner guest, smiling with his lips. "Ah—you're still here!" *Still unhurt; intact.* "And you're still trying to reach someone on the phone." *Still alive, thank God!* The eyes behind the lenses of his ponderous spectacles became moist, warm footlights.

"Of course I'm still here," Theresa replied. As usual, she nearly snapped at him. Nearly. Her head moved to the left, gaze dropping to her red-covered phone-and-address directory.

Nodding as she chose another name, another number, as if deciding whom to ask to her husband's special dinner, she rearranged the receiver in the softness formed by cheek and shoulder. "Where else would I *be* after all these years?"

He'd stayed in the entranceway, smiling tremulously. "Heaven. Hell. *No!*—Heaven, surely." Only his twitching lips moved and he was conscious of clownishness in old jeans baggy after the weight loss Doc said happened, sometimes, with older men who forgot to eat regularly, properly. But that was silly, since Theresa had made sure for forty years that anyone entering their house ate regularly, properly; heartily. Gerald added, smile settling in, "You're reading my mind again."

"You! You're as transparent as—transparencies." She was tender. "When the light's just so, I can see straight through you."

Gerald's hand, artistic slenderness covert beneath arthritis-swollen joints like small cauliflowers, moved nervously toward his shirt pocket, halted. The initialed cigarette case had been abandoned when the doctor, weighing him as well as listening to the mumbling maracas of his heart and lungs, suggested he quit. Suggested that *casually*, as if it hadn't mattered much. He turned the bumpy hand into a thumb indicating the front room, behind him, the front door, beyond. "Theresa, the light's just so now."

She was dialing again, still-dark brows curved in concentration.

"I want you to say something," Gerald said softly. "To *discuss*—what's happened."

Her clear, green eyes, more melting mint than chips of emerald, ransacked his expression before he saw her looking up. "There may not be much time."

"That's it, that's right." He bobbed a head heavy with gray snow, pleased. "There probably isn't." *And I remain alive, unlike the boy and Marge, probably.*

She put the phone back in its cradle. "I don't know what you want me to say." Her annoyance with him was concealed, as it usually was. "Or explain."

"I want to know why it didn't get us, too." He almost took a step closer, but this had to be talked out. If he held her in his arms, neither might ever speak again. "You're my science officer, Ms. Spock."

"It's because we live so far out in suburbia.

Maybe the blast didn't come this far." Theresa shrugged.

"It's within several blocks, to the south." Telling her, he was aware she already knew it, aware that he sounded accusatory. "Places down there are flat as fritters, those that remain at all. You can see through the front door window for yourself."

"Don't open that door," she said, seeing him turn slightly. As if two distinct people were speaking, she added mildly, "All kinds of showers and falls have a start and an ending. Everything—has edges."

"The hot stuff; today's showers." He proceeded mercilessly. "Do you imagine it's simply not *working* on us yet?"

"I don't think that." Her glance was to the old radio nearby, a gift to them from one of their sons, when it was new. When he still lived. But his was an old, a scarred loss. She located her crocheting and began afresh as if her lifelong hobby had no edges on either side. "We'd have known it if the radiation reached us."

"You think so, do you?"

"I *know* so."

"Dammit, Terry," he flared, "I asked why. *Why* didn't it get us, too? *Why* were *we* spared?"

The needle dipped, poked practicedly through, and rose as if independently on the opposite side. "Maybe they were wrong; the winds don't gust in every direction." Her serious eyes flashed. "Yet."

"No, it's bypassed us. Bomb and radiation alike." Scowling, Gerald shook his head. "And I think it's disgusting."

"I'm glad you're still alive," she said. Shrugged. "And I."

"Why were *we*—?"

"Perhaps it hit south of town, by miles." She made a mistake, cursed; she lay the crocheting aside with an expression of abject loathing. He'd never seen her fail to take an error in stride, and merely correct it. Maybe some mistakes really wouldn't be repaired. "How do I know *why* we survived? God—"

"*No.*" He flushed; the cheeks only, the rest of his unlined, boyish face paling. "*You*, perhaps. Not I." He half turned away. "I'm immune to nothing in this life. And *you* have been bombarded by everybody's fallout for three-quarters of a century! Who needs miracles now?"

"You said I read your mind," she murmured. "For forty years, you've secretly yearned to write all my remarks for me so I'd say what you wished me to say. Well, what was it I did right when I asked where else I could be, but here?"

He kept his face blank, buried his thoughts until he found a way to imply them. *You could have died of sickness out here, while I wept in the front room. That would have wrecked everything— our four-decade agreement.*

"I promised you," she said, believing she was again reading his thoughts. "That I wouldn't go before you."

Gerald stayed expressionless with miserable effort. He yearned to say, *That's not it; you promised me we'd go* together. *Except we know why Doc couldn't, or wouldn't, explain my weight loss. Why he never quite told* me *to quit smoking. You going first* is *the worst thing that can conceivably happen; but my going first, alone, is only second best. Surely you recall our pledge . . .*

Theresa was snatching up the receiver and pushing buttons. Precisely; tirelessly.

And this time, he went directly through the living room and opened the front door, stared to the south. To where it had finally happened. Why *here*, when there were better targets? But there might well be other places; TV had nothing to say for the first time in Gerald's experience. He strove to breathe shallowly but when he found he could not anymore, Gerald left the door open and continued looking out.

Hard to be sure, this far away. But most of Jefferson Road and 138th were gone, he thought. Two of the ruined homes he could definitely account for, three blocks away, belonged to the Wildinghams and to that Chinese American couple few of the neighbors spoke to. *I liked them,* Gerald reflected; *I like differences—a little. I didn't speak to them either.* When it occurred to him that the Lings had two infinitely tiny, infinitely beautiful daughters, Gerald's moist stare rose.

To the south, the sky reminded him of how it had looked, at dusk, that time they had attended an outdoor summer concert. The local symphony had played the *1812*, and the fireworks display had almost gotten out of hand. He'd adored it; the music, the blaze of many colors, the safe risk they'd taken, together.

No, it didn't look that way at all. The sky was like nothing he'd seen before except in modern paintings he and Theresa had avoided like the plague. . . .

Temp was stifling, yet unreadable except by his body, which pimpled, spasmed. A lonely ambulance siren sounded far off, like the old "Twilight Zone" show theme played at half speed. It stopped, suddenly, without warning; as if the ambulance could advance no farther and had been swallowed up by the burning, avaricious air. Whether he actually heard screams of agonized perishing then or the gravest stillness of his life, Gerald could not be certain. His ears were ringing. But something—some things—were afire that he'd never smelled before and he was beginning to cough and tear, simultaneously. Too much of the former's worst kind might finish him; too many of the latter might mark him a coward.

Quietly, he shut the door, hesitated, locked it carefully, as he had always locked it, even at midday. He smiled. Terry'd always assured him that there were few burglars in town brazen enough to strike before nightfall. He'd retorted that he hated thinking he was part of that innocuous or undesirable a citizenry.

He went on smiling with thoughts of his marriage after he'd gone to the writing desk in one corner of the front room. First he paused to be sure his wife was still trying to contact somebody on the phone; hearing the steady, stubborn way she went on punching telephone buttons, Gerald drew out a sheet of his uncostly, unostentatious stationery and unclipped his Papermate from his shirt pocket.

She had to believe she would reach Tim and her sister, he saw abruptly before beginning his note. *Thinking she can holds her in one piece.* Nodding, he wrote in his most legible scrawl: "I must rescue whomever I can. Go downtown, bring them back where we can tend them, if the hospitals are gone. Pray I make it, for their sakes." He lifted the pen from the paper to marvel again at her courage. Once, he'd said that he'd never seen her frightened; Theresa had replied as if she meant it, "You're underrating my intelligence. What it actually is, is that you've never seen me without fear. Consistency is what fools 'em."

And so your bravery lies in the way you've tried always to hide it, Gerald reflected. *I've never known how to do that for a full day.*

"My whole life, I've hated illogical things," he added to his letter, "and my sitting here, fundamentally alive yet surely dying soon, when

259

younger people who might make it are gone, insults my intelligence. Also, I told you that I didn't care much for heroes and have forever been the furthest cry from one. My going downtown now makes me true to some of those things I'd like to die believing in. And that is always the most rewarding and selfish thing a man may do, once he admits to himself that he's only *told* himself it is hard." Through slow, squeezed-out tears, Gerald glanced toward the dining room. Completing the note well was somehow vital, and all he could think to add was that it really appeared to be a gyp that *he* was the one to break their oldest pledge regardless of how he might try to bolt from his fate.

She was in the room with him so silently that her gaze met his at once, and Gerald instinctively covered his letter with one arm.

"The telephone is dead," she said, as if it were mildly exasperating news. As if they'd forgotten to pay the bill and might drive down to have it reconnected. She was, he thought, too full of what she was imparting to detect what he'd been up to. "So I turned on the radio. Waited. Some man with an *aw*ful accent said there was nothing whatsoever left of the Wedgewood apartment complex or of West Southgate and quite probably not the other communities southeast of them."

Marge's area. And Tim, since his divorce, had taken rooms in a dilapidated neighborhood. It was farther southeast yet, and that gave Theresa a microscopic fraction of hope that, to Gerald, she seemed indecisive about clinging to.

"I was thinking, probably he wasn't a real announcer at all." She wandered, generally, in his direction, snapping her left thumb and middle finger to internal rhythms that were accelerating, harsh. Near Gerald, she stopped to rest one icy hand on the arm hiding his message to her, and her mouth mimicked a laugh. "I think the poor man was the station manager or maybe the cleanup man; he said he'd be leaving in just a few minutes, but he went off the air in the middle of a sentence. *YOU CAN'T GO!*"

He felt her fingers dig into his arm; he'd never been more startled. She couldn't have possibly read his note and it was as if the wife he'd regarded as practical, sensible, his balance wheel, had acquired the gift of genuine telepathy or psychometry. He pressed down with his elbow, asked what she meant.

She only spun away in an encore to her vanished grace, manner frivolous and her face, when she turned, openly terror-stricken. "Before that man with the awful voice went off the air *I heard the wind*. It—*crackled*, that atrocious way cookie containers sound if you rip them open. And I heard *voices*, a studio audience, but I won't try to describe them." Her expression did not vary, despite her obvious fear for him, but she was perspiring heavily.

He captured her hands; she remained at arm's length, pulling in faint protest. He said, "I must attempt to help them."

"You can't. You *can't*. There are *too MANY*, don't you remember a *thing* you've read or heard?" Theresa was angry, vividly; her tensing musculature, her rising color, turned her decades younger. His wife was a beautiful, horrified ghost. "There's no WAY you can do anything—except *add* to the body count!"

He realized she had said nothing about the danger to herself—death—if he brought any of them home, and was sure it hadn't occurred to her. He also understood that people they knew, liked, loved, had become a *collective*, a "they."

Seeking to draw her into his arms, Theresa writhed away, shaking her head in a disagreeable, odd way. Desperately, he clung to one of her hands. "It's the way it was when people thought, now and then, about Ethiopia," he said quietly. "Remember when I became so . . . silly?"

She ceased struggling to pull away, mind engaged. *Of course that's what it takes,* he realized. *Why is it I could never remember that?* "You weren't as silly as mad to help," she recalled. "You really thought God might make you a millionaire because of your immense yearning to help—you said you'd use most of it to buy food for Ethiopian children."

He smiled with her. "People said there was nothing that could be done. That those people had to go on starving, and breeding, and again starving. That made it seem that permanent assistance was impossible. It was, only because most of us lacked any real will, faith, or imagination." He peered out of the living room window at the scar-struck sky. "I wanted to *go* to them, *do* . . ."

She stepped close with the mixed expression of big-sister teasing and womanly admiration that he'd rejoiced to see. "If you could be Emperor of the World, for three days, you said, you'd stop the horror—because then you'd have the resources to figure a way."

He patted her arm. "It was simply too far to go on an English teacher's pay."

The emerald light in her eyes said she understood at last where he was leading her. "And you added that saving any one, decent person from a peculiarly hideous, pain-wracked destiny was the Eleventh Commandment."

He kissed her small nose, then went to get what he planned to take with him. He waited for her to ask him to change out of his good clothes and, when she didn't, returned to kiss her lips. "Ethiopia," he said, "is *here* now. In a way, Terry, *it always was.*"

5.

On his feet at last, shaky, his jaw aching abruptly and leg paining him so badly that he limped, Colin inspected the total wreckage of all he'd known. In his old farming community, frozen in place, he saw it was that simple, that profound. It was garbage, twisted trash left for a mammoth trash pickup. Except that if they took the junk, and a mortician collected the human remains, nothing would be left there at all.

Edging away from the hole that had saved him when he was propelled into it, making fragmented noises deep in his throat, Colin was pummeled by the pungency of scorched flesh. All the people he saw, friend and stranger alike, were dead; yet they were few in number, and he sensed that there were others inside the few pathetic, battered farmhouse shells that stood.

Suddenly panicky, remembering, head partly cleared, Colin ran limpingly until he saw that he'd passed the place where his own house—his own people—had been, hours before. There was no trace of the home, of Mother, of Father. So he sat down on hot earth that seemed to be baking something beneath the surface, on the place where his own bed had been. He shifted, moaning, from one side of his body to the other; that keening noise he could summon to register his loss and his terror was whipped rudely away by the buffeting breezes that made his hair stand on end as if he'd been electrocuted. Nowhere—in any direction he peered—did he see, or sense, a living person, cat, dog, or bird. A dried-up old well had saved him.

He wondered bleakly, then, if there were water anywhere for him to drink.

6.

Dr. Hopper had scarcely returned to the interior of the ruined bomb shelter when he knew that the teenager's child was coming. With amazing alacrity; soon.

Yet the mother-to-be, whose name he had not learned, merely fastened her eyes' terrified gaze to her young doctor's, and struggled—labored, *worked*, with a single-minded, feminine effort that made him want to cringe. Giving birth *hurt*; it always did. But aside from a studied, purposive grunting, he saw, this one made no sound. It was as if she were listening to and obeying some wild imperative only she heard.

He marveled anew at the fact that this child was being born as civilization ended. Whether the girl and baby made it, her runaway lover, or isolated pockets of people everywhere, what they'd all termed "civilization" was over. The bleak perversity, the apparent *extraneousness* of the child on its way, obsessed Darren, and he wondered if that was because birth was a process he'd believed that he understood. It contrasted with what was *going* to happen *now*—the collective human nightmare turned real. Not the relatively recent, half-century psychological dominion of The Bomb, but an ancient, more deeply rooted bad dream.

For all those who'd died that day had faced their dreads; it was finished, for them—if continued, if cosmologically explained, in paradise. All those who were left had now to confront humankind's *paramount terror:* The Unknown at its strangest and most savage. This would be the time they discussed behind the fire they unleashed at the mouths of prehistoric caves . . .

They's no place for children, thought the doctor. Aborting it had been out of the question even before he arrived. But considering the poor thing's predetermined future, returning it painlessly to oblivion was not beyond Hopper's question. But it was very difficult to consider. (*Is that why it's coming so quickly, to get here before I can decide?*)

He worked at dredging up case histories he'd studied only a few years back, but came up dry, smarting with the injustice of his predicament. Yet it was true, wasn't it, that he'd been saved by this infant? Had its father phoned another doctor, Darren Hopper would already be a city statistic—assuming any statistician remained alive. True; his life wouldn't be long. He'd surfaced. Yet he felt fine, physically; his dying seemed, however stupidly, remote.

At the instant Darren gave up trying to remember something of his profession that remained useful, fairly recent scientific facts soared into his conscious mind—with such implications that he gazed down, startled, at the familiar, biological process—in fresh and stunning dread.

Hopper had recalled data about that section of the brain's hypothalamus called the suprachiasmatic nucleus; the "biological clock"—one more function a human mother performed for her baby-to-be, another synchronization, in a way, between her and her infant /*Was it any wonder some mothers found it hard to let go?* / involving the nerve cells, the pregnant woman subconsciously *ordered and commanded instructions* that *told* the baby *when to be born*.

J.N. Williamson

A human fetus knew the *time* in the world *beyond its womblife*, and much more; the mother's unknowing services were truly miraculous, Hopper perceived; the mechanism actually *prepared* a newborn for its entry to the world. But what would be *unusual* about a speeded-up birth under these unspeakable conditions; and what of the mother's helplessness or her sense of *guilt* in bringing a child into such a—

It was coming, now. Cursing the primitive circumstances in which he was obliged to function as he had been prepared, Hopper strove to put new fears from his mind. He told himself he was being neurotic; absurd. Unscientific, if that could still be construed as condemnation, now. Yet it *was* a fact that this heaving, sweating, silent pretty girl had spent her six months of pregnancy with the absolute faith that her Lloyd */He wanted t'kill it two months back/* and his cronies were *correct* in believing that nuclear war was inevitable, imminent; and now she *and* her baby had learned that the damn rutting cover-his-own-ass Lloyd *was* RIGHT */No place for childern now/*! And how could a responsible man or responsible woman continue to exist in a world in which a Lloyd was *more* insightful about the *basics* of human life? How—

. . . The child of humanity's tomorrows was born, and it *howled*. Not in threat, there was nothing left to threaten or even to *want*, but in an emotional resonance of knowing protest that seemed sepulchral to Hopper but which was otherwise—unidentifiable.

Averting his gaze momentarily, Hopper cut the cord and held onto the child; it took the professional, willed effort of his short career but, holding it, he turned his back to prevent the mother from seeing it. His presence of mind was sublime;

266

quite possibly self-salvationary. Then Hopper cursorily examined it.

No fingers; none. Or feet. It had no ears. It lacked skin in numerous places and appeared calcinated—incandescent. He detected the rudimentary evidence that it was male; yet it possessed no normal genitalia. Hopper grunted deep in his throat, began to sigh. He decided it was probably, beneficially, blind. There was no way to weight the infant but, in his limited experience, young Hopper had never seen a newborn who was rib-revealingly emaciated. Thinking at some wobbly level of his mind of an earlier, another holocaust, he enfolded the baby creature in the cleanest-looking rag of a sheet he had been able to find in the shelter and, at last, turned. His own eyes were madly brilliant, but he wasn't aware of that, and his smile made every tooth ache, but he intended to try to lie convincingly to this girl by shrugging off the way the poor thing looked and saying earnestly that her son had a chance at survival.

He almost slipped and fell. Because the new mother had delivered the afterbirth and gone on, gone on, gone *on* bleeding as if Lloyd or some other warped thing had repeatedly stabbed her. She was still spurting it, and an arm supported by a filthy pillow was thrust up, as if reaching, trying to take and hold her infant boy; and Hopper knew with a rush of unscientific certainty that something *fine* within this mother was making her empty herself of her life's blood; and she hadn't survived the entirety of her infinitely inhuman ordeal.

After he'd placed the newborn against her arm and her still breast, Hopper ran. *Rushed* outside, leaving the shelter door wide. *Charged* the wasted world and *screamed* at it like a man in a morgue looking for someone who wanted to fight. Soon, a buzzing fly in the distance, no more, nothing mattered to Dr. Hopper, either.

7.

Since he had no notion where else he might go, Colin stayed in the immediate region until what passed for night came queerly on, the meaty columns of smoke rising like shamans' secrets, becoming peculiarly more evident against the alien luminosity. No such colors had been seen on the planet before, and some were beautiful, mystical, eternal; it was as if Earth's surface designer of what would be considered natural had dug a deep hole near the molten core and buried such hues and tints there, saving them for this eventuality. It was as if God preferred, when the planet was done, to see it all out in a guise of original beauty that might lie to Him and say that it had not been completely a failure.

But Colin was color-blind and the wind, passing inheritor of the dead planet, was playing with itself triumphantly, cavorting like something idiotic in a series of lusty victory dances. The wind brought to Colin the ultimately pointless, arguably boring scent, of the inedible dead.

While able, Colin lay flat on his belly, groping beneath charred scraps of wood and plastic that had been chairs and other furniture, questing for something of his in the rubble of a structure wherein he'd spent his life. When, eventually, Colin found it, a spasm of ludicrous joy made him vault to his unsteady feet, automatically glance around to learn if anyone or anything had witnessed his find.

But no one, no thing, was there to see or to stop him. He carried his prize back to the deep shaft from which he'd come and crept, cautiously, into the moaning earth. Wincing and apprehensive, he slid down the slope awkwardly. But all the way down, Colin held tenaciously to his dearest possession, inordinately relieved.

At the well's bottom, falling wearily to his side, an instant need for air made Colin forget his throbbing leg. Much too late, he was suddenly ravenous, too, and all but intolerably thirsty. He felt *aglow* with his own bodily radiation; kindled, ignited. When he thought of Father and Mother in the closing chambers of his brain, it was with such anguish that he cried out and snuggled his prize close to his face. *They* had given it to him, used it to play games with him and show how much they loved and needed him. And he *wanted* them, then, he clung fiercely to their memory—

Even as their human faces, their hearty existences, began to fade from his addled and poisoned brain for good.

8.

"You'll die," she had advised him pointedly. "We were spared—but if you go, you will *die*."

Gerald thought of her warning as, again, he turned the steering wheel aimlessly, forging another path through the wreckage, the dead and dying bodies, so honest with himself that he admitted he was passing from the outskirts of shock to the boneyard of desensitization. He had driven his old pickup truck down here to hell two hours ago, finding precious few humans who were able to stand, or sit, finding himself filling with the certain knowledge that the distinction between "living" and "dead" had never been so narrow, even in emergency wards or intensive care or on death row, finding himself unable to invite into his truck those living dead who would only bestow upon him the pointless task of burying them near Theresa's flower beds.

Finding himself incapable of desiring to associate with the unattractive smoldering, the unaesthetically naked, the exhortingly praying or cursing or clearly and violent mad; learning about himself that he lacked the stomach—the heart or the soul—for a mission among the irremediably poisoned and exfoliated.

Now there were merely the trunks of trees, structures, menandwomen. The legs of tables, chairs, people. He thought then of "Alice," devouring a cake of which she knew nothing, growing until she cried, "Oh, my poor little feet, I wonder who will put on your shoes and stockings for you now, dears?" Then she'd found herself becoming small again, and shrinking rapidly, and finding out just in time; and Alice had gasped, "That *was* a narrow escape—"

Before she perceived that she "never was so small as this before, never!"

Gerald had gone; so had Theresa, neither of them surprised by that or by the fact that he had not asked her not to accompany him. They'd taken the truck because it was part of the vaguely conceived program of mercy Gerald had improvised; and three times they had stopped beside downtown shoppers or clerical workers long enough to make an offer of the sandwiches Theresa had made and carried in their picnic hamper. Two people had simply stared at the neatly prepared sandwiches until Theresa left them on the curb and Gerald drove off, accelerating faster than he had since his youth. The third person, a seemingly unmarked man in his early twenties, had taken two of the cold meatloaf sandwiches and promptly thrown them at Gerald's gravely missionary face.

Things they saw other living people doing, to the breathing and permanently out of breath alike, weren't consciously recalled for more than a block. Neither old person could have remained sane had they even remarked upon such sights.

By nightfall, a temporal circumstance mainly fixed by Gerald's wristwatch, they had covered most of the city's downtown region and found themselves farther south, yet still in what the press had called "the inner city." Thinking he might try to reach Tim's neighborhood, Gerald checked his gas gauge for the first time.

"Why, there is less than a quarter of a tank left," he said to his wife, beside him.

"That isn't enough to get home," she commented, looking from the bizarrely forming shadows of the evening slums without change of expression, to Gerald. "Or anywhere much. Is it?"

"Of course it is!" he exclaimed. He turned left and saw ahead of them, a few short blocks distant, a number of figures moving restlessly in the center of the street and in the gutter. Gerald patted his wife's hand. "No . . ." He sighed. "I don't think it is enough—quite."

Theresa didn't comment immediately. She was looking quietly at the gathering of young black people, most of them men scarcely out of their teens, whom the truck was slowly catching. "Stop here," she said suddenly, as if the burnt-out hotel she indicated might be open for dinner. When he'd pulled up to the curb, carefully parking parallel to it before killing the engine, she gave Gerald her prettiest smile. "You remember this place? The restaurant?"

Switching off the lights, he sensed the stifling shadows enfolding them. He squinted through the window. "I sure do," he said. "We celebrated our twenty-fifth anniversary here. What a

271

spread—it was a veritable *feast*!" The grin that had been making its arduous way to his mouth slipped away. "But they didn't keep the place up."

"We never went back to it," she said, nodding. A block away, loud voices, words heard only in rented movies, cut the reeking air like a blade. Theresa reached behind her seat, produced two handfuls of meatloaf sandwiches. "Hungry? *I* am!" She peeled away the wrap, took a big bite, and made a giggling, girlish noise of amusement. She held out two sandwiches to him. "I used catsup."

"Hold on," he said, groping behind the driver's seat. He came up, smiling, with two bottles of Pepsi and used a church key to snap off the caps. "Something to wash it down with," he added, handing Theresa her bottle.

Gratefully, she took a healthy swig and was breathless, pink-cheeked, when she lowered the bottle with a laugh. "Do you have music to aid our digestion?"

"But of *course*, madam!" he exclaimed, pushing a button to hear the tape deck he had slipped into place before they left the house. "I believe this may be to your listening satisfaction."

After a pause, Gerald turned up the volume. All the way.

She leaned close to him, at once smiling and very somber. "I never forgot our pledge; our promise."

He held her, kissed her. "I never really thought you did, Terry," he lied. Then he leaned back in his seat, looked out at the figures looming at the front of the pickup. *Most of us lacked any* real *resolve, faith, or imagination*, he thought a second time. *I wanted to go to them—but it was simply too far to go*. Aloud, he inquired: "Together?"

She took his hand, squeezed it. *"Together."*

He opened the door, stood in the street, found it was raining unremically. He felt as if a dark forest had sprung up around him. He chose the largest one, who was powerfully built, virtually nude, so badly burned facially and down over one massive shoulder to the mammoth fist that clasped the Saturday night special, that he was clearly out of his mind with pain. Gerald sensed that one of them, a girl, had moved round the truck to Theresa's side and was waiting, anticipatorially, by his wife's door. The *1812* was blaring so loudly that Gerald had to repeat what he'd already said for the first time in his life.

"*Nigger,*" he shouted. Scalded; he hoped God understood why he was saying it, then, again, louder: "*Nigger.*"

There was a glimpse of the black woman reaching inside the truck on Theresa's side to seize the Pepsi empty and smash its mouth against the fender, and time to feel genuine amazement that she was so very *thin*.

Something hard was rammed into his stomach, and.

9.

No one else existed in the world for Colin, whether it was a fact or not. That sort of ignorant acceptance, of complete belief, created realities, such as expiring on the floor of an evaporated well—a lightless hole in the ground. A pit that might as well have been bottomless.

Rolling over onto his stomach, Colin took the old rubber bone between his strong jaws, held an end of it down with a sizable paw, and began chewing on his prized toy, earnestly. His mood comprised simple, canine contentment and an unfearful awareness that his miseries were fanning out—from his broken hind leg to his sick belly to the other areas of his furry, sheepdog's body. When blood appeared on the rubber bone, it surprised him; but Colin went on chewing, good-humoredly mauling it, as a long night gathered on the earth he would never see again, and the light at the top of the shaft went out.

"If they had not opened the door of the south, / They would have feasted for ever."—Arthur Machen

The Writing of "A. Pyme"

Although this collection includes most of my best short fiction, it does not have all of it. I resisted the temptation to reprint, once again, "They Never Even See Me" and seven others gathered in Pulphouse's *Author's Choice* issue 24 (September 1991) with the exception of "Public Places," a particularly strong and memorable tale. That collection, with the title *The Naked Flesh of Feeling*, was recommended for a Bram Stoker award and the inference may be drawn that No. 24 had a good many readers.

Immodestly or just truthfully, I wrote some other worthwhile yarns since '91 that aren't present here because of extensive availability in other paperbacks or in prominent publications. Some of the former stories include a handful in the Gelb/Elliott *Hot Blood* series; "Just One More Thing People Do" in *Dark Seductions*; a favorite, "Frankenstein Seen in the Ice of Extinction" in

J.N. Williamson

Martin H. Greenberg's *Frankenstein: The Monster Wakes*. Some of the latter include the topical "Time Tells *Us*" in both *Pulphouse* and *VB Network*; the Sherlockian "Adventure of the Man Who Never Smiled" in *Holmes for the Holidays*; a pair of powerful pieces in handsome *Palace Corbie*; "Drowning in the River of No Return" in *Marilyn: Shades of Blonde*; and "Beasts in Buildings Turning 'Round" in Ed Gorman's *Night Screams*. The last-named would certainly be included except it was selected for *Mystery Scene*'s *The Year's 25 Finest Crime and Mysteries* anthology.

Maybe you notice that many of these later stories I cited are by no means horror fiction or horror fiction *primarily*. The next tale here certainly is not, and even though it contains elements of dark fantasy, the wife-and-husband game around which it moves isn't even fictive. It is, in a word, autobiographical. I am a man who always carried a great deal of change, or is on his way to convert dollar bills into quarters, dimes, nickels, and pennies. Read "A. Pyme," published here for the first time, and you'll learn why I never like to see a dime and a cent together!

A. Pyme

Everything about his job was turning sour, and
Ted Daggett's mood was beginning to head in the
same direction when his wife, Cathy, called to
him from the bedroom one night, "I just found
some money on the headboard. I think the fairies
left this for me."

Ted, stepping out of the tub after a quick
before-bedtime shower, automatically grinned.
"Sure they did," he said sarcastically, toweling
down. "It's my change. Actually, I left it there
when I took my nap before dinner."

Cathy didn't immediately answer. He pictured
her undressing in the next room and almost
didn't put on his pajama pants. Cath knew he was
worried about continuing to make payments on
the new car they'd bought prior to Alex Clayton
coming aboard and starting to make life miserable for Ted and his whole crew. But he *had asked*
old Mr. Loring if his job was secure, and the car

was new only to Ted and Cathy. How could he have known Clayton would be such a slave driver and take such an instant dislike to him? The bastard was—

"I checked, and not one of these coins has your name or initials on it, Ted."

Ted's mouth turned up at the corners. Some wives helped their husbands by taking phone calls from Mom and convincing them that son definitely would phone on the weekend, and other wives held well-paying jobs or planned excitingly romantic evening that made their mates believe the honeymoon had never ended. *His* wife created whimsical nonsense games for just the two of them to enjoy—delightfully silly games that never put a stress on the family budget.

All that was ever required to participate in Cathy's anxiety-relieving creations was make-believe. With this new game she was inventing, Ted knew instinctively he should follow Cath's lead while insisting he didn't believe in fairies—not exactly the hardest role to play, since he didn't.

"Well," he said, opening the door to the bedroom, "you must know the names of the fairies who leave money for you. Otherwise, no self-respecting husband could let his wife accept gifts from a bunch of strangers one or two inches high!"

She wore only her bra and panties where she sat on the edge of the bed. She turned to him with an arm outstretched, the palm up. Her eyes were almost as bright as the coins she showed him: an ordinary nickel and three pennies. "See, honey?" she asked. "The *oprickel fairy* came!"

Ted's smile widened. He turned it into a mock frown. With her enthusiasm, her short-cropped brown hair, and her intelligent green eyes wide, she reminded him of a delighted child. "How d'you know," he asked, sitting on the bed and kicking off his slippers, "the fairy was—well, whatever you called him?"

She wiggled up on the mattress to lie next to him, looking put upon. "There are three pennies, like the *Three Penny Opera*, and also a nickel. Who else could it *be* but the oprickel fairy?"

He pretended to marvel at her logic. It wasn't difficult, since he'd marveled many times at Cathy's faculty for injecting humor into their lives during nine years of childless marriage. "I do believe," he said, kissing her, "that shark ol' Mackie is back in town!"

The next morning's work went more pleasantly for Ted. He found himself thinking from time to time about Cath's new penny-fairy game and how lucky he was to have a woman such as his wife who trusted him to do the best he could on his job and preferred good-humored playfulness to a constant insistence that he earn more money.

In the afternoon, though, Alex Clayton established a goal—a quota—for Ted's sales team to achieve in the next campaign, and it was nearly 20 percent more than Mr. Loring, the company president, had ever expected. Ted knew then that his best people, Suzy Carlon and Ken Benson, would have to carry the load, because his only real friend on the team was too worried about his sick child to do better. He realized he should have fired Dick Craig months ago—"replaced him" was how Clayton would have expressed it—but the Craigs had invited Cathy and him to a dinner celebration once, and now little Brandon Craig seemed a sort of unofficial godson.

Driving home, Ted was acutely aware of the car itself and the two years of payments to make before it would really be his and Cath's. If only

279

J.N. Williamson

Loring hadn't hired that damn Clayton! What truly scared Ted was the possibility of oily Alex getting so close to the old man that Loring might believe he had to cooperate with all of Clayton's ideas—even if one of them turned out to be "replacing" the company sales manager. Lord, it was good to be going home that night.

Roughly an hour before Cathy and he usually went to bed, Ted went upstairs to slip stealthily into the bedroom. Tiptoeing and smirking, he placed a dime, a nickel, and a penny on the headboard on his wife's side of the bed.

They watched the late news together, Ted sneaking peeks at Cathy to try to decide if she too remembered the new game and might be thinking over what to say when she found a different penny-fairy had paid her a visit.

He undressed quickly in the bathroom and sat down on the john to listen to the sounds of Cathy bustling around in the next room. Then—*clink!* She'd moved something on the headboard! She'd located the change he'd left for her!

He called casually. "Any sign of fairy tracks in there tonight?"

Cath's answer drifted to him slowly. He knew she was figuring out this good fairy's name. "The best kind of sign—cold cash!"

Ted grinned broadly. "Who was this one?"

"Honey," she answered with sudden certainty, "the *pickelime fairy* came!"

Something joyful—too childlike and comprised both of make-believe and absurdity to be released in actual laughter—frolicked deep in Ted. He realized also there was another element to the fun, and it had something to do with long, loving marriages.

She was kneeling on the bed with an enormous jar between her knees when he went into the room. Beside her, propped against a pillow, was a vastly smaller jar into which Cathy was depositing the night's nickel and dime. Last night's nickel was already there.

Cath glanced up at Ted and dropped this evening's penny into the great jar, where it failed to make last night's trio of copper coins look any less insignificant. "I have a sort of hunch we'll see more of the penny-fairies themselves than the bigger ones," she explained about the larger bottle. "But it won't matter how big or small they are, because I love 'em all!"

When she lifted the two jars off the bed and squeezed them under the table where she also kept her current reading, Ted noticed she was naked.

Over the next few days, he watched the new routine in his life develop, and had very mixed emotions about it. At work, pal Dick Craig struggled badly while the more skilled Suzy and Ken tried to cover for him by improving their own sales. After the latter two started to mutter about Craig, Ted got on the phone for all three salespeople and did what he could to close a few additional sales. Clayton examined their totals each morning, shaking his balding head disapprovingly. Ted realized he saw less and less of Mr. Loring.

At home, even though he was reluctant to spoil things, he began to see Cathy's game as also becoming a routine, in part because he always needed to be sure he had change in his pocket. Feeling grouchy, he grumbled at Cathy one night when he'd accidentally left a dime and a penny on consecutive occasions. "The *pime fairy* came again tonight," she caroled at him from the bedroom. "He must like *me* a *lot*!"

"*P*" *from penny, "ime" from dime*, Ted recalled

her similar explanation of last night. "I don't think I want the damn fairies liking you. Or for the pime fairy even to come back!" he added while he was soaping his hands.

"Ted!" Cathy replied. "You *can't* be jealous of a tiny little fairy."

He got the Nuprin bottle from the medicine cabinet, shook two into his hand, and washed them down. "Well, what do we *know* about them?" He barged into the bedroom. "Miniature weirdos who hide out in the grass and under rocks, and probably don't even have any genitals!" She'd already put the dime away and he was in time to hear the penny rattle around in the huge jar, somehow underscoring his fears of being fired and left to survive on small change. "Who knows where they've been?"

Cathy picked up the true crime book she was reading, smiled at him as he lay next to her. "I know *enough*," she said.

"Okay," he grumbled, "but I won't have that horny damn pime fairy crawling around on our bed and pillows again!" Remembering himself, he kissed her cheek. "Not that you have any control over who comes, I guess," he said fondly.

On the following day he passed Mr. Loring in the hall at work and noticed two shocking things. First, the big boss was suddenly aging markedly.

Second, he didn't speak to Ted. He didn't even appear to notice him!

That night he rested two dimes inside the headboard, doing so almost by rote, and Cath, at bedtime, identified them as the "dime twins." Ted thought she sounded tired, or concerned, and knew his mood around the house hadn't exactly been sunny lately. "That name isn't very imaginative," he said when he entered the bedroom. But Cathy just showed him the pair of dimes. She asked in her usual playful manner, "What *else* would you call them?"

Ken phoned in ill Wednesday, costing the team a day they'd never get back, and Ted did his level best to fill in. Craig got in the spirit of things and produced his top day of the campaign, but Suzy was irritable over something her live-in said and barely covered her daily quota. Ted felt Alex Clayton's eyes boring into his back like ice picks all the way to the elevator when he left the place, even though it was five forty-five.

Things appeared to be going from bad to worse. He told Cathy he was thinking of unloading the car, trading down somehow, and she sought to cheer him up by reminding him there were several more days left in his campaign. He found himself yearning only to be asleep, absent from the world awhile, so it wasn't until Cath had used the bath and was heading for bed that Ted thought about the game. He loosened a few shirt buttons, irked by his own lapse, annoyed with himself, really with everyone—

And his wife announced happily, *"Somebody's come!"*

The afternoon headache was back. For the life of him Ted couldn't remember dropping any change in the customary spot. He didn't hear her identification of the visiting elf. He merely listened to the coins falling into the suitable jars and didn't press the matter.

Two days later he forgot again, but by then he had realized what had surely happened: Cathy, unwilling to close out the game when she found no coins, had obviously used some change of her own so his feelings wouldn't be hurt over forgetting.

Friday night he came home after a hideously long sales conference called by Alex Clayton, and was so worried and exhausted he only wanted to go to bed. He knew for a fact he hadn't played penny-fairy and yet, when Cath obligingly agreed to retire early too, she found loose change in the headboard. Ted was with her in the bedroom at the same time, he *saw* her pick up the coins he definitely had *not* left for her—

"The pime fairy came," Cathy said offhandedly, then reached for her familiar savings jars.

Ted saw with real, rising anger how hastily she pushed the two coins into their respective slots. Two nights before she might have been sparing his feelings; now she had not only put a dime and penny in plain view but was pretending to try to get the offending coins out of his sight. He snapped, "I *told* you I don't want that little pervert hanging around here."

Cath paused with only her blouse removed, staring at him with the guileless eyes of the child she seemed to have become. It took him a second to understand, and he didn't really get it until she spoke. "You also said you realized *I* have no control in the matter," she said, her tone an unfamiliar mixture of flat, factual statement and the lingering little-girl capacity for make-believe.

He saw it was his opportunity to halt the game then and there; and he passed.

With an icy sensation in his belly very much like fear, he realized that any other choice could lead to the end of other situations he cherished more than the whole world.

He made sure, both weekend evenings, to leave money. *But not a pime*, he thought the second night, till he told himself "they" were nothing but a penny and a dime. By the time he drove home at the end of a depressing Monday he had reflected quite a bit about the character of the "fairies" who were cheering up Cathy, and concluded they were a bunch of cheapskates and phonies. A wife who tolerated his lousy income, his small successes, deserved better, more! He made it a point Monday and Tuesday to leave a wider assortment of change, that included a quarter and a pair of pennies Monday, and *two* quarters on Tuesday. (Cathy identified the single quarter plus two cents as the "quarterenny fairy," and began to keep her quarters in one of Ted's discarded Sucrets boxes.) *So much for the horny damn pime*, Ted told himself with satisfaction before falling asleep each night.

Wednesday, Alex Clayton returned, unwelcomed, from some sort of business trip. A forty-ish man with pink skin and a hairline balding in a way that made Ted imagine he was tearing it out a few infuriated strands at a time, Clayton acknowledged that the sales crew was not far behind pace for their quota but added, pointedly, "Of course, time is running out."

So Ted took his failing friend Dick Craig out to lunch for a pep talk. First he had to listen to an update of Craig's child Brandon's latest health problems, but the business phase of the conversation went better than Ted had expected. Dick took it well that he needed to hold up his end of the campaign and produce a personal best the last few days, or the whole team could be out on the street.

But then Craig was asking Ted a question with an expression of mixed curiosity and apparent concern on his pleasant homely face. "You just got back from the cashier with several dollars worth of change. I couldn't help but notice. Ted—what do you do with all those coins?"

An instant turned into a full two or three seconds. Ted could think of nothing to say. Dick's question seemed intolerably personal, something along the lines of "How's your sex life?" But of course there was a really understandable answer, if he could just think how to word it.

What he came up with was, "Why do you ask?"

"You always have a pocketful of change these days," Craig said with a shrug. "That's all." The curiosity and concern in his face deepened, but switched their order. "We can hear you jingling wherever you are in the office, pal. It's your new trademark! Look," he said, "if it's a problem, or a big secret, I'm sorry I asked."

"Cath's coin collection," Ted said fast. The idea leaped to his mind like the rebuttal to a customer's objection. He was sweating, though, he knew. Buckets. "She's looking for . . . certain coins." Abruptly Dick's questioning seemed like interrogation, and he struck the table slightly with his fist, then tried to pretend it was just an accident. Who was this crummy salesman—who kept his job simply because Ted Daggett was too kindhearted to fire him—to cross-examine anybody?

Yet lying to a man he'd known for years troubled Ted the rest of the day, even during another brief but insulting lecture from Clayton. Increasingly it felt, Ted realized while he and Cathy munched on Big Macs he'd brought home, that the one place he could be at peace—safe—was wherever Cath was. And keeping her at this particular point of their marriage appeared to mean keeping the game going. It boiled down to Cathy making him feel loved by appreciating the way he remembered to leave change for her—giving her an excuse not to complain about how tight things had become economically—and him enabling her to pretend there was a little magic left to the world—and in their marriage.

That night, he left a generous assortment consisting of three quarters, two pennies, and a nickel—Cathy figured it out and shouted, "The puarkleuarteruarterenny fairy was here!"—and the two of them laughed like children, then made love more wholeheartedly and satisfyingly than they had for months.

"When we've both had rough days," Cath whispered as he turned off the light, "it's so wonderful that the marvelous fairies take care of us at night."

Ted scowled through the darkness in the direction of the savings jars. Alex Clayton got all the credit for what Ted and his team were accomplishing, and now the nonexistent "wee folk" were receiving the praise for him remembering to be a good husband, and he couldn't say a word about either injustice!

Before leaving the house Thursday he realized he hadn't paid the cable bill, and groused to Cathy that it might be time to dispense with such luxuries.

"It's okay, the fairies paid it," she answered, and Ted slopped coffee into his saucer. She laughed lightly. "I noticed you hadn't, so I took most of my fairy money and got a money order at the grocery. I spent all but a dollar or two, but see how sweetly they're still taking care of us?"

Embracing Cath at the door, he glared out at the first uncomfortably chilly day of winter and wanted very much—maybe too much—not to leave, but to spend the day with Cathy. Was this how agoraphobia began? "I guess I wish the little people would take care of my problems at work," he said, and departed.

Dick didn't arrive until eleven o'clock, and then it was to say he was quitting. "If you like, I'll finish out the campaign," he told a stunned Ted. "I can't go on ruining things for the team because of worry about my boy. Besides, I have a line on

287

something less risky. That creep Clayton is just too much to take."

"Absolutely, I want you to finish up," Ted answered, nervously jiggling the change in his pants pocket. "Our goose is really cooked if you quit now."

"Okay." Dick drew a sheet covered with handwriting from his briefcase. "My wife likes reading about myths and superstitions. I mentioned this obsession you have about saving change and she looked this up, copied it for you to read. Okay?"

"What obsession?" Ted asked. But he spread the sheet in front of him on the desk and read it. "Coin saving is said by some experts to have grown from the British myth of fairies who exchanged coins with mortals for favors," the first sentence read. Ted glanced at Craig with ill-concealed surprise. "Called Portunes," the article continued, "they have animal-like teeth and puff their cheeks. Wearing caps, the Portunes enjoy visiting maidens' bedrooms and doing somersaults and cartwheels on their beds."

"My wife has a theory, Ted."

"Dick," Ted said shakily, "this stuff is medieval. What is it your wife believes?"

"That everybody has these ancient memories," Craig said slowly, "and they surface when we're under a lot of stress, except the details get all confused. She said Jung even believed in a sort of collective consciousness." Suddenly grinning, Dick pointed to the floor. "Down by your right foot, buddy—some of your cash hoard got squeezed out of your pocket!"

Ted mulled over what his friend had said until he was home that evening. He knew he was turning into no "Portune"—hell, it wasn't *he* who concocted the game!—but what Craig's wife pointed out suggested he might be getting a little neurotic. Getting jealous of the "penny-fairies" last night was an example. He decided he'd leave nothing at all that night, as if it were the most natural thing in the world to do. Which it was! If Cath brought it up, he'd say directly he was bored with the game. Or if she left a few coins herself, he'd try to ignore the entire thing. If he himself didn't make a big deal of the game for a few nights, it would die a natural death. Life was real, earnest, tough; Clayton making Craig quit was a new proof of that.

The evening was both uneventful and tense, and Ted's proposal that they go upstairs an hour early met with immediate approval.

Then, "Somebody big came!" Cathy called to him in the john. He simply grunted, but she'd sounded extremely excited, or was pretending to be—Ted couldn't tell the difference any longer. "How big?" he called back. "I thought the Fairy-land Bank dealt only with small change."

He patted his red eyes with a damp washcloth when she didn't reply. Then he swallowed a rare Halcyon and went to the bedroom curious, despite every effort.

Cath had a crisp example of new folding money in her hands.

She exhibited to him an American five-dollar bill that had never been folded.

And in addition, left on the headboard on Cathy's side—but not by him, Ted would swear that!—was a damnable *pime*! No, *no*, just a penny and a dime! Ordinary coin of the realm. But he glanced to the five his wife held and back to the pair of coins that had a *name* . . .

"I can't decide if this new visitor was the *fiver* or the *primer fairy*," Cathy said reflectively, "or if *two* fairies came, making the *piverime!*"

"Stop," Ted begged, too softly to be heard. Back

J.N. Williamson

to her, he sank down to his side of the bed. "Stop this."

"You know, I think this is like an early award or something, that it means you're going to meet your quota. And Alex Clayton will change his mind about you." She wrapped her arms around him. "I think it may be a really good omen!"

He couldn't pull away, didn't want to. Cath was only striving to make him feel better when she thought he'd forgotten to leave coins, and she could do it these days by going on with the game if it drove them mad—just holding fast to what they shared. Now she was half-naked and kissing him for his nonexistent generosity in not persisting with the truth, that he had left *nothing* on the headboard this night—

Which she must know, *of course*, he thought, finding tears in his eyes as he lowered his face to kiss her where nobody else had the right. "It was a single fairy who visited. I couldn't sleep if I thought the pime was back in our room. Near you."

Alex Clayton summoned Ted to his office first thing in the morning. Looking across the desk at the balding SOB reminded Ted of how pleasant meetings had been with Mr. Loring and how Mr. L's infrequent appearances in the office now probably meant that he and Ted would enjoy no further chats.

"Your team isn't going to make it," Clayton said bluntly. "They'll come *close*, I'll give you that. But business isn't horseshoes."

"Business is reality," Ted said tonelessly, taking one of his superior's Kleenexes and trying to wipe away the sudden bad taste on his lips.

Alex continued awhile in the same vein, and

290

then stated firmly that the sales team *had* to fulfill its quota "or there definitely will be changes. From the top down."

For an instant Ted thought seriously about strangling the man. "Mr. Loring said I was so secure as manager we could buy a new car. Not exactly 'new,' but—"

Clayton raised his palm to interrupt. "Business is also dynamics, change. Mr. Loring is considering selling the company, Teddy—and retiring." Alex was the only one who called Ted that. The man touched his fingertips to his chest, beamed. "Care to surmise who plans to acquire it?"

The rest of Friday passed in a relatively merciful blur. Suzy and Craig each informed Ted at five o'clock that they had exceeded their daily quota, but Ken slinked toward the elevator with nothing but a rattling cough for farewell. That meant Ken was still ill and, in a way, was cautioning Ted that he might not make it in on Monday. Tuesday afternoon would officially end the campaign. Among other things, Ted thought.

At the evening meal he remembered it was Cathy's birthday. Though he had completely forgotten it, he used Clayton's threat as an excuse, then added something about their living expenses being so high he hadn't been able to find anything decent, as a gift, for what they could afford. He swore how miserable he felt about it, and that he loved her dearly—each was true—and proposed they go out to dinner Sunday. Her reply and expression said she understood, and she was so damn nice about it Ted was afraid she really *might* understand—how he'd become so fixed on his own daily battles that Cath's game and his was the sole meaningful contact they had left between them.

291

But he knew his wife well enough to see she was very disappointed. In him. It was a long, hollow, strained evening.

When at last they headed upstairs for the night, Ted once more recalled the penny-fairies. He groped for the change in his pocket with a depth of self-loathing and total desperation. My God, he could at least give her a handful of coins and a *reason* to *smile*!

But on the landing he couldn't think of an inconspicuous way to ask Cathy not to enter the bedroom yet, and was stuck with watching her trudge through the bath toward the bedroom, seeing with a pang how much wearier, even older, she looked than she had a mere few months ago.

He began to undress and change to his pj's with a mental image of his wife and him found someday in a crumpled, yellowing stack of sticklike arms and legs, and old Mr. Loring would read the newspaper story and gasp, "Why, the Daggetts couldn't have been much more than forty years old!"

He decided it was cold enough now to warrant wearing his pajama top as well as the pants—and Cathy burst into the bathroom. He stared at her in surprise because she usually announced the visitation of a penny-fairy while she was getting into bed.

But he hadn't enacted the role that night, and he was amazed—on her overlooked birthday—that her light-green eyes were twinkling and her beloved face was flushed with old excited joy.

She held aloft an item made of paper, but not money, he realized that at once. Cath was lifting it toward the ceiling fixture and appeared to be on the verge of a hilarious outburst, and something else: Appreciation; even love, as well.

"The fairies gave me the most money they

probably ever gave *anybody*!" she said, hugging him. "It's a check!" Laughing, she pressed her lips against his and turned the paper toward him. "Honey," she said, "the *Million-Dollar Fairy came tonight*!"

He snatched it from her hands and read the words on it with a sensation of absolute incredulity, a corner of his mind arguably insane.

The name of the bank on which the "check" was drawn had surely been placed there by hand, but it certainly looked printed: FIRST FAIRYLAND BANK & TRUST. He used a fingertip to try to smear the words, especially the last (which seemed in heavier ink), but not a letter smudged. The name "Catherine Daggett" was typed in, and so was the amount. One million dollars, just as Cathy had reported. What was going on? What?

His head reeling, Ted squinted hard at the signature on the paper. While it was nearly illegible and certainly not Cath's writing, it was altogether likely that the signatory's name—boldly scrawled— was "A. Pyme."

Cath laughed merrily, taking the slip of paper from Ted's unprotesting hands and dancing a circle as if entranced. Charmed. He gaped almost warily at her. She hugged and kissed him again, then virtually skipped into their bedroom. "You are wonderful," she cried while he stared at the open doorway. "Ted, it's perfect—absolutely perfect!" He heard her drop giggling to the bed. "Why, a million dollars is *just* what I wanted for my birthday!"

He edged inside, suddenly afraid for her, for the two of them. She couldn't conceivably imagine that the check would *clear*? Could she? He found her wearing just her underwear, smiling with pleasure, and motioning for him to join her. A year ago—B.C., Before Clayton—he'd bought her an expensive gown and taken her to one of the city's finest restaurants for her birthday, but she hadn't seemed to enjoy herself half this much.

Concentrate, man, Ted told himself firmly.

The more perplexing mystery was the origin of the absurd "check." It was clear to him now that Cath was just relieved he hadn't forgotten her birthday after all, that he'd thought to concoct a clever gag gift. But he *had* forgotten, as she surely knew; he *hadn't* dummied up one of his checks so that FIRST FAIRYLAND BANK & TRUST appeared to have been printed on it, he didn't know how to *do* such things.

Then he saw on the mattress beside his wife a small, handwritten note. He knew before she confirmed it or he even picked the note up that it had come with the "check." Written in the same strong hand of the signatory, but more legibly, it read, "Don't worry. Things will get better."

Cathy took his face between her hands when he lowered himself to the bed, and gave him a lingering, excruciatingly sweet kiss. "I meant it. This is an absolutely perfect gift when we're nearly broke!" He wanted to ask her who else she'd told about the penny-fairy game, and a hundred other questions, but he didn't. "I'm so lucky to have a husband who—well, who lets me get rich through the presents of tiny strangers."

Strangers like A. Pyme, Ted mused. He kissed her back anyway, hoping he could somehow find a way to use love and their marriage to banish all the questions, the fears, the darker elements of his own half-believing mind once and for all. But the clear facts argued that Cath or some friend of hers had created the fake check. After all, he was the only other one to know he'd forbidden the imaginary "pime" to return to their home, their bedroom, unless someone had overheard. Yet

why, when Cathy was so eager to exhibit her hap-
piness and maintain both the game and their
marriage, would she have chosen *that* "fairy" as
the make-believe signatory?

Before they went to sleep, sometime later, Ted
asked on impulse, "Where do you suppose you
can cash your wonderful check?"

"We'll look in the Yellow Pages," she said slyly,
sleepily, cuddling against him. "There might be a
branch out in the backyard!" She wriggled. "I
think most fairies are underground people."

Saturday was a splendidly lazy, recuperative
kind of day. Ted and Cathy watched a college
football game together till she tired of it and went
up to call her mother.

Sunday they went out to eat, just as Ted suggested they do. While the restaurant was nowhere
near as nice as the place to which he'd taken her
on her previous birthday, they both ate and drank
well. When she told him not to worry about the
bar bill "because I'm a millionaire now, you
know," the reference perversely reminded Ted of
the deadline he and his team faced, and he
wound up drinking much more than he usually
did. The deadline was the day after tomorrow.

Back home, after leaving an "oprickel" of three
cents and a nickel on the headboard, Ted left
Cathy to change out of her good clothes and wandered somewhat woozily out into the backyard.
"At least my lousy eight cents are real," he muttered aloud, defying any underground bombers.

He squinted into the gloom at the back fence, a
bit unsteady from what he'd drunk, and didn't
become aware of the fact that he was crying for at
least ten or fifteen seconds. He hadn't been sobbing, he didn't feel hysterical or remotely out of
control. There were tears running down his
cheeks anyway. Cath might be able to discover

the entrance to some tunnel leading to a marvelous underground bank full of colorful little tellers eager as hell to give away perfectly good money. Ted Daggett wouldn't be able to see 'em if they were doing somersaults on his bed!

"Ted," Cathy called from the kitchen window. "Phone. Dick Craig."

Great, Ted thought, drying his eyes as he went inside. The guy probably couldn't make himself stand even one more day. They could *all* become homeless simultaneously: the Craigs, Ken Benson, Suzy and her live-in, Cathy and him. He barked "Hello" into the nearest extension phone.

"I won't be quitting after all, buddy," Dick said on the other end, "not if you can put up with me till Scotty gets well."

"Why not? I mean, that's fine to hear!" Ted held the receiver closer to his ear, as if that might block out the confusion he felt. "What's up?"

"Suzy Carlon's boyfriend is a pal of Mr. Loring's son." Craig was starting to chuckle. "It's a little complicated, Ted—but the bottom line is this: Mr. Loring *canned* our beloved Alex Clayton! The bastard's replacement is already hired; he'll be at the office in the morning." Dick was laughing now. "Suzy phoned me because she couldn't find your number. Ted, old buddy—we're still in the ol' ball game!"

Asking three times if Dick was sure Clayton had been fired, his heart pounding furiously, Ted glanced through the French doors and noticed snow had been falling throughout the conversation. After he'd thanked his friend profusely for the promising news, feeling terribly giddy but more relieved than he could remember, he saw that the snow pattern formed in the yard—so light it left the ground bare in places—resembled a sequence of small, clear footprints leading up to the house. "Thanks, First Fairyland Bank," he said in a voice too low for Cathy to hear.

He went up to tell her the good news, speaking at a pitch far louder than his customary speaking voice.

Monday he was infinitely more optimistic than usual. True, the team probably would not achieve its quota, but they would come close. Mr. Loring had not retired and was approachable enough to believe Ted's opinion that their performance had actually been superior to anything else they had *ever* accomplished, under the circumstances. Once that was established, it might be possible to provide input regularly to the new guy, even to make friends with him and to dream anew Ted's old dream of a vice-presidency.

After noting Alex Clayton's nameplate was gone from the door to that office, Ted settled down at his own desk with a happy sense of anticipation. Even the text of a personal, handwritten memo he found under a paperweight did nothing to diminish his enthusiasm.

"Ted," the note began, "I've heard great things about you from Mr. Loring for weeks. It will be delightful to work with a man who has both feet planted firmly on the ground."

Ted grinned, glanced up when he heard Dick and Suzy arriving, smiled broadly, and waved to them. Ken Benson might have to go if he couldn't stop getting a cold every other week.

"It's my practice," the memo continued in its heavy, hearty man's writing, "to socialize with the managers of my departments. I'd like to visit with you and your lovely wife Cathy at the earliest and most convenient date."

Ted had to brace himself, gripping the desk. Even before he saw the signature, some familiar tone in the final sentence or two suggested what he should expect there—and in his immediate future.

His new superior had signed it, heavily and boldly, "Andy Pyme."

Clayton's old office door opened and Ted had his first glimpse of a surprisingly round-cheeked and toothy man who carried an informal baseball cap in his hand. Smiling familiarly, he was bearing down on Ted.

The Writing of "Pick-Up"

Many works of fiction, short or long, have a single viewpoint. That's fine. I confess a fondness for stories that try to do a lot of things. What I like about this tale, published here for the first time, is that it's concerned with several things, most of them rarely found in what is often termed imaginative or fantasy fiction.

As a consequence of what I've said, very little about "Pick-Up" is predictable even when you'd swear you know what happens next. This occurs through planning sudden "awareness" of what your character "is really like," or sheer serendipity. I believe it was the latter while I was writing "Pick-Up," plus the most fundamental plot points, such as the topical identities of Mackay and "Polly."

Pick-Up

The little bar wasn't quite in the middle of nowhere, but it was close. Mackay was already there mentally, so it and he were a good match. On a night as cold as this one, he thought while he walked from the minivan, maybe a cheesy joint like this could be tilted toward the middle.

And it was just possible a special guy like him might discover something *else* even at the center of nowhere.

Just inside the hard-pulling door, Mackay stopped to let his vision adjust to the darkened interior. He was a completely bald, youngish man with a stocky, squared-off kind of build. What kind of bar in the Southwest didn't keep the Tex/Mex or C&W music playing? He could care less if there wasn't any, but it seemed strange, and Mackay needed a certain level of sound to keep his thoughts reasonably safe, and *this* hole-in-the-desert was as quiet as day-old death. The kind of quiet you got when shock had worn off, things were tidied up, and the impression of being mildly haunted had vanished.

A beer or two at the bar, then back into the car to drive ten or twenty more miles, whatever it took to find what he wanted. He was en route to a bored-looking, silent bartender when he detected the other patrons. Two couples at tables. A trio of cowboys at another. Two guys squatted on bar stools a yard or two apart.

And a solitary girl siting at a table in a corner. Mackay glanced back at her appraisingly after gazing at the men at the bar so he wouldn't look obvious. Petite, head in a scarf, age indeterminate, maybe Indian, and he felt she had tracked him with her arresting black eyes.

So she brushes me off, Mackay thought, altering his course. *So she* doesn't *brush me off and I don't drive on so quickly*. All the possible experiences with women were logged in his memory—every fascinating one—and what was left, he supposed, were habit and occasional real release. You always had the former, Mackay guessed, approaching the female, and you never knew when you'd get the latter. If only beauty or the size of something had been a dependable measurement.

"Please, pardon the intrusion," he said smoothly.

She glanced up partway, expressionless. That showed him the dark, wide eyes behind bright and ornate glasses, a small nose and comparably smaller mouth, and a long, graceful throat. The head scarf was vivid and pretty, but her complexion was not dark at all, it was almost sallow. Mackay thought suddenly, gladly, *Bookish—she's bookish!* "Yes?"

"I'm not from around here, originally," he said, motivated by how the woman seemed, "and I've had some things happen to me lately that . . . well, I'm desperate to run them by someone . . . sensitive." He made a boyish gesture meant to indicate the universe beyond the bar, contriving to convey a combination of vulnerable fear, mystery, and an urgent need for advice. "I drove aimlessly for days after *it* happened, then told myself I'd go inside the next place I saw open and tell my story to the first person I saw." He shrugged and simultaneously raised and spread his hands.

"That would be the bartender," she said in a light, breathy voice, "wouldn't it?"

Mackay looked toward the quiet man in question, then turned to peer in the direction of the route he had taken to this interesting woman. A piano covered by a tarp obstructed his view. "You couldn't have seen me the first time I saw the bartender," he said unaccusingly.

"Then how did I know you saw him first?" she asked. "Or the people sitting at the tables next? Sit down, if you wish."

Mackay accepted her invitation, but was still trying to understand her little trick and not be shown up.

She didn't let him. "I should warn you not even to tell me any . . . social lies, is that the term?" Her tiny mouth turned up at the corners. "Those who know me well call me 'Polly,' after the polygraph."

"The truth detectors," he said, nodding, manufacturing a smile. *So she has a built-in shit detector, does she?* he mused. Well, they'd see about that.

"I'm not from around either," she said, "but since each of us is no longer *there*, I'm sure our origins aren't terribly important. It's the farthest thing from the truth that no one was ever hurt just listening to someone, but go ahead and tell me your story, as you called it—as long as it's interesting."

"It may be the most interesting story you ever heard, Polly," Mackay declared, finally capturing the bartender's eye and motioning to him that they required service.

The woman smiled and made a buzzing sound. "I see jagged peaks jumping above as well as below the lines." Then she sobered. "I really have heard some marvelous stories in my own travels. Fair warning, since you're promising me to be interesting."

Mackay leaned forward across the table to her, his hairless dome almost touching her forehead. "I was a member of Heaven's Gate, and I was supposed to be among the suicides the night the others left their containers to rendezvous with the mothership traveling with the comet!"

That was the point when she came closest to raising her head and looking directly into his eyes.

But the bartender hove into view silently at their table. He was a burly man who peered down expectantly at them. "Whatever the lady is drinking," Mackay said, pointing to her glass, "and a beer of any kind." He glanced toward the female with a semiapologetic expression. "We weren't allowed to drink, but that doesn't appear to apply anymore."

"I don't think your leader's death should matter," she said candidly, "if you have any faith in what he believed and taught you."

"Well, gosh, that's *just* the kind of thing I need help with now!" Mackay exclaimed. He rested his right hand on her left as if it was the most spontaneous and natural thing to do. Her flesh was cool to the touch, her hand even smaller than he had expected. "I mean, all that's left of the group is nine or ten other people like me, and we already missed the rendezvous! It's not like we were Catholic or Jewish or Baptist or something and we can simply go to another church or temple."

She moved her left hand, easily dislodging his grasp. "You could organize the others and go somewhere where there's usually UFO activity going on." She shifted slightly in her chair and one of her knees made contact with his right thigh. She didn't move away. "Unless your dedication—and need to work things out—aren't as great as you claim they are."

As nonchalantly as if his body was some detached thing over which he had no control, Mackay closed both his legs, lightly, around her knee. "*My* dedication wasn't great?" he demanded, more incredulously than with irritation. The way she sat, now, he was able to detect the sweet swell of her breasts beneath the bodice of her rather drab dress. "My name in the group was 'La,' and I can't even remember when anyone last addressed me by my real name!"

"And what is that?" Polly asked, just before the bartender returned with his tray.

"I'm sorry I didn't introduce myself earlier. I'm Dale Simpkins," Mackay said.

"And I'm Shirley Temple," she said, sipping from her new drink and laughing. "At least, that's what this gentleman's note said when I'd asked him for a drink that wasn't very alcoholic and he brought it to me. I think I like that name better than Polly."

The bartender picked up her first glass without a smile, and was starting to take Mackay's ten-dollar bill when his stubborn silence became suddenly annoying. "Why must you be so damn sullen?" Mackay demanded.

For reply, the bartender just pointed to his

mouth and shrugged his meaty shoulders, then trudged toward another table.

"I've gone from Heaven's Gate to the Good Ship Lollipop!" Mackay exclaimed, pouring himself a glass of beer with a neat head.

"I don't know what you're talking about," Polly said in her tiny voice, "if you're referring to Shirley Temple." She had long since pulled her knee back from its proximity to his legs. "We don't seem to have very much in common, alas. And my internal polygraph has gone off, so to speak, several times. Your shaven head isn't much proof of your claims, though I must admit your story had its points of interest."

Mackay smoothed a hand over his naked head, then leaned on his fist with a heavy sigh. "The first outsider I choose to—to unload on, and she thinks I'm either making everything up or I didn't have the guts to do what the rest of them did!"

Her knee, amazingly, was back between his. "I didn't say you were lying." She stripped a straw the mute bartender had left her and slipped an end of it into her small mouth. Her cheeks hollowed when she sucked it. "I merely implied that you haven't told me the complete truth." Her fingers ran the length of the straw, playfully, then squeezed it going the other way. "It's possible my built-in polygraph is registering because it distrusts your *intentions*."

"Polly," Mackay said with a disarmingly boyish grin, "that's *your* knee down there."

The knee went away. But she still held the straw to her mouth and played with it. "I confess I don't think we have *anything* whatever in common. But I read what your leader recommended the male members do to themselves and I admit that I'm curious."

"And you females always say it's men who think about sex constantly!" Mackay said with a shake of his head. He lowered the latter for a long moment and, when he stared at her again, there were tears in his eyes. "All right, I'll tell you the truth. *I was castrated*—everything I used to have between my legs—to make myself as pure as possible."

Her gaze into his eyes lengthened. She stopped sucking the straw and wadded it into a ball. "Really," she said tonelessly.

"Well, reach your hands down under the table and see for yourself!" he exclaimed. "Just *try* to give me an erection and we'll know what *your* intentions are!"

She appeared to consider it for half a second. "No, there are too many people who'd see." But she nearly sounded disappointed.

Mackay's tears were shining on his cheeks now. "I had hoped to begin a relationship with a nice woman—a friendship. Maybe to drive you home, get to know somebody normal again. I guess this is what I'm doomed to be, a nobody, a nothing!" He stopped short of adding "scorned by humanity." He paused, drew in a breath. What he said then made it sound as if he were going to rise and leave, but he merely shoved his chair back an inch or two. "I'm sorry I bothered you."

"I could use a lift," she said. Making a face, she pushed her glass away. "Two of these are too many, probably by two. I can leave now if you were sincere about riding me home."

"I was," Mackay said, standing up politely but not too eagerly. You could find females who'd go with you even when you were nearly in the middle of nowhere, he thought, meaning to hold her chair for her, if you were confident in your pitch.

Polly—or whatever the hell her name was—

glided by him, purposefully headed across the dark beer joint toward the front door that was hard to open. Mackay took his time, realizing she was the most petite woman he'd been with in ages, maybe ever. In the past he had preferred broads who were able to mix it up a little, wrestle around until his juices were really ready to flow.

He sighed with a detachment that wasn't quite genuine and started after her, confident the heavy door would slow her down. Hell, on a freezing night within range of the aforesaid nowhere's middle, he was damn lucky to find a babe of any kind who was under seventy-five. And the little broad did have a *round* ass with a wiggle to it.

Nobody was waiting by the door. For a furious instant Mackay believed she had just driven away in her own car. God knows she had a superior, stuck-up attitude to her except for the way she played kneesies with him.

He went outside anyway and saw her small figure standing by the curb. "I was getting hot in that place," she said without even turning. Apparently she had seen his face as he was exiting. "There were three vehicles left out here and I didn't know which one was yours."

"Mine is the farthest one out," he said, pointing. "The Villager minivan." He took her arm well up, mentioning the icy patches in the parking lot and feeling the outer swell of her breast on his fingers. "I guess I've been an outsider so long I automatically park quite a distance away."

"I read in the newspapers," she said in her breathily direct but almost businesslike fashion, "members of your cult gave up their money and earthly possessions. But I believe this is a new vehicle."

For a second or two Mackay wasn't sure what he disliked the most: the way her oddly flat voice rose up to him from a height he associated with eleven-year-olds; her polygraphic ferreting out of the truth; or merely the fact that she was female. Because when you got right down to it, it was the *differences* Mackay detested and frequently wanted to destroy. The differences in religion, color, size, origin by all definitions, education, belief, and class. The differences from *him*.

"Of course, you may have been a very early dropout from Heaven's Gate," she said as they reached the passenger side of the minivan and she waited for him to unlock the door. "So you could then have made several payments on the vehicle. Or you could perhaps have lied about owning it. You might also have leased it or borrowed it. Or it's not inconceivable that you stole the vehicle. Which one is it, 'La'—or do you prefer 'Mr. Simpkins'?"

Mackay got the door unlocked and stepped back, raising his head to look almost beseechingly to the hulking mountains surrounding them. In the process he saw no vehicles entering from the distant road, none beginning to exit the bar parking lot.

"I prefer only that you stop asking your goddamn questions!" he said. He heaved the female effortlessly between the two front seats, onto the floor of the minivan. Mackay knew for a fact the doors back there were locked. He wedged himself between the same seats after closing the front passenger door.

Towering above her, he opened his belt, unfastened the top button of his pants, and shoved both them and his bikini underpants to his ankles. "You stuck-up, ugly goddamn gnome, your built-in polygraph isn't worth a fuck!"

His erection needed work, but it was clear to the female using a captain's chair to get to her

knees that her assailant was in no way castrated. And staring down at her helpless condition excited Mackay enough to make his good
physical health apparent to anyone who wasn't
blind.

He dove and dragged her back down to the
floor of his vehicle, reaching for the hem of her
dress. Her glasses and scarf fell away in the scuf-
fle but it was almost dark in the Villager and
Mackay had no present desire to see her head or
face, not even if her mouth was twisted in terror.
Later, when he had fucked her, tied her up, had
gotten the heater warmed up and driven to a
safer location, he would have a fervent desire to
see what that childlike little mouth could do!

Now there were other pleasures, ones that were
even better than shocking her with the attack and
the exposure of his healthy dick and balls.
Mackay ripped the skirt of her dress almost all
the way up to her waist, then tore off her panties.
She was trying to slip out from under him, but he
shoved her back on her ass, leaned his upper
body into her, and, centering his cock in the general region he desired, drove it forward at a slight
upward angle.

"Yow!" Mackay yelped, putting one hand down
to hold his sore penis. He hadn't missed like that
in years, and it had hurt. It did not occur to him
to wonder if the head of his penis slamming
against the female had hurt her, too, since the
question of feminine readiness had never been a
concern of his with any of the females he had
raped.

Pain subsided, he inclined his shaved head to
catch a glance of his fist around the base of his
organ and again pressed forward, this time just
touching it to the area of Polly's vagina.

Nothing exciting happened. He couldn't even

J.N. Williamson

slide it in *carefully*. So he jabbed at her, here and there; and when that didn't work, he let his unsatisfied dick do whatever else it wanted and, reaching down, felt every square inch of what his victim had between her legs. No pubic hair, soft to the touch or coarse. No . . .

Mackay straightened, ordered her not to move, and switched on the Villager's interior light. At once he lowered himself to a squatting position, found his command had been obeyed, and took a thorough look from the vicinity of her knees.

No, there was—nothing. Not an aperture of any kind. And maybe it was the automotive lighting, but—in addition to the way her body simply narrowed sleekly at her legs and continued smoothly around to her back—her skin didn't actually look like human skin. It wasn't only that the flesh was nearly gray at close inspection, it was as if she had *no blood* beneath it, coursing through her veins . . . as if she might be dead, or a vampire or something, maybe—

Mackay lifted his face away, his entire body upward, needing now to see the female's face, He rocked her forward into a cross-legged sitting position, his masculine hands clamped to feminine biceps that felt like moderately pliant stone under his fingers.

His head of hairless skin and bone shone in the illumination provided by the minivan's lighting— and *so did hers!* Now he understood why she had kept her scarf on even inside the bar. But just as strange and terrifying to the half-nude, newly flaccid man were her eyes now that her spectacles had also been knocked off. Mackay thought only that they were particularly wide eyes. He hadn't imagined they extended approximately to her temples and looked hollowed, uncannily depthless. Added to her alopecian absence of hair, her

310

tiny nose, and virtually lipless mouth, the female was hideous.

"I've heard males like you admire the female bosom." She began to claw her torn dress higher. "Do you want to fondle and kiss mine? I don't possess true breasts, because *we* don't nurse our young, but I *am* female, and my torso has a pleasing incline."

Mackay edged hastily back between the front seats. He threw down an arm and hand in quest of the pants he had somehow kicked aside, but was unwilling to conduct a visual search. It felt vital not to stop looking at her, not even for a moment.

"I knew it each time you lied." She cast the dress aside and stood. The sight of her entirely naked body merely made matters worse. "I felt sure you wouldn't have castrated yourself, but my only means of verification at the time was an abhorrent prospect to me."

"You're not exactly Miss America, sister," Mackay blustered. He spotted his shorts and pants, but they were partly beneath his driver's seat, closer to her than him. He covered his shrinking penis with his hand and had enough finger length left to hide his balls. "What's with the 'polygraph' shit anyway? At least I'm a real guy!"

She took a step away from the captain's chairs. Toward him. "I've told you no lies, and who or what I am was and *is* my business. She raised an arm toward him and a tiny finger shot out, described a circle around his right nipple. Even through his jacket and shirt, it felt cold. He edged as far away as possible. "We seek only truth. The world you created is one of falsehood and deceit. In your flight from truth, you even lie to yourselves. Correcting that is why we are here."

Then she cupped her hands and lowered her

arms, easily dislodging Mackay's grip on himself. The fingers of one small hand opened.

He got the passenger door open behind him and half jumped, half fell from the Villager.

Sitting naked from the waist down on his ass, Mackay looked up at searing light, believing for an instant he was caught in the high beams of a vehicle leaving the parking lot.

But the blaze of light was coming, not going— *above* him. Its immediate departure point had been the mountains encircling the bar and its lot, but he heard no sounds. The female was there with him when the light basically wrapped itself around Mackay and her, and he realized at a remove that the two of them were . . . ascending.

Mackay shook his head to clear it, glanced around, and saw that he was sitting on the frozen ground high in the mountains. How the hell he'd gotten there, he had no idea. He didn't see his Villager anywhere, or any living being. Suddenly he was aware that he was *terribly* cold, began to rise, and was filled with sickening pain. Afraid not to do so, Mackay looked down his body for the first time since his head—

Where were his *pants?* God, how many hours had he been out bare-assed in such freezing temperatures? And where had that searing pain come from—

Mackay spread his knees very gingerly and peered between them. The stare confirmed his fears.

His balls and part of his dick were frozen to the hard-packed earth!

Time passed in dollops of misery and terror. He did see his bikini shorts and his pants folded neatly, mysteriously lying on a big rock no more than five or six yards away.

The truth was, Mackay realized, his clothes might as well have been on Mars.

Down below him, he saw, a small bar sat in the center of a parking lot. A petite woman was headed toward the entrance, and Mackay shouted "Help!" at her awhile, then screamed it. The door closed behind her a second later.

And half an hour later, with night coming on and temperatures dropping, Mackay came to realize another truth: He could stay where he was, waiting for a car to venture up there, and probably die. Or he could tear most of himself loose from the earth, hold his pants tightly against his crotch, and try to make it down to the bar before he bled to death.

That would mean, of course, two or three sacrifices and some real dedication to bear life!

Mackay lay down again to think things through. He simply didn't have the balls to reach a decision just yet.

The Writing of
"It Does Not Come Alone"

"It Does Not Come Alone" is probably the first story for which I've written an afterward, and I was grateful to editor/publisher Ken Abner of *Terminal Fright* for running it. This novella is studded with characters ranging from my late paternal grandfather, Lowell, to many people I've known and whom he never met. My notion in part was that Pop would have been liked by people of all ages— as always—and good for them to know, whether most of them were young or old. "Ageless" was one of several words that fitted Pop most of his long life.

As for the others I've known, they're sketched in quite simply, not intended to be people subjected to word-portraits of anything but usefulness to this look at a long-standing social group that loses its first member to old age.

It Does Not Come Alone

"Fear old age . . . for it does not come alone."
—*Plato*

1.

"They're predicting the first real snow of the season this weekend," Harold said. He managed to appear apprehensive and wistful simultaneously. "Gosh, if I could just borrow Drew's new Sentra we could take turns driving and be in Florida by Saturday night!"

"Even if you did," Jim said, reaching for the huge bowl of buttered popcorn and tugging it nearer, "I doubt Drew would let you keep his new wheels down there for the rest of the winter. There'll be more snow, y'know."

Bos shifted his bulk in one of the host's two

easy chairs, his small blue eyes gleaming. "I could get us to Jax by Saturday morning if we took off by noon tomorrow." Bosworth had always had a heavy foot on the accelerator and was the only one they knew who bragged about it. "Remember when we were running late for the concert in Noblesville and I put us in our seats before the show even started?"

"I just remember being afraid I might piss my pants," Allen said, looking—as always—like an aggrieved stork with better things to do. Except Allen had never figured out what they were. He turned to the dark-complected, nervous Harold, who had brought up driving south. "Say, Harold," Allen began, "just what *is* 'real' snow? Or *fake* snow, if you prefer to answer that question?"

Johnathan and Ray, seated on the floor against the sofa, chuckled. Stuffed into one of his beloved Irish wool sweaters as ever, Ray raised his current beer and sighed at the same time he belched. "Shit, Hal, if it was your own new car, I wouldn't be allowed to go along. My folks would figure I might not take one of my insulin shots—or that I'd find some cute babe who was sun-blinded and wanderin' around the beach since spring break!"

Lowell, the host, was the youngest one in the gang—now and then they called him "the Kid"— but he hadn't chuckled over Harold's idea at all. That was unusual for good-humored, round-faced Lowell, so they turned collectively to stare at him as he sat straight in his easy chair.

"You know, boys," he began, "there isn't a single good reason for any of us not to go to Florida for a few weeks if we decided to do it." His wide smile was as youthfully infectious as ever. "Ray, I'd keep an eye on when you needed your shots; you know I would. Bos, I've driven to Florida before, so we could take turns at the wheel with

Harold and Johnathan. And Harold, we don't need Drew's new Sentra—because we could chip in and rent a *van*, if we wanted badly enough to do it!" He had kept his fingers laced, but unclasped his big hands now, and leaned back with what seemed reluctant resignation. "Not that we'll go. We all know we won't."

"It was easy for you to say we could do it," Johnathan said, more than a little huffily. His winter beard was half grown back and he might have appeared raffish if his eyes weren't permanently and carefully dulled by the many wonders he had dreamed of and abandoned as far too risky. "Your wife died, so you can go where you please, when you please."

"But he used to take Franny everywhere," Harold said. He felt grateful for Lowell's defense of his remark, even if he had not been remotely serious about it as a suggestion. "Truth is, none of us does much of anything. I wonder why that is?"

"Evidently the Kid has some ideas on that," Jim Kleiner said, shoving the mammoth, half-empty popcorn bowl in their host's direction. A six-footer with a full mustache, Jim had a way of crossing his legs, wrapping his arms around himself, and practically fading from sight. "Why did you say we all know we won't go anywhere, Lowell?"

"Let it go, Jimbo," Lowell said, cramming a fist filled with popcorn to his genial mouth. "How about I make up another batch of Orville's finest, fellas? Ray? You ready to dig into some fresh, hot popcorn? Jim—or Bos?"

Phil Bosworth got to his feet and stretched. Ostensibly, that was why he had stood. But it also reminded the others he was a good two inches taller than Jim Kleiner and weighed at least thirty more pounds. Bos had played on the football team. "First, Kid, I think everybody would like to have an answer to Harold's and Jim's question." He inhaled, adjusted his belt. "About the crack you made."

Lowell was about halfway out of his chair, ready to head for the kitchen. Suddenly a terrible pall lay across the front room, tension existed where none had materialized since they'd stopped asking a guy named O'Brien to their get-togethers, and—improbably—the most popular member of the gang had created the tension.

The odd part, Lowell thought, settling back down in his chair, *is that I* meant *to create it*. "All right, boys, we've never kept any big secrets from one another. I said there was no reason not to go on a trip—and showed I could prove it—and that we knew we'd never do it because... well, because you're *too old*."

Bos called him a name, executed a little complete circle with his big feet, then slumped into his chair. The springs squeaked, and the former athlete, always red-faced, grew more crimson. "He said *we're* too old, fellas—notice how he left himself out of that!"

"No," Lowell said with a grin, "notice how Bos insisted on pointing out that I'm younger. And see how silly this is: I'll turn seventy-five my next birthday, but all you boys make a big deal out of being older than I am—because *you're* closer to *eighty*!" He broke off with a hearty laugh. "Our children and our grandchildren think we're all older than Methuselah, and the fact that I'm around two years younger than you are means *nothing* to them!" The Kid's laugh deepened. "It's like the two cents in a dollar ninety-eight!"

"Since you brought it up, Lowell," Johnathan, a

retired banker, pointed out, "the fact that we average nearly eighty years of age might explain why we didn't jump at the idea of driving to Florida with Harold." He turned his head to look for support and both lanky Allen and enormous Bos provided him with tentative nods.

"Why?" Lowell demanded. "Were you planning to *push* the vehicle, or just stand up until we got there?" Laughs rose from Ray, Harold, and even Allen. Lowell leaned forward. "What got me started, boys, was something odd. I remembered when we were in our teens—*and had the same basic discussion as this!*"

"I remember it, too, Kid!" Allen exclaimed. His long face was enlivened by the memory. "I brought the subject up, back then. Mom was upstairs, and Dad had just showed everybody his new Packard—and we were a little bit too young to ask him to borrow it just for a joyride!"

"So what age *is* the right one," Jim sighed, "if we're too old now? Did it just come and go and I didn't notice it?"

Lowell lit a regular Camel—which he knew to be an unfiltered one, because he'd begun to smoke long before filters were common, so unfiltered *was* regular—aware that he was the only smoker left in his old gang of pals. "Jimbo, you know we're not just talking about long trips now, don't you? It was Harold who mentioned that none of us does much of anything any longer. Do any of you want to argue with him? If not, why do you believe we've gotten to such a stage and do you think we should be ashamed of it?"

"Well, *I'll* argue with him!" Johnathan Masters exclaimed, twisting in his chair to glance as amiably as possible at Harold. The ex-banker had never broken his habit of wearing a suit, even among old friends, although he had eschewed his customary tie. "I weed my own garden and I mow the yard at least once a week. That's doing things!"

"Are you planning to do either of those things after the first 'real' snowfall Harold mentioned?" Lowell inquired pleasantly.

Johnathan glared at him, started to speak, and thought better of it.

"Don't forget I have to use a cane just to get around," Jim Kleiner said on a note of mild pique.

"Hell's bells, Kleiner," Ray Reilly said scornfully, "you're the only man I ever knew who was *glad* to have a little hip problem—so you have an excuse to sit around on your ass all the time!"

Everyone laughed, and even Jim didn't lose his temper. After some sixty years of gatherings similar to this, each man understood the roles played by all the others, and had long since accepted them.

But Lowell Striker, the Kid, seemed to be entirely out of character. One by one, his guests— his closest friends—swiveled their heads until they were facing him, wondering why he had chosen to challenge and possibly distort the particular comfort zone they found solely in one another's familiar company. Budding resentment showed—if not reproach—in more than one pair of bespectacled eyes.

"Some of us depend on social security or pension plans," Lowell said. He didn't nod even scantly toward Allen Hoffer or Jim Kleiner because there was no need. They had known each other so long and so well they were all potential biographers of the rest and they no longer could have said whether they even liked the others. It probably didn't matter. "But I think everyone can agree there are many interests that require no more than gas money."

Everybody started to disagree, but remembered just in time such things as saving stamps from envelopes, libraries and museums, card games. Nobody was enjoying anything much but television, and these get-togethers.

"When we were young," Harold volunteered, almost shyly, "we used to talk about the exciting things to explore if we didn't have to go to work the next day." Reflectively, he rubbed his chin with its perpetual five o'clock shadow.

"And a few of us," the Kid said, white brows raised, "retired fifteen years ago or longer and haven't done any of them."

"Like the man said," Reilly sighed, " 'youth is wasted on the young.' "

"They're the enemy, all right," Bos declared with a somber bob of his big head. "Once the enemy was our folks, then the soldiers we met in war, then one political party or the other." He laughed explosively, derisively. "Now I know that when we become fathers, we're begetting the enemy!"

Nearly all the old men chuckled, some with empathy. But bearded Johnathan, who'd reared a rebel of his own, said softly, "I take it Eric isn't running the company, again, the way you did." And Bos smiled ruefully.

Lowell lit a new Camel. "Each of us, once upon a time, was younger than everyone else in his own family. That would mean the fellow who drew *Pogo* was right—if *you're* right, Bos—and the enemy really *is* us! But I don't think it's that simple."

"Go ahead, Kid," Jim prompted him.

"I quit smoking years before it was popular to do it. You know that. I'm not proud or ashamed that I started puffing again when a lot of folks who had never smoked were joined by a bunch of converts and began to make smokers sound worse than heroin or cocaine addicts." He eyed them through a trio of neat rings he created. "But I finally realized it wasn't for the reason I gave you, that I was already in my seventies anyway."

"Then what *was* your reason?"

Ray Reilly had asked and, for an instant of travel back to the time when the overweight and sweater-clad Reilly had taken nothing whatever serious but his mom, Lowell thought Ray was being sarcastic. No such luck. "I realized everybody is scared half to death about *something*, and I decided to show I wasn't. Or," Lowell added with a nearly imperceptible rumbling chuckle, "I wasn't going to join any of the bunches who bind together as if theirs will be the group that is— spared." He glanced away, embarrassed. "When I realized I belonged to a bunch like that already, I brought it up. Now I'm sorry I did. Nobody knows what I'm talking about, so let's change the subject."

"No, let's not," Johnathan Masters replied, pinching the creases in his suit trousers and trying to sit with dignity on the floor in front of the sofa. For the first time in any of their recent memories, Johnathan's blue eyes were sparkling with animation. "You've told us we're lazy old loafers, and now you're accusing—what, all Americans?— of running scared! If you don't like a lot of yellow, aging bastards any longer, why do you keep inviting us to your house?" Johnathan snorted and looked to the others for agreement. "Or do you fail to put up chairs for Ray and me, so we have to sit on the floor, to—to toughen us up?"

Lowell paled and jumped to his feet, heading for the closet where he kept two folding chairs on which he and Franny had sat to play card games and Scrabble for decades. "I didn't think, Johnathan," he said, red-faced with embarrassment. "It's just that you and Ray have sprawled on the carpet as long as I can remember."

"Johnathan," Ray muttered, turning his head to speak softly to the retired banker, "you told me you got here first today. You could have sat anywhere. Hell, you could have taken the chair Bos has!"

Johnathan was rising to help Lowell unfold the old chair the Kid had brought him. "That's where Bos always sits," he said, distracted. He shoved a second folding chair toward Reilly, but Ray—still on the floor—was taking a pull from his beer bottle.

"There's a lot to be afraid of, these days," Allen Hoffer remarked. He passed a hand over his white, close-cropped pate, as if he might be making a magician's pass. "Everyone knows they're going to do something to social security and probably Medicare too."

"And with crime rates what they are," Harold said, "my Sarah is afraid to go to the grocery after the sun goes down."

"Well, you gotta keep your eyes open for those vampires, Hal," Reilly said, with a wink in the Kid's direction. Then he sobered. "I don't doubt *something*'s going on in Washington. They can't do enough, these days, for either the ladies"—he managed to make the word derogatory—"or that other bunch that likes to dress up like women and spread diseases."

Jim Kleiner had never really shifted his gaze from Lowell, and when the latter sank back in his chair, Jim stared at him from beneath hooded eyelids. "I don't think the Kid is accusing anyone of anything, just trying to say he'd noticed some changing views of his own. Like back when he was trying to get laid." Most of the gang laughed, glad there was another tension breaker. Kleiner grinned, under the heavy mustache, but waited to see what Lowell would say. "Go on, Kid. I've been misunderstood by my family and almost everybody I know but you fellas for so long, and let it go, I suppose I'm a card-carrying coward!"

"Golly, Jim, I'm no expert in anything," Lowell Striker said honestly. "I just said what I'm seeing, and none of you changed my mind just now. But you did remind me of something I've been thinking about since the Persian Gulf War, although I realize now it started when the Berlin Wall came down."

Bos grumbled, "I don't see how we can have anything involved with—"

"Let me answer the question I was asked!" Lowell interrupted. "You're like so many people I meet, Bos, you believe everything can be laughed off or answered 'yes' or 'no,' and that's just not true!" He drew in a deep breath. "For most of our adult years, even when we wouldn't have admitted it, we were afraid of an enemy we couldn't see who might attack us in our beds, then annihilate us so *fast* that maybe even the good Lord couldn't keep track of us and bring our souls to heaven. Or if we weren't destroyed where we lay, we might be terribly altered forever by the same invisible enemy—or even if we weren't badly injured ourselves, the nation we live in *would* be, so there'd be famine, no retirement plans, and life would be every man for himself."

"But the Cold War ended," Bos said, starting to understand.

"And the Soviet Union broke up," Allen picked

up the thread, "and it looked as if communism was destroyed—"

"And," Lowell finished, "the threat of nuclear holocaust appeared to go away, magically. Nearly overnight." He blew another smoke ring and waited until it dissolved into nothingness. "For a short while—till the war in the gulf—it seemed we no longer had much to fear except for what drugs were doing to our young." His voice rose. "Most of us didn't like it when we sent troops to defend a nation we never heard of, we didn't know why we did or didn't care for the reasons we were given. But we seemed to be winning easily, and polls showed Bush setting records for voter approval—"

"But he wouldn't let our troops pursue Saddam," Ray Reilly broke in, "and finish the bastard off!"

Lowell nodded his big head. "So he lost the election, we went back to distrusting the government, and we've been a fractured, frustrated, and frightened people since then—now, with a gigantic difference."

Harold, increasingly fascinated, asked, "What difference?"

"Without the atomic bomb in the picture, so far as we know," the Kid said, "we had to become scared silly by . . . other things. You fellas mentioned many of them: Fear that money you counted on won't be sent any longer. Crime in the neighborhoods. Changing morals and attitudes in the young, to the point that we could joke about *our own kids* being the *enemy*! And notice that since a lot of bigwigs saw we can't stop illegal drugs, folks who don't happen to have smoked have begun calling other folks like them positively *terrible* things! And one more observation, okay?"

A few of the other men nodded.

325

"I've described how people used to go to sleep halfway expecting an invisible enemy to come change us, or everything, forever; remember? Well, that's the way most UFO abductions begin—and sooner or later, those folks report that they're shown scenes of this planet laid waste. It's as if their former fears were just shoved way deep inside and rearranged a little, isn't it?"

"He's right," Jim said. Excited, he fished in his jacket pocket for his pill dispenser, shook out two aspirin, and washed them down with lukewarm coffee. "I've read about abductions too, and people are usually taken from their beds, or automobiles, often by beings they don't even see! And most of these people either discover new skills or ESP or think they've been changed by weird objects put in their noses or somewhere!"

"I am *not* afraid of being kidnaped by little people from another planet!" Johnathan said with firm, massive dignity.

"I believe you, Jonno," Lowell said sincerely. "But since we *don't* do the things we'd like, is it because we stubbornly insist on being young again?"

"Lord, no!" Johnathan said, laughing in a way Lowell hadn't heard from him in uncounted years. "I can't bear the idea of Mother watching all I do, and censoring what I read—or of Dad with those 'expectations' of his that I always let down somehow. Not," he added swiftly, "that I wouldn't give practically everything to see them again."

"If they weren't the same people anymore," Reilly said under his breath.

"Or they'd become mute," Jim Kleiner said beneath his mustache. He looked around, followed up on Lowell's question. "Anyone here want to be young again? I think the Kid's come up with some magic potion. I pass."

Harold wafted a slight hirsute hand. "And find girls to date, then wonder why they won't go out for *second* dates?" He chuckled. "Not on your life, thanks!"

"Same here," Ray said, stifling a belch. "But I'll tell you something odd about that. I *would* have said I'd give anything to be a footloose young bachelor again if you'd asked me right up until . . . well, around the period of time you mentioned, Kid."

Lowell saw that he had the attention, then, of every man in the front room. He drew in a deep breath. What he was on the verge of asking veered sharply into the one territory each of them knew, without being told, was forbidden. "I have a big question now, boys, and of course you don't have to answer it if you're, well, superstitious, or if you simply prefer not to: Are you, like me, not exactly *afraid* to *die* anymore? I don't mean that we're in any big rush to go, and I know there were points in each of our lives when death was positively unthinkable. But am I right that you're no longer *frightened* to die?"

Studiedly blank faces regarded Lowell. If he halfway recognized an expression, it was the astonishment of betrayal. For an instant that lengthened in proportion to each white-haired man's discomfiture, it appeared to Lowell there would perhaps be no reply. Or perhaps no answer they were inclined to share, companions of many decades or not.

"Jesus, Kid," Reilly said at last, head drooping as if in a curious embarrassment, "you tryin' to sell us life insurance or what?"

"I'll give you an answer," Bos told Lowell, rising. The motion suggested he was thinking of leaving now. "I'm ready to check out today. Have been since that damn prostate surgery three years ago."

"Well, I attend church regularly," Allen Hoffer spoke up, straightening. "I won't be afraid when my time comes."

"I admit I'm curious," Jim said, eyes narrowed in reflection. "Both about what death feels like, and—afterward. I think you're right, Kid. At some point people—a lot of them—stopped being afraid to conk out." His face crinkled with thought. "But other things keep scaring us!"

Johnathan commented without turning toward Lowell. "I suppose I feel pretty much the same way," he said; and Ray Reilly said, "Yeah, okay. Yeah."

Harold squirmed as the others' gazes inexorably drifted in his direction. Very few times had they heard this quiet and passive man with the once coal-black hair opt against agreement with the group will. They had not expected it just now. "Count me out," Harold said tightly.

"Hal," an exasperated Reilly told him, "it's not like we're casting a *vote* to die or not. That'll just *happen* some day!"

"Well, like I said," Harold said firmly, arms crossed, "I'm against it!"

Lowell spoke rapidly. "Ray, I don't think Harold is arguing the existence of dying as a fact. He has a right to be afraid of death if that's how he feels." He watched Reilly trying to keep his wisecracks to himself. "But most of you agree with what I said, and what Jim offered—that other things *do* scare us. And, as I've said, they can frighten us into immobility, into doing almost nothing at all."

"And what *are* those things, in your opinion?"

Johnathan asked. Seated on his folding chair, on the same eye level as Lowell, the retired banker appeared for the first time to be both less defensive and more genuinely interested. "Clearly, you have been devoting considerable attention to the matter by now." He managed one of his affably kidding smiles of old. "Are we to start entering track meets, or begin an affair—or perhaps join one of those 'polar bear' winter swim clubs?"

Lowell grinned, and shuddered. "Golly, I hope it's not that last activity you mentioned, Jonno!" Most of the men chuckled because of the two activities he didn't exclude. "It wouldn't be up to me to tell any of you fellas what to do—but it's funny how you all seemed to think I was recommending that we do anything *specific*."

"Then what?" Ray demanded.

Lowell drew in a fast breath and started the rest of what he wanted to convey to these peers who were all the friends or companions he had in the world: "Whatever keeps us from looking like any of the dead old folks we've seen lying in their coffins!" They gaped at what he had found the nerve to say. "Walk into any mortuary, head toward the guest of honor, and the *first thing you notice* before you're close enough to view the remains, boys, is"—Lowell paused—"absolute *inactivity! Motionlessness!*" He rushed on while the group was listening avidly. "You could *shout* at the corpse, sit it *up* or—or *stand it on end*, and you won't get a protest from it, a laugh, or a question about why you've done such a thing!" Lowell was on his feet. "Boys, you won't see a reaction—or please not, *any* action! He lowered his level of enthusiasm a notch. "That's what I had in mind when we were discussing your need for interests, becoming passionately involved, and taking action! They're the *opposites* to *deadness*, and they are our obligations to ourselves with business over and the kids grown—while we can still *do*, still *act*! While we're still alive!"

For all the rest of them, Johnathan arose from his folding chair to ask, "Your point, then, is that we're afraid of—what, 'deadness'? But *not* death? I'm sorry, Lowell, but I don't really get the distinction you're making."

"Because there isn't much of one," Lowell said agreeably, "except appearances, and I don't imagine a man who's conked off is obliged to hang around his boring remains for long! Jonno—*here's* what I believe most people are afraid of, and especially us: *Continuing* to get older!"

"You already said our children think we're old as Methuselah," rangy Bos objected from across the room. "I don't necessarily disagree, Kid, but why should we be terrified of what we've already done?"

"Well, first, Bos," Lowell answered, "I don't know where the expression comes from, but check your Bible. Methuselah wasn't even the oldest bird in his family! Second, because we were already terrified of turning thirty; forty seemed like sheer torture—and when I turned sixty-five I went creeping around obediently, pretending to be an old man, a damn 'senior citizen,' till I realized there just wasn't any percentage to it!"

"You're saying," Jim began, rising without his crutch, "we're more afraid of *getting* old than we are of *being* genuinely old? Or of death?"

Lowell laughed. "Once a doctor could put down 'old age' as a cause of death, but my own physician says that's hardly ever the case in America any longer. That that's been a cop-out for a couple of decades and that nobody should think of advanced age as some sort of disease or sickness."

Harold looked up, keen-eyed, interested. "But it

seems to be the case, Kid," he began, "that bad hearts or cancer kill the most people, and that the majority of those cases consist of . . . well, folks of 'advanced age.'"

"Those are killers of all ages, Harold," Lowell replied. "Sometimes they get kids too. But think about these things, fellas: Children *mostly* die from diseases of childhood—right?" Lowell waited until they acknowledged that he was correct so far. Then, with a broad smile, he added, "But I doubt there's anyone anywhere who would say those boys and girls died of the *opposite* of old age! Which *is*," he cued his companions, patiently waiting until each man not only knew the answer but had entirely followed his reasoning.

Youth was the word that passed the lips of the other six men. Nobody was said to die of youth; of "young age." And as they understood that their own most youthful member was correct, they came to the collective realization that what they had unconsciously feared the most—aging—was as toothless as were they, and only became a fanged phantom through neglect, heredity, inaction, and terror.

It had already robbed them of too much pleasure in retirement, too much life, and each man, in his own way, began to get busy again.

2.

During the next three weeks, Jim Kleiner, who had always wanted to paint, put some art supplies on an almost tapped-out credit card and began, finally, to paint.

Phil Bosworth ran into the widow of an old business associate and asked her for a date. She granted it. *Maybe I can't hope for the kind of culmination I once would have wanted*, he thought,

J.N. Williamson

shaving on the evening in question. *But I always liked Lin's company*.

Harold had a special interest he had never confided to his friends. He borrowed his son Drew's new Sentra, drove to a used bookstore, where he spent too much money, and changed his mind about that before finishing the first book he read. Flushed with excitement and intense curiosity, he realized suddenly that he couldn't even remember the color of the Sentra!

Johnathan Masters initiated sexual contact with his wife—the first time he had even tried for years—and she amazed him by turning into his arms with a happy smile. It was so wonderful, he wept. The next day he bought her roses and smiled a lot.

Lowell Striker did several things in that period of time that were enjoyable and stimulating to him. He accepted an invitation to play Scrabble with two old-maid ladies he had known for years. He agreed to substitute for a sick member of a barbershop quartet he had sung with regularly until they acquired a second tenor who was consistently flat, and loud. He went to dinner with his son, daughter-in-law, and grown grandson and *his* wife, then picked up the bill despite the flow of unsought advice from his daughter-in-law of four decades. He also continued to read a Dean Koontz novel, and he played banjo with some records—LPs—spinning on his twice-repaired stereo. Nightly, he prayed to be reunited "someday" with Franny. None of these events was much of a departure for him.

Allen resumed his attendance and Mrs. Hoffer's at a Wednesday night pitch-in for his church, and when the pastor asked him to go back to teaching a Sunday School class "if you're up to it," he knew he was. And Ray Reilly went on a diet without telling anyone about it, began puffing again on an occasional cigar, and left the Al-Key an hour earlier—plus an equivalent number of brews less—seven successive nights.

There was approximately a week and a half to go before the next scheduled get-together of the seven old chums when Harold died. None of them had had a clue the heart attack was coming, and it was in Harold's house—in his beloved rec room—that they were to have met.

For five members of the group, the sadness experienced was of a nature anyone might have anticipated.

But Lowell Striker immediately feared that his remarks might have motivated Harold to undertake some strenuous physical activity that proved responsible for the fatal attack. Guilt-ridden but speaking to no one about his feelings, he very nearly skipped his old friend's funeral.

Then he realized Harold would have allowed nothing to prevent him from paying his own final respects, if their positions had been reversed, and entered the mortuary scant minutes before services were scheduled to begin.

Wearing the black suit he had not donned since Franny died, Lowell stared toward the front of the parlor where Harold's son and daughter-in-law were obviously waiting for any last-minute arrivals. *And I'm it, darn it*, Lowell thought, beginning the long, painful walk. As usual, he had to slow his natural pace to maintain the guise of dignity expected—by younger folks—of older ones. He caught glimpses of the other fellas in the group, already seated among the small number of (in all probability) family members, and thought a mild swearword. How many people did a fella meet in eighty years of life? Even the deaths of a lot of peers couldn't entirely account for the paltry turnouts at the formal send-offs of most old people. Lowell reflected—not if they had stayed busy, involved in living, anyway.

What was it he had told the boys, including poor Harold? "The first thing you notice before you're close enough to view the remains is absolute inactivity! *Motionlessness!*" Well, dammit, it was *true*! Whether he'd accidentally influenced Harold wrongly or not—and he was certainly sorry if he had!—he hadn't told the lovable old coot to go overexert himself! *Or prove I'm wrong, Harold*, he thought, trying to send a message to the dead man in the coffin; *just* wave *to me*—communicate *some way*!

"I wouldn't let Mama come today," said Harold's son Drew, "because she just isn't up to it." He placed a paper sack in Lowell's hands with a whispered, "Dad wanted you to have this." In ordinary tones he added, "Mom will be as glad you came today as we are, Kid." A shorter version of Harold, he tried to turn Lowell to the coffin. "They did a wonderful job on Dad."

"Not a good enough one, Drew." Lowell fully averted his gaze from the you-could-sit-it-up-or-stand-it-on-*end* version of Harold, patted the arms of the son and daughter-in-law, said "I'm sorry for your loss," and walked back to where Ray Reilly sat, closest to the open sliding doors.

"Haven't seen him budge once," the irrepressible Irishman grunted as Lowell lowered himself to a folding chair. "But I don't think it was vampires."

Lowell grinned despite himself. "Pass the word, Raymond, the get-together's still on. My place again, since there isn't much time to make new arrangements."

"Sounds good to me," Reilly said, shaking hands with the Kid.

Lowell was struck by how fit his friend looked. He wasn't as red in the face. "What kind of gag would you have told if it was me up there, and Harold sat down next to you?"

Reilly did not hesitate. "I'd've told Harold I guessed you were old enough now to be inactive. To lie around and do nothin' much like the rest of us!"

3.

The object Lowell pulled from the sack Drew gave him, from Harold, at the mortuary, was a book. A fairly old, used book from the looks of it.

Then he spotted the note in his late friend's familiar handwriting, left inside the front cover, and switched on a floor lamp before sitting in his favorite easy chair. *Astonishing to get a letter from Harold immediately after his funeral*, Lowell thought. The one thing he could think of as comparable were the letters GIs scribbled in foxholes and reached Mom and Dad, or Betty or Alice or Flo, just about the time that the Purple Heart arrived. *He must have written this to me just before he died, poor guy.*

The note said, on the very top, "Please give this book and letter to Lowell Striker when I'm gone. Love, Daddy."

Then it started right in: "You were absolutely right in everything you said about having more interests and forgetting about a fear of aging, Lowell! I've had the time of my life reading whatever I wanted to read, since we all got together last, for the first time since I got married!

"No," Harold's letter continued, "you don't need to leaf through the book to see if it's pornographic. It's not, even if there are references to pretty strange beliefs about parts of the human body. Back before my getting hitched, I always wanted to learn more about people, and why we believe and do the things we do. After you spoke, I realized that I *still* wanted to learn, and I'd better begin right away if I was ever gonna do it!"

Lowell paused to light one of his unfiltered Camels, still uncertain if his remarks had somehow led to his friend's death.

"The thing I wanted you to know, Kid," the note went on, "was that the study I'd meant to make wasn't in psychology, history, anthropology, religion, or anything else there's an accurate name for. But whenever I wondered out loud some of the stuff you finally discussed, the other fellows, my folks, and my lovely bride looked at me as if I was a *nut*! And after Sarah had her stroke and got afraid of everything, and Drew became a successful businessman, I basically tried to *stop thinking*, period.

"And I didn't realize that was literally true, till you spoke your mind," Harold's handwriting proceeded. "Then I got it through my head that folks can't *stand* it when we step out of the line they put us on; that individual thoughts and insights aren't really allowed, because there are supposed to be educated *experts* for just about everything, and they are the ones who can have unusual ideas, experiment and investigate, and so on. Meanwhile, everyone else gets crammed into niches with nice neat labels, and we wind up looking like crackpots whenever we elbow the sides of our niches—or actually try to climb *out* of them!"

All this time, Lowell thought wonderingly, *Harold and I were kindred spirits, and I thought he was a little bit slow because he was just trying not to make any waves and to be liked—just like me!*

Harold's long note went on, "Twice in the last year I think I had little bitty heart attacks. I didn't tell anyone because I'm the only caretaker Sarah has, and Drew would put us straight into a nursing home. I couldn't take that, Kid, but I know Sarah would actually feel safer there. Well, an attack nearly took me away yesterday, so I had to write to you today, to thank you for freeing me from my fears while I still had some time, and to make sure *you get this book*! Look at what I underlined, please, under the heading of *Senescence*. It's been great knowing you, Lowell, and being a part of the gang! I hope to see you again 'someday,' but take your time about it, and go on enjoying life—I wish I'd begun to do it sooner!"

Lowell removed his bifocals to pinch the bridge of his nose. When he lowered his wide hand he pretended his fingertips weren't wet.

The title of the used book Harold had given him was *Man and the Beasts Within*; written by Benjamin Walker in 1977, it had been published by Stein and Day with Scarborough House. Lowell opened it to the section his late friend had recommended, reading instantly an underlined statement that "very little" was known about the aging process. The author went on that what people desired wasn't just longevity but "the health and vitality to appreciate it," a viewpoint Lowell himself had stressed.

So Harold decided to lead a better life, the Kid realized, *partly by trying to understand what was really* happening *to him due to the so-called aging process*. Perhaps he'd reasoned that he might *stop* that process—not get magically younger, just halt the aging—and not reach the point when he might suffer some "scheduled" fatal heart attack. That had never been Lowell's idea, or desire, but for a few moments it attracted him. Exercise and some perfect diet obviously weren't the answer, or were, at best, a part of the solution.

Reading more, Lowell saw that this entry in

Walker's book wasn't any kind of how-to at all, but a summary of both knowledge and beliefs on the subject. In the latter realm there were the Scythian old folks, who believed that awaiting death was morally wrong, so they set themselves afire! The Siberian Buriats paid tribute to their old in a formal rite, then murdered them! Lowell read descriptions of another few horrors along the same lines, relieved to spend his life at a time that seemed slightly more enlightened.

Then he encountered a long list of words all too often associated with old people, automatically grading himself in terms of whether each one defined him or not—doddering, incontinent, envious, low vitality, dull-witted, forgetful, unreasonable, morose, miserly, and intolerant were just a few. The Kid decided forgetfulness was truly the only word he might have to claim. But then, Franny told him he almost always forgot where they parked their car—and that was at least thirty years ago, when he was in his forties!

He raised his chin to peer across the room at a framed photo of the petite, dark-haired woman he had loved, reflecting. It wasn't nice, but most of those insulting words occasionally applied to the fellas in the group. So was he being honest with himself, or patting himself on the back? Or was he, perhaps, being too hard on his friends? Yet Harold had underlined a few words himself.

And was he being guilty of sharing this attitude Walker said the young too often felt about the very elderly, that they represented both an "encumbrance" and "the done-with"? But that viewpoint angered him enormously, and Lowell much preferred what he read about the occult view that a "particular virtue resides in the aged," an increasing "psychic energy"—and that an old man's blessing or curse "is more effective."

"Well," he muttered aloud, possibly to Franny, "I don't remember ever trying literally to *curse* anybody." He paused, smiling at the image of the beloved face. "Or, for that matter, to say anything aloud like 'Blessings on you.'" Of course Lowell recalled praying *God bless you* on behalf of others, but they'd always been folks in some physical distress—or beyond that, when it was the departing immortal soul for which he was asking the Almighty's blessing in Jesus's name.

What he was inclined to disbelieve, in what he was reading, was that he or the others in their group had any psychic abilities whatever, let alone the psychic energy to bestow on others. Any time he'd had a strong hunch, the best way to bet was the opposite of it! Yet it was this brilliant fella, the writer Walker, who was saying the "barrier" to the spirit gets very thin with age, and a lot "of great importance comes to their understanding," even "the ancient wisdom of humanity."

Well, Lowell thought, laying ol' Harold's gift aside to light a Camel, *I'd like to believe all that*. And maybe a great many middle-aged folks made a huge mistake by overemphasizing and pursuing the interests of a young bunch to which they could never return, instead of leading, moving ahead.

And it seemed pretty likely to the Kid that Harold had bought this stuff about the boys in the group having some special powers, and maybe was trying to figure out how to use 'em when his old ticker gave out.

Lowell sighed and returned to reading Walker's unusual book.

There was just a chance he might find something useful for the group when they got together next.

J.N. Williamson

4

They straggled in one at a time for a bit more than a half hour, offering no explanation and wearing—each quite elderly man—expressions of startling similarity.

Part of that, Lowell perceived, stemmed from the fact that this was their first gathering with a regular missing. No, the Kid corrected himself, not missing, but forever gone. Yet this sadness, this grief, did not appear to reach out and embrace the others as he supposed he had expected. It was oddly personal; indrawn, even questioning.

And it was only when all his guests were seated—he'd remembered to put up two folding chairs, one swiftly taken by Johnathan, the second ignored by Ray in preference for a seat on the floor—and conversationally catching up that Lowell got an inkling of their general mind-set.

Each man in his own way had become busier and had done meaningful things since their previous get-together. Just as Harold, they had heeded Lowell's advice—

But Harold had died very suddenly, and each survivor was basically looking to Lowell for his answer. The question, obviously, might have been stated, "We feel better and we're happier, but is it going to kill us, too?"

Lowell gazed around at the five men who he guessed were his closest living friends. Bos had announced boastfully that he was seeing a "real looker" twice a week. Ray Reilly had asked for a Vernor's ginger ale instead of a beer and had clearly dropped ten pounds. Cranelike Allen had confided that he was teaching Sunday School again and actually thanked Lowell for "telling us to stir our stumps while we still have any to stir!"

Johnathan Masters glanced toward Bos, as if he didn't intend to be outboasted, and let them all know (as he put it) "Hostilities with Mrs. Masters have been suspended, and normal relations—for people around age forty!—have been restored!" That earned him a round of masculine applause.

And Jim Kleiner, blinking back tears, exhibited for his gang a portrait he had painted "from memory" in tribute to "our late, great friend Harold." More than a few men were glad Jim had identified his subject, and a couple of them believed he showed genuine talent.

"What should each of us do now, Kid," Jim put it into words, "with poor Harold dying so suddenly, out of the blue the way he did?"

So this was it, Lowell Striker mused, reaching for his Camels and Djeep lighter even while he finished chewing the popcorn in his mouth. He had been the first one of them ever to offer a little well-meant advice, and to express some opinions on matters deeper then an upcoming mayoral election or the rising prices for decent automobiles. Now he was the group guru, nominated to hold all their lives in his hands and not close his fingers too tightly. Swami Lowell Striker, whose most arcane experiences had to do with long ago becoming a thirty-second-degree Mason.

Well, I'll try, the Kid thought, and unconsciously rose to his feet. "Harold was trying to learn more about aging, and its mysteries, when he had his attack. I'll tell you the same things I learned from a book he gave me, and you can judge for yourselves." He peered from familiar face to familiar face and explained that little was known about why people age; that certain people had venerated the old while others brushed the aged aside like gathering dust; and that some special psychic "virtue" was available to old folks.

Then, mentioning that just as Bos said, the young were their "enemy," he cited some of the humiliating words certain youth routinely applied to those of many decades. To his amazement, Lowell observed, only Allen even glanced up at him, and no one reacted with irritation or anger. *I think I'm losing my audience*, he realized, and paused to ask if anybody needed something to drink, or a "potty break."

But no one spoke, or even budged, so he quoted Benjamin Walker that there was "an eternal and elemental conflict between youth and age." His friends appeared to take that for granted, since nobody stirred. "It's just my notion, fellas, but I think I understand the reason for conflict: Old or young, we come from the same Source; God, heaven, whatever name you want to use. Toddlers are adorable because they're not far from the Source, but teenagers and those we call young *are*— so they're directionless, want to create their own rules, and see old geezers as being in the way." He was warming to his topic and, gesturing, shifted from foot to foot. "The old are even *longer* from the Source, so it seems a bit uncertain and shadowy— until we realize we're just on the way to *returning* to it. Which is when we begin to develop that psychic energy I read about! Now, I want to give you boys something really *hopeful* I learned about—"

No one was listening, Lowell saw with a chill of terror that left him standing in front of his chair with his mouth open. No one was even looking at him, not even Jim and Johnathan, who *faced* him with *open eyes*. He turned his own gaze from friend to friend, remembering something else he'd told them in a different context: *Walk into any mortuary and the first thing you notice is absolute inactivity! Motionlessness!*

"Dear Lord," Lowell whispered audibly—"I'm the first guy who was talking and literally *bored* a lot of people to death!"

Strangely, though, Lowell realized as he moved shakily forward to approach the nearest unmoving man, it did not quite *feel* that way to him. He wanted desperately to *do something*, but was fearful of even touching them. No, it felt like he himself, Lowell J. Striker, had reached some different level of knowing, of vitality, without any intention. It really seemed he had moved on, achieved a certain *speed*, or rate of vibrations, and was living at a rapidity of being that left him and his pals of more than half a century beyond mutual contact. In separate dimensions or different plateaus of existence, so that neither they nor he were necessarily . . . dead.

Harold sat calmly across the room in his customary place!

Not sure of the proprieties in this situation, Lowell merely looked back at his old friend, becoming gradually aware that he wasn't really afraid of him—why should he be afraid of Harold in death when he'd never been afraid of him in life?—but surprised, caught off guard.

"H'lo, Lowell," Harold said. He scratched the dark hairs on the back of one hand, chuckled shyly. "You haven't forgotten who I am already?"

"Golly, Harold, not likely," Lowell replied. "You're looking good."

"Fine, then I got it right." He rubbed a jaw guilty of the familiar five o'clock shadow. "Franny told me to say hello. She's almost finished fixing up the place you two will have, and she said there's a new card table up, plus two new decks of cards. Whenever you're ready."

Lowell swallowed, tried not to think too much

about that message. "What are you doing back, Harold," he asked, "if it's really nice . . . up there?"

Harold nodded with more decisiveness than the Kid had seen in him before. "It's wonderful. But where else would I be on the evening of a get-together? Besides, I knew you'd read what I gave you, and I was afraid you'd have some problems trying to help this bunch of close-minded old galoots."

"Well, I do," Lowell admitted. "Looks like they up and died on me."

"No, I'd know that," Harold said easily, not bragging. "It's pretty much what you were thinking, Kid, to the best of the knowledge I've picked up here so far." He paused, giving Lowell the opportunity to realize this wasn't mind reading they were doing, but regular talking. "You just developed your psychic energy enough," Harold added, "that added to your regular beliefs—to who you are—you temporarily passed our other old pals by completely."

"So this is strictly temporary?" Lowell asked.

"Absolutely," Harold said with a nod. "You're a living human being. Within ten minutes after I've left you, you'll be pretty sure you had a miniature stroke or something and imagined all this." He shrugged. "When we're alive, we fight a battle for all our years between faith and doubt. It's a precious few folks who can believe anything with all their hearts for more than a half hour at a time. Happily, it's considered good enough to know, more times than not, that we *ought* to have more faith in God and His things—which is the whole ball of wax, minus the stuff we all know is bad."

"Well, how am I going to get these fellas back," Lowell began, "or put *me* back *with* 'em? It's pretty darn awkward this way! And what can I do or say to make them stop wasting the rest of their lives?"

Harold sat up straight. "First, wait until you no longer see me, then reread the list of words about the old that angered you. When you find one that *frightens* you because, as you age, it *might* fit you then, your faith will be tested and all your friends will slip onto the same wavelength again. I'll stay for the rest of the get-together, but you'll no longer believe it."

"I bet I will," Lowell said with affable challenge. "And how can I help them, Harold?"

"See you in fifteen or twenty years, Kid!" Harold cried with a wave, fading. "Give or take how well you use your psychic energies to bless or curse!"

"Doggone it, Harold," Lowell shouted with an irked grin, "you didn't—"

But he found himself standing only among his living but motionless cronies, and stopped speaking. Then he pulled his notes from his pocket and read the terrible descriptive words again, senses alert.

There; *that* one: *Miserly*. That mustn't ever describe him, Lowell thought with a shudder. And another one: *Intolerant*. He had never been a close-minded man, a bigot—and he'd been generous, whenever he could be, not a self-serving old fart! It was *terribly* important to his self-respect, his self-worth, that nobody should think of him that way, or as a hater, he—

"Are you just going to stare at that scrap of paper," Ray Reilly asked from his seated position on the floor, "or tell us the rest of what you wanted to say to us? There's a Pacers-Bulls game on the tube, remember?"

Lowell automatically turned his head and gazed expectantly across the room. There was nobody sitting where he had imagined he might see Harold.

Jim Kleiner had noticed Lowell's reaction. "He's gone, Kid," he said in a kindly manner. "He probably has a lot more important things to do now than haunt a bunch of old earthbound characters like us. I hope!"

"We all share your hope, Jim," big Bos said from where he sat. "And maybe we think it's a little more realistic now that we're all trying to look more alive than dead, by getting busy and interested in things again."

"That's really almost all I was going to add," Lowell said, slipping back into his chair. Who was he, now that he thought about it, to ask anybody to be what they weren't or hadn't become over the years? "It's wonderful that you're losing weight and not drinking as much, Ray. Jimbo, your painting is a grand tribute to Harold—and to your own courage in beginning, now, to develop your talent. Bos, you've grown up just by realizing you're lonely and learning to grow fond of a woman simply because of her personality. And we all applauded you, Johnathan, for rediscovering the qualities in your wife that made you desire her." He hesitated and smiled at skinny Allen, once more in Sunday School. "As soon as I tell you fellas the other thing I learned from Harold's book, I'm turning the chair of advice-giving over to Allen. He's much more qualified for the job than I am, anyway!"

"We wouldn't have done these things without you, Kid," Allen murmured.

"I don't know," Lowell said, "if that's true. Now, that other matter I mentioned: According to that book Harold and I were reading, human blood vessels already show evidence of hardening at age seven. But only five years later, at twelve, we're less apt to die than at any other age—at the same time that, becoming teenagers, we're starting to come down from that pinnacle, our vitality beginning to diminish."

"But what do twelve-year-olds have to do with us?" Johnathan asked.

"I believe there's a *second* pinnacle or peak available to human beings when we reach seventy-two!" Lowell told them, almost breathlessly. "My Franny practiced astrology and taught me the number six is man's number. And because the sixth sign is Virgo, and it's tied to efficiency, our daily lives and methods, and also negative or neurotic notions, six times the child's twelve is seventy-two."

"Gosh, Lowell," Reilly snorted, "thanks for the arithmetic lesson!"

"Wait!" Lowell said, lifting an index finger. "Most folks these days are in pretty good shape at seventy-two—but we become scared of aging further, as I said last time, and too many of us make our daily methods sitting around being *careful*—or reading all the patent medicine bottles in the drug store, taking naps, and imagining we're 'coming down with something'! But Virgo is also the sign of planning, and if we live that way, what do we have after another twelve years?"

"A really old fart!" Ray snapped. "Hell's bells, Kid, that's age eighty-four!"

"Right!" Lowell exclaimed. "And the busy, involved, *not* negative guy reaches that age while he's enjoying life, and his psychic energies enable him to help others while he no longer has a concern about death! That kind of attitude gives him a chance at another twelve developing, growing years, maybe even a shot at living to one hundred!" He spread his arms, beaming at them. "None of you is even eighty yet, so there's still time—maybe *lots* of it. I'm saying I believe every dozen years is a growing-up time, fellas, and the period in between is like the teenage—the 'between years' of age—all over again!"

"Prove it," said Johnathan, not unkindly. His winter beard was fully grown again and it was shot with more white than Lowell remembered. "I'd like to hear any evidence at all."

For a long moment Lowell could not answer. He hadn't made up what he'd read in Harold's book, but he had thought of the rest of it spontaneously, created it out of vanity, responding to challenge, or to help his gang further—maybe for all those reasons.

Then he had it! "What does science claim," he said, softly, "is the age we human beings are constructed to achieve? You've all read it, I'm sure. Fellas, what's the *maximum* supposed to be, according to experts?"

Allen answered the question first, but everyone chipped in with the same figure: *"One hundred and twenty years!"*

Lowell nodded, and grinned. "Correct. And one hundred and twenty is ten times . . . age *twelve*!"

Johnathan arose from his folding chair, clasped Lowell's hand in both of his, and sat down again—on the floor, where he had sat for years without complaint.

While the gang of old friends rooted the Indiana Pacers to an upset of the Chicago Bulls, three separate food fights—*snack* squabbles, in reality—broke out.

They had a great time, and told Lowell so as, smilingly, they meandered out into a snow-shrouded night.

Lowell stood another moment with the door halfway open even after he saw the last man into his car.

"I didn't forget," he said without turning. "Come again anytime, Harold—preferably when I can see you."

A warmth, not a chilliness, touched the Kid's upraised, open palm. But when he closed his fingers, they curled without obstruction.

Afterthought by the Author

"It Does Not Come Alone" might be said, by some, not to be either a supernatural or a horror story, but I beg to differ. There is no reason the supernatural should unfailingly frighten us, and elements of this tale—fear of dying and death; the loss of good friends; how one approaches those ages for which there is no perfect guidebook—involve some of those terrifying stages of life common to all.

But I'm here with this Afterthought to say the story is a tribute to the most remarkable man I've known, my late paternal grandfather, Lowell J. Williamson. He was the only person I have met who was liked or loved by everyone, on sight, and managed to be his own man. Maybe that's true because he may have loved life more than anyone else I knew, and delighted in bringing smiles to as many people as he could amuse or just please.

The real Lowell had cronies, but the range of

people he called his friends wasn't measured by age; they were very young, young, middle-aged, elderly, old, and very old. Unlike the fictional Lowell, the only unsought advice he ever gave came in the form of his own admirable lifestyle, because people wanted to be like him. When his wife Frances died in her sixties, he said he couldn't stay in town because it would be too easy to get old among loved ones. He went off to Ocala, Florida, and alternated between living there—in a mobile home he bought—and Harlingen, Texas, wearing a ten-gallon hat and becoming the photographer he had always wanted to be.

Just past his seventy-fifth birthday, Pop—I called him that, as most people did—wrote a letter to me to ask how I thought his son (my father, Lynn) would handle the news that he was remarrying. His primary concern was that the lady, named Jane, was younger than Lynn—around forty! Since I knew Lowell's assets consisted of his trailer, car, and social security, I was delighted for both of them. The marriage lasted a few years, then fell apart by mutual agreement.

I expressed my sympathy to him on one of his visits to Indianapolis, and he gave me the only sharp look I got from him: "I'll never be sorry I married Jane, boy," he said. "We had some great times." Then he inclined his big head and reflected. "I'm only sorry she couldn't keep up with me!" he remarked. "Guess some folks get old and tired out sooner than others!"

At the age of eighty-three, Lowell sent me the most exuberant letter of his life or mine. Despite the fact that he had assumed the hospital costs of my youngest son, John, when he broke his leg, Pop had existed on very little throughout his retirement (which was never quite *that*). But an extremely distant female relative had died, and her attorney had just notified him that another kinsman and Lowell "stand to inherit around forty thousand dollars apiece!"

Well, the attorney was still trying to locate the second beneficiary, and Lowell came back up to Indy to collect his inheritance in person, not to mention to share his glad tidings with everyone. Off to the legal office he went, dazzled by such a windfall at his age.

But he got out of the car gingerly, on his return, his broad face a controlled mask. I was dreadfully concerned for him and immediately asked him, "What's the matter?" He shook his head a bit and sighed. "Well," he began, "they located the other old boy—I don't know him, either—and, well, he died not long ago." Lowell's face brightened and went on brightening. "It looks like I'm the *sole beneficiary*—of *eighty-three thousand dollars!*"

And he was.

What Lowell did next was, I believed, extremely intelligent as well as generous. He said he did not want to be "nickel and dimed" for the rest of his life—with "loans" of $100 or $200 periodically requested—"because it'll ruin all my relationships in time." So he would give himself a single big trip, take care of the future by prepaying for an apartment in a retirement home "for when I need it," and "have fun giving the rest of the money away!"

That's what he did. After paying his taxes and those of a loved one, he visited his grandchildren with gifts we'd said we hoped to get "someday," all with a maximum price he had set (to be sure there was enough left for the things on his own list). Knowing we had most of our kids still at home without transportation, he showed up one unforgettable, sunny afternoon behind the wheel of . . . my new automobile! (I still think he went a little over budget, but he was crazy about my wife Mary's spaghetti and gigantic meatballs.)

He sent his ex-wife Jane a gift check and was off to Belgium for a couple of months. After returning home, Jane and he ignored the family scandal and went on a Caribbean cruise for the time of Pop's life.

My grandfather Lowell wasn't afraid of aging, and did precious little of it for a man who lived almost ninety-three years. His thoughts on dying were his own. When he decided it was time for his real retirement, he drove straight through from Florida, came to our house for spaghetti, and played Scrabble with us until 2 A.M. Years before, he'd stayed up with us and then-young children to see the first moon landing and, filled with awe, he hadn't seemed appreciably younger then. He was flat on his broad back on a gurney the last time we saw each other alive, and I know he hadn't lost a fraction of his intelligence or charm. "Don't worry about me, boy," he said, clenching my hand firmly and smiling. "I'm gonna be fine now, by golly!" He would die soon, yet I believed him. I still do.

There were more people present to mourn our loss than I've seen in a mortuary, before or since. Row after row, the people animated as they shared story after story about Lowell. I don't remember being more proud; it was nearly not one of the saddest days of my life.

I suppose he was old enough by then to lie around and do nothin' much, like the rest of us.

But barely. Just barely.

The Writing of
"The Field of Blood"

Again I must be careful in how I discuss this
short-short story to avoid giving away the ending.
Primarily I can say that everything begins somewhere, even supernatural beliefs, and if *this* particular belief had an origin in reality, it could
have begun in the manner I've depicted.

I once heard a few horror-writing icons express
the belief that there was no such thing as actual
or real evil. My reactions were in such nearly violent opposition that I did not comment, and I
wish I had. Then I heard such further opinion
offered as the psychological (there's mental illness, and everything is subjective) and the irreli-
gious (it's all a carryover from times when people
read the Bible and believed everything in it).

Why is it that people who claim to believe in
nothing they can't see or touch fail to understand
that *that* is a belief? And why do you suppose
that, unless they're writing about human murder-

ers, they're writing in a genre that's also known to some as "dark fantasy?"

The reason I asked the second question is because the first tough problem all us writers of rue and wrath face is persuading our readers to suspend their disbelief.

The Field of Blood

For a period of time that seemed to him as painful as the impact of the length of rope from which his body swung, the man endured the punishment of the damned—specifically, what he considered an apt punishment and an agony suitable to one who believed himself literally damned. The noose had tightened so abominably at the point when he had begun his drop that he'd imagined he could no longer breathe, that he was, in fact, dead.

But when he had whispered every anguished and guilt-ridden word of prayer he knew, and when it occurred to him he was simply *thinking* about the condition of lifelessness—when he realized that the bite of the noose had not broken his neck and he still occupied a body that should perhaps be dead but was not—

He accepted that his flight from the terrible last deeds of his life would not be as swift as oblivion, and that his true punishment might prove far worse than sudden death, or even the tortures of hell.

By the time he had laboriously unknotted the tight noose with arms enfeebled and fingertips seeping blood, and tumbled to the earth beneath the tree, the man was uncertain whether he was truly alive, dead, or a tenant of some unmapped terrain between the extremes. His throat was so badly bruised that he doubted his ability to whisper, and he sprawled atop the shadow-painted hill to squint fearfully into the darkness of late night. He saw that no one was afoot beneath the hill; no living soul had witnessed his futile attempt to end his existence, yet the night was not still. Sounds of furious voices and others that pleaded, entreated, rose up the hill like phantoms, disembodied but (he knew) given life—given *reason* for the clamor—by his own difficult and convoluted acts. Those who muttered with anger would not welcome him should he descend the hill and return. Even if he had acquiesced to their will, they had demanded he be gone from their sight forever.

And those whose sad, plaintive voices drifted to his bramble-sharp ears might wish him dead. Although he had once attempted to fulfill their wishes as well, he suspected now he could not conceivably explain to or please them either. There was nowhere to go. In life or in the community of the dead.

Above him night wind sifted through the ancient tree with a replication of mourning. He glanced up quickly with all his old terror of the unknown and cried out, shrank into himself with a simultaneous yearning for the strange. Intuition told him his deeds of this day had only made him a part of that which had always brought fear

J.N. Williamson

to his breast. He saw the rope he had used dangling from the red-bud tree, forming an X or a cross with a shivering, outflung branch. The image provoked from him a moan, but he did not know why. Shuddering, hands trembling, he pulled up the hood of his calf-length garment till his entire head and face were hidden in it, except for his blood-filled and staring eyes.

Fleeing somewhere seemed his one choice. Running elsewhere, in the crouch of a beast doomed to constant travel in an endeavor he recognized as futile to evade both the crowd commissioning his treachery and the one that would see him now as irretrievably evil—that was all he could imagine doing.

Erect, his thin shoulders hunched, he peered once more down the hill and detected the tentative emergence of daylight. He saw it, self-damned, as merciless tendrils of vengeance bound to find and expose him, to grope for the bruised throat that hadn't broken, and remorselessly pull from it the inexplicable living breath that sustained him like some grotesque, unpitied miracle of unguessable midnight gods—

Except it was not in fact inexplicable, incomprehensible, he saw. Those glimpses of the future could always be relied upon when the source of prediction and prophecy was itself unimpeachable. With those so lately his companions, he had been assured that there were some in the company who would not taste of death until their leader assumed complete authority. Yet he himself, this night—for reasons he truly could not fathom—had lost sight of that unimpeachable pledge! What had come over him, overpowered both his judgment and memory, and overwhelmed his faith in their leader?

Cursing his confusion and culpability alike, he

lurched down the other side of the hill, wanting to escape the dawn and what he felt it would mean for him. When he had wandered aimlessly till he was lost in the countryside, he knew a rage was beginning to build inside him unlike any other. Of his sins he had little doubt, but he had striven to inflict self-punishment and yet remained afoot, staggering on until a more complete awareness of his plight filled him with incipient fury. He *was* part, now, of the frightening unknown—of the ambiguities and impenetrable mysteries that had drawn him, in part, to his leader. He was obliged now to continue this mockery of life without guidance, enlightenment, companionship, or anything except a mostly unspecified point in the future which *might* free him, too. Why wouldn't he lash out in vengeance, take what he pleased, make others suffer as he, now, must suffer?

But it was not a real question, and he was suffused then with a mixture of thirst and hunger—plus a great need to relieve the dryness of his battered throat—so like one another he could not distinguish hunger from thirst. Reaching the banks of a stream, he fell to his knees in an approximation of a man at prayer, and started frantically to scoop water into his mouth.

I can scarcely swallow it! he thought with agony. And that water he did get down came up again at once! His manic urge was to hurl back hood and head, then howl at the day-dappled sky. Yet now the sun had almost risen, and even the glimpse of light, after his miserable and interminable night, seared his vision and seemed nearly to melt his sallow cheeks and forehead! *Has a man ever been so exquisitely punished?* he wondered. *Has any man before me ever become . . . undead?*

J.N. Williamson

It was not until—moving in a crouch now—he arrived at a potter's field he had never witnessed before, wended his way among the graves of the destitute and the unwanted, then knelt at a pool ringed with glorious wildflowers, that he experienced any alleviation of his torment. Perhaps there, with the dead, it would remain comfortingly shadowed, overcast; there, and possibly in other such places, he might for a while lose himself.

But when he had sipped cautiously at the contents of the pool, the man neither marveled at the fact that it was *not* water he was keeping down but blood, nor thanked his Creator that he would be able to sustain himself with it.

His only thought was that he required more. And more.

He felt color flushing his cheeks, his lips. Nothing of his peculiarly combined thirst and hunger was sated, yet the strength of many seemed to course through his veins. When a field mouse scampered within arm's reach, he caught it with astounding ease, ripped away its tiny head, and drained the hot body as if it had been a goblet.

And more, he thought avidly, pushing himself to his feet. However, it was time now, this blazing morning, to locate a place of concealment. There he would remain, trying to rest, until the hour of his faithless deed returned by night, and he had, once more, to attempt the most futile of flights.

His eyes filled with blood matching the color of the new sun as he loped and ran for a hiding place. He bit his lip with teeth that seemed oddly longer, sharper, than they had been. When he found an empty grave, he jumped into it, intentionally dislodging a great pile of round objects that descended upon and concealed him. *Golgo-*

tha, he remembered the name of this awful field. "The place of skulls." It was perfect.

For the remainder of that day and, subsequently, for many days afterward, Judas thought about the kiss he had given Jesus in order to identify Him to the soldiers. Haste had seemed very important under the circumstances, and the Master was taller.

The kiss had not been on the cheek, but the throat.

> *"And he cast down the pieces of silver . . . and went and hanged himself. (They) took the silver pieces, and said, It is not lawful for to put them into the treasury, because it is the price of blood. And they . . . bought with them the potter's field, to bury strangers in."*

"Wherefore that field was called, The Field of Blood, unto this day."

—*Matthew 27:5–8*

Original Appearance Credits

"Reality Function," Robert Bloch's *Monsters in our Midst*, TOR hardcover, 1993.

"Public Places," *Pulphouse* magazine #1, 1988.

"Watchwolf," *Footsteps* magazine, 1986.

"The Sudd," *Pulphouse* magazine #5, 1989.

"Mercy," *2AM* magazine, Spring 1988.

"The Mother Pact," *After Hours*, #25, Winter 1995.

"Small Gift From Home," *Whispers* magazine, #21-22, 1986.

"Origin of a Species," DAW, 1996.

"Child of the Sea," *Pulphouse* magazine, Fall 1994.

"Everyone Must Know," *Dead of Night* magazine #2, 1989.

"The House of Life," John Maclay's *Nukes*, 1986.

"It Does Not Come Alone," *Terminal Fright* hardcover, 1997.

"The Field of Blood," *Pirate Writings* magazine, Fall 1994.

THE NIGHTMARE CHRONICLES

DOUGLAS CLEGG

It begins in an old tenement with a horrifying crime. It continues after midnight, when a young boy, held captive in a basement, is filled with unearthly visions of fantastic and frightening worlds. How could his kidnappers know that the ransom would be their own souls? For as the hours pass, the boy's nightmares invade his captors like parasites—and soon, they become real. Thirteen nightmares unfold: A young man searches for his dead wife among the crumbling buildings of Manhattan... A journalist seeks the ultimate evil in a plague-ridden outpost of India... Ancient rituals begin anew with the mystery of a teenage girl's disappearance... In a hospital for the criminally insane, there is only one doorway to salvation... But the night is not yet over, and the real nightmare has just begun. Thirteen chilling tales of terror from one of the masters of the horror story.

___4580-X $5.50 US/$6.50 CAN

Dorchester Publishing Co., Inc.
P.O. Box 6640
Wayne, PA 19087-8640

Please add $1.75 for shipping and handling for the first book and $.50 for each book thereafter. NY, NYC, and PA residents, please add appropriate sales tax. No cash, stamps, or C.O.D.s. All orders shipped within 6 weeks via postal service book rate. Canadian orders require $2.00 extra postage and must be paid in U.S. dollars through a U.S. banking facility.

Name_____
Address_____
City_____State_____Zip_____
I have enclosed $_____ in payment for the checked book(s).
Payment <u>must</u> accompany all orders. ❏ Please send a free catalog.
CHECK OUT OUR WEBSITE! www.dorchesterpub.com

MASQUES

BILL PRONZINI

Mardi Gras is a time of madness when an entire city seems to lose its mind. But for Steve Giroux, the madness has become all too real. A mysterious voice on the phone wants something from him—evidence of an unspeakable murder—and will use all the forces it commands to get it. Suddenly Steve is cast into a swirling nightmare of voodoo, black magic, and blood, a nightmare that can only get worse until he delivers what the voice wants. But how can Steve deliver what he's never had?

___4451-X $4.99 US/$5.99 CAN

Dorchester Publishing Co., Inc.
P.O. Box 6640
Wayne, PA 19087-8640

Please add $1.75 for shipping and handling for the first book and $.50 for each book thereafter. NY, NYC, and PA residents, please add appropriate sales tax. No cash, stamps, or C.O.D.s. All orders shipped within 6 weeks via postal service book rate. Canadian orders require $2.00 extra postage and must be paid in U.S. dollars through a U.S. banking facility.

Name_____
Address_____
City_____State_____Zip_____
I have enclosed $_____ in payment for the checked book(s).
Payment <u>must</u> accompany all orders. ☐ Please send a free catalog.
        CHECK OUT OUR WEBSITE! www.dorchesterpub.com

BLOODLINES

J. N. WILLIAMSON

Marshall Madison disappeared the night his wife committed suicide. She saw the horrible things Madison did to their son, Thad, and couldn't deal with the knowledge that their daughter, Caroline, was next. Caroline is taken in by a kind, hardworking family, and Thad runs off to live by his wits on the streets of New York. But Madison means to make good on his promise to come for his children. And as he gets closer and closer, the trail of bodies in his wake gets longer and longer. No one will keep him from his flesh and blood.

___4468-4 $4.99 US/$5.99 CAN

Dorchester Publishing Co., Inc.
P.O. Box 6640
Wayne, PA 19087-8640

Please add $1.75 for shipping and handling for the first book and $.50 for each book thereafter. NY, NYC, and PA residents, please add appropriate sales tax. No cash, stamps, or C.O.D.s. All orders shipped within 6 weeks via postal service book rate. Canadian orders require $2.00 extra postage and must be paid in U.S. dollars through a U.S. banking facility.

Name_____
Address_____
City_____ State_____ Zip_____
I have enclosed $_____ in payment for the checked book(s).
Payment <u>must</u> accompany all orders. ❑ Please send a free catalog.

DRAWN TO THE GRAVE
MARY ANN MITCHELL

"A tight, taut dark fantasy with surprising plot twists and a lot of spooky atmosphere."
—Ed Gorman

Beverly thinks that she has found something special with Carl, until she realizes that he has stolen from her. But he doesn't just steal her money and her property—he steals her very life. Suddenly she is helpless and alone, able only to watch in growing despair as her flesh begins to decay and each day transforms her more and more into a corpse—a corpse without the release of death.

But Beverly is not truly alone, for Carl is always nearby, watching her and waiting. He knows that soon he will need another unknowing victim, another beautiful woman he can seduce...and destroy. And when lovely young Megan walks into his web, he knows he has found his next lover. For what can possibly go wrong with his plan, a plan he has practiced to perfection so many times before?

___4290-8 $4.99 US/$5.99 CAN

Dorchester Publishing Co., Inc.
P.O. Box 6640
Wayne, PA 19087-8640

Please add $1.75 for shipping and handling for the first book and $.50 for each book thereafter. NY, NYC, and PA residents, please add appropriate sales tax. No cash, stamps, or C.O.D.s. All orders shipped within 6 weeks via postal service book rate. Canadian orders require $2.00 extra postage and must be paid in U.S. dollars through a U.S. banking facility.

Name_____
Address_____
City_____ State_____ Zip_____
I have enclosed $_____ in payment for the checked book(s).
Payment <u>must</u> accompany all orders. ❑ Please send a free catalog.

ATTENTION HORROR CUSTOMERS!

SPECIAL
TOLL-FREE NUMBER
1-800-481-9191

Call Monday through Friday
10 a.m. to 9 p.m.
Eastern Time
Get a free catalogue,
join the Horror Book Club,
and order books using your
Visa, MasterCard,
or Discover®

Leisure
Books

GO ONLINE WITH US AT DORCHESTERPUB.COM